# BACK TO YOU

## BAD BOYS OF RED HOOK

# BACK TO YOU

## BAD BOYS OF RED HOOK

# ROBIN KAYE

A SIGNET ECLIPSE BOOK

SIGNET ECLIPSE
Published by New American Library, a division of
Penguin Group (USA) Inc., 375 Hudson Street,
New York, New York 10014, USA
Penguin Group (Canada), 90 Eglinton Avenue East, Suite 700, Toronto,
Ontario M4P 2Y3, Canada (a division of Pearson Penguin Canada Inc.)
Penguin Books Ltd., 80 Strand, London WC2R 0RL, England
Penguin Ireland, 25 St. Stephen's Green, Dublin 2,
Ireland (a division of Penguin Books Ltd.)
Penguin Group (Australia), 250 Camberwell Road, Camberwell, Victoria 3124,
Australia (a division of Pearson Australia Group Pty. Ltd.)
Penguin Books India Pvt. Ltd., 11 Community Centre, Panchsheel Park,
New Delhi - 110 017, India
Penguin Group (NZ), 67 Apollo Drive, Rosedale, Auckland 0632,
New Zealand (a division of Pearson New Zealand Ltd.)
Penguin Books (South Africa) (Pty.) Ltd., 24 Sturdee Avenue,
Rosebank, Johannesburg 2196, South Africa

Penguin Books Ltd., Registered Offices:
80 Strand, London WC2R 0RL, England

First published by Signet Eclipse, an imprint of New American Library,
a division of Penguin Group (USA) Inc.

ISBN 978-1-62090-757-3

PUBLISHER'S NOTE
This is a work of fiction. Names, characters, places, and incidents either are the
product of the author's imagination or are used fictitiously, and any resemblance
to actual persons, living or dead, business establishments, events, or locales is
entirely coincidental.

The publisher does not have any control over and does not assume any responsibility for author or third-party Web sites or their content.

To my real-life heroes: Susan Reed, my dear friend, and Isabelle Kawczynski, my daughter.

You never fail to amaze me with your ability to overcome incredible obstacles and beat all the odds with an unparalleled zest for life, generosity toward others, enormous talent, humor, and above all else, courage. You are my inspiration.

*"Courage is more exhilarating than fear and in the long run it is easier. We do not have to become heroes overnight. Just a step at a time, meeting each thing that comes up, seeing it is not as dreadful as it appeared, discovering we have the strength to stare it down."*

*— Eleanor Roosevelt*

# ACKNOWLEDGMENTS

Writing is a solitary endeavor, but a writer's life is anything but. I'm lucky to have the love and support of my incredible family. My husband, Stephen, who after twenty-three years of marriage is still the man of my dreams. My children, Tony, Anna, and Isabelle, who in spite of being teenagers, are my favorite people to hang out with. They make me laugh, amaze me with their intelligence and generosity, and make me proud every day.

My parents, Richard Williams and Ann Feiler, and my stepfather, George Feiler, who always encouraged me, and continue to do so.

My wonderful critique partners, Deborah Villegas and Laura Becraft. They shortened my sentences, corrected my grammar, and put commas where they needed to be. They listened to me whine when my muse took a vacation, gave me great ideas when I was stuck, and answered that all-important question: Does this suck? They helped me plot, loved my characters almost as much as I did, and challenged me to be a better writer. They are my friends, my confidantes, and my bullshit meters. I owe a debt of gratitude to their families, who so graciously let me borrow them during my deadline crunch. So, to Robert, Joe, Elisabeth, and Ben Becraft, and Ruben, Alexander, Donovan, and Cristian Villegas, you have my thanks and eternal gratitude.

I'd also like to thank my writing friends who are always there when I need a fresh eye or a sounding board: Grace Burrowes, Hope Ramsay, Susan Donovan, Mary Freeman, R. R. Smythe, and Christie Craig.

I owe a debt of gratitude to Kevin Dibley, the best marine architect out there. When I e-mailed him asking for an eighty-footer, he sent me the plans for *No Censor Ship*—it's not just a figment of my imagination. It really is that nice. Any mistakes I might have made on the sailing scene are my own.

I wrote most of this book at the Mt. Airy Starbucks, and I have to thank all my baristas for keeping me in laughter and coffee while I camped out in their store. I also need to thank my fellow customers who have become wonderful friends: Cory, Melissa, Liz, Barbara, Cheryl, Mitchel/Michelle (he becomes one of the girls when we're reading the love scenes aloud), Jennifer, and Phil.

As always, I want to thank my incredible agent, Kevan Lyon, for all she does; my team at NAL; the cover artists for the beautiful job they did; and my editors, Kerry Donovan and Jesse Feldman, for all their insight, direction, and enthusiasm. Working with you has been a real pleasure.

# CHAPTER 1

"I think you killed him."

Ten-year-old Nicoletta said it with such immutable calmness, Breanna Collins wondered if this wasn't the first time a strange man had entered Nicki's room at three in the morning and been taken down by a woman wielding a cast-iron frying pan.

Bree's heart traded punches with her sternum, winding her more than a ten-mile run uphill. She sure as hell hoped Nicki's assessment of the intruder was right. Better a dead burglar than a live one.

The dim glow of a streetlight outlined the shadowy figure lying facedown on the carpeted floor between Bree and Nicki. Dropping the skillet, Bree skirted the body before grabbing Nicki's arm, pulling her off the bed, and shoving her toward the door.

The man groaned, and, like something out of a horror flick, a vise-like grip closed around Bree's ankle. She landed hard, kicking and screaming. She reached for the frying pan, only to be flipped like a tortilla on a hot griddle and covered with one extra-large serving of man.

"Get off me!"

He held her hands on either side of her head as his breath washed her ear. "I'm not going to hurt you."

"Yeah? Well, I'm going to hurt you."

"You already have."

Light flooded the room, causing temporary blindness. When Bree's vision cleared and she saw he wasn't an intruder, she wanted to crawl under the pink princess canopy bed and hide. Instead, she dove right into the turbulent, ocean blue eyes of an enraged Storm Decker—the past occupant of Nicki's room. Storm Decker—a man Bree had known since before she started wearing sexy underwear. Storm Decker—a man who epitomized the reason women bought the lacy, uncomfortable stuff in the first place.

"Breezy, a frying pan? That was the best you could do?"

Bree hated that nickname—maybe because Storm was the only one who dared to use it. It didn't help matters that the sound of it rolling off his tongue had always been enough to make her breath catch. She struggled, trying to slide from beneath him, but succeeded only in pressing her body against his. His heat scorched Bree through her Mr. Bubble boxers and matching tank top. She couldn't believe Storm would be a witness to the remnants of insanity caused by a wild shopping spree at the Walmart in Secaucus. Women built like her shouldn't wear tank tops—not even to bed.

Storm didn't move a muscle, keeping her pinned beneath him. He didn't behave like a gentleman should and get off her, help her up, and make sure she was all right—not that she was surprised. Storm Decker was a bad boy, and he had the rap sheet to prove it.

He had the nerve to shoot her his guaranteed-good-time grin, the one that made any woman in the vicinity want to remove the sexy underwear she'd purchased with him in mind. "If I were out to hurt you, you'd be in a real tight spot right about now."

"No, she wouldn't."

Storm's attention snapped to Nicki standing in the doorway, holding the phone in one hand and the frying pan in the other.

"You'd be out cold again, and the cops would be on their way. Now, do you want to get off her, or am I gonna have to use this?" She waved the frying pan and did her best to look menacing.

Nicki was too cute to manage that, but Bree gave her points for trying.

Storm turned back to Bree, their noses almost touching. "Who's the kid?"

"Storm, this is Nicki. Nicki, meet Storm Decker, Pete's son." She tried not to think about Storm's proximity and concentrated on the pained and confused look on his face. He wasn't the only one confused. "What are you doing here?"

Storm rolled off her. She thought she'd be able to breathe better without two hundred pounds of man crushing her, but she was wrong. No, the breathlessness was still there. Crap. She was twenty-eight and a far cry from that seventeen-year-old caught in Storm Decker's wake.

"Logan couldn't get away from the vineyard— something about harvest season. He got ahold of me and told me Pop was sick. Since Logan was unable to make it, I was elected. I've been traveling for"—Storm glanced at his watch—"twenty-three hours, and this is the welcome I get? No wonder I haven't been home in years—"

"Eleven years." Bree sat and hugged her knees to her chest.

"So you did miss me."

"Yeah, like a rash."

"I might not have seen you, but I've been home a few times. The last time was five or six years ago. You were probably away at school."

Bree rose and brushed herself off, just to have something to do with her hands. "You must have left quite an impression. Funny, no one mentioned it to me." She took the phone and the pan from Nicki. "It's late, sweetie. Go back to bed."

"Aw, Bree."

Dropping a kiss on Nicki's forehead, Bree cut her off. "I'll see you in the morning."

Storm rose to his feet. He'd looked a lot smaller when he was out cold. He picked up his duffel bag with a grunt, one hand held against his head over what must have been one hell of a lump.

Bree waited for Nicki to climb into bed and curl around a big teddy bear before pulling up the light cotton blanket and brushing a hand over her hair. "I'll be in the next room if you need me."

"Okay."

Bree followed Storm out, doused the light, and closed the door behind her. Without looking at him, she headed straight to the kitchen, grabbed a bag of frozen peas, and tossed them at him. "Are you okay? Do I need to take you to the emergency room to have your head examined?"

He sat on a barstool and winced when he placed the bag against his head. "I'm fine."

She looked him over—his pupils were equally dilated. "Any nausea?"

"Why, Breezy, if I didn't know any better, I'd think you cared." The side of his mouth quirked up.

"I don't. I just don't want to be charged with murder. Now answer the question."

"No, I'm fine." His phone rang, sounding like a foghorn. Pulling it off his hip, he checked the caller. "I'm sorry. I have to take this."

"Fine." Bree started out of the kitchen, but he wrapped his fingers around her wrist and held on. The tingle shot straight to her breasts. She didn't dare look down.

"Storm Decker." He listened for a moment, and a smile spread across his face as her cheeks ignited. His black hair was cut short, much shorter than she remembered. It only served to accentuate the chiseled features of his face, while his strong square jaw covered with dark stubble added to his dangerous look. Blue eyes watched her and changed color with his mood. When he'd been on top of her, it had been like looking into an angry sea, and now his eyes were the color of a summer sky—deep blue and full of promise. When he smiled, his perfect teeth gleamed white against his tan skin. His voice was as soothing and buttery as a bottle of Macallan's fifty-five-year-old single malt scotch. At $17,500 a bottle, she'd bet a case of it that the person on the other end of the line was female.

"Hi, Sandy."

*Bingo.* Bree twisted her wrist and pulled away, breaking his grip.

"How are things at home? Any problems today?" Storm's gaze lingered on Bree's chest before moving to his pricey watch. She wondered if they sold cheap knockoffs on the street corners in Auckland. She doubted it. It looked more expensive than the run-of-the-mill Rolex. They probably charged extra for the dive watch to withstand the pressure of the ocean's depths or the corner office. Then again, maybe his watch had been a prize for winning the Sydney to Hobart Yacht Race. So okay, she'd Googled him and found a picture of Storm and his team holding the Rolex Cup. It was just her luck the photo hadn't done him justice.

"Tell Laurel I'll be back in plenty of time to go to the yacht club dinner. This should only take a week, two tops."

Bree did a quick boob check while she wiped the already-clean kitchen counter and tried to look as if she weren't listening to every word of his conversation. Unfortunately, the girls were standing at attention. Still, it didn't keep her from wanting to smack him upside the head with the damn frying pan again on general principles. A one- or two-week visit was no help. She had called Logan because she needed someone responsible to stay for the next couple of months at least. It sounded as if Storm's plan was to blow in, stay just long enough to assuage his guilty conscience, then leave for the next eleven years or until Pete's funeral, whichever came first. It was disappointing, but not unexpected. He probably had Peter Pan tattooed on his incredible ass.

Storm snapped his phone shut. "I guess I should thank you for the great homecoming. Now, do you want to tell me just what the hell is going on and who that kid is in my old bedroom?"

"Who are you to walk in here and start demanding answers? You ignored Pete for years, and now . . ." Storm was . . . God, he was *here*. Her energy level bottomed out, and she leaned against the counter for support. "Why couldn't Logan have come? And if he had to send someone, why couldn't he have called Slater?" After all, Slater was safe. "Slater's in Seattle. And last I checked, Seattle is a hell of a lot closer to Brooklyn than New Zealand, if you're still in New Zealand." With the Storm Chaser, one never knew.

"I get that you're not happy I'm here. Deal with it, Breezy, because like it or not, I'm all you've got."

"Lucky me. When it comes to helping someone other than yourself, you were always as useless as an inflatable dartboard."

Storm's head snapped back, and his chin followed, as if Oscar De La Hoya had hit him with a right cross. "People change."

She'd won this round. She'd pinned him against the ropes with the two-ton weight of her gaze, willing him to explain his disappearance years ago, but his eyes told no tales. "Pete collapsed at the Crow's Nest. Heart attack. They did bypass surgery, and he's not handling it well." She threw the sponge into the sink and wiped her hands on a towel. "I have a hard enough time managing the restaurant and Nicki single-handedly. I can't take care of Pete too. I need help. I'm surprised Logan called you, but I'm even more surprised you came."

"Why wouldn't I have come? Just because I moved away doesn't mean I'm not close to Pop."

"Oh yeah, I heard you friended him on Facebook. I'm sure that means so much to him." Bree took a deep breath and released it slowly. "He's at Methodist Hospital, and with any luck, he'll be out in a few days. He needs to heal, and I don't know how much he'll be able to do once he's back on his feet."

Storm stood and in two steps was around the breakfast bar. "Breezy? Is Nicki yours?"

"Mine?" She stepped back. "Why would you think that?"

"Why wouldn't I?"

Bree ran her hand through her hair and tucked it behind her ear. "No. Nicki is Pete's."

"Pop's? Since when?"

"It's been a few months now." If Pete hadn't told him about Nicki, it wasn't her place to do it. "Look, I'm tired. I'm going back to bed. Help yourself to whatever you want. There's beer and leftover pizza in the fridge. The guest towels are in the linen closet. I'm in Logan's old room. You can stay in Pete's room tonight—the sheets are clean. Good night, Storm." She brushed by him on her way out of the small kitchen.

"Good night, Breezy."

Bree felt his eyes on her the whole way back to her room. She closed the door and thought about locking it—not sure whether it would be to keep him out or keep her in. Climbing into bed, she fought the searing memory of the last time she'd seen Storm Decker. He'd been running out that same door and leaving her behind.

Storm's gaze locked on Breezy as she moved away. Reddish brown hair framed her face and gave her that hot, tussled, just-rolled-out-of-bed look women spent a fortune to duplicate—Breezy did it without trying. But then she *had* just rolled out of bed. He couldn't help but smile at the way her big green eyes sparkled with humor or anger whenever she hit her target. She had a hell of an aim, and not just with frying pans.

Her face had softened with time but still showed off those high cheekbones, the short, upturned nose, and the wide, full mouth. Her face wasn't the only thing that had changed. At seventeen, she'd been a skinny kid, but she'd filled out in all the right places. Her tank top showed off an abundance of cleavage, and those breasts were one hundred percent natural. He could tell. The rest of her body did anything but disappoint, and it put her in the realm of fantasy material. Damn, leave it to Breezy to be the only woman alive who could make those stupid cartoon pajamas look better than anything he'd seen as a teenager in the Victoria's Secret catalogue—the poor man's *Playboy*.

Storm fingered the goose egg on the back of his head. Shit, he was going to kill Logan when he got his hands on him. Logan failed to mention Breezy worked for Pop. But then, Storm had never asked about her either. The last thing he needed was a reminder of Breezy—hell, he'd dreamed about her every night for at least a year after almost having sex with her.

Storm pulled the phone off his belt and called Logan. He didn't give a shit what time it was. While the phone rang in his ear, he looked around the apartment he'd grown up in. It hadn't changed much except for some new carpet, paint, a big-screen TV, and a leather couch. Pop's favorite recliner still sat in the corner. Even though smoking in New York had been outlawed, since the apartment was above the Crow's Nest, it still held the faint scent of stale tobacco and beer. It smelled like home—something he hadn't realized he missed until he'd walked through the door. That was ... right before Breezy beaned him with the frying pan.

"Do you know what time it is?" Logan didn't sound happy. Good, neither was Storm, and it was three hours earlier in California. Hell, Storm didn't even want to know what time zone his body thought it was in.

"It's twelve forty-five your time. I guess the better question would be, do I care? I'm home, and you have a lot of explaining to do."

"What do you need explained exactly? Pop's in the hospital, and one of us needs to help him until he's back on his feet. I'm in the middle of a harvest, and Slater is doing an internship for school. You were elected. Besides, it got you out of the winter blues down under, so what the hell are you complaining about?"

Storm raked his fingers through his hair, momentarily forgetting about the goose egg until his hand traveled over it. He sucked in air through his teeth, the ones he was currently grinding. "Logan, you never told Bree I was coming. The first thing she did when I got here was hit me upside the head with a frying pan. She thought someone had broken into the apartment." The deep chuckle on the other end of the phone irritated him.

"What did you want me to tell her? She asked for help, I sent help."

"You also failed to tell me about the kid." Storm didn't know what to do with a kid, especially a girl. Women, sure. Girls, no way.

"What's this about a kid?"

"You didn't know either?"

"What the hell are you talking about? What did Pop do now, take in another stray?"

"This one is a little kid. *Her* name is Nicki."

"Did you say *her*?"

"Yeah. Her, as in 'Congratulations, it's a girl.'"

"How old is she?"

"How the hell do I know? She's not walking around with her date of birth stamped on her forehead."

"Well, is she two? School age?"

"Definitely school age." He tried to think back that far. He didn't see many kids, so he didn't have much to compare her to. "She's at that awkward age when nothing quite fits together. Her legs are too long and skinny; her teeth are too big." She was old enough to have the same look in her eyes he'd seen every time he'd looked in the mirror as a kid. Nicki was on a first-name basis with pain and fear and the dirty underbelly of society. Still, that knowledge came to some really young. "I don't know, somewhere between eight and twelve."

"Why didn't Pop tell me?"

"How the hell do I know?" Storm kicked the wall under the breakfast bar, something that never failed to get him a smack on the back of the head from Pop when they were kids. "I guess I shouldn't feel so bad since he didn't tell you either. After all, I'm the black sheep." Pop had never forgiven him for leaving without a word, even though he'd planned to join the merchant marines. He never explained why he'd shipped out two months earlier than expected—explanations were always messy.

"When did the kid show up?" Logan asked.

"Bree said it's been a couple months. Why the hell has it been months since you've talked to Pop?"

"Look who's talking. I've been busy at the vineyard."

"And Slater?"

"School and work. Pop came out last winter, and the three of us got together in Vancouver."

Storm hadn't been invited. Not that he would have flown to the West Coast, but shit, he used to be one of them. An invite would have been nice.

"It must have been before he got her. Pop never said anything about a girl. He never said anything about a heart problem when he was with us either."

"A quadruple bypass is a little more than a problem."

"I was shocked when Bree called and told me he'd had a heart attack."

"Yeah, I know. Looks like he's closer to Bree and Nicki than to any of us."

"What are you waiting for? The pity platoon to come rescue you?"

Storm groaned. Even to his ears that sounded whiny. After all, Pop had rescued him, Logan, and Slater from foster care and loved them as if they were his own. Then they'd grown up, and Storm had moved on. Hell, he'd left Red Hook, but not because of Pop. He left because he had no choice—he couldn't disappoint Pop, and he couldn't stay. There was no future for him in Red Hook, only a past he wasn't proud of.

"Are you going to see him tomorrow?" Logan asked.

"No, I came all this way to hang out at the bar. Of course I'm going to see him. I'll be at the hospital first thing."

"Good, get some sleep. And Storm, you might consider buying a helmet."

"Don't laugh. I might do more than just consider it. The woman has one hell of an arm."

"I'm glad you're home."

"Yeah, well, I'm here. But I need to get back in two weeks."

"Two weeks?"

"I told you, this is the busiest time of the year for me. I just landed a commission for a Class 40 racing yacht. I'm slammed with tight deadlines. As much as I love the old man, I can't stay in dry dock forever."

"Okay, I guess we just have to hope Pop's better. I'm in the middle of harvest, and it's not something I can take care of from Red Hook."

Storm ended the call and stared at Breezy's door, wishing he had X-ray vision. Even after all these years, he hadn't needed the lights to know who lay beneath him. One breath and Bree's scent—an intoxicating blend of citrus and spice—tossed him back eleven years, landing him in the exact place he'd been before. On top of her. Between her legs. Hard.

"Fuck."

He wasn't sure what had him reeling more—the conk on the head or seeing Bree.

He'd done the right thing eleven years ago. He'd left because he knew he wouldn't have had the strength to walk away from her again. Bree was like a daughter to Pop, and Storm had broken the cardinal rule: Don't mess with Pop's little girl.

Storm rounded the breakfast bar and tossed the wet bag of once-frozen peas back into the freezer with more force than necessary. Being in Red Hook with Breezy was as dangerous as sailing through the Bermuda Triangle—he couldn't afford to get sucked back in.

Tomorrow he'd go to the hospital, size up the situation, and figure out what to do. If anyone thought Storm planned to stay here for more than two weeks, he was a few hands short of a full crew.

Mug in hand, Bree waited for the coffee to brew. She looked away from the pot when Storm walked through the front door, wearing running shorts and a sweat-stained T-shirt. The sight of him stole all the oxygen from the room, maybe the whole building.

"Morning, Breezy."

"Morning."

Storm lifted the hem of his shirt and wiped his face, baring his washboard abs and revealing the treasure trail of dark hair disappearing into the waistband of his shorts. Rounding the breakfast bar, he set two bags of what smelled like bagels and all the fixings on the counter, then grabbed a water from the fridge. As he downed the entire bottle, his Adam's apple bobbed with each gulp.

"Coffee?" She cleared her throat, hardly recognizing her own voice. She grabbed another mug and, without waiting for the machine to finish, poured two cups.

Flashbacks, like grainy sex-tapes of the last night she'd seen Storm before he'd left, ran through her mind. Every. Humiliating. Moment. She took a slow, deep breath.

Storm stared at her.

She raised her chin and stared right back. He'd changed—physically at least. He was broader and more muscled. His tall, skinny frame had filled out in manhood, and the angles of his face had sharpened. His nose was narrow and a little crooked, probably the result of all the fights he'd gotten into as a kid. His square jaw was more defined, and his neck was corded with muscle. He was solid, heavy, dangerous, and so full of charged energy, he seemed to barely kept it in check.

Needing something to do, Bree opened the bags and peeked in. "Thanks for picking up breakfast."

"Anything to keep you away from a frying pan."

She winged her eyebrow as she snatched the first salt bagel she saw, ripped a piece off, and stuffed it in her mouth.

"I didn't know what you and Nicki liked, so I got a little of everything—just to be safe." He pulled his shirt off and dragged it across his neck and chest. "I'll just grab a quick shower."

She stared at his six-pack. Why couldn't it be a keg?

"Hello? Breezy? Did you hear me?"

"Uh, yeah." She handed him his coffee and watched him walk to Pete's room. Wasn't she just chock-full of inspired repartee? She wasn't out to impress him or anything, but sheesh, she'd sounded like a member of the dim-bulb club.

Nicki padded out of her room in her Hello Kitty nightgown. "He's still here?"

"Shh. He might hear you."

Nicki smiled as she climbed onto the barstool. "I can live with that."

"What, that Storm is here or that he might hear you?"

"Both, actually. I bet Pop will be happy to see him." Nicki tilted her head to one side. "How come Storm's been gone so long?"

Bree closed her eyes and rubbed the spot on her temple that throbbed with every beat of her heart. God, she was in no mood for twenty questions. "I'm not sure." She knew why Storm had left, but not why he stayed away. "I guess you'll just have to ask him."

Bree poured a glass of orange juice and slid it across the bar. "How did you sleep?"

"Fine after you took Storm down. Man, that was epic. You were like Wonder Woman with a frying pan instead of the rope."

"Yeah, that's me. Wonder Woman with her frying pan of truth." Bree arranged the bagels on a plate and grabbed another for the whitefish and lox. There must have been seventy-five dollars' worth of lox, not to mention the schmear. She handed the plates to Nicki. "Why don't you set the table so we can eat? We need to get down to the hospital, and I'm already running late."

Nicki walked around the table, placing the napkins on top of the plates.

No matter how many times Bree corrected her, she couldn't break Nicki of the habit. "Food goes on the plate. Napkins belong under the fork or on your lap."

Nicki stopped. "When you sit down, the first thing you do is put your napkin in your lap. What's it matter if the napkin's under the fork or on the plate?"

Bree sighed. What was the point? They'd had the discussion thirty times. It never changed the way Nicki set the table, and it only served to remind her of Nicki's first dinner at Pete's, the day Bree fell in love with the little scamp.

Pete had asked Bree to come because Nicki seemed uncomfortable alone with him. The poor thing had just been abandoned by the only parent she'd ever known. She was hurt, scared, and thrown into the care of a big bear of a man.

Nicki had spent the meal hunched over her plate, guarding her food. She'd even hidden some in her napkin for later. Bree's heart broke every time she thought about it. She placed her hands on Nicki's shoulders.

"What?" Nicki gave her that look—a little confused, a little shy, and still, even after almost three months, a little scared.

Bree pulled her close and held her, resting her chin on the top of Nicki's head. She loved Nicki as much as she imagined any mother loved her child. She'd always wanted a family—a traditional family like the one she had before her father died. She remembered what it was like when she had two loving parents and then what her life was like after her father had died. She was afraid of being the same kind of single parent her mother had turned into—smothering, obsessive. Bree wouldn't do that to a child. No, unless Bree found a man and was happily married, she'd never have a child of her own. Many single women had children and were fabulous parents, but the deep fear of becoming like her mother was enough to make her not want to take the chance. "I love you, Nicki."

Nicki snuggled in. "For always and forever?"

Bree held her tighter. "For always and forever. No matter what."

"Even if I never put the napkin in the right place?"

Bree felt a smile tug on the corners of her mouth. The little brat was testing her. "Even then. I love you for who you are, not what you do." She kissed the top of Nicki's head and looked up to find Storm leaning against the doorjamb. The curious look in his eye had Bree hugging Nicki tighter. She wasn't sure what Storm was curious about, but then, she didn't know Storm Decker—not anymore and maybe not ever.

It was an affront to all womankind that Storm could take a five-minute shower and come out looking edible when it took Bree an hour just to come out looking not scary.

Bree kissed the top of Nicki's head again, released the little rascal, and then reached for a bagel for Nicki. Cutting it in half, Bree stopped just short of slicing her hand. The damn man made her nervous.

"Good morning, Nicki." Storm sat at the head of the table while Nicki piled her bagel with lox. He took up more room than any man should—all spread out, as if he didn't have a care in the world.

"That's Pop's chair."

"Yeah, well, you're sitting in mine."

Nicki snorted. "Doesn't have your name on it."

Bree watched as Nicki sized up Storm. He looked

loose and comfortable, as if his father weren't in the hospital; as if he hadn't been away for more than a third of his life; as if he ate breakfast with her and Nicki every day.

Storm set his coffee on the table and sat straighter in his chair. "What grade are you in?"

Holding her bagel with both hands, Nicki continued to eye him. "I'm going into fifth grade." She took a big bite of her bagel and struggled to keep it in her mouth.

Bree stopped herself from telling Nicki to take human bites. The girl didn't eat food; she inhaled it.

"So that makes you how old?" Storm asked, either not noticing Nicki's lack of table manners, or ignoring them.

Bree pushed Nicki's juice toward her. "Ten."

When Nicki finally swallowed, she shook her head. "Ten and a half."

Bree snuck glances at Storm as she fixed what was left of her bagel. Licking the remnants of schmear off the side of her finger, she lifted the bagel to her mouth to lick what had escaped.

She caught Storm staring. She remembered that look; no matter how many times she'd tried to forget it, it returned to her in her dreams. It was the same look she'd seen in his eyes right before he'd shut down and run away from her all those years ago, leaving her naked and needy. Fidgeting in her chair, she crossed her legs before wiping her fingers on her napkin, and tried to erase it from her inner hard drive.

Bree saw Nicki goggling at Storm. God only knew what would come out of Nicki's mouth next. The girl was not only perceptive, but she said whatever went through her mind. "Nicki, why don't you run and get dressed.

Don't forget to wash your face and brush your teeth. You can take the rest of your bagel with you and eat it on the way to the hospital."

Nicki looked at her plate.

"I'll wrap up the leftovers so when we come back, you can make another bagel to bring down to the restaurant if you want."

"Okay." Nicki rose, still looking longingly at her half-eaten bagel, and then swiped her tongue across the schmear.

Bree cringed—as if anyone else would eat it. "Just leave it. I'll put it in a sandwich bag for you. And don't forget to bring a sweater. It's always chilly in the hospital."

Nicki did the patented teenaged eye roll and headed to her room, muttering, "Bree, I'm not a baby."

Storm turned the full wattage of his smile up a few degrees and aimed it at Bree. "The kid's still protective of her food after three months? I'm surprised she didn't spit in her juice."

"Like you never backwashed your Coke. At least she doesn't hunch over her plate anymore." She picked up Nicki's bagel. "Are you going to eat anything?"

"I guess I should. She didn't lick anything else, did she?"

"You should be safe. She's had all her shots."

He fixed a monster bagel while Bree made another for Nicki and grabbed a juice box.

"Where'd Pop find Nicki?"

Bree shrugged and pulled out a few sandwich bags. "You need to talk to Pete about that. All I know is one day Nicki was here. Pete said he'd known her mom years ago and that she couldn't care for Nicki anymore, so she signed over all parental rights and left Nicki with him."

"Who's her mother?"

Bree stashed the food in the fridge. "I don't know, but it doesn't matter. Right now, it's more important for Nicki to know she has a real home where she's loved and wanted."

Storm's straight dark brows drew together as if he didn't believe her. Well, that was his problem. She didn't owe him anything, but she owed Pete her life. Pete had been her father's lifelong friend and partner on the force. He'd taken her under his wing after her dad's death, loving her and supporting her like a surrogate father. Pete gave her a safe place to escape her mother, he gave her guidance, and eventually he gave her a job and a home. She'd do anything to protect Nicki and Pete.

At the thought of Pete, she realized Storm was going to have one hell of a shock when he saw him.

Bree stopped what she was doing. "Storm, Pete's changed a lot. He's aged. He's not the same big guy you saw six years ago."

"People don't change that much."

"They do after open-heart surgery."

# Chapter 2

Storm ate and watched Bree work in the kitchen as if she lived there. He hadn't been back since she graduated from college. Before that, when he visited, he made sure she was at school. He talked to Pop often enough—or he thought he had until now. When he called, they enacted their own version of don't-ask-don't-tell. He had thought the only taboo subject was Breezy, although now he was beginning to wonder. How could Pop take in a little girl and not tell him or his brothers?

Breezy wore light capri pants, and a tunic. It skimmed her curves without highlighting her assets. When she was seventeen, she kept them hidden. Now she made a man work for it, pay attention, notice. That might discourage other guys, but he'd seen her in a tank, and he knew exactly what was beneath that top. A man would have to be dead not to notice breasts like those, and he wasn't anywhere close to being six feet under.

She reached across the bar to grab the plate of bagels, and a flash of pink caught his eye. A pink bra? He smiled at the mental picture. Taking a bite of his bagel, Storm tried to erase the vision his imagination painted of her in a tight tank top and a pair of barely there lace panties.

No matter what he might want, Bree was still off-limits. She'd never been the kind of girl who could handle sex without strings. It was still written all over her pretty little face. Besides, he was only here until Pop was well enough to take care of himself and Nicki.

Nicki ran from her room. Her fluorescent green Vans made her feet look about three inches too long for her body. Sticklike, gangly legs were topped with madras shorts, and an orange T-shirt covered her torso with the face of a smiling monkey.

Bree smiled and held out her hand. "Nicki, bring me your brush. You missed most of it."

"I did not."

"Good, then I should have no problem running a brush through your hair again."

"Fine, I'll do it myself." Nicki stomped off, and Bree followed Nicki into her room.

Storm listened to Nicki's protests. It reminded him of bath night before he and his brothers discovered girls.

When the kid reappeared, she wore a ponytail—the kind he was sure little boys would like nothing better than to pull. Pop was going to have his hands full in a few years—again. "Everyone ready to go?"

Bree grabbed her purse and the brown paper sack containing Nicki's breakfast. "I'm parked just across the street. I'll drive."

Storm locked the apartment with the key he'd kept all these years and followed them to the street.

Nicki, full of energy, skipped along chattering as Bree walked with a graceful kind of determination. She held her back straight, something he didn't remember her doing before. When he'd known her, Bree had always seemed to make herself look smaller. She was taller than he remembered, probably five feet nine, most of which was leg. She had been skinny as a kid. He remembered how shocked he'd been at age eighteen to find out what kind of body she had hidden beneath the oversized clothes she always wore.

"Do you think Pop's coming home today?" Nicki asked as she stepped on and off the curb, turning in circles as if doing an intricate dance beside a little blue Ford Fiesta.

"I know he wants to, but it's not up to him. It's up to his doctors. We'll find out when we get there."

"Do you think Pop's using the heart pillow we made him?"

Bree clicked the remote to unlock the car. "He'd better be if he wants to come home."

Storm folded himself—knees to nostrils—into the car and pushed the seat back as far as possible. It wasn't far enough—he'd have to remove the front seat and sit in back to do that. "Why does he need to use a heart pillow?"

Nicki stopped the dance midstep and climbed in, pushing her skinny body between the front seats. "Duh, I thought you came from New Zealand, not New Dorkland."

"Nicki." Bree closed her eyes and rubbed her forehead. "You don't say duh to adults."

"Sorry."

Storm looked out the window to hide his smile. The kid was anything but.

Bree gave him an apologetic shrug. "After open-heart surgery, patients need to cough, and it doesn't hurt as much if they hug a pillow to their chests. We made Pete a big, fuzzy, heart-shaped pillow to use."

Storm swallowed a boulder-sized lump in his throat. The whole idea of Pop being sick was surreal. Pop never got sick. Even when Storm and his brothers were down with the flu from hell and he was surrounded by three puking kids, Pop didn't catch it.

"So, do you think he uses it?" Nicki bounced in the backseat as Bree started the car.

Bree looked in her rearview mirror. "If you want to find out, you'd better buckle your seat belt. You know the rules."

There wasn't enough room to shift his shoulders, so he opened the car door to reach his seat belt. "You might need a can opener to get me out of this car."

Bree snorted. "I've got WD-40 and a crowbar in the trunk. No worries." She waited for the telltale click from Nicki before she put the car in gear and pulled into traffic. Every time she shifted, her fist slid against his thigh. He was going to need a moment before she pried him out of his seat.

The day was a little overcast; it would be muggy as hell in an hour. In summer, it was so humid, residents developed iron lungs. Everyone else needed scuba gear. There was nothing worse than Red Hook in the summer. Hell, in his estimation, there was nothing worse than Red Hook any time of the year. What Pop ever saw in this place was a mystery.

Storm sat back and watched Red Hook fly by. The abandoned buildings he and his brothers had avoided as they walked home from school were all he saw. Bree drove by the empty lot where they had played baseball until they'd found it surrounded by crime-scene tape and a few of New York's finest outlining the body of a murder victim on top of the hubcap that was second base. It was one of the hookers who'd routinely worked Van Brunt Street.

He shook his head as the memories followed him past every street corner, toward the Red Hook Houses—the projects on the bad side of town where he'd spent his first twelve years. His grip on the sissy bar tightened until his knuckles turned white as he tried to clear away the memories. He'd survived his life in the projects before Pete, the badass ex-cop, had opened his home and his heart to three ragtag kids who'd never met before they were rescued.

Bree sped past the first place he'd ever gotten arrested. His graffiti art had long ago been covered over by some other kid with a spray can and a colorful vocabulary. "This place hasn't changed much."

Bree's smile was strained. "It's changed a lot. I've been on the Revitalization Committee for five years working on Red Hook's regeneration. The committee's been meeting for more than a decade, and the results are really beginning to show. They demolished the old sugar factory; Ikea opened and brought a lot of jobs and shoppers who take advantage of the free ferry from Manhattan; and the Fairway Market opened at the end of Van Brunt by Pier Thirty-nine. It's been wonderful for the community."

They passed a teen wearing pants so big he had to take giant steps to keep them from ending up below his knees. An unbuttoned black shirt hung from his skinny frame over a wife beater. The kid looked too much like Storm had when he'd been a trouble magnet. "It takes a lot more than a few coats of paint, a couple of shops, and a shiny new condo here and there to change a community."

Bree looked in the rearview mirror at Nicki and then back at him as if planning his demise. Well, shit, what the hell did she expect? It had been years since he'd had to face his past—something he never wanted to do. Now they were headed straight to the one place on earth he'd sworn he'd never return to. He was sure she was doing this to get back at him for their one-night fiasco. If she was, she couldn't have picked a better way to unman him.

Bree walked into the hospital, signed for guest badges for her and Nicki, and slid the clipboard toward Storm.

She didn't know what his problem was, but throughout the drive, Storm had looked like he was reliving a nightmare. His breathing had grown choppy, and even with the air-conditioning turned down to arctic, he'd been sweating.

She still fumed over his comment about it taking a lot more than a few coats of paint and a couple new condos to change a community.

As if she didn't know that. She'd dealt with a lot of naysayers over the years and bested most of them. The only way to win a point when people threw out thoughtless, unsubstantiated comments was to inundate them with facts—show proof positive of the results of the plan. But not this time. No, she'd just shut her mouth, not willing to get into it with Nicki sitting in the backseat.

Nicki took Bree's hand and pulled her toward the elevator, hitting the UP button as she bounced on the balls of her feet. Bree kept her eyes locked on the elevator doors. If she didn't look at Storm, maybe he'd go away—again.

The UP arrow blinked, and a bell dinged. Nicki pulled

Bree in, pushing the number of Pete's floor. Storm stepped in beside Bree, and she moved away.

He leaned toward her, invading her personal space. "Do I make you nervous, Breezy?" he whispered. His breath was warm against her ear.

She stayed still, refusing to step back, refusing to show any reaction. "No. Is that what you're going for?" The scent of the sea, laundry detergent, Irish Spring soap, and something she couldn't put her finger on surrounded him. She remembered it, both from last night and that night so long ago.

The elevator dinged again and the doors slid open; before Storm answered the question, Nicki and Bree stepped out. He glanced up and down the hallway. "Hey, Nicki." Taking his billfold from his pocket he asked, "Why don't you run down the hall and grab us three waters out of the vending machine? I don't know about you, but all that lox made me thirsty." He handed Nicki a few bills, took Bree's elbow, and pulled her away from the elevator, crowding her against the wall. "Now, Breezy, why don't you tell me what's got you so pissed off?"

"Nothing special, just you." It was something she was sure he didn't hear often, especially from women. His brows drew together, and she had the urge to smooth them with her fingers. "You've been here less than twelve hours, and you think your mere presence will make everything okay."

"Give me a break, Breezy. I never said that."

"Don't call me Breezy. I don't like it. My name is Breanna, or Bree."

"You didn't mind when I called you Breezy before."

\*    \*    \*

Storm watched Bree's cheeks flame.

"That's ancient history."

"Obviously not, since you're still thinking about it."

Her bright green eyes glittered with anger and darkened with what looked like arousal. "Don't even go there."

Her eyes alone proved his point. Shit, he'd been going there for the last eleven years. It was nice to know he hadn't been going there alone.

"Here you go, Storm." Nicki ran up and handed him a water, which had the same effect as shooting him with a fire hose.

"Thanks." He cracked the cap and did his best to put out the flames.

Nicki danced around Breezy, who was having a difficult time opening hers.

Storm took the bottle from her, and unscrewed the top.

She mumbled her thanks and snatched it away as if she were afraid to touch him.

Nicki didn't seem to notice Bree's shaking hands, her flushed face, the awkward silence. She galloped down the hall, her oversized sneakers slapping against the linoleum floor, before rounding the corner and racing out of view. Bree hurried after her.

Storm hated hospitals. His pace slowed as memories resurfaced of the times that, thanks to his father's beatings, he and his mom had ended up a few floors below in the emergency room. The very memories he'd run from and never wanted to revisit were popping up faster than stars in the night sky in the middle of the South Pacific. Yet here he was, back in Red Hook with no escape.

He turned the corner just in time to see Bree stroll into a room. Nicki's delighted squeal was met by a deeper, quieter tone — Pop.

Storm pasted a smile on his face and walked through the doorway, taking in the picture of Nicki, holding an obnoxious, red, fur-covered pillow, and climbing onto Pop's bed. But the man he'd expected to see wasn't there. Sure, it looked a little like Pop, but the man who had saved Storm wasn't the same man folding Nicki into his bony arms. Swallowing back the breakfast threatening to make an unwelcome appearance, Storm gulped for air, stepped back feeling as if he'd been gut shot, and plowed blindly through the door.

He leaned hard against the wall. It felt cold against his clammy skin. Tilting his head back, he closed his eyes and locked his knees, trying to stay on his feet, trying to breathe, trying to come to terms with his new reality. "Fuck."

Bree followed him out and quietly closed the door. "I tried to warn you."

He took a sip of water, washing away the bitter taste of bile. "God, what happened to him?"

Bree rounded on him as if ready to bare fangs and strike. "Years of working too hard, a major heart attack, and a quadruple bypass."

"I . . . Pop's never been sick a day in his life." If he kept repeating it, maybe it would be true.

She gave him a shove. If his back hadn't already been against the wall, it would be now. "Pete's been slowing down for the last year and a half."

He grasped her wrist. Her pulse raced beneath his fingers. "No one told me."

"You never asked." She pulled away and gestured wildly. "You've been too busy gallivanting around the other side of the world to notice. So pull yourself together." She pointed down the hall. "There's a restroom down there. Go splash water on your face or something, and don't come back until you've gotten a grip. I won't let you upset Pete. And don't you dare say anything about leaving either. Not until I can figure out what I'm going to do." She turned her back to him, and the realization of what she'd been faced with hit him like a boom coming about in a typhoon.

He cleared his throat. "Breezy . . . I mean Bree."

She spun around as if expecting a fight. "What?"

He reached out and took her hand, gave her a tug, and she tumbled against him. He pulled her close, not wanting to see the warning he knew was on her face. "I'm sorry."

She relaxed in his arms, as if she needed a hug just as badly as he did.

"Do you need a minute, or are you good?"

A smile threatened, but he tamped it down. He was real good, or so he'd been told, but that wasn't what she was asking about. She was asking if he could walk into that room, see a shadow of the man he considered a father, and not lose it or make a complete fool of himself. He nodded, his chin rubbing the top of her head.

She leaned back, watching him, thigh-to-thigh, pelvis-to-pelvis, his hand holding hers, his arm looped around her waist. When she really looked at him, her face held a mixture of pity, concern, and awareness that caused a pretty blush to cover her cheeks.

"I'm okay now. I just wasn't expecting—"

She patted his chest with her free hand. "I know. Pete

will get through this. We all will." Bree looked over her shoulder at the door. "I can't leave Nicki in there alone with him much longer. She's probably already told him you're here. We'd better go in."

Storm pulled her close and held on for just a second longer, thankful she let him. He took a deep breath; the scent of citrus and spice, the scent of Breezy, replaced the antiseptic odor of hospital, and he wished he didn't have to let her go. He'd sailed through gales, survived more than one close shave during a yacht race, but he'd never been more scared.

He released her and held her gaze.

Bree looked as if she were deciding whether to allow him in. "Okay." She took his hand and gave it a squeeze. "You'll get used to it."

He doubted he'd ever get used to seeing Pop looking weak and sick. He nodded and didn't let go of her hand until she pushed open the door.

# CHAPTER 3

Pete raised the head of the bed to sit as he listened to Nicki chatter on about whatever ten-year-old girls chattered about: her favorite show on Disney, the joke that led to her belly laugh, the meaning of which got lost in translation, though he followed it with a chuckle, if for nothing more than the pleasure of hearing her laughter.

He was tired—more tired than he could ever remember. His eyes felt heavy as the comforting warmth of Nicki's body seeped into his side.

"And then Bree was like Wonder Woman and hit him on the head with her frying pan of truth. He was knocked out, lying on the floor. All that was missing were those cartoon birds flying around his head, tweeting."

"What?" Pete came alert, wondering what was fact, and what was fiction. Nicki had one hell of an imagination, something she shared often.

He was relieved when the door to his room opened and Bree walked in, followed closely by someone. Not someone, *Storm*. All other thoughts evaporated.

"Hey, Pop. I came as soon as I heard." Storm walked

around the bed and enveloped him in a careful half hug that had him rattled.

Nicki slid away as Pete stared, unbelieving. "God, it's good to see you, son." Pete felt old and at a loss as tears clouded his eyes. He patted Storm's back, careful not to snag the IV line, and looked over Storm's shoulder at Bree. "You called Storm?"

Storm drew away and fortunately turned so he didn't notice Pete's loss of composure. "No, she called Logan and he couldn't come, so he called me. You could have called me yourself, Pop. I had no idea. . . ."

Storm looked good—strong, a little pale under his tan, but he was a welcome sight. "I didn't want to bother you. You've got your own life to lead and a business to run." When Storm faced him again, Pete saw anger and hurt. "I didn't think it was a big deal. Turns out, I was wrong. I'm glad to see you. It's been too long."

Bree moved beside Pete and brushed his cheek with a kiss, running her hand over his balding head. "I love the new pj's." She straightened the collar. "You wear them well."

He let out a laugh, which turned into a cough, and he grabbed his pillow, pulling it to his chest. Once he took a cough-free breath, he swallowed the pain and did his best to continue as if it never happened—not an easy thing to do while hugging an oversized, furry, heart-shaped monstrosity of a pillow. "I don't know about that, but it beats the hell out of having my ass flopping around for all the world to see."

Bree laughed. "Nicki and I are going to take a little walk and give you two some time to catch up, okay?"

Pete nodded and watched something pass between

Storm and Bree, a warning look and something else that had been brewing since they were kids. He'd always hoped they'd figure it out eventually, but then Storm had taken off.

There were still so many unanswered questions, the least of which was why Storm had left so suddenly. In the long run, Storm had taken the right path. Pete just wished he hadn't bolted. Leaving and running were two very different things. If Storm had left, it wouldn't have taken him years to find his way home again. "Why'd you run?" Pete watched a wave of shock break over Storm's face before an eerie calm replaced it.

"Why are you asking me this now, Pop? It's not going to change the past."

"You'd think after all this time you'd be able to tell me. I'm not getting any younger, and Lord knows, I might not get too much older either."

Storm blanched.

"Don't worry. I'm not bellying up to the big bar in the sky—at least not yet. But I gotta tell you, there have been times I would have killed to order a Guinness from St. Peter."

"You think there's Guinness in heaven?"

"Good God, I hope so." Pete pulled his blanket up and cursed his inability to get warm. "If not, I'll be spending a hell of a long time in purgatory."

Storm smirked and leaned forward in his chair, his elbows resting on his thighs, his fingers laced together. "You might not have much of a choice about that. Guinness or no."

"Was there a woman involved?" It was amazing how fast a smirk could disappear.

"Yeah."

Well, shit. "Who?" When Marisa, Nicki's mother, dropped her on his doorstep, she'd claimed Nicki was his granddaughter. As he looked back at his three sons eleven years ago, the first one who came to mind was Storm. Back then Storm had been antsy and impulsive. He'd run from something. Pete studied Storm and saw what looked an awful lot like pain, guilt, maybe even remorse.

Storm closed his eyes, shook his head, and looked away. "I'm sorry, Pop. I can't . . ."

His son may have been gone a long time, but some things never changed. Storm was shutting down. It was time for a different subject. "Have you been by the Crow's Nest yet?"

Storm shook his head and then rubbed the back of it as if he had a headache. "Not yet. I flew in late last night."

"Bree's done some fine work—classed it up a lot. You're not going to recognize the old place."

"How long has she been working for you?"

Pete knew an accusation when he heard it. "I never hid the fact that Bree worked for me, and you never once asked about her. She's worked for me since she graduated college. I made her the manager and gave her the one-bedroom apartment above the bar that we always used for storage. She's been with me ever since. Hiring Bree is the best business decision I've ever made. She's worked hard and has become one hell of a business-woman. I might own the place, but the Crow's Nest is all Bree's."

"What's the story with Nicki?"

"I knew her mother, and when she couldn't take care of Nicki, she brought her to me. What can I say? Nicki's a great kid. You'll see when you get to know her."

"Yeah, Pop, I'm sure she is. I'm just wondering why you never called to tell me about her. What are you hiding?"

Pete looked away and thanked God when Storm continued. He was tempted to cross himself when he realized Storm wasn't waiting for an answer. "Taking in a kid is a big deal. Then again, so is heart disease."

"All you boys have lives of your own. I didn't want the lot of you feeling as if you had to run home to meet Nicki—besides, it hasn't been easy for her to settle in."

"She's close to Bree."

"Bree's easy to love. They both are. They've been good for each other."

The door swished open, and Bree peeked in. "How are you two doing?"

Storm stood and slid his hands into his pockets. "Good."

Nicki bounded over and jumped back up on Pete's bed as Bree filled the water glass from the pitcher on the table. "The doctor said they're going to keep you around until tomorrow, and if all goes well, he'll spring you after his rounds. You should be home in time for dinner."

"Great." Pete hoped to hell he sounded excited, because right now it was all he could do to stay awake.

Bree took Nicki's hand, then bent over him and kissed his cheek. "We've got to get back," she said, checking her watch. "I'm running late."

Pete waved her away before giving Nicki a kiss. "You be good for Bree and Storm."

Nicki rolled her eyes. "You know me. I'm always good." She waited a beat and then smiled. "Except for when I'm not." She slid off the bed.

Bree threw her arm around Nicki. "Which is usually. Come on, kiddo. I have to get to work."

Storm came closer and smiled. "I guess I'll see you tomorrow, Pop. Take care."

"Sounds good. And, Storm, the keys to the car are on my dresser if you need it."

Storm leaned over and gave him a hug. "Thanks, Pop, but there's really nowhere around Red Hook I want to go."

Storm followed Bree and Nicki out of Pete's room as they headed toward the elevator. He still felt a little green around the gills seeing Pop like that. He had a bad feeling Pop was going to need more than two weeks before he was recovered enough to take care of himself, no less to take care of Nicki. Shit. He was stuck there for the duration. He didn't have a choice.

Even as sick as Pop was, it hadn't taken him long to start his interrogation—not that Storm blamed him. Pop deserved some kind of explanation. But with Bree working and practically living with him, Storm didn't think it was right to kiss and tell.

Bree leaned against the wall as they waited for the elevator. "How'd it go with Pete?"

"Good, I guess. He spent most of the time talking about you."

Bree shrugged. "We've worked together for years. I guess it's not surprising."

After taking the elevator down, they handed in their badges, and Storm stopped. "You two go on ahead; I'll get back on my own."

Bree looked at him the same way she had earlier, when she was deciding if she should let him in Pete's room.

"See you later, Nicki. Bree." It wasn't as if he needed

her permission. He turned on his heel and headed in the opposite direction. Unfortunately, that hallway took him to the last place he'd wanted to go—the emergency room.

"Storm, Storm Decker? Is that you, man?"

All the hair on the back of his neck stood up. He turned, expecting a punch, but instead found himself staring into the eyes of a man covered with blood. He knew he shouldn't have come back home.

"Hey, I thought that was you. I haven't seen you since—"

"That fight by the old sugar factory." Frankie was two years older than Storm, and all through school, Frankie had used him as his own personal punching bag.

At least Frankie had the decency to look embarrassed, which just added to the weirdness of the situation. "Yeah. I guess that's true."

Storm shook his head, wondering if he had stepped into some strange alternate reality: Pop was in the hospital, and Frankie "the Bruiser" DeBruscio hadn't threatened Storm's life yet. "Don't you need to go get some help?"

"Me?" Frankie looked down at himself. "Oh, right. I was just going to the locker room to grab a quick shower and a pair of scrubs when I saw you."

"So all that's not yours?"

He tugged on what Storm realized was a uniform shirt. "The blood? Hell no. An occupational hazard."

"Vampire?"

Frankie laughed. "Paramedic. Look, I know your old man is here—"

"How do you know that?"

"Bree and I are close."

Storm fought the urge to put Frankie through a wall to find out just what he meant by that.

"Give me five minutes to get cleaned up; then maybe we can grab a cup of coffee. Catch up, you know?"

Storm must have nodded, but he wasn't sure. He was in a state of shock. Frankie DeBruscio was a paramedic? Storm had always figured he'd be in the state pen, serving multiple life sentences by now. He took a seat as close to the door as possible and rubbed the lump on the back of his head. Maybe Breezy hit him harder than he thought. He wondered if concussions caused hallucinations.

A few minutes later, Frankie met him by the door. He was built like an oversized fireplug—Storm had a few inches on him, but Frankie still outweighed him by a good fifty pounds. Frankie reached out to shake hands, and Storm didn't know how to avoid it. They shook, and Frankie shocked him again when he pulled him into a guy hug. "Come on, let me buy you a cup of coffee. I'm off duty and about a quart low."

Storm really wasn't up to socializing with the terror of Red Hook, but he found himself walking out with him. "So, Frankie—"

Frankie laughed. "I go by Francis now."

Storm stopped. "You're kidding me. You used to beat the shit out of anyone who called you Francis."

Francis shrugged and continued on. "Yeah, well, people change."

"Funny, I said the same thing last night ... or was it this morning? I can't remember."

"Jet lag will do that to a guy. You're supposed to drink a lot of water. It will help. When did you get in?"

"Last night ... or this morning—"

"You don't remember, right?"

"Maybe I'm trying to forget."

"That bad, huh?"

They went into a Starbucks and ordered. Francis grabbed a large water and tossed it on the counter. "Do you want anything else?"

"No, coffee's fine." Storm pulled out his billfold. "I'll get it."

Francis shook his head. "Nope, this one's on me. You can buy me a beer the next time I'm in the Crow's Nest."

Maybe the bar hadn't changed that much after all. "You hang out there?"

Francis laughed and grabbed their drinks. "Pete pulled me off Logan one time and made me pay for the fifteen stitches Logan needed after the tussle. He said it was either that, or he'd call the cops. He let me work it off at the bar. Your old man's the one who set me straight—I owe him. I still help out at the Crow's Nest when I'm not on the job. With four days on and three off, I go in as often as I can. I've been helping Bree out a lot since Pete got sick."

Storm sat at a round table and shook his head. He never thought he'd be shown up by his archenemy.

Francis sat across from him and stirred his coffee. "Over the years, Pete showed me all the articles in those sailing magazines about you and the boats you design. He's so damn proud of you. He has a whole wall at the Crow's Nest filled with framed pictures and articles following the careers of you and your brothers." He stopped and looked embarrassed. "Ah hell, why am I telling you that? I'm sure you've seen it."

"No, I haven't. I haven't gotten down to the bar yet. I flew in and went straight home. Bree, Nicki, and I came here first thing."

"How's Pete holding up?"

Storm shrugged. "Hell, I don't know. I didn't even know he was in the hospital until Logan called me a few days ago. I grabbed the first flight out, and I had no idea what I was walking into. It's surreal."

Francis looked at his watch. "How are you getting home?"

"I hadn't thought that far ahead. I just needed some time to wrap my head around this whole thing with Pop and being back."

"I called my wife and told her we were stopping for coffee, but she's got a hair appointment in an hour, so I have the kids. Let me give you a lift home; it's on the way."

"You're married?"

"Do you remember Patrice Taylor?"

"Everyone remembers Patrice—she was the hottest girl in school."

"Yeah, well, I married her."

"No shit! And you still live in Red Hook?"

Francis smiled. "Where else would I live?"

"I don't know. I just thought with kids you'd want to live somewhere safer."

Francis downed the rest of his coffee. "You've been gone a long time, my friend. Red Hook isn't the same place we used to terrorize when we were kids."

Storm finished his coffee, and Francis pushed the bottle of water toward him. "This is for you. Drink up; it'll make you feel better." He stood. "Come on, I'll give you a ride home. If Patrice can find a sitter, maybe we'll see you tonight at the bar. If you're lucky, I'll even let you dance with her."

Storm tossed his coffee cup and took a swig of the water. "Don't you think you should see how Patrice feels about that?"

"I'm pretty sure she won't have a problem with it. Hell, I always thought she had a thing for you. Why do you think I beat on you so regularly back in school?"

"And all this time I thought it was just my personality—I had one, unlike someone else I knew. But you're wrong about Patrice. She never knew I existed."

"Oh, she knew. She was just shy. It took me a lot of years to figure it out."

The music for *The Twilight Zone* repeated in Storm's head as he followed Francis to a black Jeep Liberty.

Francis unlocked the car and climbed in as Storm followed suit. "How's Nicki handling Pete's being sick?"

"I can't really say. I just met her."

"Nicki's a tough kid; she'll be fine. She's great with my two rug rats. She has a way with them. She's incredibly empathetic for a kid so young, but then she's been through a lot."

"She's also a real smart aleck, but she seems like a good kid."

"Any kid lucky enough to be taken in by Pete is a good kid. Just look how well you and your brothers turned out."

"And you. It seems like Pete's got a magic touch when it comes to juvenile delinquents."

Storm was glad Francis laughed. "That he does."

He pulled up in front of the Crow's Nest and waved away Storm's thanks. "Bree has my number. Give me a call if the jet lag gets to you and you want to meet up with me and Patrice another night."

"I should be fine."

"Good. I'll probably see you later, then. Tell Bree I said hi."

Storm shut the door, and while Francis pulled away, he looked at the bottle of water in his hand. Maybe he'd be better off replacing it with a beer and a shot. Maybe then things would start making more sense.

Storm walked into the Crow's Nest and was tempted to step back outside to make sure Francis hadn't pulled a fast one on him. The only thing he recognized other than Bree was the bar itself.

The antique carved-mahogany bar had always looked out of place beside the cheap vinyl-covered, metal-runged barstools Pete had favored. The ones that fronted the bar now were the high-backed swivel kind, and if he wasn't mistaken, the deep hunter green seats were leather, or at the very least pleather. The stained, drop-tile ceiling had been replaced by what looked like antique tin, trimmed with matching carved crown molding. Cracked plaster walls had been ripped down to show off beautiful exposed brick, and the other walls were painted a deep, rich gold. Small round tables were positioned between the bar and high-backed booths with deep maroon cushions. Tasteful art and Tiffany glass lighting gave it warmth and richness.

Bree stuck a pen behind her ear and walked away from the woman she'd been talking to at the bar. "You've come back."

"Disappointed?"

"Not disappointed, Storm, just wary."

"Yeah, that's coming in loud and clear, but thanks for spelling it out for me."

"My pleasure."

"And mine too, I hope." The tall woman Bree had been talking to had somehow snuck up on him.

It was hard to believe, considering this woman would stick out in Times Square on New Year's Eve. She wore one of those loose tank dresses that looked too long to be a top, but too short to be a dress, though that was how she wore it. Not that he was complaining about the prodigious amount of gorgeous leg she displayed, and her high-heeled sandals made her legs look longer still. Bleached blond, choppy hair, cut short around her ears, tapered down her long, graceful neck. A hot pink streak sliced through her bangs, covering one eye. The other eye was a brilliant blue he'd seen only in the Mediterranean or on girls wearing colored contacts.

"I'm Rocki O'Sullivan—the lead singer of Nite Watch, the house band."

"Storm Decker—the prodigal son, if you believe Bree here."

Rocki smiled and didn't release his hand. "I usually like to reach my own conclusions when it comes to men. My taste and Bree's differ considerably. I like them; she, for the most part, doesn't."

"So her dislike of me is nothing personal then?"

Rocki graced him with a sexy grin. "It's too soon to tell. Bree didn't so much as mention you—odd, considering she's my BFF."

"Pardon?"

"Best Friend Forever."

"Good to know." He dropped Rocki's hand and turned back to Bree, who glared at him. "I hardly recognized the place. Wow, Bree. You've worked miracles here. When Pop said that you'd classed up the joint, I had no idea what he'd meant. You've completely reinvented it. It's amazing. It looks like you."

"Thanks."

If he wasn't mistaken, she blushed. "I have some work to do upstairs but thought I should see if there's anything I can do to help you here first. You never know when you'll find yourself in need of an inflatable dartboard."

"No, I'm good, but thanks for the offer." Bree turned her back to him and walked around the other side of the bar, pouring a soda.

He leaned a hip against a barstool and checked out the wall of fame that Pete had made. Framed and matted copies of every article published about him and his brothers hung beside the bar. He'd had no idea Pop had followed their careers so closely. He'd always known Pop was proud of him and his brothers; he just never imagined he'd do something like this. He swallowed hard, returned his attention to Bree, and watched her work. When she looked up, her surprised gaze shot across the polished bar. What did she think—that he'd run off like a good little servant?

"Thanks for stopping by, Storm. I'll yell if I need you."

"Oh, I almost forgot to tell you. Francis DeBruscio says hello. He and Patrice may be coming in tonight." He ignored Bree's surprised look and turned to Rocki, who seemed to be keeping score. "It was nice meeting you, Rocki. I look forward to hearing the band."

"Don't get your hopes up, Storm. What we lack in talent we make up for in volume."

"Thanks for the warning, and keep me up-to-date on any conclusions." He shot her a wink and turned to leave.

Bree drank the cold soda, wetting her suddenly dry mouth, and wished she could pull a vanishing act. She looked around the bar to see who'd witnessed the exchange. Nicki was tucked into the booth closest to the kitchen, hidden by the high back. Bree stepped to the far end of the bar to check on her. She was sketching something and seemed content with the new markers they'd picked up on the way home from the hospital. Dick, one of Pete's old cronies, had a copy of the *Times* spread out beside his club sandwich and beer. Neither of them had seemed to notice. Unfortunately, the only one who did notice was the one person Bree wished hadn't.

Rocki was already warming up, the light of inquisition shining brightly in her eye. "The prodigal son? I thought you called Logan."

Bree blew out a breath, ruffling her own bangs. "I did. He sent Storm."

"Do you think if I called Logan for help sometime, he'd do the same for me? Lord knows, Storm's the kind of help every single woman pushing thirty needs."

Bree pretended she didn't hear that. "Do you want something from the kitchen? I think I'm going to get the special, Moroccan stuffed cabbage. Are you game?"

Rocki wrinkled her nose. "I'll take a bacon cheeseburger with the works, extra guacamole, and sweet potato fries. Then all I need is for you to tell me the history between you and the prodigal son."

Bree punched the order into the computer. "Nicki, what would you like for lunch?"

"The usual."

"One peanut butter and bacon on toast."

Rocki sipped her Orange Crush, then placed it back on the cardboard coaster. "You can ignore me all you

want, but I'm not going away. Let's just skip all the pre-
liminaries. How was he?"

"What are you talking about?"

"Pretend you just pulled the question out of a fortune
cookie."

Bree still had no clue what Rocki was getting at, but
she had a very strong feeling she wasn't going to like it.

Rocki shook her head and gave her that I-can't-
believe-I'm-best-friends-with-an-idiot look. "Don't you
know? Every time you read a fortune cookie, you add 'in
bed' at the end. So, answer the question."

"What question?"

Rocki pinned Bree with her gaze. "How was he?"

The words "in bed" ran through Bree's head as she
tried to think of what she should tell her BFF.

# CHAPTER 4

Storm trudged up the stairs to set up his work space. He didn't know why he'd flown halfway around the world if Breezy wasn't going to let him help—not that he didn't have enough work for three people on his own.

He booted up his computer, only to realize the bar had wireless, but he didn't have the password, nor did he relish the thought of another awkward conversation with Breezy to get it.

He'd searched Pete's room for a jack last night, hoping to check his e-mail on his laptop instead of his phone. Knowing Pete, he shouldn't have been shocked not to find one. He doubted there was one in Nicki's room—she was a little young for a computer or the need for Internet access—at least he thought she was, but then what the hell did he know?

Maybe Logan and Slater's room still had a jack. After all, Slater had discovered the Internet before Al Gore, and he'd been hacking into computers well before most people knew about Internet security—which was probably why the Crow's Nest's wireless router had a password.

The moment Storm stepped into his brothers' old room, the scent of Breezy hit him like a sledgehammer. She only lived across the hall, but her computer sat running on Slater's old desk. He wondered how long she'd been staying at Pop's. He was tempted to peek into her files to see what he could find out about her, but he didn't. He did, however, check to see if her computer was hooked up to a network outlet, and he thanked God that it was. "Looks like we're going to be sharing more than just an apartment, Breezy."

What choice did he have? It was the only network outlet in the apartment. He shut down her computer and made room for his Toshiba Satellite with a seventeen-inch screen, which meant moving a pile of neatly folded, silky, and very intriguing lingerie.

No matter how hot Breezy's lingerie was or how great she looked in it, she had to get over whatever the hell had her so pissed so he could help. And he would be here to help for as long as she needed him, or at least until Logan got his ass out here and took over. Unfortunately, attacking him with a frying pan hadn't seemed to lessen her rage.

Storm leaned back while he booted up his computer and felt the lump on the back of his head. That old William Congreve line, "Heaven has no rage like love to hatred turned, nor hell a fury like a woman scorned," came to mind. Good old Will had that right—maybe a pissed-off spitfire of a redhead went after him with a frying pan too. Storm just wished he knew what else Breezy would hit him with.

He wasn't sure if what he and Breezy had back then was love. How the hell would he know? He refused to believe whatever his parents had together could be considered love. He knew Pete and his brothers loved him and Storm loved them, but the whole man-woman thing was still a mystery.

Sex he knew. Lust, desire—he had those down cold by the time he was sixteen. But with Breezy, everything had been different. Sure he wanted her—he always had and suspected he always would, but it had always been more than just the need to get into her pants.

Maybe the intensity of the attraction stemmed from Breezy's having been off-limits—and Storm had never seen a line in the sand he hadn't wanted to step over. That was what made him such a damn good marine architect. Designing yachts involved working to a rule. He knew all about rules; he learned when designing to come up with the best solution for that rule. He had to learn the rules before he could break them, and designing taught him there were only a few rules that were truly unbreakable. The laws of physics, motion, and gravity—those were written in stone. But when it came to everything else—those rules were up for discussion. He thought outside the box, he defied the old ways, and he always looked for more—more money, more speed, more power in his boats, his life, himself. He pushed the limits until they broke.

Maybe he wanted Breezy so badly because he couldn't or shouldn't have her.

Unless Breezy had changed a whole lot more than her bra size, which he now knew was a 36-D, he wouldn't have her any time soon. She had always been the most stubborn person he'd ever known.

He checked his watch; it was one thirty, which meant it was four thirty a.m.—tomorrow in Auckland. "Shit." Too early to call Sandy. He supposed he could go through his e-mail and create a pile of work for her when she got to the office. At least it might get his mind off Breezy, her red bra and matching panties on the top of the pile he'd moved, and the scent of her that filled the room and left him panting like a fucking virgin.

He had over a hundred e-mails—proof that no matter what happens, life goes on.

"Bree is gonna have a cow when she finds out you're in her bedroom."

Nicki had snuck up on him. He'd been thinking too much about Breezy's unmentionables for his own good. "It's not hers—it's Logan and Slater's room."

"Yeah, but she's stayin' in it, and you're invading her space." Nicki's face wore all the false indignation a ten-year-old could muster while wearing a peanut butter and milk mustache.

It made him smile—his first real smile since learning about Pete. "Are you going to run to the bar and tattle on me? No one likes a tattletale."

"I don't know." She ground the heel of her sneaker into the carpet. "What's it worth to ya?"

"Not a whole hell of a lot. The first rule of bribery is to make sure you're holding something big over the other person's head. And in this case, you're not. You tipped your hand, and now I know I'm holding all the cards. That's a bad mistake on your part. I doubt very much that a straight arrow like Bree would appreciate your trying to shake me down."

"Tipped my what?" Nicki's forehead wrinkled.

"Your hand." He swiveled the chair around so they were eye to eye. "You see, life is like a poker game. You have to be pretty sure that whatever cards I'm holding—in this case it's my working in the room Bree's temporarily occupying—are worth less than the cards you're holding, which is the knowledge that Bree's not going to be happy about that. But what you didn't consider was the ace up my sleeve—which is that I couldn't care less if Bree is pissed about my working here."

"Well, sh—" Nicki clasped her hand over her mouth and stared at him with wide eyes. "Shoot." She wiped her now milk-and-peanut-butter-covered palm on the monkey face covering the front of her shirt.

"What did you want the dough for?"

"Nothin'." Nicki bit her lip.

"Okay." He spun the chair back to face his computer and scrolled through his e-mail, searching for anything that couldn't wait while Nicki chewed her lip and ground her heel farther into the carpet.

He'd just about given up on the girl when she threw herself on Bree's unmade bed, her too-big feet swinging back and forth over her butt like a pendulum, and let out a long-suffering sigh. "Do you like kids?"

"Yeah, I guess." He'd been watching her in his peripheral vision; he turned his gaze toward her. "I don't know many of them. What's that got to do with money?"

"You got a lot of money?"

"I get by."

"You're probably the richest guy in Red Hook. At least you look like you are."

"There's not much competition in Red Hook, or there never used to be, but I've been away a long time."

"Yeah, like for my whole life. How come?"

"Not your whole life. I came back five or six years ago to see Pete. But I live on the other side of the world. Do you know where New Zealand is?"

"Not really."

He waved her over, and she rolled off the bed and stepped beside him. He pulled up Google Earth and programmed a flight from Red Hook to Auckland—if only it were really that simple or that cheap. He sat back and watched the wonder flit across Nicki's face.

"Wow, that's way far."

"You can't get much farther." He didn't mention that for too many years he couldn't afford to come back. He'd saved every cent so he could to fly back and see Pete, Logan, and Slater the few times he had. He'd found out Breezy had come home after college, and he hadn't been back since. If he could have avoided this trip, he would have. "It's not an easy trip to make. You have to fly from Auckland to LA, and then LA to New York, but you used to have to fly from Auckland to Hawaii, Hawaii to LA, and then to New York, so it's gotten easier."

"Wow, you've been to Hawaii too?"

"I've been just about everywhere, kid." He'd searched the world for a place that felt like home. He'd never found it. Auckland was fine—it was where he lived and worked, but deep down he knew it wasn't home. It never would be.

"Where is she?" Bree asked Rocki when she noticed Nicki wasn't at her designated table. Bree turned off the PBS station she kept on when no customers were around.

"I saw her sneak out the back through the kitchen. Maybe she's in the alley, or she could have gone up to the apartment." Rocki shrugged it off, as if having a ten-year-old playing in a dirty alley was no big deal. But Nicki was Bree's responsibility, not Rocki's.

Rocki stood on the stilts she called shoes. "I thought she was just going over to beg sweets from Rex. You know your chef, for as tough as he is, he has a soft spot for Nicki."

"Ask him to check the alley. I'll just run upstairs. Be right back."

Bree took the stairs two at a time, cursing herself for being stupid enough to give Nicki her own key. She banged into the apartment. "Nicki, are you up here?"

"Yeah, she is." Storm appeared in the doorway to her room, holding Nicki's still-bony shoulders.

Relief vied with anger. "What the heck are you doing in my room?"

"Trying to work."

Nicki bounced on her heels. "I told him you'd be mad." She ran to Bree and grabbed her hand, tugging her toward the bedroom and bouncing more than Tigger. "You gotta see this cool program on Storm's computer. We flew all the way to New Zealand." She pulled Bree into the last place she wanted to be—her bedroom, hell, any bedroom with Storm. "Storm's been to Hawaii. Do you believe it?" Nicki pointed to the computer that took up most of the desk.

The desk where her computer and lingerie had been.

"Look, Bree. This is so cool. Storm, show her. Fly to New Zealand again."

"You couldn't find anywhere else to set up your computer?"

"Not with a router." The left corner of his mouth tipped up. "Sorry."

He looked anything but.

"I just shut down your computer and moved your stuff." Storm raised an eyebrow and smirked as he eyed her pile of bras and panties.

"Pervert," she mouthed over Nicki's head.

"No, if I were, I'd be wearing or collecting them. I just pictured you wearing them. That's just a healthy-guy thing."

Oblivious to their grown-up exchange, Nicki tugged on Storm's hand. "Show Bree. Do it again. Please, Storm."

"Okay." He sat in Bree's chair as if he owned the place. But then Storm had always looked as if he owned whatever space he took up. Damn him. He'd always had that indefinable quality that made people step aside when he walked into any room, but not in fear. Storm Decker just moved within an impenetrable bubble. She was certain if he stood before the Red Sea, God would come down and part the waters. He was just that kind of man. She'd spent her life watching other men, waiting to find anyone with that ability. She never had. Maybe she needed to get out more.

Storm clicked a few buttons, and the planet Earth took up the big screen. The United States was outlined on the globe; then it rolled across to the Pacific and down to the tiny-looking islands that made up New Zealand.

"Isn't that cool?" Nicki bounced beside Storm.

He glanced at Nicki and grinned—his face as bright as morning sunshine. He typed in an address, and a harbor with a boatyard and docks filled the screen.

"Your home?" Bree had always wondered where he lived. The high-rises beside the harbor with million-dollar views would suit him. All she knew was that they must cost a pretty penny.

"My office. Here's the view from my desk." He clicked on something else, and a photo filled the screen with a breathtaking view of hundreds of sailboats filling slips, others sailing, and a beautiful bridge in the distance.

"Not too shabby. It's a wonder you get any work done at all." It was a far cry from Red Hook; even now, as much as Red Hook had improved, the two places were in different hemispheres—literally and figuratively. No wonder he couldn't wait to get back and be able to look at that view every morning when he went to work. She couldn't imagine living in a place so beautiful, so perfect. "You've really made something of yourself. You must be proud."

Storm did his one-shoulder shrug she'd seen since the first day she'd met him. The man never could take a compliment.

"Did you build all those boats, Storm? Pop says you draw them and then somebody else builds them."

He opened up another file. "Here are some of the boats I've designed." A slide show of 3-D graphics of hulls flew across the screen. She didn't really know what she was looking at, so she looked at Storm instead. "Impressive," Bree murmured.

"Awesome. You made all those boats?" Nicki whispered.

"I designed them and worked with the boat builders, but I'm not the one building them."

"You must be really good at drawing then, huh?"

"Most of the drawing is done on the computer, but yeah, I hold my own with a pencil. I like to sketch ideas before I draw them on the computer and see if they'll work."

"Will you teach me how to do that?"

Storm's eyebrows rose, and he speared Bree with a look as if he were asking permission or direction tinged with a healthy dose of fear. Fear of what? Was he afraid of spending time with Nicki, or was he afraid that she'd say no?

Bree put her hand on her hip and tugged on Nicki's ponytail. Nicki's eyes met Bree's as she leaned into Storm. "You left your sketch pad and markers in the restaurant when you disappeared—which is against the rules. You need to tell me where you're going. I freaked when I came out of the office and saw you were missing."

"You were on the phone, and Miss Rocki was playing the piano. You know how she gets when she's playing."

"Then you wait for me to get off the phone; you just don't take off."

Nicki looked down at her shoes. "Sorry, Bree."

"Okay. Just don't do it again. I've got to get back downstairs, and I'm sure Storm has work he needs to get done. Maybe you two can schedule a lesson over dinner."

"Aw, Bree. Can't I just bring my markers and paper up here now?"

"No. Miss Patrice is coming to pick you up for a playdate in a little while. She's going to take you and her girls to the park. You wouldn't want to miss that, would you?"

"I guess not." Nicki didn't look so sure as she dragged her feet all the way out of Bree's bedroom.

Bree turned back to Storm. "We have wireless, so there's really no need to work in my room."

"I didn't have the password, and this is a more secure connection—especially while I'm downloading files." Storm smirked at her again. "I promise not to disturb your stuff. Besides, after Pete comes home, you'll be moving back to your place, right?"

She hadn't thought that far ahead. For her, the last few weeks had been a one-day-at-a-time kind of thing, but she couldn't imagine leaving Pete and Nicki with only Storm to take care of them. What if Nicki had nightmares? What if Pete needed her? "You could go stay at my place if you want."

Storm stood and moved closer to her, filling the small room with his presence. She was tempted to step back, but she didn't. She craned her neck to look him in the eye. If she took a deep breath, her chest would hit his. Damn him.

"Why did you ask for help if you were just going to refuse it? Why the hell did I drag my ass halfway around the world to come here?"

"I don't know. Why did you? You're just going to take off again." Bree turned and stepped toward the door—the door he shut before she got there.

He practically vibrated with what looked like barely contained anger. The closer he came, the bigger he seemed. "What the hell do you want, Breezy?" He breathed into her ear. "An apology for something that happened eleven years ago?"

"I want nothing from you." She meant that to sound indignant; instead, it came out sounding breathless. She couldn't think when he was this close. She stepped back and hit the door.

Storm slammed a hand against the doorframe, trapping her. "That's too bad, Breezy, because I want a hell of a lot from you." His mouth came down on hers, but she wouldn't call it a kiss—not like any kiss she'd ever had. It was more like a war. She wasn't sure whether he was fighting her, himself, or whatever this thing was between them.

He shuddered beneath her hands, against her body. His thigh slid between hers as he dragged her closer and pressed her back against the door. Passion—hot and furious—exploded between them. And God help her, she dug her nails into his shoulders, and held on, taking, giving, melting and inciting him, wanting more.

A knock sounded. "Bree, Patrice is here. Are you coming?"

Storm dragged in a breath close to her ear. "Not yet, but you're close."

She wanted nothing more than to kick him right in the balls—she would have too if her legs hadn't been wrapped around his waist.

The look on Breezy's face was the only thing keeping Storm from laughing. She looked pissed enough to do bodily harm, but since he was holding her up, she didn't dare, and he was in no mood to unhand her ass. Damn, she felt so good against him, he'd almost come in his pants.

"Be right there, Nicki. Grab your backpack on the counter." She stabbed him with those ice-cold green eyes. "Let me down."

"We're not finished."

"We were finished eleven years ago when you ran out the door. Naked."

"That was then; this is now. I'm not the one running, Breezy. If anyone is running, it's you." He slid her down his thigh, pissing her off even more, "Go see Nicki off, and then we're going to talk."

She put her hand on the doorknob and turned back to him. "I have a bar and restaurant to run, I don't have time to talk, and I don't take orders from you." She sashayed out, slamming the door behind her.

She might not want to talk to him, but she would. He would hound her every step until she cried uncle and they figured out how to work together. Hell, he wasn't even sure whether she was pissed because he'd left or because he'd come back. With his luck, it was both.

Another minute and they'd have been ripping each other's clothes off. He sat on the edge of her bed. He'd heard of makeup sex, but never fight sex, and damn if it wasn't the single most spectacular make-out session he'd ever had, and he hadn't even gotten her out of one piece of clothing. He couldn't imagine how hot it would be when he did.

Bree made sure Nicki was buckled into the back of the Jeep and did her best to avoid Patrice's questions. Of course, Storm was all anyone wanted to talk about. That went for Nicki, Rocki, Patrice, and from what Patrice said, even Francis.

Patrice flipped her newly relaxed, sexy blond-highlighted long hair over her shoulder, making her look even more like Beyoncé, and shot Bree one of her knowing looks. "That's okay; I was able to get a sitter for tonight, so Francis and I will be back later. We'll just keep Nicki with our two and drop her off with you tomorrow. This way you'll get a break, and I'll get all the information I want straight from the horse's mouth."

"Horse's ass is more like it. Besides, there's nothing to say." What was it with people? It was as if they'd never seen a man before.

Patrice got behind the wheel and started the car. After Bree waved to Nicki, she ran into the bar.

Leaving the bar in the not-so-capable hands of Rocki was usually a disaster. But Bree would have gladly spent the rest of the night picking up after Rocki not to have to deal with what—make that who—she found there.

Storm poured a drink as though he knew what he

was doing. He smiled at something the customer said. His eyes never left her face, which, even Bree had to admit, was amazing, considering the woman was almost climbing over the bar to give him a cleavage shot. He took the twenty she handed him and turned back to the register.

Bree hurried behind the bar and pulled the bill out of his hand. "What'd she have?"

"Stoli on the rocks with a twist."

When Bree started punching the order into the register, he waved her away. "I've been working behind the bar all my life—first as a bar back and then as a bartender. How do you think I paid for marine architecture school, Breezy? I'm more than capable of ringing up a drink."

"That's all fine and good, but I don't want you in my till."

"Do you honestly believe that I spent three grand to fly here just so I could steal a few hundred from your till? Give me a break."

If it had been Logan or Slater helping, she'd be kissing his feet, but this was Storm. It was impossible for her to be grateful for his help. Unfair—definitely, but who the hell said life was fair, and how could she be grateful for his help when his mere presence caused her more pain and stress than she'd had dealing with everything alone? She sucked in a deep breath and let it out slowly. Fine, if he wanted blunt, she could do blunt. "This is my bar, and I don't want you here."

Storm leaned back against the beer cooler and crossed his arms. "Last I checked, this was Pete's bar, and he was awfully relieved this morning when he found out I was here to help out, so get over yourself. I'm here. I'm going to help. If you don't like it, I'll be happy to fight about it later—just not in front of the customers."

He shot a brilliant smile at the walking plastic surgeon's catalogue, punched in her order, totaled the sale, and counted out her change, slamming the drawer shut with his hip.

"Fine." Bree stomped into her office and was so angry, she slammed that door too—only it didn't slam. She looked over her shoulder and found Rocki protecting her face. "Sorry."

"I guess if you really want to, you can slam the door now. I'm just glad I have great reflexes." Rocki took a seat on the other side of Bree's desk.

"I have work to do."

"No, what you have is a bad case of beard burn. You might want to put some cream on that. Maybe next time you and Storm go at it, he should shave first. Still, that whole scruffy, didn't-get-the-chance-to-shave-this-morning look really works for him. But then, what wouldn't?"

"We had a fight."

"Why make love and not war when you can do both? That must have been one hell of a reunion, huh?"

"I think I preferred the one last night when I clobbered him with a frying pan."

Rocki laughed. "Oh, to have been a fly on the wall . . . but knowing you, you would have hit me with the frying pan too."

"This is not funny. He's behind my bar."

"I know—that's usually what happens when you request help running a bar."

"He's supposed to help. Not take over. Not mess with my head. And not look as if he belongs here when he's just biding his time until he can run away again."

Rocki slid forward in her seat, "Just think of all the women he's going to attract. We should publicize it. Of course, Patrice is already on the job, so you'd better be prepared for one hell of a night. Storm Decker is going to be quite the draw. He's all that with a Brooklyn Kiwi accent—a tantalizing combination."

"Why do I bother?" Bree sat at her desk and held her aching head in her hands. "You're supposed to be my best friend. You're supposed to commiserate with me and give me 'poor babys.' Instead, all I get is skin-care advice and the nauseating job of holding your drool cup."

"I hardly drooled, not that he's not worthy." Rocki crossed her legs and did that annoying heel-to-sandal slap with her waggling foot. "I'm not sure what's more interesting, watching Storm or watching you watch Storm. Girl, you've got it bad."

"I do not. I can't stand him."

"Yeah, I can tell by the beard burn." Rocki reached into her bag and took out a tube of cream. "If you don't want to advertise what you two were doing upstairs, you'd better use this." She tossed it across the desk, stood, and headed for the door. "It's about time you let a man close enough to scrape some of that fair skin of yours off. The blush works for you too. It really brings out your eyes."

Bree hung up the phone after her daily call from Slater asking about Pete's condition and ran up the back stairs to her apartment. If she was going to have to deal with Storm Decker and loaded questions all night, she was going to do it looking as good as she could, and preferably without noticeable beard burn.

She piled her hair on the top of her head and jumped into a hot shower, doing her best to wash the scent of Storm off her body.

As if it weren't bad enough that he rubbed all the skin off her face with that coarse bristle, she'd spent the afternoon squirming in her chair. Instead of doing a beer order, she relived every second of that kiss—or whatever the hell it was. Remembering the way he'd picked her up, how her thighs cradled his erection, the taste of his anger and the second it had changed to need, want, and pent-up frustration.

What was it about him that had her thoughts making a right-hand turn toward eroticaland? And what the hell was she going to do with him? He could piss her off and turn her on just by breathing. How could she fight something like that, especially with her Irish temper?

Bree tore the ponytail holder from her hair and soaked her head. It was no use; nothing helped. She was beyond horny, edgy, and exasperated with herself and with him. She'd never been one to fall all over a man. No one had ever left her wanting; no one had ever affected her to the point of madness; no one had ever made her fall in love. Except for Storm.

# CHAPTER 5

Storm stood behind the bar, sipping a club soda and studying the menu. It contained a hell of a lot more than the burgers and fries Pete had always offered. The new menu had appetizers, soups, salads, entrées, and desserts.

The bar had been busy since he'd come down and relieved Rocki—something else that hadn't happened when Pete was running the place, but not everything had changed. The menu still had everything he'd craved when he was away from the States: Red Hook's famous lobster rolls, Key lime pie, and, most of all, beer from Sixpoint Brewery—all in all the perfect meal as far as he was concerned.

The two servers working lunch were well trained, and by three o'clock, the bar service had picked up and there was still a busy late-lunch crowd at the booths and tables.

Bree hid out in her office. If she was waiting for him to fall on his face and beg for help, she'd have a long wait.

Storm had already introduced himself to the kitchen staff and asked about the specials. He'd even received a quick lesson on how to place an order on the bar computer from one of the servers. It was an easy-enough program to pick up. Sure, he had to figure out some of the intricacies and get an employee code of his own, but for now he was using Bree's—which must have really chapped her ass. And what a fine ass it was.

"What's that smile all about?" Rocki pulled up a stool and leaned toward him across the bar. "And what the hell did you do to piss off Bree so badly?"

"Which time?"

"Touché."

He leaned back, held her gaze, and waited for it.

Rocki, instead of peppering him with questions, settled for a stare off. Her eyes held questions, warnings, along with a good bit of humor. Storm had a feeling that once he got to know her, he'd like her as much as Breezy seemed to, even if the girl couldn't tend bar to save her own life. It had taken him an hour to clean up the mess she'd made in a quarter of that time.

Storm wasn't sure how long they'd stared at each other before she finally nodded and slipped off the stool. "I'm glad we understand each other."

Storm gave her a mock salute. "Perfectly."

She stepped behind the bar, turned off the music, and flipped another switch before sitting down at the piano to take requests for the next hour from the regulars who came in with briefcases and loosened ties for a mixture of standards and Brahms. Yeah, Storm was pretty sure he was going to like Rocki a whole lot.

He fell back into the routine of tending bar as if he'd never stopped. By five, the place was hopping—delivering Storm directly into the weeds. He was just about to send one of the servers to find Breezy, when a big guy wearing a black polo and khaki pants came around the bar and logged onto the computer, switching out the cash drawer.

"I'm Simon. Who are you, and where's Breanna?"

Storm didn't like his tone but couldn't really blame him. "Storm Decker, Pete's son. I came to take some of the pressure off Bree."

Simon relaxed and shook his hand. "Good to see one of you finally showed up."

"I just found out the day before yesterday—and it's a twenty-four-hour flight. Pop's not much of a communicator."

Simon blew out a breath. "I've been worried about both Bree and Pete. I'm glad you're here. Bree's been running herself ragged."

"Yeah, well, my presence here won't make much of a difference if she won't let me help."

Simon stopped midswipe. "She's got a real stubborn streak, and from what I gathered, you're not her favorite of Pete's kids."

"Thanks for the news flash."

"Hey, Breanna—looking good."

Storm looked up from the order he was pouring. Bree walked toward the bar, wearing black trousers paired with sex-on-stilts, pointy-toed shoes that made her legs look a mile longer than usual. She topped it with a black tank under some kind of long, formfitting blouse that shimmered—seemingly changing color from fuchsia to purple every time she moved. She'd done something to her hair. It still had that just-got-out-of-bed tousle, but it didn't look accidental. It looked as if some man had just spent the last twenty minutes running his hands through it—and he hadn't been that man.

Her blush brought out the emerald green of her eyes as they raked over him. Damn, the woman could get him half hard with just a look.

Bree bit her lip, which was still slightly swollen from their earlier escapades. "You can leave, Storm. Simon and I will handle it from here."

"No, thanks. But you're welcome to take off if you want some time."

"It's my shift." She came around the bar with eyes flashing, and he had the urge to pick her up and carry her to her office for round two.

"I'll take that end of the bar," Simon said as he turned away. "Storm, let me know if you have any questions."

Storm couldn't help but smile at Bree as she fumed. There was nothing he liked more than taking Breezy down a peg or two, well, except for kissing her.

"Fine. Do what you want." Her phone announced a text message, and she checked it, making sure to keep the screen pointed away from him. Whatever.

Bree answered Daniel Knickerbocker's text asking about the Harbor Pier fund-raiser. She'd put him off before, even though her presence was expected, because she didn't know if Pete would be home. Since she was suddenly free and her easy-escape allies—Rocki and Patrice—were already settled at the bar for the night, she jumped at Daniel's offer to get out of the uncomfortable situation Storm had put her in.

She stepped aside and tried to avoid the bucket of ice swinging from the bar back's gangly arm and ran right into Storm. "Excuse me." She waited for him to move— he didn't. "With the three of us and Cory running around, it's too crowded behind the bar."

"I'm making margaritas. I need the blender. Where do you suggest I go?"

"New Zealand would be good."

She was being hard on him, she knew it, but when it came to Storm, she had no filter. She just couldn't control it. He had no right to come here and stir up old feelings and emotions. He had no right to crowd her. He had no right to make her want him.

Storm expertly salted the glasses and poured, shooting a look toward the door. "There are a few people waiting to be seated; maybe you should give the hostess a hand. Simon and I can handle the bar."

As she turned to glare at him, the too-high heel of her shoe stuck in one of the small holes peppering the floor mat, sending her reeling right into Storm.

He caught her.

Bree wasn't sure if she was thankful or not. It would be a lot safer to fall on the floor than to fall for Storm Decker—something she swore she'd never do again.

In heels, Bree was almost eye to eye with him. His eyes turned an amazing shade of blue shot with green. She sucked in a breath and got a lungful of Storm-flavored air, which didn't help matters.

"Hi, Bree."

Patrice. Bree closed her eyes and willed Storm's hands off her body.

"Storm. It's nice the two of you are getting along so well. Picking up where you left off, I see."

Of course Storm hadn't let Bree go; if anything, he held her closer. When she opened her eyes, Storm had his good-time-guy grin aimed at Patrice.

"You're as beautiful as ever, Patrice." Storm's hold tightened on Bree, and he lifted her off the offending mat as if she were an inanimate object. He tugged her closer, wedging her between him and the corner of the bar—leaving her no escape. "It's great to see you." He nodded toward Francis. "Glad you could make it."

Simon came closer. "Cory and I have the bar under control. Why don't you two take a break with Patrice and Francis before the rush?"

"Sounds like a plan." Storm's hand lowered, and he brought his mouth to her ear. "After you, Breezy."

"Remove your hand from my ass," she said, speaking through a smile so Patrice wouldn't be able to read her lips, "or you'll need a surgeon to reattach it."

Storm let out an annoying, sexy chuckle, ushered her to an empty booth, and then squeezed in beside her.

Bree had always thought the booths were roomy until she sat in one with Storm Decker. His thigh pressed against hers, heat searing through her thin crepe pants, his broad shoulders straightened and crowded her. She pressed against the wall until his arm came around and pulled her to his side. He grunted when her elbow dug into his ribs.

Patrice settled on the bench across from them and leaned into Francis with a contented sigh. "How's Pete doing? I haven't been able to get to the hospital for a visit in a few days."

"Great," Bree said.

"He looks like crap," Storm said at the same time. He glanced at Bree. "I can't believe the change in him."

They looked at each other, and Patrice raised an eyebrow.

Bree cleared her throat. "He looks a lot better than he did before you got here. You should have seen him last week."

"I would have had I known he was in the damn hospital." Exasperation either at himself or at her filled the small booth.

"Yeah, so you say. He's been in the hospital for over a week; where were you? Oh right, you were yachting in New Zealand."

"You knew how to reach me." He turned his shoulders and leaned into her until they were nose to nose.

Bree pushed against his chest. "I did not, and why would I bother?" He didn't back off, so she kept her hand hard against him, afraid he'd come closer. "I called Logan when I needed help. I thought he was more dependable. I guess I was wrong. After all, he sent you."

"I didn't hear any complaints." His deep voice rumbled against her palm.

"Oh, you mean when I knocked you out? I doubt you heard much of anything."

"What was your excuse earlier, Breezy?"

"Temporary insanity."

"Yeah, we seem to have that effect on each other." His hand covered hers, and she realized she'd curled his shirt in her fist. His lips drew into a half smile. "I'm not complaining."

"You're impossible—"

"To forget, or so I've been told."

"In your dreams." God, she sounded like Nicki. She felt her phone vibrate at her hip—and from the way Storm jumped, so had he. "Excuse me." She slid her hand into her pocket and down Storm's thigh since his was pressed against hers, grabbed her phone, and smiled at Daniel's text, "Pick u up in 15."

Bree felt Storm tense beside her. She didn't think he could see the message, but then with Storm, she never knew. He had a way of seeing way too much.

Bree realized the menus were already on the table. When had they been delivered? She opened hers and studied it as if she'd never seen the damn thing before. Forget the fact that she designed it.

"What's everyone having?"

Bree wanted to kiss her favorite server, Wanda, who stood with her pad at the ready. She always had perfect timing.

Bree gave her a grateful smile. "Why don't we just start with an appetizer?" That was all she had time for. They could order dinner after she left with Daniel. "Does everyone want to split the artichoke dip?" She kicked Francis under the table.

"Sure. Sounds good," Francis answered as Bree pocketed her phone. She ended up sliding her hand over Storm's side again.

Bree took a gulp of water, ignoring Patrice's pointed stare. What Bree wanted was scotch, preferably a full bottle, but with Storm around, she'd be better off sticking to water.

Storm wanted to kick his own ass for offering to take over the shift for her—especially with her dressed like a walking wet dream and sending and receiving texts from God knew who. He didn't know what Breezy was up to, but he'd bet a year's commissions that she was up to no good.

He took a deep breath and tried to calm his hammering heart. He had planned to crowd Breezy, hoping to upset her equilibrium, but hadn't considered what her closeness would do to his. Damn, she smelled amazing and looked even better. He definitely had to get his mind off the woman pressing against his side. "Patrice, tell me what you've been up to since I left. You graduated the same year Bree did, right?"

"Yes. I went to nursing school and got my RN. I work in the ER at Methodist part-time, three days a week. Francis and I got married right after I graduated from college, and we had Cassidy a year and a half later. She's five and Callie is three. They're a handful, but I love being a mom. What about you? What are you up to?"

Storm leaned back, and Bree's hair tickled his arm. "I design yachts, both sailing and motor. I do everything from coastal cruisers to full-out racing yachts, and I race every chance I get."

"It's been years since we've seen you, and that's all you're going to tell us? Come on, Storm."

"There's not much else to tell." And wasn't that the truth? He'd built his company and nothing else. "I've been busy working, building my business."

"And your social life?"

"That's pretty much business related too. You know how it is."

Patrice raised an eyebrow. "No, but I can imagine. I hear boat people are *very* friendly."

Storm felt more than saw Bree's spine stiffen.

"How were the girls at the park today, Patrice?" Bree rolled her napkin in her lap—it was going to be a mangled knot before their food was delivered. "Was Nicki good for you?"

"Oh, you know Nicki; she's always great. Now, Storm, how long are you staying? Any chance of your coming back home for good?"

Home? Red Hook? No, Red Hook couldn't be home. When he left, he'd sworn he'd never come back—not for more than a visit. Shit. Cell doors slammed shut in his mind; the sound echoed in his ears. His throat tightened and his scalp tingled. He'd been in jail only once, but that was enough to know what being good and trapped felt like. He never wanted to relive the experience.

Bree continued to roll her napkin in her lap. He didn't miss the tremor in her fingers.

"I'll stay as long as it takes for Pop to get back on his feet or until Logan or Slater can pull himself away from what each of them is doing. Then I'll go back to Auckland."

"But until then, you're staying with Bree?"

"No, I'm staying at Pop's."

"And so is Bree, so you're staying with Bree."

Francis put his hand on Patrice's and gave it a squeeze. "Patty, behave."

Storm had the urge to run; he checked the bar, hoping Simon needed help. But no, everything was under control. Simon was a damn good bartender—much to Storm's dismay.

"I'm just trying to get the facts straight from the horse's mouth." Patrice gave Bree a strange look, almost as if daring her to say something, and then ran a hand over Francis's chest before nuzzling his ear. "Besides, you like me better when I'm naughty."

"Yeah, but I don't think Storm and Bree appreciate it."

"No, but Bree appreciates it when Storm is—like this afternoon, right, Bree?"

"He wasn't . . . I didn't . . ."

Francis shrugged and gave Bree his what-can-I-do-she's-your-friend-too look.

Relieved to be out of the line of Patrice's fire, Storm laughed and pulled Bree closer to whisper in her ear. "Oh yeah, I was, and you certainly did."

The server delivered the artichoke dip and saved Breezy from making a fool of him. And he was a fool. What the hell had he been thinking kissing Bree like he had?

Bree took a chip and ran it through the steaming, cheesy, creamy dip.

Hadn't he learned anything from when he'd made that mistake the first time?

Bree slipped the cheese-covered chip between her lips, and his dick twitched. Apparently not. Fuck.

Storm's words reverberated in Bree's head, making her panties moist and her bra feel a cup too small. He was impossible, and she could only imagine what he would do if he knew what his words alone did to her.

Stuffing a chip in her mouth, she wondered if Patrice and Francis would notice if she smashed her spiked heel through Storm's foot. She wished she had more room under the table to really put some weight behind it. At least Daniel had been only a few blocks away when he texted her. He should be here any moment. She kept one eye on the door and the other on Storm.

As if she'd conjured him, Daniel Knickerbocker stepped into the bar and scanned the room. A little kernel of guilt skittered through her. She wouldn't have thought to accept Daniel's offer if she wasn't just a little bit desperate. She'd gone out on one date with him—which was a mistake. Not only was it a bad first date; it was the last date she'd been on. It had been a while. . . . Okay, so it was six months ago—February, if she remembered correctly. Right after yet another depressing Valentine's Day. In Bree's book, there was nothing worse than watching a bar full of couples make eyes at each other for sixteen hours straight. Valentine's Day made single women everywhere a little desperate and was the sole reason a woman would go out with someone she would never ordinarily date and do things she'd just as soon forget.

Daniel stood taller than most men and wore his summer-weight suit the way James Bond wore tuxedos. As a matter of fact, now that she thought about it, he even looked a little bit like the new James Bond. He might not blow her skirt up, but from the way other women followed his progress through the bar, it didn't look as if Daniel ran into that problem often.

"Oh good, Daniel's here. You guys have a good time catching up. Maybe I'll see you later if you're still here when I get back." Bree waited for Storm to release her from the booth. "Excuse me."

Storm didn't move.

"Storm, I need to leave."

"And go where?"

"None of your business. Now move."

He stiffened as she raised her arm and waved at Daniel. And when Daniel's gaze zeroed in on her, she heard Storm curse under his breath. Storm and Daniel were both hunters but in different ways. Daniel was the more refined, gentlemanly type—always far above it all, like a highly skilled sniper, whereas Storm was the lone wolf. He was wild, untamed, and had instinctive skills honed by survival in a kill-or-be-killed world. He slid out of the bench seat.

Patrice put her hand over Bree's. "You'd rather go out with Daniel Knickerbocker than stay here with us?"

Bree raised an eyebrow and looked pointedly at Storm. "Definitely." She ran her hand through her hair and cursed all the mousse and paste and hair spray she'd used. "I haven't had a night off in weeks. Besides, we're going to a benefit for the Harbor Pier, and since Daniel and I are spearheading the project, it's important for us to show a united front."

Daniel stopped in front of the booth, ignoring the death glare from Storm. Maybe next time he'd think twice before he told her to go help out the hostess.

Bree stepped between the posturing males and pasted on a now-boys-behave smile. They gave her quite a show. Her gaze flitted from one to the other. If they'd been peacocks, she was sure their tail feathers would be fanned out, showing off their goods. If she was honest with herself, if it were a competition, Storm would win.

Daniel was a nice-enough guy, and working closely with him on the Red Hook Revitalization Committee had been productive, if nothing else; he definitely was not her type—too bad he was missing that special something. It wasn't as if there was anything wrong with him. He was good-looking, successful, and charming. Unfortunately, Bree had never met a man who measured up to Storm Decker on her Richter Scale of Hotness, but Storm didn't need to know that.

"Daniel Knickerbocker, this is Storm Decker, my boss's son. Storm's here to help out while Pete's recovering. Storm, this is Daniel." The guys nodded to each other. "Well, I'm sorry to break this up, but we're going to be late if we don't leave. I'm just going to grab my purse. Storm, Simon has my number if there are any problems. Patrice, Francis," she said, stepping away from Storm and taking Daniel's arm, "have a good time tonight. I'll see you later."

\*     \*     \*

Storm sat and watched Bree and Captain Superior walk away with his hand on her lower back, entirely too close to her ass. Damn.

"I never liked that guy; he's too slick by half," Patrice said as she dunked a chip in the still-gooey dip. Storm couldn't agree with her more.

"Now, Patty—" Francis interrupted.

She stuffed the chip in her mouth without the finesse Bree had recently displayed. "Don't 'now Patty' me, Francis." She covered her mouth and spoke around the food. "I have every right to say what I think, and I never cared for that man. Sure, he's doing all the right things, but I can't help but feel that he has his own agenda. He's the star of his own show, if you know what I'm saying. His philanthropic work is all fine and good, but I can't imagine him doing anything unless it helps line his own pockets."

"Spoken like a true cynic." Francis slid his arm around his wife.

"I'm not a cynic. I'm a realist, and a good judge of character. I saw through you, didn't I?" Patrice shot Storm a smile. "I saw the marshmallow within the body of an ogre."

"An ogre, huh?" Storm laughed. "I missed the whole marshmallow thing. Maybe it was because Francis was too busy using me as a punching bag to see anything but his big fat fist."

Storm never thought he'd see the day Frankie "the Bruiser" DeBruscio blushed, but then he never would have believed he'd be back in Red Hook watching Breezy leave with a slick bastard in a thousand-dollar suit either. "So, this Daniel Knickerbocker, what's his story?"

Patrice leaned forward. "Daniel bought a bunch of real estate when Red Hook was just starting to clean up its act. Now, he's on the Red Hook Revitalization Committee with Bree—as I said, doing philanthropic work to line his own pockets."

"You don't know that, Patty. Maybe he's just taking an interest in his community, just like we are. You can't fault the progress the committee has made."

"No, and he's not complaining about the increased value of his real estate holdings. And if the Harbor Pier gets off the ground . . ."

"The Harbor Pier?" Storm's ears perked up.

"Yeah, Daniel and Bree are spearheading a program to get the city to buy one of the old piers to be used as a park with stores and condos surrounding it. It would be great for the community, and Daniel is right there with Bree. Seems to me he's orchestrating everything, and I have a bad feeling about it."

"Why?"

Patrice shrugged. "I don't know. It's nothing I can put my finger on—just female intuition, I guess."

Francis looked up from his drink. "I don't know how she does it, but over the years, I've learned not to take Patty's feelings lightly. She's usually right, and it's bitten me in the ass too many times to discount. Still, there's not a whole hell of a lot we can do about it other than to keep an eye on Knickerbocker." Francis swirled his half-empty beer around the mug, "Bree is a smart woman, she knows what she's doing, and she's been doing a whole lot of good for Red Hook for a long time. Ever since she came home from college, she's been revitalizing everything she touches." He motioned around the restaurant. "Look at this place. Hell, she had to sell every single idea to Pete—not an easy job. Whoever said you can't teach an old dog new tricks never met Bree Collins—she's made a huge difference with the bar and the community."

Storm found himself smiling; Bree put her personal stamp on everything and everyone she touched, including him. "She's always been a dreamer with her head in the clouds and her feet firmly planted in reality."

Patrice smiled. "You really do know her, don't you?"

Storm just shrugged. He knew things about Bree no one else did, but he wasn't going to tell Patrice that. He wasn't sure what Bree had shared with Patrice. She was a very private person, and she hadn't had an easy life since the day her father died on the job. Her crazy-ass mother became so intent on keeping Bree safe, she wrapped her in cotton and controlled Bree's every move—or tried to, making dangerous people like Pete and Storm off-limits. Bree had rebelled, sneaking off every chance she could to spend time with Pete, her father's partner on the force, and the closest thing to a father she had after his death. For a long time Bree was just a fixture in Storm's life, until the summer after he graduated from high school.

"You two used to date, didn't you?"

"No, Bree was like one of Pete's kids."

Until the day when all of a sudden Bree had become a whole lot more than a fixture—she'd become a focus, a fantasy. And Storm had become a fool—a fool for her.

"That's not what it looked like from where I was sitting."

"That's ancient history." No matter how Storm had tried to ignore Breezy, no matter how he'd tried to treat her the same way he had before, something had changed. He couldn't say how or when it happened. He just remembered one day she'd snuck out and come to Pete's, and what began as a friendly hug turned into something else entirely. That was the beginning of the end.

Storm looked at the dip and realized he'd lost his appetite. "Why don't I get out of here and let you two have a nice romantic dinner? You don't need me hanging around, and the bar is starting to pick up, so I'll get back to work."

Patrice patted his hand. "He doesn't mean anything to her, you know."

Storm shook his head. "Patrice, what Bree does outside of this bar is none of my business. I'm here to help Pete, not for anything else, and I'm not staying any longer than I have to. As soon as Pete's back on his feet and able to take care of himself and Nicki, I'm history."

"Sure, okay." She waved her hand. "I don't buy it, but by all means, go ahead and spout your nonsense. Maybe if you keep telling yourself that, you'll start believing your own brand of bullshit. If Bree went out with Daniel to get a rise out of you, she succeeded."

"Bree getting a rise out of me has never been our problem. Our problem is just about everything else. Enjoy your night out."

Storm waved over Wanda as he strode to the bar. "When you have a chance, take Francis and Patrice's dinner order. It's on me tonight, but don't tell them that until it's over, okay?"

Wanda wiped the top of her tray. "Sure thing."

Storm slid behind the bar and took a beer glass to a pile of napkins, fanning them, doing his best to keep his mind off Bree and that jerk she was with.

Wanda stuffed her order pad in the pocket of her apron. "When's Bree coming back?"

"I don't know. She doesn't clear her calendar with me. If there is any bar business that needs to be dealt with, I'll take care of it."

"Great."

Storm wished Wanda would just get back to work and let him get his mind on anything else, but she rested her tush on a stool and settled in for a chat. "It's good to see Bree finally go out with Mr. Knickerbocker. He's been asking her out as long as I've been working here."

Part of him wanted to tell Wanda the only reason Bree went with the guy was because Storm had practically dared her. He'd heard of a pity date, but never a revenge date. "Why didn't she go out with him?"

Wanda shrugged. "Hell if I know; he's pretty hot. Bree doesn't go out much. She gives new meaning to playing hard to get."

Storm just hoped ol' Daniel wouldn't be getting any tonight. The glass he used to fan the napkins cracked in his hand. "Shit."

"Sore subject, obviously." Wanda raised an eyebrow. "I'll just go and take Francis and Patrice's order now."

"Probably a good idea." Storm swept the stack of cocktail napkins and the broken glass into the trash. It was going to be a long night.

# CHAPTER 6

Bree mentally filed her nails as Daniel held her close while they danced to a Sarah Vaughan look-alike singing one of Bree's favorites, "You're Mine, You." She looked deep into Daniel's too-pretty brown eyes and felt nothing. No sparks, no connection, no future, no nothing—at least not on her part. Unfortunately, the bulge pressing against her told her the same couldn't be said for her dance partner. How did one get out of a situation like this?

She wished she felt something—anything—for the guy, and the fact that she didn't was not only an utter disappointment, but it made her feel guilty. God, when had she become the type of person who would use someone? When Daniel had asked her to the benefit, she'd told him she'd go only as a coworker. She probably should have reiterated that by text, but her mind had been so full of Storm, all she'd wanted to do was rub his nose in it, even though it meant absolutely nothing. She checked her watch, wondering how much longer she'd have to wait to claim exhaustion.

"When did Pete's son arrive to save the day?"

"Storm?" God, could he sound any snarkier? Not that

she hadn't thought the same thing, but it wasn't Daniel's place to point it out. "He flew in early this morning—or late last night."

"How well do you know him?"

A picture of Storm passed out on the floor of Nicki's room brought a smile to her lips. "Better than I ever wanted to. Why do you ask?"

"Storm Decker has quite the reputation. The stories Pete tells about his boys are enough to make you wonder why they're not all in jail. I don't know if I like the idea of him living and working so close to you."

Bree stopped dancing. "Daniel, first of all, Storm and I have known each other since we were kids." And no one had the right to talk about Storm but her, dammit. "But that's beside the point, because when it comes down to it, who I spend time with is no concern of yours."

"What if I wanted to make it my concern?" His voice dropped an octave, and he pulled her closer.

Bree pushed against his chest, and, smart man that he was, he loosened his grip. "That's not an option." As she disengaged herself, she remembered all the reasons she'd never accepted a second date with Daniel; that itchy feeling she got whenever he walked her home from their committee meetings and the way he always seemed to stand too close.

Great, this was the perfect time to come to her senses and remember that kissing Daniel had been like kissing a cross between a lizard and an octopus. Shit. "You know, I've been working such long hours"—she pulled away and headed toward their table—"and it looks as if the night was a success, so I'm going to head back to the bar. I need to make sure things are running smoothly before I get some much-needed sleep."

"Let me walk you back."

"In these shoes?" She looked at her favorite toe-stranglers. "I don't think so." She was used to being on her feet, so wearing heels wasn't much of a problem; she just didn't like the possessive look in Daniel's eyes. "I'm going to grab a cab. It was important for us to show a united front for the sake of the project, but this wasn't a date. I don't want you to get the wrong idea."

"I want to make sure you get back safely. I insist." Daniel's grip tightened on her arm.

Bree scanned the still-busy club and saw all the deep-pocketed people who'd paid a lot of money to support her favorite project. It certainly wouldn't help if they got into a knock-down, drag-out fight. "Fine." She gave him what she liked to think of as her glacial look and then stared at his hand on her arm. He released his grip, and his calm and collected mask slipped back into place.

Bree made her way to the door, making sure the doorman got them a cab, as the last thing she wanted was to be alone with Daniel. When she alighted from the cab, she was surprised to see Daniel get out behind her. "I'm going to check on the bar, and then I'm going home. Alone."

"I'll just come in for a nightcap."

"I'd really rather you didn't. I'm tired." She ignored him, or at least tried to as she stepped into the bar.

As if he had some kind of weird radar, Storm caught her eye when Daniel put a possessive arm around her. She rolled her eyes before turning to Daniel. "Thanks for seeing me in. I'm just going to check on a few things in the back and then head upstairs. I appreciate your letting me pal around with you tonight."

"Come on, Bree."

Daniel was doing the arm-holding thing again, and she seriously considered saying to hell with their working relationship, and breaking his arm. Of course, she'd have to break his nose first to surprise him, and she really hated blood. She planted her feet, ready to do battle. "Daniel, if you don't let me go right now, I'm going to embarrass you, hurt you, and probably ruin that Zegna suit you're wearing. Bloodstains are always so difficult to get out."

"Bree, we're over here." Francis hurried toward her.

Daniel dropped her arm when he saw a tank in human form striding toward them.

"Francis, I'm so glad you and Patrice are still here. Daniel was just leaving. Weren't you, Daniel?"

Daniel threw his shoulders back and smiled. "Actually, I think you talked me into a nightcap. Francis, Bree and I would love to join you and Patrice."

"And Storm." Francis shrugged. "I don't know if you were around much before Storm Decker left."

"I know him only by reputation."

Francis shook his head. "You can't believe everything you hear, unless it's good; then you kind of have to give him the benefit of the doubt." Francis let out one of his shotgun laughs and pulled Bree into a hug and away from Daniel. He gave Daniel a friendly slap on the back, which sent him reeling ahead of them.

"Thanks, buddy," Bree whispered. "I was trying to get rid of him."

"Don't worry about it. Storm sent me over. He'll take care of Daniel, and I'll make sure no one ends up in jail. I have a feeling Storm will have no problem with the likes of Knickerbocker."

"Great, that's all I need."

"Bree, you should have thought of that before parading Knickerbocker in front of Storm. Next time, you might want to make sure the guy's not such a big dick."

"I can handle him."

"Sure, but when you have friends like me and Storm, you don't have to—it's a good thing Storm spotted you. Just make sure you don't do this again. There's a reason Patty doesn't have a good feeling about this guy. I don't like the way he was touching you."

That made two of them. She planned to give Daniel a wide berth from now on. All she needed was a way to get rid of him—that didn't involve Storm Decker, blood, or the police.

Rocki finished up the fourth set with her band and watched the air crackle in an electric arc between Storm and Bree. Man, if she had that much chemistry with anyone, she wouldn't be blasting him with visual darts or dangling another man in front of him, that was for sure.

At the piano, she adjusted the mic while the band broke down the stage, and she let the two people she'd watched with growing curiosity and annoyance inspire her solo set. She wasn't scheduled to do one, but what the hell? Maybe Storm and Bree would take the hint.

She started the intro into Lifehouse's "Broken" because that was what she saw when they looked at each other. They were two broken people, each dealing with their own demons, the residual pain of losing whatever it was they once had, circling, trying to find their balance with the changes they discovered in each other and in themselves, fighting the attraction, fighting the addiction, fighting each other.

Her fingers itched for a pen and paper as she sang

about broken hearts still beating, about not knowing how to find a way home.

She rolled it into a Norah Jones. The dance floor filled with couples holding one another close and shuffling their feet. That always brought a smile to her lips. Her fingers flying over the keys like a caress down a lover's spine, she closed her eyes and belted out the song, the music exposing a piece of her soul to those aware enough to look.

Rocki let the last notes resonate through the quiet bar before she opened her eyes and watched what she hoped was Storm and Bree's mating dance. Whenever Bree was near, Storm stood too close to be polite, his chest expanding as if drinking in her scent. And no matter how hard Bree tried to stay away, she was drawn to him, seemingly against her own will.

Rocki signaled her guitarist, who sat beside her as she played the intro to a Lady Antebellum song they'd been working on, thinking maybe the duet would give Storm and Bree the extra push they needed. Frankly, Rocki wasn't sure how much more of this she could take. She was ready to just knock their heads together.

Bree would normally head upstairs, but instead she sat at the end of the bar, toying with her drink and fending off unwanted admirers—only one of whom was Daniel Knickerbocker. Her plan had backfired. It wasn't that she wanted Storm; she just wanted him to know there were plenty of other men who wanted her. Unfortunately, Daniel, the creeper, wasn't the man she wanted to make that point. Not that Storm even noticed—he was too busy dancing with Patrice.

Francis dragged a stool next to hers and put his arm

around her shoulder, pulling her toward him. "If you want to dance with Storm," he whispered, "why don't you ask him?"

"I don't."

"That's not what it looks like to me. What is it with you two? You've been fighting all night. I thought you wanted help around here. He's helping, and you're acting like it's an imposition."

"I wanted someone to help, not take over."

Francis groaned. "Oh, so this is a woman thing."

"Excuse me?"

"You know, one of those things where a guy is in the doghouse and in order to get out, he's expected to read the woman's mind and say or do exactly what she wants, even though it makes no sense to anyone but her. In other words, Storm is screwed."

"This has absolutely nothing to do with me."

"You're wrong. It has everything to do with you. He's been dancing around you ever since he got here. He's willing to stand on his head, do whatever it takes, but he doesn't have the first clue as to what that is. The problem as I see it is that I'm not sure you know what you want either."

"I don't want anything from Storm, except for him to leave me the heck alone."

"If you're going to lie, Bree, you'd better work on your body language, because from the male perspective, you're saying the complete opposite." Francis stood. "Come on. Let's dance."

He took Bree's hand and muscled her off the barstool. What was it with men moving her around like a pawn on a chessboard? "I don't want to dance."

"No"—Francis dragged her to the dance floor—"you

just don't want to dance with me or Daniel—who looks like he's getting busy with the girl who was after Storm for most of the night while you were AWOL. Don't worry, though. I'll take care of your partner problem in a minute."

"What are you talking about?"

Francis pulled her into his huge arms. "You'll see. Just give it a few minutes."

She and Francis became friends when Pete gave Francis an ultimatum—work at the bar to pay off the stiches Logan had to get due to the beating Francis inflicted on him or Pete would call the cops. Pete's influence had ultimately helped Francis turn his life around.

Dancing with Francis was not new to her. Hell, he'd taken her to her senior prom; of course, he'd spent most of the night mooning over Patrice. It hadn't bothered her—Francis had always been a good friend and nothing more. It took Patrice a while to figure out that under that cocky, muscled, rebel-without-a-cause exterior beat the heart of a gentle soul.

"I remember you crying on my shoulder after Storm left. I didn't know it then, but you were in love with him."

"I don't want to talk about it."

"I'm not talking about it. I'm just stating the facts. Was he in love with you?"

"Don't be ridiculous. The only one Storm has ever loved is himself."

"I wouldn't be so sure if I were you."

"Yeah, and why is that?"

"Because even though he's dancing with my wife, he looks about ready to kill me. Look for yourself."

Francis turned, and sure enough, Storm was scowling.

"Maybe Patrice is raking him over the coals. She's not much for respecting a person's privacy. She'll dig and dig and dig to get what she wants out of someone."

"Either way, I'm going to solve the problem."

Before Bree knew it, she was in Storm's arms, staring into angry eyes. She didn't know how to disengage herself without making a scene. "Someone piss in your beer or something?"

"Or something."

Rocki and Jake were singing about it being a quarter after one, which it was; about being a little drunk, which she was; and feeling all alone—she wasn't even going there. Bree got sucked into Storm's fathomless eyes just as Rocki belted out the words, "I need you now," and the tension in his body became palpable.

"We're leaving."

"Why?" Bree pulled her gaze away from Storm and realized he'd danced her right to the door to the back stairway.

"You and I have things to settle before tomorrow if we're going to make this work."

"Make what work?"

"Upstairs."

"We haven't said good-bye to Francis, Patrice, and Dan—"

"Now."

"But—" Bree's feet left the floor; she let out a squeal and wrapped her arms and legs around Storm. He took the stairs two at a time. Bree held on; she was afraid of falling. "I'm not a piece of furniture you can put anywhere you want."

"Don't I know it."

He set her down to open the door, and she slugged

him. The jerk didn't even grunt. His stomach was as hard as his head.

The door yawned open. "Get inside."

Bree crossed her arms. "No."

Storm had spent the entire night on a slow burn. The damn woman was driving him insane. "Move it, or I'll move you myself."

"You wouldn't—"

He picked her up, carried her inside, kicked the door shut with the heel of his boot, and tossed her on the couch instead of where he wanted her—his bed. He scrubbed his hand over his face as she scrambled up and shoved him.

"I'm not going to take this crap from you, Daniel, or anyone else for that matter. Don't ever pick me up again."

"I never treated you like Daniel—don't go there if you know what's good for you. We need to talk. Alone. So stop arguing with me." She looked about ready to blow. "I asked nicely—"

"You did not. You demanded. I don't work for you. You work for me. And nobody manhandles me. Nobody kisses me—" Bree looked as if she shocked herself by admitting it. Tonight alone he'd counted no fewer than a dozen guys trying to pick her up—not including Dan. If no one but he was kissing her, it wasn't for lack of interest on anyone's part but hers.

"Sounds like a personal problem. And if you remember, I wasn't the only one doing the kissing." Damn, he wanted her. He took a step closer, invading her personal space, and got a whiff of her scent, citrus and scotch. "You kissed me back."

She sputtered and then clapped her mouth shut. She seemed to be counting to ten, trying to rein in that vicious temper of hers. "What do you want to talk about?"

"Us."

"There is no us." Her spine stiffened, and every muscle in her face and neck did too. So much for counting to ten. "There's nothing to talk about."

"Could have fooled me. If there's nothing to talk about, why did you go out on a revenge date with that asshole Dickerbocker, and why have you been avoiding me ever since you returned?"

"I went to a benefit with Daniel. We were not on a date, and it had absolutely nothing to do with you."

"Right, try selling that somewhere else, Breezy. Too bad it backfired on you."

"News flash, Storm. The world doesn't revolve around you. Daniel and I are—"

"Finished. If he ever lays a hand on you again, I'll break it off and mail it back to him via China."

"I'm more than capable of protecting myself. I thought you learned that lesson last night."

"Just remember who ended up on top. But that's not the point here. The point is that we"—he pointed to her and then to himself—"meaning you and I—the two of us have to figure out how to work together before Pete comes home tomorrow. We're not going to do it by you sniping at me, avoiding me, parading Dan-the-man or some other sorry excuse for a date in front of me, or by telling me to pack up and go back to Auckland."

"I don't snipe—"

"Liar." He tried very hard not to smile. But damn, it was difficult. He didn't think there was anything more attractive than a pissed-off Breezy Collins.

"Fine." She blew her bangs out of her eyes and stepped back, avoiding him again. "You want to get along? Just do what I tell you to do from now on and leave me alone the rest of the time." She crossed her arms, which only showed off her cleavage, and his mouth went dry. "There, it's all settled. I'm done. Good night."

She spun around so quickly, he almost missed when he reached for her. "Not so fast. I'm not good at following orders, and I don't work for you." He didn't mention that the last thing he wanted to do was leave her alone. No, he wanted to leave her screaming his name, begging for more.

"You do when you're in my bar—"

"Pete's bar—"

"I'm the manager. I run it. I'm the boss."

"Do you think I'm going to ditch my career and steal your job?"

She took a deep breath, as if the thought that he might scared the hell out of her. "No."

"Good, because there's no way in hell I'd ever work the bar again. So, if you're not afraid of me taking over your territory, why are you having such a problem with this?"

"It's not this, Storm. It's you. I don't like you, I don't want you here, and I don't trust you as far as I can toss the Statue of Liberty, one handed."

"Because of what happened between us—"

"I told you. There is no us. There never was."

"Bullshit. You can't have it both ways. You can't tell me that you don't like me, don't trust me, and don't want me here because I left, and then deny that my leaving hurt you. I'm sorry I hurt you. I'm sorry I let it get out of hand. I'm so sorry I left like I did."

"You didn't leave; you ran." For a moment he saw the look that had haunted him for the last eleven years; it was the same look he saw on her face when she realized he was taking off. Then she blinked and it was gone, replaced by a pissed-off woman.

"I . . ." Fuck, he'd panicked. He'd run when he realized she was a virgin. "I was afraid." What must that have done to a seventeen-year-old girl? He didn't have much of a code of honor back then, but he'd never taken anyone's virginity. "I had to leave. I couldn't stay, and I couldn't take you with me. And Pop—if he thought I ever . . . I couldn't do that to him."

"You ran away from me because of Pete?"

"No. Not because of Pop. This is coming out all wrong." He scrubbed his hand over his face and remembered the fear. The enormity of the emotions being with Bree had brought to the surface. She wasn't just another fuck, and that was all he'd ever had, all he wanted to have. Until Breezy. "If I had stayed with you, if we had made love, I would have been trapped here." He would never have been able to leave her. Hell, if the ship hadn't set sail that next morning, if there hadn't been miles of ocean between them, and if he hadn't been ten stories above the surface, he would have jumped off the damn boat and swum back to her. Losing her almost killed him. "In the end, it was better for both of us that I lost you."

"You didn't lose me." She stared at him with hard, cold emerald green eyes. "You threw me away."

"I did you a favor."

"Well, thanks for nothing." She turned on her heel, went into her room, and slammed the door behind her.

\*          \*          \*

Bree was trapped in her room, planning her escape as she hugged the pillow to her chest.

It would have been nice if she'd thought to use the bathroom before she made her door-slamming, thanks-for-nothing exit. She'd waited hours and couldn't hold it any longer. It was three in the morning. The coast had to be clear—heck, she hadn't heard a sound since she'd stopped crying hours ago. Right now, her teeth were floating, and she could really use a handful of aspirin to combat the headache she got every time she spent more than a few minutes crying. She hated to cry. Worse yet, she wasn't one of those pretty criers. No, her face got all blotchy, her eyes swelled, and her makeup ran like a racehorse. With her, there was no such thing as waterproof mascara.

She wasn't sure which emotion had been stronger, anger or sadness tinged with regret. Not that it really mattered—both made her cry. She was the only person she knew who teared up when spitting mad. Now, she was angrier with herself than with anyone else. Years ago, she'd sworn she'd shed the last tear over Storm Decker. She'd been wrong.

Bree rolled out of bed and blew her nose. Talking about it, something she'd always refused to do, hadn't helped like everyone had said it would. No, it just hurt more. It was much easier to take all that nastiness and lock it in the deep recesses of her mind. After all, it wasn't as if she wanted to forget; she just wanted to survive. Remembering should keep her from making the same stupid mistake. As she fought through the anger and tears, she'd made a very important decision. She was going to take whatever Storm had to offer. She couldn't afford to let her guard down around him; she wouldn't fall in love with him again. But then, sex had nothing to do with love—that she'd learned from experience. She was a grown woman, in control of her own emotions, and she couldn't think of one good reason not to have her way with the man. She threw on a ratty old T-shirt and boxer shorts, then crept to the bathroom. She'd talk to him in the morning and tell him exactly what she wanted. She wanted him, no illusions, no strings, just sex. Maybe then she'd figure out what all the fuss was about and get him out of her system.

Bree took care of her near-bursting bladder, brushed her teeth, and washed her face. She turned off the bathroom light and snuck out, patting her blotchy, wet face with a towel on the way to the kitchen and the Excedrin. She turned into the dark living room and ran into Storm Decker's naked chest.

Stepping back, he hit the lights. From the way his 501s were buttoned halfway, he wore nothing else. Damn him.

"It's about time you came out. I was worried about you."

"Hate to break it to you, Storm, but I'm hardly the suicidal type. I have too many people depending on me."

"I heard you crying."

She stepped around him and slipped into the kitchen, opened the cabinet to the left of the sink, and grabbed the Excedrin bottle. It gave her something other than Storm to wrestle with. "I cry when I'm pissed, and believe me, I'm as pissed as you are arrogant." She popped the childproof top and threw four into her mouth, turned on the spigot, and drank right from the tap before swiping her mouth with the towel.

"Arrogant?"

She turned, avoiding his eyes and stared over his shoulder. "Did it ever occur to you that I knew you were

leaving back then? I mean, everyone knew you were going into the merchant marines—you might as well have
put it on a billboard. Did you think I planned to trap
you?"

"Not consciously, no. But that's how it would have
turned out."

Bree didn't know whether to laugh or cry. "God,
you're such a conceited ass."

He crossed his arms over his gorgeous chest, looking
at her as though she'd lost her mind. Maybe she had.

"I never wanted you."

His eyes just about bugged out, and streaks of red,
either from anger or embarrassment, slashed across his
well-defined cheekbones.

"Okay"—she patted his chest—"I wanted you, but
not for more than a month or two. Not for more than sex.
Believe me when I say I've never named our future children."

"What?" He took a giant step back, as if the thought
might be enough to send him packing—it probably was.
That was so not her problem. As a matter of fact, she
enjoyed knowing she could scare him.

"I was seventeen, madly in love with you, and I
wanted you in every way my dirty little mind could imagine. I may have been young, but I was never delusional.
I knew you were leaving. I had plans for a life and a future for myself without you." Okay, so she made them
the night he walked out on her. "I didn't wait around for
you. I put an end to that."

"An end to what?"

Was she speaking a foreign language? An end to believing in love. "An end to being the oldest virgin in Red
Hook."

"You were seventeen."

She rolled her eyes. "Yeah, I remember. I learned from the experience of falling for you. There will be no more dangerous men with no staying power who run away and don't come back. No, the next time I fall in love it's going to be with someone slightly boring and very safe, someone whose most dangerous act is jaywalking, someone who will show up for dinner every night." She tried to picture it, but the only person she saw walking through the white picket fence was Storm. She took a mental eraser and ran it over the image. "I'm all grown up now. I'm finished with fantasies. Who would have thought my mother would be right after all? Now I just want to sleep with the bad boy of my dreams before I settle down with a nice, safe accountant."

"Wait. What?" Storm's eyes were huge and brightened either with excitement or shock; she wasn't sure which. "You want to use me?"

She bit the inside of her cheek to keep from telling him in no uncertain terms and explicit detail how she wanted to use him.

"We can use each other." She stepped closer, not touching him, but just a hairbreadth away, her mouth close to his ear. "It'll be mutual." Heat radiated from him, attracting her like a cat to a patch of sunlight. "You've made it very clear you're leaving. I may have loved you way back when, but that's history. You'll never be safe and boring. You're so not that man."

His mouth dropped open, as if he were going to argue. She placed two fingers over his lips, and he let out a groan instead.

"No," she said, sliding her hand to his chest, "you're dangerous, hot, sexy, and guaranteed to leave. You were then and you are now. Knowing that, I'm safe. And I'm not even going into the whole thing with Pete."

Storm's hand came around hers, stopping her progress but not removing it. Instead, he pressed her open palm over his heart. "Breezy, Pop thought of you as his little girl. He would have disowned me if I hurt you."

"You big dope." She gave him a push, removing her hand. "I was going to be hurt whether we made love or not. I may have had stars in my eyes back then, but I don't now. You're guaranteed to leave, which makes this even better."

"It does?"

Bree stared into his eyes and saw something she'd never seen before—Storm Decker completely dumbfounded. She hid her smile, moseyed over to the couch, and sat.

Storm followed and sank down beside her.

She turned to face him. "The only way I'd ever sleep with you now is if there is absolutely no way I'd be able to keep you. You'll make sure of that, because if there is one thing I've learned about you, Storm, it's that you'll never settle down."

# CHAPTER 7

"Breezy, what do you want from me?" Storm let the question dangle like one of Rocki's piano notes reverberating through the room.

Bree snuggled up to him on the couch, her breasts pressed against his side as he replayed their conversation in his head on fast-forward, trying to take everything in and waiting for her reply.

Breezy wanted him.

Breezy had loved him.

Breezy didn't want him for anything more than sex.

Yeah, there was a total disconnect with that last one.

He didn't know whether to be relieved or hurt. All he knew was that Bree had just given him a get-out-of-jail-free-card with benefits.

"I want the same thing I've always wanted." She kneeled next to him and tossed one leg over his. Facing him. Close enough to kiss. "I want you." She sank onto his lap, straddling him, and scooted closer.

His breath caught, his temperature shot through the roof, and his dick sprang to life.

Her gaze held his. "I want you for as long as you're

here." She kissed the corner of his mouth; her hands slid over his chest. "I want you every way I can have you."

He grabbed her waist, tugging her closer still. She tilted her hips, pressing his erection against her heat.

"I know you'll leave." Her breath was sweet, fresh, minty. "I'm worried about Nicki and Pete. But that's a whole other issue, one I have no control over. Still, it has nothing to do with us."

"Us?" He stared into her bright green eyes, searching for any hint of uncertainty. Determination stared back at him.

"Yes, us. You and me. For as long as it lasts." Her breath raged in his ear. "For as long as you're here."

"Why?"

"Because I'm selfish." A sexy smile curled her lips. "I want you before I settle for that nice, safe, slightly boring guy."

The thought of Breezy with anyone but him had him tightening his hold. How could she even think of letting someone else touch her?

"Being with you is like going to Coney Island and riding the Cyclone. I want to enjoy the wild ride as long as it lasts, but I don't want to spend the rest of my life on a roller coaster. I did that with my dad, always waiting for the day he wouldn't come home. He loved us, but not enough to give up his roller-coaster ride." The sadness etched on her face was the same one that had haunted him all these years.

"The day my dad died, my whole life fell apart. I don't want to be in that position ever again, and although you're not a cop, you're just as dangerous. You're far too risky for more than just a quick and hopefully thrilling ride."

"No pressure there." Storm couldn't think straight with Breezy sitting on his lap, her breasts pressed against his chest, her eyes looking straight into his as if she could read his mind. Still, there was a niggling doubt, something was wrong, something big, but for the life of him, he didn't know what. "You make me sound like a daredevil." Breezy knew the score, and she still wanted him. Who was he to let her down? "I sit at a desk all day and design boats." And when Pop recovered, Storm could leave—go back to Auckland and never have to see her with that boring, safe guy she'd settle for. "The only danger I've encountered besides you and your frying pan is a paper cut."

Bree snorted—she was the only woman alive who could make a snort sound sexy. "Get real. I read all about that accident you had a few years ago in the Sydney-to-Hobart race. You and your crew were almost killed. Your boat was lost at sea for two days. They called Pete. We thought you were dead."

"Shit, that was nothing." Nothing he'd discuss with her. That stormy night in the Bass Strait, his boat fell off a wave and capsized. For a while he'd thought he was a goner too, and the only woman he thought of while he waited to die was sitting on his lap right now, wanting him.

He wasn't sure how long they'd been capsized. Thirty seconds, two minutes—it was a blur. When another monster wave hit, the force of it righted the boat and ripped off the mast. He and the crew worked frantically to save the boat, hacking at the rigging that punched holes into the vessel, turning it into a sieve.

A box of chocolate PowerBars burst in the capsize, water filled the hull, and the PowerBars got sucked into the bilge pumps, clogging them. He and the crew spent two days bailing water, waiting to sink until he was able to get the engines running again so they could limp back to Eden. In the three years since, Storm hadn't been able to even think about a chocolate bar without wanting to blow chunks.

He'd watched his life flash before his eyes for two days, over and over and over, on a continuous loop. Leaving Breezy was his only regret.

"Storm, what do you want?"

To love her for as long as she'd let him. Sure, he wasn't convinced he knew the meaning of the word *love*, not really. All he knew was whatever he felt for her was stronger than anything else he'd ever experienced. There was only one other word that covered everything. "More." He tangled his fist in her hair and tugged her face toward his. "Now."

He kissed her, letting all the feeling he'd held in check for so long flow into her, like wind into an unfurled sail. The kiss was hot, wild, but just when he thought he was kissing her, she turned the tables and changed the dynamics.

Bree took over. She attacked his mouth, swamping him with sensation, taking all he had and shooting it back at him tenfold. Damn, for a woman who claimed not to allow men to kiss her, she sure knew what she was doing.

She sucked on his tongue, raking her teeth over it, sending a lightning bolt through his entire body.

He slid her T-shirt up her back, learning the feel of her, the nip of her waist, the softness of her skin, the play of her muscles under his roughened fingertips.

She pulled her mouth from his and ripped off her

T-shirt. She'd definitely changed since the last time he'd seen her topless, and with her breasts at eye level, he let his mouth do the communicating while he pulled her boxers as low as he could get them. His hands slid up her thighs to her heat. Her scent was intoxicating. He wanted to lay her out before him and taste every inch of her body. And he didn't want to do that here on the damn couch. He pulled his mouth away from her breast. "I'm breaking one of your rules. I'm picking you up and taking you to bed." He flipped her into his arms and stood.

Her boxers slid down to her ankles, and she kicked them off. "Okay, I won't punish you just as long as you don't run out naked again. Once in a lifetime was enough."

"I'm not running, but I'm not averse to punishment either." He waggled his eyebrows and then kissed the tip of her nose, watching her eyes cross. He bit back a laugh.

"Hurry."

Storm set her on the bed and took his time running his hands over her, memorizing the texture of her skin, and her reaction to his touch. "Breezy, you're even more beautiful than you were before. I didn't think that was possible."

A blush crept from her chest to her face, her pale skin opalescent in the light that stole through the open door.

He followed the path of her blush to her lips and sank into her mouth, taking his time, teasing her with his tongue, his caress, listening to the sounds she made, the way her skin jumped under his hands.

"Storm, please."

"I'm trying, Breezy, but pleasing you will take some time. Good thing we've got all night."

"You don't understand. I need—"

He slid his hand between her legs and filled her with two fingers. She was tight. She was hot. She was wet. She was his.

Bree pushed herself onto her elbows, and the sight of her with the light pooling around her, the tip of her pink tongue wetting her bottom lip, her hair falling around her shoulders, just about knocked the wind out of him. He hadn't had many special times in his life like this. This, he knew, was a biggie. He stared, memorizing every nuance, every image that made this moment one he would recall until the day he died.

Bree reached for the button fly on his jeans.

"No, not yet." His hand stilled hers, pressing it against his bulge.

Her tongue peeked out as if she couldn't wait to taste him. She ran her hand over his erection and squeezed. He held back a groan and sucked in air.

Breezy rose to her knees, scooted to the edge of the bed, and brought her mouth to his stomach—her wicked tongue traced the muscles, her hand pressed against the front of his jeans.

Having her mouth so close to his dick sent all the blood in his body flowing south. "Bree, you're killing me, babe."

With a yank, the buttons popped, and his erection sprang free. She took her time looking. "I didn't get to see you the last time we were together. The only thing I really saw was your bare chest, and your naked, retreating ass."

She ran the tip of her finger over the sensitive head, and her touch had him locking his knees to keep from falling. He gritted his teeth.

"You were so busy driving me crazy. Your mouth and

hands seemed to be everywhere all at once." She looked into his eyes and reminded him of a cat cornering a mouse. "At the time, I didn't know how to please you."

"God, Bree."

"But I do now."

In theory.

Okay, so Bree talked a good game, or she thought she did anyway; she just wasn't sure she could live up to it. She'd had sex a few times, but frankly she didn't know what all the fuss was about.

Her first time had been miserable. She didn't even know the guy's name. After Storm left, her virginity had become a curse she'd wanted to vanquish. At the first opportunity, she'd snuck out her bedroom window, went to a party, and hooked up with the first guy who noticed her.

Bree lost her virginity in a bedroom the size of a walk-in closet that smelled vaguely of dirty socks, but then it could have been the guy—a guy who unfortunately seemed as inexperienced as she. It had been as pleasurable and lasted as long as the polite conversation one might have after dialing a wrong number.

Still, the deed was done, and she'd been hopeful the second time would be incredible—or at least not awful. She'd read her share of romances; she'd heard all about the fireworks, the rush of pleasure, the way the heroine looks into her lover's eyes and is transported to another dimension.

After the third try, she'd given up on the idea of an orgasm that wasn't self-induced. Since she was much better at getting herself off than were any of the men she'd dated, she figured dating and sex were a complete and utter waste of time. Still, she dated a little—she didn't want to be a nun. She'd gone after the safe, stable men her mom would approve of, but they all left her cold and bored. It was easier to bury herself in work than to face the constant disappointment. No one had ever made her feel half as much as Storm did just by looking at her.

Storm lifted her chin, bringing her back to the present. His eyes dark, his pupils almost blacking out the beautiful blue irises, his breathing as erratic as hers, heat pouring off his body.

"This shouldn't be so hard."

He quirked a smile, which shocked her. Smiling had never been part of sex—at least not in her limited experience. "Breezy, if it wasn't hard, we'd have a real problem, or at least I would."

She closed her eyes and felt her face flame as she tried to swallow, but her mouth was so dry, it took a few tries. This was just one more in what was becoming a long line of sexual disasters. Could her sex life get any worse? Yeah, but only if he ran away; then again, maybe that would be a blessing.

"Breezy? Look at me."

"Do I have to?"

The bed dipped beside her as she sank down on her heels.

"What's the matter? Changed your mind, have ya?"

His Brooklyn Kiwi accent was almost comical. She didn't know whether to laugh or cry. "No, I'm just . . . you know, nervous."

Storm's arm came around her, and he kissed her neck, "She'll be right."

"What's that supposed to mean?"

"It's a Godzone saying. It means don't worry. Everything will work out."

"Would you mind speaking English—the Brooklyn kind, please? What's a Godzone?"

"New Zealand. It's like a perfect place; people call it the Godzone. Sorry."

"Oh." Great, Storm would take off for the Godzone, and she'd stay in Red Hook. Granted, all the work she'd done had made it a better place to live, but it was still a far cry from the Godzone Storm had run to. She slid off the bed. "You know, maybe this wasn't such a good idea after all. I—"

He kissed her, cutting off whatever it was she had planned to say. The words left her brain as quickly as his tongue slipped between her lips. This wasn't an it's-okay-I-understand kiss. This was more of an I'll-die-if-I-don't-take-you-now kiss, the kind she'd read about in all those romances. Damn, it was as good as the up-against-the-door, I'll-kiss-you-to-keep-from-strangling-you kiss he'd planted on her earlier, but different. There was no anger now. There was frustration, sure, but this frustration was of a purely sexual nature. A hand slipped around the back of her neck, sealing her mouth to his, and his arm banded around her waist. He held her against him as if she were made of fine china he was deathly afraid he'd drop and break.

Bree had waited a decade for this one moment, this one night, this one finite space in time. Storm was hers, and she was his until he left. This was what she'd been missing all these years.

"Breezy." The roughness in his voice slid across her skin like sandpaper, scraping her every nerve.

She slid his jeans down until he could step out of them. His taste and scent were nothing short of amazing—the same as she remembered. Fingers skated down her spine, and Storm slid his leg between hers before he tumbled them back onto the bed.

He kissed her chin and nipped it before moving along her neck. His hand skittered down her side to her hip, pulling her closer as his mouth blazed a wet trail to her breast, sucking it deep into his mouth as if wanting to drink her in.

He was doing it again—overwhelming her. Everywhere he touched drove her higher. All she could do was grab his head and pray he never stopped. With his every touch, need formed like a fireball within her. She didn't know what to do to reciprocate. God, she felt like such a loser.

"Storm?"

"Hmm?"

He didn't stop—well, only long enough to switch breasts. Not that she really wanted him to, but some direction would be helpful.

His hand slid over her stomach and lower; his mouth followed, coming dangerously close to—"Oh, God."

She tried to pull away, but he held her hips and pulled her closer. She could only imagine that the shocked look on her face caused the smile he shot her before he dipped his head.

The first touch of his mouth knocked the wind out of her. Her heart, already pounding against her ribs, shot into overdrive, and when he found that one spot, she saw stars, and if she hadn't been imagining things, she might have screamed.

Bree had read *Cosmo*; she'd heard all about oral sex from Rocki; but no matter how incredible it sounded, it could not be compared to the real thing. Bree grabbed the sheets and held on as if anchoring herself against the tidal wave of feelings bombarding her. She writhed beneath the assault of his mouth, his teeth, his tongue, filling her and making her feel empty at the same time. She wasn't sure how much more she could take, but damned if she didn't want more. And Storm gave it to her—she was on a roller coaster, and they hadn't even hit the first drop. She saw stars, and fireworks that would rival those on the Fourth of July over the Hudson River.

Storm held Breezy as she lay boneless in his arms. Her words ricocheted through his mind: *I don't like you, I don't want you here, and I don't trust you....* There wasn't much he wouldn't do to please her, except sell his soul. As he lay there looking at her, he realized suddenly that was what she'd asked. She turned to him with a smile on her lips, and when she looked into his eyes, it faltered.

"Bree . . . I can't do this. I'm sorry." He forced himself to let her go and slid off the bed. Grabbing his jeans, he tugged them on, thankful he didn't have a zipper to deal with. In his condition, that could have been painful.

"Again?" Breezy bolted to a sitting position and stared at him. "You're doing it again? You're running away?"

Storm couldn't meet her eyes; he didn't want to have to come up with an excuse. Instead, he picked up her robe and handed it to her. "I'm not running."

"Could have fooled me." She speared her arm through the sleeve and scrambled to the other side of the bed. "Get out." Her voice rose and quavered. Bree belted the robe so tightly, it looked as if she'd cut off her circulation, and her gaze skittered around the room as if searching for something. "You know what? Never mind. I'll leave."

She tossed a big handbag over her shoulder before skirting the bed.

"Breezy." Storm held up his hands and stepped in front of the door. "Can't we talk about this?"

She tried to get past him, but he blocked her so she got in his face, well, as much as she could, considering she was barefoot. "You want to talk?" she yelled. She stepped back, cocked her hip, and crossed her arms. "Well, by all means, let's talk about why I'm such a sexual pariah that you ran out on me twice."

"Bree, you're not a pariah. I've never wanted anyone the way I want you. I'm not running. I just can't—"

"What can't you do, Storm? Close the deal? Stay the course? Finish the job? Fuck me?"

"I can't use you."

"I gave you permission. Hell, I wanted to use you too."

"Yeah, I know. You made that very clear. The thing is, I don't want to use you, and I don't want to be used either. I'm not your boy toy, your one last fling. Don't you get it? This isn't just sex to me. It never has been, and it never will be. If sex is what you want . . . If that's *all* you want . . . I can't do it. I want . . ." He closed his eyes and shook his head. "No, I need more."

"More? More of what? According to you, this is a two-week thing, and then you're leaving to go back to New Zealand."

"That was before I saw Pop. Before I knew about you and Nicki. Everything has changed. I'm staying for as long as it takes."

"You'll stay until Pete can take care of himself and Nicki—I know. But then as soon as that happens, you'll be out of here so fast, you'll leave skid marks." Bree laughed, and not a funny laugh either. "You know, Storm, I thought between the two of us, I was the coward. I've stayed here where I felt safe and cared for when I could have gone anywhere, and I've waited for a boring prince charming, but at least I never lied to myself."

"Breezy, I ran away once, and I've spent the last eleven years regretting it. I'm not the same man I was then."

She scoffed. "The only differences I see are about thirty pounds of muscle, that scar bisecting your left eyebrow, and a different haircut."

"Then you don't know me at all."

"Maybe not, but I know me. This is the end. I'm going home tonight. I don't need you breathing down my neck, so when Pete comes home, you can stay *alone* at my place across the hall until you turn and run again."

"That's where you're wrong. You can stay here, or you can stay at your own place. Your choice. Where I stay is mine, and I'm not leaving—not even to sleep across the hall. Deal with it."

Breezy looked about ready to rip him a new one. She stood shaking, furious. He squashed the urge to kiss her as he had earlier, and he wondered what it said about him that seeing her all fired up and mad was almost as much of a turn-on as seeing her naked.

"From now on, Storm Decker, you stay the hell away from me. Are we clear?"

"Crystal." Bree was back to hating him. Maybe he deserved it. He should have said no when she climbed on his lap. He'd thought he could take what she offered but then realized he couldn't. Okay, well, he could have; all the parts were working and then some, but then his conscience got in the way. She might say she wanted a relationship with no emotional attachments, but he didn't believe it. It would hurt her. He wouldn't allow that to happen again. It might kill him, but he would wait until Bree was ready for a serious relationship with him. "I'll work at the bar, I'll take care of my family, and I'll prove you wrong. I won't touch you until you want more than just a fuck. If you want to make love to me, Breezy, you let me know."

He was through with regrets. Before this was over, he'd prove to Breezy and himself that he was worthy of her respect, her trust, and, although he had no idea how he'd manage it, her love.

# CHAPTER 8

Storm took the last sip of his quad-shot Americano and checked the address he'd scrawled on a piece of paper. Francis and Patrice's house was a rehabbed row home in a gentrified neighborhood about a block from Coffey Park. There were still signs of the ramshackle neighborhood he'd pictured while taking down the address, but the neighborhood had changed and Francis's home was one of the nicest in the area.

He climbed out of Pete's ancient Jeep Cherokee and locked it before rubbing his tired eyes. He hadn't slept for shit. He spent most of the night roaming the empty apartment and kicking his own ass before he gave up and went on a punishing sunrise run. Nothing helped.

Francis opened the door, holding on his hip a beautiful toddler, who, thank God, looked just like her mama. Francis's smile fell. "You look like crap."

"Thanks." Storm looked past him into the formal living room to find high ceilings, crown molding, and beautiful hardwood floors with surprisingly formal couches. A flat-screen TV hung from the wall, and a big plastic dollhouse sat in a corner littered with half-naked Barbie dolls, plastic furniture, cars, and doll clothes.

"Nicki," Patrice called as she walked out of the eat-in kitchen, wiping her hands on a towel, and stopped at the bottom of the steps, "your big brother is here."

Brother? Shit. Storm rubbed his aching head. He'd never thought about it, but he guessed he and Nicki were related—the same way he was related to Logan and Slater. He had never thought of Nicki as anything more than a kid he had to deal with. What kind of big brother did that make him? Damn.

Nicki ran down the hardwood stairs in socks and slid to a stop in front of him. One of her pigtails was tied higher than the other, making her look crooked. "Where's Bree?"

Storm couldn't very well say she was at home wishing him dead, so he just shrugged and handed Nicki a bag of clothes he'd scavenged from her drawers. He didn't know what little girls wore, but he tossed a few things together after Patrice reminded him to. "Why don't you go change so we can go pick up Pop? He's coming home today."

"Sure. Is Bree meeting us there?"

"No need, kid. I'm here now."

She gave him a worried look. "Bree always picks me up. How come she's not here?"

"Because I am."

Nicki took the bag from him, looked inside, and glared at him. "Bree knows I hate these shorts."

"Yeah, well, I didn't. You can change later if you don't like what I brought."

She let out a groan and headed back upstairs, but not before shooting him that universal pissed-off-female glare.

Francis, Patrice, and their squirming daughter watched

him. He was batting a thousand today. He stuffed his hands in his pockets and rolled his neck. "What do they do, Patrice? Pull girls aside in preschool and teach them how to shoot daggers at unsuspecting males?"

"No, I think it's a genetic trait."

"Good to know."

"So," Patrice said, stepping toward him, "I take it things didn't go well last night."

"That's putting it mildly." He pinched the bridge of his nose. "It's probably better this way."

Francis laughed. "Could have fooled me. You look like you've crawled through the nine circles of hell since you got back."

"I have. I've been back less than forty-eight hours, and people wonder why I rarely come home."

Francis handed the ankle biter off to Patrice and punched Storm in the arm. "It has nothing to do with coming home; it has to do with the way you left. You need to make up for sins of the past."

"Frankie, if I wanted to talk to a priest, I'd go to confession."

"If only it were only that simple." Francis picked up a stray Barbie shoe. "It's going to take a lot more than a few Hail Marys and a couple trips around the ol' rosary to solve all your problems. But it will be a hell of a long visit unless you and Bree get your shit worked out."

Patrice put the little girl down and gave her a pat on the tush. "Little ears, Francis. Little ears and big mouths."

Francis put his arm around Patrice and kissed her temple. "Sorry, babe."

Storm blinked his gritty eyes, wondering if he was seeing things. Frankie, Patrice, kids . . . It was too weird. "How long is Nicki going to take? I've got to get Pop home."

"You can leave Nicki here with me, and I can drop her off later."

"Thanks, Patrice, but I'll take care of Nicki and Pop."

"Oh, you will, huh?" She threw the towel over her shoulder. "Did you think to go grocery shopping?"

"No."

"When were you planning to do that?"

Shit. "I don't know." He hadn't so much as looked in the refrigerator. "Pop owns a restaurant; I'm sure I can order something up."

"He's on a special diet."

"He is?"

Patrice rolled her eyes. "A heart-healthy diet. Lean meats, low cholesterol, no processed food, fruits, and vegetables."

"I'll take care of it."

"I guess you'll have to arrange a visiting nurse."

"I will?"

"Didn't you talk to Bree about any of this?"

"No."

"I see. Does she even know you're here?"

"Not exactly. I told her last night that I'd take care of Pop and Nicki, and that's what I plan to do."

"All alone?"

"Hey, I'm a capable guy. If Bree can do it and run the restaurant, then I should have no problem handling Pop and Nicki."

Patrice shook her head. "Bree couldn't do it. That's why she called Logan. At least she was smart enough to know she was out of her depth."

"Are you insinuating I'm not?"

"I'm not insinuating anything—I'm stating a fact." She crossed her arms and raised an eyebrow. "If I were you, I'd get on my fancy cell phone, call Bree, and at least tell her your plans. The two of you are making this a lot harder than it has to be."

Patrice had no idea how hard it was last night to let Bree go. He kept telling himself he was doing the right thing, but he didn't know why it felt so damn wrong. "I'm the last person she wants to talk to."

"It doesn't really matter what either of you want. We're not in high school anymore, Storm. It's time the two of you started acting like adults. You have Nicki and Pete depending on you now."

"Don't you think I know that? Hell, that's why I'm here in the first place. If it weren't for Pop and Nicki, I'd be a world away."

"Right now you're working at cross-purposes. Unless you and Bree figure out how to work together, you might as well go back to Auckland. They'd all be better off without you."

Patrice couldn't have done more damage if she'd had Francis take him out back to beat on him. His mouth opened, but the invisible grip she had around his windpipe hadn't relaxed, so he was unable to choke out a response before she turned on her heel and went upstairs, hopefully to hurry Nicki along.

Francis leaned against the wall, his eyes following Patrice's progress up the steps. "Looks like you really stepped in it this time." Storm wasn't sure if he was talking about with Patrice or Breezy. "What the hell happened last night?"

"Nothing."

"Nothing? The way you carried Bree up the stairs didn't look like nothing to me."

"Mind your own business, Frankie."

"Hey, man. I'm trying to help you out here. Did you talk at all? I've been married for a while now—long enough to pick my way through a female minefield or two. You don't stay married and alive without surviving a few of them."

Storm rubbed the back of his neck, hoping to relieve some of the tension. "I'm not looking to navigate Bree's minefield. I just need to take care of Pop and Nicki and stay as far away from Bree as I can."

"Good luck with that." Francis laughed. "You're living in the same apartment, bro."

"She went home."

"Storm, you do realize she lives across the damn hall, don't you?"

"After what happened last night, I couldn't be any farther away from Bree Collins if I were sitting in an igloo in Antarctica."

Francis whistled through his teeth. "That bad, huh?"

There was no need to answer. Storm just shoved his hands deeper into his pockets and rocked back on his heels.

Francis checked his watch and then snatched his uniform shirt off the banister, dragged it on over his T-shirt, and looked up the steps. "Patrice, girls, I have to leave for work."

Patrice and three little girls—one of whom was Nicki—ran down the steps and took turns hugging and kissing Francis good-bye. Storm had never seen anything like it. It looked like something out of a freakin' 1950s TV show. All that was different were the clothes and Patrice's lack of pearls. Francis pulled Nicki into his arms and gave her a smacking kiss on the cheek before tugging on one of her off-kilter pigtails. "You keep Storm in line for me, Nicki. Okay?"

Nicki nodded, looking as uncomfortable as Storm felt. They were two outsiders looking in—afraid to get too close, afraid to get too big a dose of the happy-family vibes ricocheting around them, afraid to want to be part of something like that. It cost too much to want what Francis and Patrice had—people like him didn't get happily-ever-afters. Storm didn't deserve one, but Nicki did.

As soon as Francis released Nicki, she backed away and wrapped her arms around herself like a shield. Storm looked down to find he'd done the same thing. Damn. He had to help the poor kid out, so he put his hand on Nicki's shoulder and gave it a squeeze. Nicki looked so all-alone watching the Red Hook version of *Father Knows Best*. "Come on, kid. Let's go pick up Pop."

Patrice squatted down in front of Nicki. "Give me a hug and a kiss good-bye, sweetie."

Nicki shuffled her feet and allowed Patrice to envelop her in a hug. She stood stiffer than one of the Queen's Guards outside Buckingham Palace. Shit, couldn't Patrice give the kid a break? Didn't she see how uncomfortable all her hugs and kisses made her?

Nicki pulled out of Patrice's hold as soon as she could and turned to the door. "Can I go home?"

"Don't you want to pick up Pop?"

She shook her head, looking at her sneaker, which was trying to dig a hole in the hardwood floor. He'd seen that before; the kid was hiding something.

"Sorry, kiddo. I need to pick up Pop, and I don't think you're old enough to stay alone. You're stuck with me." He opened the door and turned back to Patrice. "Thanks for everything. We'll see you around."

Patrice sashayed to him, pulled him into a hug, and

gave him a smacking kiss on the cheek too. Nicki smiled up at him, enjoying his obvious discomfort. Damn, he wasn't used to all this touchy-feely crap any more than Nicki was. He gave Patrice an awkward pat on the back, not exactly sure of what to do.

"Get used to it, Storm." Patrice rubbed something off his cheek, probably lipstick. "People who care about you want to hug you."

"Yeah, just don't let your husband see you doing that. He's beaten the crap out of me one too many times already."

Patrice rolled her eyes. "Francis has changed a lot more than you know. He's fine with me hugging friends. You'll get used to it if you hang around long enough."

"Not gonna happen. Thanks, though." He didn't think she bought the gratitude, but right now, he was so damn uncomfortable, he was past caring. He grabbed Nicki's arm and dragged her along with him. "Is she always like that?" he asked under his breath.

"Like what? Hugging and stuff?"

"Yeah."

"Pretty much. I can't leave without getting a hug and a kiss. It's weird."

"Tell me about it." He feigned a shiver.

"You kind of get used to it after a while. It's not as awful as it used to be."

"Good to know." Storm crossed the street and went around the car to open the door for Nicki. When he looked around, she wasn't there. He looked across the street and saw her standing on the curb. "Nicki, come here, kid."

"I can't."

"Why the hell not?" He slammed the door and went back around the car.

"'Cause I'm not allowed to cross a street without holding a grown-up's hand."

"Aw, for crying out loud. That's ridiculous."

"Yeah, but Bree said she'd ground me for a week if I tried it again, and she's got spies everywhere." Nicki looked over her shoulder to the house where Patrice watched through the front window.

"Fine." Storm crossed the street in three strides, took Nicki by the hand, and walked her across the street, cursing under his breath. He opened the passenger door and waited for the kid to get in.

Nicki stood there, wide-eyed.

"What's the problem now?"

"I'm not old enough to ride in front. You gotta be twelve years old or ninety pounds, and I'm neither."

"Seriously? Who the hell made that rule?"

Nicki shrugged and climbed into the backseat. She fastened the seat belt, and Storm tossed the bag of dirty clothes in beside her. He got in and looked at her through the rearview mirror. "Hell, I was younger than you the first time I drove a car."

"Really?"

"Yeah." He didn't mention that he and a few of the guys in his gang hot-wired it and took it for a joyride.

"Can you teach me to drive?"

"Sure. We have some time to kill before Pop will be ready." He looked around and turned down a street that looked familiar, heading toward the docks. There were always empty parking lots around the falling-down warehouses. He pulled into one and opened the driver's side door. Nicki jumped out and came around. He pointed out the gas pedal and the brake, showed her how to shift from park to drive and reverse, and slid across the bench seat of the old Jeep. She crawled in behind the wheel, and he adjusted the seat until she could reach the pedals. "Okay, now, be gentle with it. Don't go stomping on the gas, or we'll go flying. Just get a feel for it."

"Okay." Nicki pressed on the gas, and the car lurched forward.

"Lightly, kid, and don't forget to steer." He helped turn the wheel so they didn't run over the grass separating the parking lot from the street. She let off the gas, and the car rolled along. "Okay, step on the brake, and then back up."

Nicki slammed on the brake, and the two of them—neither of whom was wearing a seat belt—slid forward. "Maybe you should buckle up."

"Yeah, okay."

He grabbed Nicki's seat belt and pulled it around her little body. The kid was so small, she could barely see over the dashboard. Was he ever that little? He didn't think so, but he must have been. He braced his hand on the dash. "Now put the car in reverse like I showed you, and look over your right shoulder so you can see if anyone is behind you."

"I can't see over the seat."

"Yeah, next time, we need to bring a pillow or a phone book for you to sit on."

The kid looked over at him and smiled so wide, she nearly blinded him. "You're gonna let me drive again?"

"Sure, you're a good driver. You haven't hit anything yet."

"There's nothing to hit."

"Kid, when I was your age, I could find shit to hit. You're doing great. Really." He patted her knee and was surprised to find himself smiling back at her. "Okay," he said while looking over his shoulder, "throw it in reverse and remember when you're going backward, you turn the wheel in the direction you want the back end to go, but watch because the front end will swing the other way. Give it some gas, hold the wheel, and I'll help you out."

He turned the wheel toward himself, and the car moved slowly toward the right; then he turned the wheel to the left, and together they made an S.

"That's so cool!"

"Yeah, I guess it is." He checked his watch. "Okay, kiddo. Time to go pick up Pop. I'll drive."

"Oh, Storm, do we have to? Can we take one more run around the parking lot?"

"One more and then you promise not to pout?"

"I don't pout."

"Yeah, right. You're female; you pout."

"Boys don't pout?"

"No. Women pout; men brood."

"What's the difference?"

"When pouting doesn't work, it leads to crying. When brooding doesn't work, it leads to fighting."

"I don't cry."

"How come?"

"It doesn't work, and it makes me feel bad. Why bother?"

"Crying is a little girl's way of getting rid of hurt feelings and frustration—it always works."

"You don't cry much, do ya?"

"Nope."

"Then what do you know?"

"Not much, I guess." The longer Storm hung around Bree and Nicki, the less he knew. Patrice was right—he was completely out of his depth.

*          *          *

Storm leaned over the counter of the nurse's station. "What do you mean, Pete Calahan left?"

The nurse checked her notes. "His daughter came to pick him up about twenty minutes ago." She looked back at him, bemused. "He went willingly."

Storm scrubbed his hand over his face. "Yeah, but they told me they wouldn't release him until noon. I was early."

"Sir, I'm sorry you and your wife got your wires crossed."

"She's not—" There was no point in telling the nurse that Breezy wasn't his wife. "Thank you for your help." He turned and made sure Nicki was with him. He'd almost lost her once today. On the way to Pop's floor, Storm got on the elevator and didn't realize Nicki hadn't made it in before the doors closed. After nearly having a heart attack, he got off at the first opportunity, ran down two flights of stairs, and found her waiting in front of the elevator bank. He wasn't going to take any chances with losing the kid again. He reached for her hand.

Nicki looked up at him. "Patrice was right; you should have talked to Bree."

"What do you have, bat hearing? You were upstairs when Patrice gave me that talking-to."

Nicki shrugged and pushed the button for the elevator. "Voices carry in their house."

"I'll have to remember that."

They turned in the visitor's badges on the way to the parking garage. "Let's get home and see what's going on."

Storm drove through his old neighborhood—the Red Hook Houses, the projects, and did his best to ignore the

memories beating on him with all the force of a battering
ram. He wondered when he'd be able to drive through
the area without breaking into a cold sweat. He turned
up the blower on the air conditioner.

"Storm, are you okay?"

He checked the rearview mirror and saw Nicki watching him from the middle seat. "Yeah, I don't like driving
through here. I used to live here when I was about your
age."

"I lived here too, with my mom and one of her boyfriends. He wasn't very nice."

"Yeah, neither was my dad."

"Pop wasn't nice to you?"

He stopped at a stop sign, remembering a time when
it wasn't safe to stop after dark. "Pop's not my birth father. He's my foster father, same as he is to you."

"Did your parents give you away too?"

"No, I was taken away. Though, if they knew someone
would take me, I think they'd have gladly given me away
just to be rid of me."

"My mom said she couldn't take care of me anymore.
I think she just didn't want me anymore either."

Storm didn't know what to say to her. He wouldn't
have believed it if an adult had told him his parents
loved him. Since Nicki's mom dumped her on Pete's
doorstep, chances were the kid was right. "Pop loves you
and he wants you and you're his. You'll be his forever.
When you're my age, he'll still love you and want you.
He's a forever kind of man. That's all that matters."

"Is that all that matters to you?"

No. If it had been, he wouldn't be gripping the steering wheel so tight, he might break the damn thing. Still,
he didn't have the heart to tell Nicki that. "It's all that

should matter. Pop loves you, and he'll give you everything you need to be happy, healthy, and safe. You have Bree and Patrice and Francis. When you grow up, you can be anything you want to be, Nicki."

"You have Bree and Pop and Patrice and Francis, and I know I'm just a kid, but you have me too."

Storm tried to swallow past the lump in his throat. The kid just told him she loved him, and he didn't deserve it—especially since he hadn't added himself to the list of people she could count on. What kind of brother was he?

Storm tried to clear his mind of memories and regrets as he turned onto Van Brunt and spotted an ambulance outside the Crow's Nest. "Oh shit."

"Storm, if you say that in front of Bree, you're gonna be in big trouble. Why's an ambulance here?"

"I don't know." He parked and wasn't sure what to do with Nicki. If something was wrong with Pete, he didn't want her to see it, but he couldn't very well leave her in the car, could he?

"Come on, kid. You stay behind me, okay?" He pulled her out of the car and took Nicki's little hand in his. He was struck again by how small she was, how fragile she looked. He did his best to put it in the back of his mind and steeled himself to deal with the next disaster.

Storm pulled the door open to the bar and almost ran into Francis. "What's wrong? Is something the matter with Pop?"

"Pete's fine. He just needed some help getting upstairs, and you, my friend, were MIA, so Bree called me. You have one very P.O.'d lady upstairs."

Storm looked up the steps and cringed. "Thanks for the warning." He pulled Nicki out from behind him. "Go ahead upstairs, Nicki. I'll be up in a minute." He watched the kid run upstairs like a cat with her tail on fire before he turned to Francis. "So, on a scale of one to ten, how pissed is she?"

"Fifteen. You should have listened to Patrice."

"Yeah, but that ship's left the dock. If you want to be helpful, you'll tell me what the hell I'm supposed to do now."

"Duck?" Francis gave Storm a pat on the back that pushed him a few feet toward the steps. "I'd love to stay and watch the fireworks, but I'm on the job. Call me if you need me to come back and patch you up."

"Don't laugh." He rubbed the knot on his head. "It's a possibility. Bree's already given me a concussion, and that was before she was pissed."

"Which is why I married a brunette. Redheads are too fiery for my tastes, and when Bree is fired up, man, she makes a lit box of dynamite look like a sparkler."

Storm just shook his head. "Thanks for the help. I owe you, man."

"Yeah, I just hope you'll live long enough to repay the debt." Francis turned to leave.

Storm started up the steps, feeling like a dead man walking. "When I fuck up, I do it royally." At least Nicki was around. Bree wouldn't ream him out with Nicki in earshot. He needed to keep the kid around as a buffer. He took a deep breath and pushed the door open.

# CHAPTER 9

"Hey, Bree. I'm home." Nicki banged into the apartment, her footsteps sounding like elephants running through Madison Square Garden minus the building shake, but then she was still pretty small.

Bree had called Patrice to see when she was going to drop Nicki off, only to be told that Storm had already picked her up. She was still on a slow burn over that one. "Hey." She pulled Nicki into a hug and rubbed her chin on the top of Nicki's head—enjoying the scent of Johnson's Baby Shampoo and little girl. Bree didn't like not knowing exactly where Nicki was; the tension she'd been carrying slid off her shoulders. "Did you have fun?"

Nicki pulled away and leaned against the counter. "Yeah, it was okay. Did you miss me?"

Bree flipped Pete's three-egg-white asparagus omelet, and returned her gaze to Nicki, who was chewing her lip. "Of course I did."

"But you didn't come with Storm to pick me up."

What was she supposed to say to that one? *Are you hungry for lunch?*

"Storm picked out these shorts for me to wear." She plucked at the khaki material. "You know I hate them."

Nicki didn't take the hint. "He didn't ask my advice, sweetie. You can go change if you want."

Nicki didn't move toward her room; she just eyed the apartment door.

"Is something wrong?"

"No." She shifted her weight from foot to foot. "It's just I've been gone for like forever."

Bree slid the omelet onto a plate and grabbed a piece of toast. "Less than twenty-four hours."

"Yeah, but it feels like forever. Me and Storm went to pick up Pop, but—"

The door slammed open and Storm stomped in; the look in his turbulent eyes reminding her that he was aptly named.

"I said I would take care of Pop and Nicki."

Bree took a deep breath and did her best to sound as if she weren't still reeling from last night's fiasco. "Oh really?" She turned to face him. "If you were so willing, where were you? You certainly weren't at the hospital."

Nicki climbed up on a barstool. "Storm was teaching me to drive. He said we didn't have to pick up Pop until twelve."

Bree gave up on the whole deep-breathing thing—it was all she could do not to hit him with the frying pan again, and this time it was hot. She faced him; her heart beating a mile a minute, her hands fisted, and reminded herself not to scream at him with an audience. "You let Nicki drive a car? She's ten years old."

Storm shrugged. "Not on the street or anything. I let her drive around a deserted parking lot. It was no big deal."

"Did you teach her how to hot-wire it too?" The look on Storm's face made her want to back up a step; instead, she just raised her chin.

"She's my sister. I think I'm capable of deciding what's best for her. Besides, every kid should know how to drive in case of an emergency."

Bree heard a weird buzzing in her ears, and her scalp tingled as if she had just been turned into a human pincushion. She reached out and grabbed the counter to steady herself. "Right." Her voice sounded as if it were coming through a tunnel. She blinked and continued. "Like you have so much experience with kids. She's not allowed to cross the street by herself, but it's okay to drive?"

"She's ten. I've been crossing the street by myself since I was—"

"Way too young. Do you really want her growing up like you?" She thought she saw a flash of horror cross his face, but it disappeared before she could be sure.

"I turned out all right."

"Says who? I, for one, think that's highly debatable. You practically had to be begged to come back home and help your own father—"

"There was no begging involved. I came as soon as I heard."

"Yeah, and you've been so helpful."

"I have. I was going to pick Pop up from the damn hospital, but you beat me to it. I told you I'd take care of Pop and Nicki—"

"Oh, right. So I was supposed to do what? Assume you even knew what that entailed? Did you think that maybe Pete would need clothes to wear out of the hospital?"

By the color slashing across Storm's cheekbones, it

was evident he hadn't considered clothes or anything else for that matter.

"That's what I thought. Excuse me while I take Pete his lunch. He needs to eat on a schedule so he can take his medicine. He can't wait around until you decide to make an appearance."

She slammed the pill case she'd spent the last half hour filling with Pete's medication for the week onto the tray along with his omelet, toast, decaf coffee, and juice, and then she left Storm standing in the kitchen with his mouth hanging open.

Bree looked forward to facing Pete only slightly less than going another round with Storm, and that was saying something. Pete would be as big a pain in the ass as Storm once he saw what she'd made for lunch. It wasn't as if she had the opportunity to do anything special. She still needed to go shopping and couldn't trust Storm to buy what was on the grocery list. Storm wasn't the type to follow any kind of direction. If there was a chance in hell of getting Pete to stick to his diet, she needed to do the shopping herself. Maybe Rocki would stop by for an hour or two to keep an eye on Pete, Storm, and Nicki so Bree could stock the kitchen.

Stepping into Pete's room, Bree found him dozing. The trip home from the hospital and up the steps had drained him. God only knew how long it would be until he could go back to work. Right now she wondered if he would ever be well enough. She sat beside him on the bed and patted the hand that held his covers under his chin. "Pete, lunch is ready."

He let out a snore, and she shook him harder. "Come on, wake up, you big bear. Time to eat. You hate it when your eggs get cold."

Pete's eyes blinked open.

Bree set the tray on his bedside table and slid farther up the bed, pushing pillows behind his back for him to rest against.

"Eggs for lunch?"

"It was all I found in the refrigerator. It's time to do some major shopping." She set the tray on his lap.

Using his fork, Pete peeked inside the omelet, looking none too happy.

"You need to eat, and you have to admit, it's better than anything they fed you in the hospital."

"True, but that's not much of a yardstick." He brushed his thumb over the bags under her eyes. "You don't look like you've slept much, Bree. Are you okay?"

"I'm fine."

"I thought with Storm here, it'd give you a break."

She didn't think he'd appreciate it if she told him the only thing Storm was breaking was her chops. "I'm just a little tired. Now, eat up."

"Where's the salt?"

"In the kitchen. You're on a low-salt diet, remember?"

He took a tentative bite and made a face Nicki would have been proud of. "Come on, Bree. How's a little salt going to hurt me?"

"It raises your blood pressure, which is already way too high. Next question?"

"You know, you're worse than a mother hen."

"I love you, and you scared the hell out of me and Nicki. I don't ever want to see you gasping for breath again, so deal with it."

He snuck another look at her and cut a piece of omelet. "Okay."

"You need to take your meds. I put all your pills for

the week in this box." She handed it to him. "There's a section for morning, afternoon, and evening of every day. Today is Sunday, so take all your afternoon pills. Can you get it open?"

"I'm not an invalid."

She raised her chin and slapped her mouth shut. Snapping back at him wouldn't help matters.

"Hey, Pop." Storm's voice behind her had every muscle in Bree's body jumping. "Bree's trying to help. You don't need to rip her head off."

No, that was *his* job. Bree didn't turn to see Storm; the angry look on Pete's face was off-putting enough. She patted his hand. "It's okay."

Pete turned his hand over and caught hers. "No, it's not." He deflated like a week-old balloon. "I'm pissed at myself and taking it out on you. I'm sorry."

"There's no need." She stood and smoothed the bedcovers. "I have work to catch up on, so I'll let you guys visit." She turned toward the door and wished Storm would move out of the doorway. He didn't. "Excuse me."

Turning sideways, Storm sent her a silent dare, forcing her to face him in order to slip out. "You okay for a minute, Pop? I have to talk to Bree."

Bree headed for the kitchen and as far away from Storm as she could get without leaving the apartment.

"What do you think?" Pete grumbled.

"I think you're a pain in the ass. I'm glad you're home anyway."

Bree shook her head at Storm's retort. Men.

"What's the head shake for?"

She jumped—he was so close, his breath washed down the back of her neck. So much for staying away from her. "Must you corner me?"

He took a half step back. "You didn't answer the question."

"I choose not to." She took the frying pan off the stove and did her best not to smile when she turned and he took a giant step away. "Is there something you need?"

"Do you know where Nicki is? She's not in her room."

"Shit." Bree scanned the apartment. "She was standing right here when—"

"You ripped me a new one—"

Bree slammed the pan back onto the stove. "Well, if you hadn't attacked me—"

"You know, right now I couldn't care less about your delicate feelings. I'm more concerned about Nicki." He grabbed his cell phone off the counter and hooked it onto his belt. "You stay here with Pete, and I'll look for my little sister. Call my cell if she comes back. You have my number."

"Yeah, I've had your number for a long time, and it hasn't changed."

Storm turned in time to make sure Bree didn't see his reaction to her latest slap-down. After less than forty-eight hours at home he felt as if he'd gone nine rounds in a cage with an Ultimate Fighter.

He stepped out of the apartment and congratulated himself on not slamming the damn door. It would have felt good, but he had more to worry about than his dented ego. He had to find his little sister, and he didn't have a clue where to look.

He took the steps two at a time to the empty bar and looked around. Maybe she'd gotten hungry for some real food and gone to raid the walk-in refrigerator. Storm pushed through the swinging door to the kitchen and did a quick scan. No go. He checked out the storage closet where the potato chips were kept—that was where he'd always gone when he was a hungry kid. Fries were the only thing better than chips, and the fryer was turned off—thank God.

He considered looking in the liquor-storage closet but figured Nicki was too young to be sneaking booze. Besides, after finding him and Logan in the throes of a guzzling contest when they weren't much older than Nicki, Pete had put a lock the size of his fist on that door.

Storm didn't know how Pete handled three boys on his own when Storm couldn't keep track of one little girl. He took a deep breath and tried to put himself in Nicki's fluorescent green Vans—not an easy thing for a man pushing thirty.

The alley—if she wasn't in the kitchen, she'd either gone out the front door or the back. Since he was closer to the back, he'd check there first.

The door was held open by a block of wood— probably the same one he and his brothers used when they didn't want to get caught sneaking back in. He slid out quietly and found Nicki on her knees, hand feeding a big-ass dog slices of leftover fifty-dollars-a-pound lox. She pulled the top off the tub of schmear and held it out for him. He looked like a German shepherd/golden retriever mix and was a far cry from growing into his huge feet—still, he looked to be about seventy pounds, so he was hardly a cute, cuddly puppy. The dog buried his snout in the Styrofoam tub. "That's not such a good idea, kid."

Nicki spun around and did her best to hide the mutt, but the animal wasn't having any of it. He stuck his cream-cheese-covered nose through Nicki's legs and stared at Storm.

"Your friend's gonna get the runs if he eats too much schmear." He leaned against the brick wall. "We should probably just buy him some puppy food—he's gonna be a big son of a— I mean, he's gonna be a big dog when he grows into those paws."

Nicki's mouth hung open, and the dog pushed through her legs, almost knocking her on her ass.

Storm crouched down and held out his hands for the dog to sniff and to keep the mangy thing from jumping on him. "How long have you been hiding him back here?"

Storm watched Nicki as her little brain raced— weighing her answer to get in the least amount of trouble, her sneakered foot digging a hole to China. She finally shrugged. "I found him just before Pop got sick. I was going to ask if I could keep him—"

"But things went crazy, huh?"

Damn, the kid put her arm around the mutt, and they leaned into each other. Storm didn't have the balls to tell Nicki she couldn't keep the dog. No, if anyone was going to be the bad guy in this scenario, it would be Bree, and it would serve her right too. Still, he had to take care of a few things before Bree found them. He grabbed his phone and told her to call off the dogs—if she only knew. He put his phone back on his belt and got down to business. "Do you have a leash or anything for the pup?"

Nicki's eyes went wide; she puffed up her chest and did her best to keep the mutt behind her. "Why? What are you gonna do with Dee—Oh—Gee?"

"I'm not going do anything. If you're going keep him, he needs his shots and a bath—not necessarily in that

order, and then we need to go to one of those big pet
stores where we can buy him food, bowls, a leash, and a
collar."

Nicki looked as if she didn't believe him.

"Nicki, you can't very well bring him home looking
like he's been rolling around in a sewer and expect Bree
not to completely freak out, can you?"

"You mean you're really not gonna take D.O.G. to the
pound?"

"Hell no." He'd been in the human equivalent of the
pound, and he didn't want to be responsible for putting
anyone else in there—not even a mangy-looking mutt.
Storm put his phone in his pocket and took off his belt,
looping it around the dog's head and handing the end to
Nicki.

His phone dinged—Bree texted him back. He smiled
at Nicki. "Bree said she'd deal with you later. The good
news is she's going grocery shopping, so we can sneak
what's-his-name upstairs and give him a bath. Hold on
to him, and I'll make sure the coast is clear."

Nicki grabbed the belt and tugged to keep the dog
close. "His name is D.O.G., sheesh."

Storm ran through the restaurant just as Bree left
through the front door. He turned on his heel and
headed to the alley, holding the door open. "Come on,
kid."

Nicki tugged on Storm's belt and dragged the shaking
mutt through the bar and restaurant to the steps. She
went up a few steps, but the mutt planted his front paws
on the first step, halting her progress, and whined.

"Come on, boy," she called to him.

The dog took a tentative step up and looked as if he
didn't know what to do next.

Storm stood behind the dog to keep him from turning tail and dragging Nicki along with him. "The mutt doesn't know how to go up stairs."

Nicki rolled her eyes. "Well, it's not like he ever needed to learn."

"Yeah, and we don't have time for puppy practice now either." Storm held his breath—the mutt really stank—and picked him up. The dog rested his head on Storm's shoulder—he seemed as trusting as Nicki. "Nicki, you run interference. Close Pop's door and open the door to the bathroom, okay?"

"Sure."

Nicki did the honors, and Storm carried D.O.G. into the bathroom. He started the taps, and the dog stuck his nose under the spigot, lapping at the water in the tub. Storm's four-hundred-dollar Ferragamo belt was history. "Shit."

Nicki planted her hands on her hips and shook her head like a miniature Breezy. "If Bree hears you talk like that, you're gonna be in big trouble."

"That's nothing compared to what she's going to say when she sees this dog if we don't get him cleaned up real quick."

As Storm set the dog in the tub, the scent of wet dog slapped him in the face and the double whip of the dog's tail hit his cheek.

The mutt slipped on the slick porcelain surface, sloshing the water everywhere, and clawed at the side of the tub, trying to escape. The only thing keeping him in the water was Storm's grip on the belt around his neck.

A knock on the door set the terrified dog into a fit of barking. "What the hell is going on in there?" Pete hollered over D.O.G.'s yelps.

Nicki opened the door. The wet mutt slipped the makeshift collar, and Storm's Ferragamo belt fell into the tub of filthy water.

D.O.G. ran for his life, knocking Nicki over in the process. Muddy water splattered everything four feet off the floor down as the dog made a beeline down the hall, past Pete.

Storm loped after him and made it to the living room just as D.O.G. stopped, splayed his legs, lowered his head, and wound up for the shake of his young life.

Time slowed, as a Spirograph of muddy water cascaded through the air, hitting everything—the curtains, the ceiling, the window, the walls, the couch, the lampshades, the coffee table—nothing, including Storm, was dry. The scent of wet dog mixed with raw sewage permeated the apartment.

Pete leaned against the wall, held his sides and laughed, the laugh turning into a cough. "Well, you'd better get that mutt back into the tub and clean up after him or Bree's going to kill you. I'm just glad you're going to have to explain it and not me."

Storm grabbed the dog by the scruff of the neck. "I don't have to explain anything to Bree."

Pop laughed and coughed some more. "You just go ahead and keep thinking that, son. I'm gonna have a great time watching you squirm. You're on your own with this one. I'm already stuck eating tasteless egg whites, and if Bree blames this on me, she'll have me on a tofu diet."

"That's really helpful. Thanks, Pop."

Storm looked at the disaster of an apartment. He needed to finish bathing the damn dog before he could even think of dealing with everything else. "Nicki, bring me my belt."

The little girl slid down the wall and peeked at him from behind Pete. "You're not gonna hit D.O.G. with it, are you?"

Pete slipped his arm around her and pulled her against him. He raised his eyebrows as if waiting for Storm to deal with her.

Storm loosened his grip on the dog slightly and schooled his expression. "No, I'd never hurt an animal, kiddo. It's not his fault he got scared in the tub. I just need to keep him under control, and I can't do that unless I have some kind of collar."

Nicki nodded and took a tentative step forward, holding the belt behind her, gauging his mood.

"I'm not gonna hurt him, Nicki. I promise. We'll get him cleaned up and then start on everything else. It'll be okay."

Nicki smiled up at him, and Storm felt as if he'd just won something precious. She looped the belt around D.O.G.'s neck. "He won't hurt you, boy. He promised," she whispered to the shaking mutt.

Since Storm was already soaked, he picked the big lug of squirming dog up and carried him back to the bath. "Okay, boy, let's try this again."

It was only a few blocks to the Fairway, but Bree took her car. She had a grocery list as long as her arm for Pete, and as if that weren't enough, she had her mother's list too.

The only good thing about her mother's reluctance to leave her own home was that she'd stopped showing up while Bree was at work or sleeping. Her mother hated the fact that Bree worked somewhere as unsafe as a bar and was never one to take Bree's late nights/early mornings into consideration. In Bree's mind, there was little worse than being woken up way too early by her loving mother. Contrary to popular belief, Bree needed more than three hours sleep a night—not that she'd been getting it, especially since Storm sailed back into her life, wreaking havoc.

She did her best to put Storm Decker out of her mind and concentrate on shopping for two households.

Bree let herself into her mother's house and carried in the groceries. "Mom, it's just me. I went to the store for you." She slid the ice cream into the freezer. Just as she shut the door, her mother stepped into the kitchen. It had been a few weeks since Bree had seen her mom— she hadn't had time since before Pete's heart attack, and Bree was taken by how beautiful her mother still was. Her red hair, almost the same shade as Bree's, was a little sun streaked, and she had a healthy-looking tan. She even had a smile on her face for once. "You look good, Mom. Have you lost weight?"

Her mother gave her a quick hug and shrugged. "I don't know; I might have. I've been using the treadmill you gave me for Christmas, and I've been working out in my garden almost every day. It's really coming along." She pulled a few cans from one of the bags and put them in the pantry. "You look tired. You're working yourself to death."

"Pete just got out of the hospital today, so I've been juggling a lot. I didn't sleep well last night." She hadn't slept at all, but that wasn't her mother's business. The woman was always insanely worried about her, and the last thing Noreen needed was more ammunition to use against her. She had perfected the fine art of guilt.

It hadn't always been that way. Bree thought back to her childhood and tried to recall when it had all changed.

They'd been happy, or at least that was what Bree remembered. On her father's days off, they'd picnic in Prospect Park and fly kites while her mother cheered them on from a blanket in the shade where she sat reading a book. Bree remembered the three of them hiking in Forest Park and going to Coney Island in the summer where she would play in the surf. She remembered her parents holding hands and how she'd squeeze in between them for a hug every night when her father came home safe and sound. She remembered family dinners full of conversation and laughter and Pete and other guys from the force coming over on weekends for barbecues in the backyard—she remembered the good times.

"Coretta told me Storm is back in town."

Bree had arrived wearing a smile that quickly deflated to a grimace. Leave it to Patrice's mother, Coretta, aka the Town Crier, to make sure Bree's mother missed nothing. "Storm flew in a few days ago and will leave just as soon as humanly possible."

Her mother's face transformed from the pretty fiftysomething woman to that of a shrew. Even without makeup, she could be a stand-in for the Wicked Witch of the West.

"Don't start, Mom. There is nothing between Storm and me except hostility. The man is insufferable. He just sails in like some kind of savior and does nothing but make matters worse."

"Since Storm's here to take care of Pete and that child he took in—"

"That child has a name." Bree tossed the empty reusable shopping bag back on the counter and tried to control her temper. "Her name is Nicki, and she's a wonderful little girl."

"Still, now that Pete has help, there's no need for you to be involved."

"Mother, just stop. I'm tired of fighting about this. I have my life and you have yours. I'm an adult, and I'll live my life the way I see fit."

"Oh, and you're doing such a good job of it. Look at yourself, Breanna. You work all hours in a bar, and you have no one. By the time I was your age, I had you and your father. I had a full life."

"I like my life just fine." Bree emptied the last of the groceries and folded and stacked her reusable grocery bags. "Mother, I have to go. I have groceries melting in the car. I'll call you in a couple of days."

"You're leaving?"

"Yes, Mother. I have a lot to do."

"But it's your day off."

"And I have errands to run and an apartment to clean. I haven't had a day to take care of my own things in weeks."

Bree gave her mother a kiss on the cheek. "I love you, Mom."

Her mother turned around and walked away without another word—just like she always did.

Bree swallowed back disappointment, walked toward the front door, and heard the echoes of long-forgotten sighs of relief her mother let out every night when her father's car pulled up in front of the house. She remembered the hours her mother paced in front of the bay window waiting for him; the stress in her mother's shoulders if her father wasn't home on time. She remembered the hard looks, cold stares, and the catch in her mother's throat as she swallowed back her fear and frustration. And, yes, Bree remembered the fights her parents had after she'd gone to bed, and how she'd pull her pillow over her head to muffle her mother's wails and tears and recriminations and pleas.

Her mother had begged him to get a safer job, begged him to leave the force, or at least take a desk job, begged him to leave Red Hook. Bree remembered her mother's constant refrain—if he loved them enough, he'd want to be there for her and Bree. It was always followed by the sound of her dad's deep, calm voice explaining over and over and over that he would always be there for them and it was his dream to make Red Hook a safe environment for her mother and a wonderful place for Bree to grow up in.

Things had gotten worse even before her father was killed by a snot-nosed kid robbing a convenience store. Her mother had changed. Little things stuck in Bree's mind, such as her mother taking to walking her to school again, holding her hand so tight it hurt. Her mother waiting by the fence to walk her home and the fear in her mother's eyes if Bree took too long getting her books together or had to stop to talk to a teacher. She remembered the first time her schoolmates noticed that her mom was weird, and the last time she invited a friend over to the house, and the first day she recognized the feeling of being smothered.

But most of all, she remembered the day Pete came to the house to take them to the hospital, where, after what seemed like a lifetime, her father died on the operating table, confirming her mother's worst fears and sending her over the edge. Her mother had to be sedated, and Pete took Bree home and held her all night, telling her he'd always be there for her and her mom. But her mom had never wanted Pete's help and stopped answering his calls after the funeral. Bree wasn't sure why. Did her mother blame Pete for her father's death, for her father's refusal to give up his job? All Bree knew was that her mom didn't want Bree to do anything without her. She refused to allow Bree to see Pete, and later, after he'd taken in Storm and his brothers, she didn't want Bree to see the boys.

No matter what Bree did to try to help her mother, it wasn't enough. After college, she'd taken on her father's dream of making Red Hook a safer community. Her mother refused to be involved, and her hatred of Red Hook grew.

Bree wasn't enough to keep her mother from sliding down the long, slippery slope of despair. Bree had never been enough to make anyone happy, to make anyone stay, and after what had happened with Storm last night, she knew she never would.

Bree slammed out of the house, dragged in a deep breath to push away the feeling of utter suffocation, and pulled the phone out of her purse. She texted Rocki on her way to the car to give her a heads-up and see if she needed anything, only to find out that she was still on the ferry. She tossed the bags and her purse on the passenger seat, started the car, and groaned. "Note to self: Check to see where someone is before asking them to stop by and check on Pete and Nicki. Shit." She'd been gone over an hour. Lord only knew what kind of trouble Nicki and Storm could get into.

Bree heard Nicki's startled cry and ran into the apartment. The stench hit her before her feet slid out from under her, landing her on her ass on the wet linoleum. Nicki's scream had Bree scrambling over the scattered grocery bags and running to the hall. She opened the bathroom door and was bowled over by a wild animal. For the second time in two days Bree had the wind knocked out of her. All she saw was an animal with wild eyes and enormous teeth. She dragged in a breath and screamed, crab-crawling away. The next thing she knew, she was standing on the kitchen counter—still screaming. The animal—a huge rabid-looking wolf—ran straight for her. She eyed the distance between her and the top of the refrigerator. She might be able to make it.

"Bree, stop screaming."

Storm. Of course he'd have something to do with this.

"He won't hurt you." Storm had the nerve to smirk at her as the wild animal jumped up, his front paws clawing the counter.

"Get that . . . that thing away from me."

"Calm down. It's just a puppy."

"That's not a puppy. It's a rabid wolf."

"He's not foaming at the mouth; that's just baby shampoo. D.O.G. isn't a fan of baths, but he's harmless."

Nicki ran toward the animal and grabbed a big leather strap.

"Nicki, get away from him! He's dangerous."

Nicki shot Storm a questioning look, and Storm winked at her. "Try to get him back into the bathroom while I handle Bree."

Bree watched as Nicki put her arm around the neck of the vicious animal and whispered in the ear that stood straight up, tugging him along with her.

"You let her touch that . . . that . . . thing?"

Storm had the nerve to smile. If she could reach the pan on the stove, she'd smack that smile right off his face and see how he'd handle her then. Storm stared at her.

His gaze started at her painted toenails and traveled the length of her legs. She should never have worn her white shorts, which, thanks to Storm, were soaking wet and probably see-through. His gaze continued past the short-sleeve filmy top she wore over her red tank, zeroing in on her breasts. Somehow they'd gotten wet too, probably from being knocked down by the wet wolf he called a puppy.

The air-conditioning kicked on, not doing her any favors. She wrapped her arms around herself to stop the shaking. She wasn't sure if it was from fear, cold, or an adrenaline overload—but then, it could be from the way Storm stared at her.

"Come on." He held out his hand. "Let me help you down." When she didn't move, he stepped forward and plucked her off the counter.

"Don't touch me." She dragged in a breath and almost gagged. "God, you stink!"

"Yeah, well, you shouldn't talk. You're not smelling too pretty either." He set her down. "I've got to finish giving the mutt a bath, and then I'll clean up everything else. Don't worry."

Nicki let out a yelp and flew by them, holding on to the end of the leather strap for all she was worth. Grocery bags flew—their contents scattered and rolled as the dog lay down and bit into a one-pound package of beef bologna—holding it between his front paws and tearing the bag to shreds.

"He's eating the food!"

Storm shrugged. "Yeah, sorry about that. I'll clean it up. Come on, boy." Storm knelt and, ever so smoothly, pulled the bag out of the dog's mouth. "Let's get you back into the tub. Nicki, you stay here with Bree and pick up whatever food is salvageable—save that meat for after he's finished with his bath as a treat, okay?"

Nicki started picking through the groceries while Bree stood there in shock.

"When Bree comes back around, find out if there are any ratty old towels I can use to dry him off when I'm done. And no matter what, don't open the bathroom door. Understand?"

Bree opened her mouth to ream him. He held up his hand, stopping her. "Don't worry. I'll take care of everything. I'll replace all the food he's ruined—just make a list, and I'll clean it all up too. You know, why don't you just go back to your place until we need you?"

"What?"

"Well, I've got to get him to a vet and have him all checked out, get his shots, and then buy him some puppy food and supplies."

He couldn't be serious. "You're not planning on keeping this . . . this—"

"Puppy. He's Nicki's dog. She's been taking care of him since before Pop's heart attack."

"No she hasn't—" Bree looked at Nicki who was suddenly grinding her sneaker into the wet, dirty carpet.

"All those times you went missing, you were with this—"

Nicki looked at Storm, who put a hand on her shoulder, while the other firmly held the leather strap constraining the dog lapping up the broken eggs. "His name is D.O.G., and he's real nice, Bree. Storm promised he wouldn't take him to the pound."

She really wanted to kill Storm now. "He did, did he? Well, we'll just have to talk to Pete about this."

Storm gave the back of Nicki's neck an affectionate

squeeze and smiled. "Oh, don't worry about Pop. He's already on board." He gave the strap a tug, forcing the dog to sit, and then picked up the huge dog with all the gentleness he'd used when he held her just last night— right before he stomped all over her heart. No, that last phrase needed some serious editing; she wouldn't give Storm that much power. She settled on a reworded phrase: before he'd tap-danced on her feelings. Yes, that was better. She stood there, unable to move, watching Storm laugh as the dog licked his ear and rested his head on Storm's shoulder. She almost felt sorry for the poor, stupid mutt; he was in for one hell of a disappointment, and from the look of trust and hero worship Bree saw in Nicki's eyes, the puppy wouldn't be Storm's only victim.

# CHAPTER 10

Rocki raised her hand to knock on Pete's apartment door just as a disheveled Bree stepped into the hallway and slammed it behind her. Bree looked like a drowned rat and smelled twice as bad. "What the hell happened to you?"

Bree shook her head as if she couldn't speak. She looked as if she were about to explode.

Rocki wondered if it would be in tears or temper. The way her eyes were filling, maybe both. She was tempted to give Bree a hug—she looked as if she could use one, but the stink permeating the air had her taking a step back. "I'll give you a hug after you take a shower."

Bree unlocked the door to her apartment, and Rocki followed her in, barely making it through before Bree slammed that door too. Rocki covered her nose and mouth with her hand. "What is that smell?"

"Wet mutt."

"I've smelled wet dogs before, but never like this. Is it part skunk?"

"I'm going to kill him."

Rocki set her Coach bag down on the table. "Storm or the dog?"

"Both."

"Why don't you get a shower while I open the windows to air the place out, and then you can tell me all about it?"

Bree pushed her wet hair out of her eyes and spun around—the scent swirling through the apartment had Rocki pushing open a window. "Who does he think is going to take care of that . . . that beast after he flies back to the Godzone? Isn't that just like him? He comes here, makes a mess of everything, and leaves."

Rocki opened the bifold doors to the closet that held Bree's washer, dryer, and cleaning supplies. "Do you have any Febreze in here?" She slid cleaning products around, looking for the familiar blue spray bottle. Once Rocki's brothers hit their teenage years, she should have bought stock in the company. It was the only way she was able to live in the same apartment with them. She hoped it worked as well on dog stink as on boy stink.

"I can't believe Pete is going to allow this." Bree pulled off the shirt she wore over her tank top and tossed it in the washer. "Pete can't walk up the steps by himself or take care of Nicki; how is he supposed to handle a hundred-pound dog?"

Rocki covered her nose and mouth again to face Bree. "I'll run down to the corner and buy a bottle of Febreze—or six."

"Nicki looks at him as if he walked on water."

"The dog?"

"No, Storm. He's been here two days, and he's already taught her how to drive and given her a puppy. The next thing you know, he's going to buy her a damn pony. How am I supposed to compete with that?"

"Storm taught Nicki to drive? She's only ten."

"That's what I said." Bree went into the bathroom.

Rocki was thankful to hear the shower starting. "Why do you need to compete with Storm?"

"I love her. It's taken me three months to get her to trust me; he walks in and, in two days, he's stolen her heart."

"Nicki's heart is big enough to love you both."

"He's going to leave, and then what is she going to do?"

"Whose heart are you concerned about, Nicki's or yours?"

Rocki turned toward the kitchen; she didn't need to hear the answer to that one. She knew it as well as her own name. Bree, on the other hand, was the queen of denial. "Toss your other clothes into the hall, and I'll start the wash." Rocki searched through Bree's kitchen drawer where she kept her cooking utensils and wrapped her hand around the plastic-covered handle of a pair of barbecue tongs, held them up in the air, and snapped them together. "Bingo." There was no way she was going to touch those smelly, wet clothes.

After Rocki picked up Bree's clothes and had the wash going, she went back to Pete's apartment and knocked on the door. "Is it safe to come in?"

Nicki opened the door a crack. "I don't know. Storm is using Bree's hair dryer in the bathroom. I'm not sure if it's for him or D.O.G. I'm cleaning up what's left of the groceries, but from the way Bree looked, I don't think anyone is safe, especially not me."

Rocki did her best to smile, even though the scent of the place was coming through the open door. The last thing she wanted to do was go into the stinky apartment. Sometimes this best-friend crap really sucked. She dragged in a deep breath of fresh air and stepped inside.

After a look at the dripping Nicki, Rocki figured Nicki needed the same treatment Bree got. "Don't worry about Bree—she's young; she'll get over it." Eventually . . . maybe. Her gaze swept the apartment. The entire place was covered with what looked like splattered mud. "I just threw Bree's clothes in the wash. She's in the shower now. Since your bathroom is occupied, why don't you go grab some fresh clothes and run over to Bree's so you can shower after she gets out, and we'll toss your clothes in with hers? How's that sound?"

Nicki pulled her wet top away from her skin and shrugged. "I don't think Bree wants to see me right now. Or ever."

Poor kid. "I think you're wrong. Come on." Bree was so gonna owe her for this one. Rocki grabbed Nicki's dirty hand in hers, stepped over what was left of the mess, and dragged Nicki to her bedroom. "Let's pick out your clothes and get back to Bree's before the prewash cycle ends."

Nicki looked up at her, her brows all scrunched to-gether. "You sure?"

"Positive. Here, I'll get the clothes so you don't dirty them. Just tell me what you want to wear."

Nicki pointed out an outfit that reminded Rocki that the poor girl needed some real fashion advice, but now was not the time. She stopped outside the bathroom door. "Storm?" She yelled through the door.

The hair dryer turned off. "Yeah?"

"It's Rocki. I'm taking Nicki over to Bree's to get cleaned up."

"Okay. Send her back when she's done."

Nicki still didn't look comfortable with the idea, so Rocki rested her hand on the base of Nicki's neck and walked her back to Bree's place. She grabbed a fresh towel from the linen closet and knocked on the bathroom door. "Bree? I brought Nicki over to get cleaned up. Are you finished?"

The door opened, and Bree stepped out in a towel. She took one look at Nicki and smiled.

Rocki pushed Nicki toward the bathroom. "Your turn, Nicki. Take your clothes off and jump into the shower, or do you want to take a bath?"

Nicki kicked off her shoes. "No, I think I've had enough of baths for a while. I'll just get in the shower." She finally looked at Bree, her head tilted with uncertainty. "You sure you don't mind? You were awful mad."

"Nicki, I wasn't mad at you, but even if I was, you're always welcome here. I love you; that doesn't stop when I get mad. Do you stop loving me when you're mad at me?"

"No, I guess not."

Rocki rolled her eyes. "Okay, you two, enough of the syrupy-sweet stuff. Bree, get the kid out of those clothes so I can put them in the wash—she's stinking up the joint."

As soon as Rocki had the clothes in the wash, she tossed the tongs in the sink and then let herself into Bree's bedroom.

"Do you mind?" Bree held her top in front of her.

Sheesh, it wasn't as if she were naked. She had a bra and shorts on already. "No, it's nothing I haven't seen before." Rocki flopped down on the unmade bed. It looked like someone either had had wild sex in it or a really restless night. From the trash can overflowing with tissues and Bree's less than perky disposition, Rocki figured it was the latter. "So, no hot monkey love with Storm last night, huh?"

"That's none of your business."

"I'll take that as a no."

"Rocki, please, leave it alone."

"No. You might as well just tell me what happened before Nicki gets out of the shower. Knowing that kid, you have about five minutes." She waited.

Bree said nothing.

"Don't make me ask Storm."

Bree yanked a tank top over her head. "You wouldn't dare."

Rocki checked her manicure. "Are you willing to bet on that?"

Bree shoved her arms through and stepped toward the bed. "Remind me why you're my best friend?"

Rocki gauged her distance to the door in case Bree decided to throttle her. "Because I know the good, the bad, and the impossible sides of you, and I still love you. So do us both a favor and tell me what the hell happened."

Bree turned toward the window and looked out. "He did the same thing he did last time—he ran."

"He didn't run." Rocki slid off the bed and stood beside Bree, watching her reflection in the window. "When I brought Nicki over here, Storm was in the bathroom with the dog and a blow-dryer."

"I didn't say he ran far." Bree swiped at her eyes, wiping away angry tears. "One minute I was lying naked in his arms thinking finally we were gonna . . . you know—"

"Make love?"

"And the next, he was pulling his pants on and walking away." She turned and seemed to deflate. "He said he couldn't do it."

"Equipment malfunction?" Rocki did her best not to laugh. Storm was the last person she'd imagine having that problem. He always looked so physically . . . capable. Damn. What a letdown.

Bree's eyes filled. She swallowed hard, and then blew out a breath. "No, that would have hurt less."

"What did he say?"

"What does it matter?"

Rocki figured it mattered a hell of a lot. She hadn't seen Bree this upset since . . . Well, she'd never seen Bree this upset. She shook her head and started toward the door. "Looks like I'm going to have to talk to Storm after all."

"Rocki, please, don't."

"Why?" She stopped and faced Bree.

"Because"—Bree sank down on the bed and pulled a tissue out of the box—"because I told him I wanted him for sex for as long as he was here, and when he leaves, I would find myself a nice boring accountant type."

"You actually said that?"

"Yeah, why else would I want to sleep with someone like Storm?"

"Because you're in love with him, and you've been in love with him since you were a kid."

"I am not. I may have been in love with him years ago when I was young and stupid. I'm not even sure I like him now; I'm just attracted to him. I told him that too. I was completely honest."

"You told him you didn't like him, but you wanted to sleep with him? No wonder he left you naked on the bed. You hurt him." Bree's righteous indignation wavered a bit, and if Rocki didn't misread her, it was replaced with a touch of shame. Good. "So what did he say?"

"He said he didn't want to be used and that he

wouldn't use me, but if I wanted to make love to him, to let him know. Do you believe him?"

Rocki held up her hands. "Wait. Let me get this straight. You think Storm's the bad guy in this scenario?"

"Of course I do. He didn't have any problems with it until we were in bed."

"When did you tell him you didn't like him?"

"When we were making out on the couch."

"Bree, I know you don't have much experience with men, so let me clue you in on something. When men are trying to use both their big head and their little head at the same time, it takes them a lot longer to respond to verbal stimuli than physical. Men are not natural multitaskers—especially when there's a naked woman involved. Frankly, I'm impressed that what you said even registered, and I'm even more impressed that Storm put on the brakes. It serves you right."

"What?"

"You insulted him, you hurt him, and you're surprised he didn't want to . . . well, not to be crude or anything, but you're surprised he didn't want to fuck you? Because, girlfriend, that's what you asked him to do in no uncertain terms. If a guy sweet-talked me like that, I'd have left him on the bed—unconscious. I hate to say it, but he was a lot nicer than I would have been. You owe him an apology."

"Me? He walked out on me—again."

The shower stopped, and Rocki got off the bed. "Storm ran out on you years ago. It was wrong, but Bree, he was practically a kid. You're an adult, and now you treated him like a piece of meat."

"I was being honest."

"Oh, and that makes it all right? Did you even consider his feelings?"

Bree didn't answer.

"I'm going over to check on Pete and help Storm clean up. It sounds as if he could use a friend." She stopped at the door and turned. "When Nicki gets dressed, send her back to Pete's. I think Storm has plans for her and that dog of theirs. Since I don't have anything better to do, I'll hang out with Pete until they get back."

"You're leaving?" She looked dumbfounded.

"You asked me to come by and look after Pete for a while, and that's what I'm going to do. Besides, you need some time alone to think about what happened with Storm, what you said to him, and put things in perspective. I've never known you to be cruel, Bree, not even to people like Daniel who deserve it. Storm doesn't."

"I didn't intend to hurt him."

"Didn't you?" Rocki opened the door. "I think it was Ian Percy who said, 'We judge others by their behavior. We judge ourselves by our intentions.' It's always stuck with me. Sometimes our intentions and our behavior don't match. Just sayin'. I'll see you later."

Storm stepped out of the shower wearing nothing but a scowl and a towel, and he found Rocki washing the walls of the hallway. "Hey, Rocki. You don't have to do that."

Rocki blew the pink part of her bangs out of her eyes and sat back on her heels, looking up at him. "Oh, I know. I thought you could use some help. I checked on Pete—he's sleeping—and Nicki should be back any minute. Where's your furry friend?"

"I locked him in my room." He clamped his hand on

the towel that was slipping down his hips. "I'm going to get some clothes on. I'll be right back."

"Sounds like a plan."

Rocki returned to scrubbing, and he slipped past her into his room, making sure D.O.G. didn't escape. Storm found the dog asleep on the bed. One eye opened and watched him warily. Storm had never had a dog before, but after one look at D.O.G., he understood where the term "dog tired" came from. He was tempted to join him. It sounded a lot better than dealing with the mess he'd made of the apartment and whatever was left of his relationship with Bree. "Don't get too used to sleeping there, boy. That's my bed, and I'm not into sharing it with dogs." He'd hoped to share it with Bree, but if last night didn't kill his chances, bringing a stray dog home had probably done the trick.

Storm reached for his belt and remembered it was ruined. He added a new belt and a dog bed to the list of things to buy as he pulled on his clothes and slipped out without waking his new roommate.

Rocki had moved on to wiping down the leather couch while Nicki kneeled on the kitchen counter, putting away canned goods. All the windows were open, but the place still smelled like wet dog with a twist of Lysol— an improvement.

"Rocki, thanks for helping out."

"What are friends for?" She tossed the rag into the bucket and stepped closer. "You doing okay?"

Storm figured she was asking about more than just his health. "I'll live." The last thing he wanted to do was talk about his disaster of a relationship with Bree when Nicki was in earshot. "Nicki and I have to take off for a little while. Would you mind hanging around here for an hour or two so we can get D.O.G. his shots and pick up a few things? There's a store that has a vet right there. I called them, and they said to come right over."

"Go ahead. I'll just clean up and keep an eye on Pete until you get back."

"Oh no. You don't have to do that. I'll clean the rest when I return."

"Okay." She dropped the rag into the bucket. "But you might want to stop by Bree's before you leave and tell her your plans. Just a suggestion."

Storm rubbed the back of his neck. "Okay. Nicki, are you ready to go?"

"Uh-huh. I'll get D.O.G."

"I'm going to talk to Bree. I'll be right back." He took a deep breath and stepped into the hall. He knocked on Bree's door before he lost the nerve.

She opened the door but didn't invite him in.

"Hi. I just wanted to tell you I'm taking Nicki and D.O.G. to PetSmart to get his shots and buy a few things. Rocki said she'd stay with Pete until we get back."

She nodded.

"Look, I'm sorry I didn't discuss the whole dog thing. And you have every right to be pissed at me, but you weren't around and Nicki loves the mutt. I didn't have the heart to disappoint her."

"No, you figured you'd leave that to me."

He rubbed the back of his neck again. Guilty. So, okay, it wasn't his finest moment. "I'll take care of everything."

"Sure you will. Good luck with that."

"Thanks." Storm rested his hand on the doorframe. He hated this false politeness. She started to shut the door; he stuck his foot out, stopping it. "Bree, don't do this."

"What?"

"Don't shut me out. We need to talk. We need to make plans we can both live with."

"Okay, but now is not the time."

"You're right." Still it felt wrong. Everything felt wrong since last night. "I guess I'll catch you later."

This time when she closed the door, he let her. One problem at a time, and the problem he had to deal with now had four legs, mismatched ears, and a little girl who loved him desperately.

Bree sat at the end of the Pier in Louis Valentino Jr. Park, staring at the Statue of Liberty without really seeing it. The late-afternoon sun beat down on her head and shoulders as the brackish-scented wind off the bay swirled around her and tugged at her hair, sending it flying around her face. Teenagers waded at the water's edge by the boat ramp; others climbed the rocks precariously placed atop the jetty across from the pier. Painted like children's building blocks, the rocks spelled out Red Hook.

Voices all around her were muted by those in Bree's mind. Visions of Storm replaced the sight of the sun casting diamonds on the water. She'd been cruel; she hadn't stopped reacting to her feelings long enough to consider his. Guilt burned her as surely as the sun's rays.

Someone sat on the other side of the long bench, but Bree was so immersed in her own turmoil, she took no notice. She continued to stare off into space, fitting the puzzle pieces scattered throughout her mind while unsuccessfully trying to visualize the big picture. She didn't know what the big picture was, but she had a feeling it wouldn't be pretty.

"What you need is a good rain; it looks as if it would fit your mood. Too bad it never rains when you want it to."

She almost laughed. What she needed was a good storm—just not the one sitting beside her. "I look that bad, huh?" Bree couldn't believe she'd been so lost in her thoughts that she hadn't noticed Storm's presence. She'd always had a weird kind of internal Storm warning system. The hair on the back of her neck seemed to rise whenever he was within a hundred yards of her—today she hadn't noticed.

"A good rain washes away all the crap so we can see things more clearly." His arms rested along the back of the bench. His long legs were kicked out and crossed at the ankle, and his trusty dog was lying quietly beside him, panting and eyeing the seagulls screeching overhead.

"You're probably right."

Storm's brows rose. "That's a first."

"I'm sure you've been right before, although I'll admit it's the first time I noticed. Is the dog okay?"

"D.O.G. is one hell of a lucky dog. The vet said he's in pretty good shape for a stray, but then Nicki's been taking care of him for a while. He wasn't too happy with the shots and the blood test, but he doesn't have heartworms—whatever the hell they are. He has to take a pill once a month to avoid getting them, and he needs to gain a few pounds, but the vet assured us he'd be fine."

Storm shook the paw D.O.G. placed on his leg. "Nicki really loves him, Bree, and he's good for her. Every kid needs a dog."

Bree shrugged and looked over at the beast. "Why did she have to get such a big one? Couldn't she have found a toy poodle?"

D.O.G. sniffed around her feet, which she quickly moved away. He backed up, dropping his front paws and chest to the dock, his butt high, as if preparing to jump on her, and let out a bark. Before she registered moving, she was standing on the bench and looking down at a laughing Storm Decker.

"Keep him away from me."

Storm held the leash a little tighter and rose, smiling up at her. "I didn't think anything scared you, but now I know your secret. You're afraid of dogs."

"I am not."

"Right, that's why you climb anything in the vicinity when he's around."

"He was going to attack me . . . again."

Storm patted the dog, who leaned against his side. "He was playing."

D.O.G. sniffed at her feet, and she stepped as far back on the bench as she could.

Storm grabbed her hand. "Watch you don't fall over backward. He's not going to hurt you; he's just saying hello."

She held his hand like a lifeline. She was afraid her palms were sweating; being this close to a big dog was almost as flustering as being too close to Storm, so she got a double whammy—lucky her.

"Do you want to take a walk?"

"With him?"

A slow smile quirked his perfect lips. "And me."

"Not really." Bree looked away. "It's nothing personal."

"Right, I'm not sure which one of us you're avoiding more, D.O.G. or me."

"Does it matter?"

"You can't avoid us forever."

No, but she could try. But first she had to apologize. "I'm sorry." There, she'd said it. Now it was done.

Storm's eyes widened as if she'd hit him with a Taser. "I suppose I should ask what exactly you're sorry for?"

"For what I said."

"Breezy, you've said a hell of a lot in the last couple of days. Can you be a little more specific?"

"You're not going to make this easy on me, are you?"

"I'm not trying to make it more difficult. I just don't know what you're apologizing for."

"I was cruel last night. I didn't mean to be, but it came to my attention that I didn't take your feelings into account."

Storm's eyes zeroed in on her. "It came to your attention? How?" He stepped closer, getting into her face— or trying to. It was pretty hard since she was still standing on the bench. It was nice to have the height advantage for once.

Bree stared at Lady Liberty, since looking into Storm's eyes was too difficult. "Rocki mentioned it."

"And how did Rocki know what happened?"

Wow, he did a pretty good Dirty Harry impression. She looked down at him and then wished she hadn't. He wasn't too pleased. "I sort of told her."

Uh-oh, now he had that whole I'm-gonna-kill-you-or-kiss-you thing going on, which for some sick reason, turned her on to no end. She wondered what it said about her. God, he made her so nervous, she flapped her arms like a damn goose until she brought her hands together and stopped herself from wringing them—or his neck. "I was mad at you."

"Yeah, I caught that." He still seemed to be debating

whether to kiss her or strangle her when he stuffed his hand in his pockets.

Bree'd rather have one of those hot, heady, angry kisses than the distance she felt now. "Rocki mentioned a few things, and, well, she might have had a point."

"And what point would that be?"

"Do we really have to get into specifics?"

"It might help."

He was right; it might help. She just wished she knew for sure that it wouldn't hurt. If things got any worse, she'd end up in the bay. "Fine." She was more unnerved by Storm than by the dog, so she jumped off the bench and stood by the railing, holding on to it for dear life and looking anywhere but at him and his damn dog. "Rocki said I was the bad guy. She said I treated you like a piece of meat." She let out a breath, waiting for some kind of response.

Storm was right behind her, but he didn't say anything. He didn't need to. Even the dog felt it—he whined, and it was not a happy whine either.

She could relate. Damn, Storm was going to drag her over the coals and force her into a full mea culpa. "That wasn't my intention."

"No, your intention was to turn me into your boy toy."

"True, but I didn't think it would hurt your feelings."

"It didn't."

"See, I told Rocki you don't have any feelings for me."

"Yeah, well, that's where you're wrong."

She turned and looked at him. He didn't look mad now, not that he looked happy, just resigned. "I really am sorry."

"Breezy." He stepped so close, his body blocked the sun. "We have feelings for each other—some good, some bad, some X-rated.... We need to get to know the people we've become before we can really figure out where we stand. I'm no more that kid who left here eleven years ago than you are the girl who stayed. We're different people, and except for your aim with a frying pan, and your annoying habit of bringing up ancient history, I like what I've come to know about you so far. I like it a hell of a lot."

"But I don't know anything about you."

He raised an eyebrow. "Don't you?"

That movement alone was enough to have her heart galloping in her chest. When she added the deep, gravelly voice to the mix, she was surprised she didn't melt like an ice cube in the summer sun. How did he do that?

"You know what I do for a living, you know I'm going to be here for a while, and you know we're practically combustible."

"I also know we fight like cats and dogs and we have nothing in common when it comes to what we want out of life."

He stepped closer and placed his hands on either side of her, blocking her in. "How do you know that? You've never asked me what I want from life—just what I want from you. You assumed my life's goals are the same goals I had a lifetime ago. Maybe you should put all your preconceived notions aside and get to know me. You might be surprised by what you find—unless you're chicken."

"I'm not afraid of you."

"Prove it. Go out with me."

"How? We're supposed to be taking care of Pete and Nicki, remember?" When had he leaned into her? His chest pressed against hers, his eyes daring hers to look away.

"We'll get a sitter. Pete and Nicki will be well taken care of, and you and I can spend some time together. I've got it covered—Rocki's not working tonight, and she offered."

Rocki was a traitor. "Isn't that convenient?"

"I thought so." His smile was back. This time, she couldn't see it, but she sure as hell could feel it against her cheek, and the rough stubble of his beard, his breath on her ear, which had liquid heat pulsing through her.

"You don't play fair."

"All's fair in love and war."

"This is lust, not love."

"Lust is definite; we'll have to see about the rest." His mouth hovered close, so close, she shut her eyes and waited for the fire she'd feel when he touched his lips to hers. The fire she always felt. The fire she all but craved. Then the sun's light shot through her closed eyelids. When she opened them, he'd stepped back. "I'm going to finish D.O.G.'s walk. I'll pick you up at your place at about seven." He turned, and with a snap of D.O.G.'s leash, man and dog walked away.

# CHAPTER 11

Storm stepped off the pier and looked down at D.O.G., who looked back at him with questioning eyes. "There's a method to my madness." And it was madness—instead of kissing Bree, he'd walked away, and now he was talking to a dog. "Always leave them wanting more, boy." He pulled his phone out of his pocket, reminding himself he still had yet to replace his brown belt, and dialed his friend's number. "Thomas, it's Storm Decker."

"Wow, it's great to hear from you. How are things down under?"

"I don't know. I'm in New York. In Red Hook, actually. My dad just got out of the hospital, so I'm helping out for a while."

"Is he going to be okay?"

"I think so. Listen, Tom. I need a favor. Would you consider lending me your boat for the night?"

"Just for a night? Hot date?"

"Yes and yes. I know it's late notice, but I really need to impress her. You know, dinner, a moonlit sail, and privacy. Can you help me out?"

"Sure can. I'll have my assistant arrange everything, Lord knows, she's done it often enough for me."

"Carly works on Sundays?"

"The news never sleeps, remember? Neither do newshounds. Carly's always on call, not usually for things like this, but I have a feeling, for you, she'll make an exception. If not, we'll figure something out. One of us will give you a callback within the hour. Is there anything else you need?"

"A brown belt — a nice one."

"Do I want to know the story behind that?"

"I'll tell you over a beer this week. I owe you one, my friend."

"No, you don't. It's the least I can do. I'll send the belt with my car and driver. What time are we talking?"

"I said I'd pick her up at seven."

"Good. I'm thinking drinks, dinner service, and dessert. Does she prefer Italian or French?"

"Whichever is more impressive. Breezy isn't a picky eater."

"French it is. I've got *No Censor Ship* docked at the North Cove Marina at Battery Park. Text me your address for my driver and your waist size and call me tomorrow."

"Will do and, Tom, thanks for everything."

"Enjoy her."

"Are you talking about the boat or the girl?"

"Both."

Storm had a smile on his face when he heard the call disconnect. Oh yeah, he'd definitely enjoy Breezy, and as for the boat, well, a boat like *No Censor Ship* was impossible not to enjoy.

*    *    *

Pete had seen neither hide nor hair of Bree since Nicki and Storm brought the dog into the house. Rocki had stayed with him all afternoon, as if she were taking over for Bree. It wasn't like Bree to just up and disappear.

Storm came into his room and saved him from another game of spider solitaire. "What the hell is going on? Where's Bree?"

Storm sat at the foot of his bed, looking pleased with himself. "She's at her place, I think. She's afraid of dogs."

"Well, shit. He's just a pup."

"I didn't say it was rational. That dog would sooner lick her to death than hurt her, but that doesn't seem to make a difference. Bree will come around; just give her some time."

"That's what I thought about the two of you, but time doesn't seem to be helping matters there either."

Storm shot him a smug look. "You're wrong. I'm taking Bree out on a date tonight. Rocki's agreed to baby, mutt, and old-fart sit for me."

"I don't need a damn babysitter."

"I know that, and you know that, but do you think Bree would leave you and Nicki alone with a wild mutt? Besides, you're in no shape to walk D.O.G. yet, and Nicki can't take him out alone. Bree won't even let her cross the street by herself."

Pete shrugged. "Bree's a bit overprotective, but can you blame her? Her mother made sure she saw a boogeyman around every corner."

"It would have been nice if you'd clued me in on that. Bree had a fit when she found out I let Nicki drive."

"You did what?"

"You heard me. I let Nicki take a spin around the parking lot down by the docks. It was no big deal."

"I'm sure it was to Bree."

"Yeah, I gathered that. Nicki sure had a good time, though."

"I bet she did. Great, now I'll have to start hiding my car keys again."

Storm cracked a smile. "I'm surprised you stopped."

"I kept forgetting where the hell I put them."

"In your empty humidor."

"And how long did it take you to figure that out?"

"About three days. The guys and I turned the house upside down one night while you were working."

"That's not all you did while I was downstairs working."

Storm looked as if he had no idea what Pete was talking about, and that was fine for now. Pete had to figure out how to play this. His long-term plans changed the day he ended up in the hospital. Now he needed to do whatever he could to make sure Nicki was taken care of in case he wasn't around. His heart attack scared the shit out of him and proved he wasn't as invincible as he'd thought. "So, what time is this date of yours?"

"I told Bree I'd pick her up at about seven." Storm stood. "How does stir-fry sound for dinner?"

"Are you cooking?"

"Yup. I learned a few things while I was away. I haven't poisoned anyone yet, and I promise not to put any tofu in it. I'll make sure there's a lot of chicken so both you and Bree will be happy."

"Fine, but I'd rather have a nice rare steak."

"If I fed you steak, Bree would kill me. You really scared her, Pop."

"She's not the only one. It scared me too. I've got to talk to her."

"Why don't you wait to talk to her tomorrow? I hope she'll be in a better mood then."

Pete took a good look at Storm; his boy looked nervous. "You'd think she'd be in a good mood now. Isn't she happy about going on a date with you?"

Storm rubbed the back of his neck. "Not really. I had to dare her. You know Bree can't refuse a dare."

"I hope to God you've got one hell of a date planned, because Bree isn't one to just let someone steamroll her."

"Tell me about it. I pulled out all the stops, Pop. If she doesn't like the date I have planned, then that will be the end of whatever the hell this thing we have between us is."

Pete laughed. "Son, if you don't know what's between you and Bree, then you have more problems than I thought. There's only one thing between the two of you, and it's the one thing you've been avoiding all your life."

"Yeah, what's that, oh wise one?"

"Love."

Storm took a step back and all the color drained from his face.

"Not the answer you were expecting, huh?"

Storm didn't reply.

"You know, son, I've known since you two were kids, but she was too young and you had things you needed to do. I always hoped that maybe someday, after you got your head on straight, you'd use the brains God gave you and figure it out on your own. I thought I'd better let you know since it's as obvious as the nose on your face how you still feel about her, and I'm not getting any younger.

Besides, you've got some fancy footwork to do if you're going to get past the wall Bree built up after you ran off. You broke her heart, and she's never forgiven you for it."

"I don't know if I broke her heart, but I sure pissed her off."

"And you're still not going to tell me why you lit out of here as if you were being chased by the hounds of hell?"

"Pop, it's not going to change anything."

Pete wasn't so sure. It just might change Storm's whole world, but now wasn't the time to get into it.

Storm rose, took a step toward the door, and then turned around.

"What is it?"

"I just wanted to say thanks." Storm stuck his hands in his pockets and then rocked back on his heels. "Thanks for everything you've done for me, taking me in . . . well, everything. I don't think I ever thanked you for being there for me all the time—even when I didn't want you around."

Pete laughed to keep from crying. "You're my son. I love you. You'll always be my son no matter where you go or what you do."

Storm looked at his feet and nodded. "The feeling's mutual. You're the only dad I ever knew. You gave me a family. I don't think I ever really understood it before now."

Pete let out a breath and hid a smile. The boy still struggled with emotions. Pete hoped to hell he'd get a handle on it before Bree gave up on his ass.

Storm cleared his throat and backed away. "I'll start dinner. It should be ready in about forty-five minutes."

"Okay." Pete leaned back on the pillows and knew

that tomorrow he'd have to have a heart-to-heart with Bree. He hoped what he had to say wouldn't break her heart all over again.

Storm stood in front of the bathroom sink with a towel wrapped around his waist and smiled. He hadn't spent so much time in the head since he started out as an ordinary seaman. His first two days on board were spent cleaning every head on the ship. It didn't take long to decide he needed to move up the ranks quickly, which was what he did.

He'd just finished spreading shaving cream over his face when Nicki walked in and took a seat on the john. "Don't you knock?" He checked the towel around his waist, making sure it was secure.

"Not usually, no."

"You should." Storm wiped the shaving cream off his sideburn with his finger and slid the razor from his sideburn down before rinsing it off.

"Why? Pop lets me watch him shave all the time. He makes funny faces."

"I'm not Pop." He was also not wearing pants, which was a definite concern, but he thought it best not to mention that.

"You don't make funny faces?"

"I don't know. I've never shaved with an audience."

"Keep going. I'll tell you if you do."

"Great. Thanks."

"Pop said you're taking Bree out on a date."

He rinsed his razor and tapped it against the side of the sink. "Uh-huh."

"How come?"

"Because I want to, and she said yes."

"Do you want to marry her?"

He pulled his upper lip down under his teeth to shave above it but stopped. "Why do girls automatically jump from dating to marriage?"

"Because that's what happens, right? You wouldn't marry someone you didn't date, would you?"

"No." He tried to shave above his lip again. He got two swipes of the razor completed.

"Are you gonna marry Bree?"

Shaving with an audience while having a conversation was proving more difficult than he'd anticipated. "I've dated a lot of women, and I never married any of them."

"But you could."

"I guess it's within the realm of possibility." Yeah, it was right up there with winning the New York Lottery on his first try.

"I'm guessing that's a solid maybe."

"It's a not so solid maybe, so I wouldn't bet on it. Bree doesn't like me much."

"Then why's she going on a date with you?"

"I dared her."

"Oh, that's not good." Nicki's pigtails swung around her somewhat-dirty face. "Bree doesn't like it when people corner her."

Great, that was exactly what Pop said. It didn't bode well for his date. Maybe the whole dare thing wasn't such a good idea. "She's young; she'll get over it." He hoped so, and decided to go for the other sideburn rather than the tricky chin and neck.

"Only if you don't mess everything up. Did you buy her flowers?"

"No."

"Girls like flowers, and not that kind you get at the corner market either. What's-his-face bought Bree some, and she wasn't impressed."

"Who bought Bree flowers?"

"That guy Daniel from the community board. I don't like him. He has mean eyes."

Storm rinsed his razor and tapped it on the sink with more force than necessary. He thought it best not to say anything about that asshole, especially when shaving. Shaving while angry was never a good thing.

"He sure likes Bree, though."

Storm took a slice off his chin. "Shit."

Nicki's eyes went wide. "You really need to work on the not-cursing thing, Storm. Bree is real strict about that."

"How do you know Knickerbocker likes Bree?"

Nicki rolled her eyes. "Because he's always calling her and asking her out and stopping by. I'm not a baby. I know stuff, and I know he doesn't like kids. He's just like all my mom's boyfriends. They were always telling me to get lost."

Storm stopped shaving and did his best not to lose his temper. How many times had his parents told him the same thing? They'd also told him to take a long walk off a short pier, and to play on the dotted yellow line in traffic. He knew exactly how it felt. "Daniel told you to get lost?"

"Yeah."

"When?"

Nicki shrugged. "Whenever I'm around Bree when he stops by." She took a deep breath. "Storm, you're making a face, but not a funny one."

"No one tells you to get lost. I might tell you to go to your room or something, but if anyone tells you to get lost, you come to me and I'll take care of it. Okay?"

Nicki nodded.

"Did you tell Bree what he said?"

"No."

"You should have. Bree wouldn't put up with someone talking to you that way. She loves you. Sounds to me like the only one who needs to get lost is Daniel."

Nicki was paying an awful lot of attention to her swinging feet, and she wasn't saying anything. The kid wasn't normally quiet. Storm took a towel from the rack and wiped off his face. "Nicki, when Bree and I didn't know where you were, it scared the hell out of us."

"Really?" She looked up at him and squinted as if doing her best to see if he was lying.

"Yeah, really. From now on, no taking off without telling one of us where you're going. I never want you to get lost, and neither does Pop or Bree. Got it?"

"I got it."

"Good. So, do I make funny faces when I shave?"

"Not as funny as Pop, but that's okay. I still like watching you shave."

Storm tugged on one of Nicki's pigtails. "I'm going to get dressed. Rocki should be here in a little while. Maybe you should pick out a movie to watch and make some popcorn."

"What'cha gonna wear?"

"Clothes."

Nicki rolled her eyes. "Duh. What kind of clothes?"

"Nice ones?"

"Okay. Go get dressed and then come out to open the popcorn bag. Bree won't let me do it by myself."

"You're wearing that on a date?"

Bree scowled at Rocki, who had charged into her

apartment as if she owned the place. Rocki always looked ready to take on the town—she'd never seen Rocki in comfortable clothes. Bree, however, was a different story. She looked at her comfy jeans and clean T-shirt she'd tossed on after her shower. "It's not a date, date. It's a let's-figure-out-how-to-deal-with-each-other-without-wanting-to-kill-each-other date."

Rocki shook her head. "He's wearing dress slacks, a tie, and a jacket."

"You're kidding." Bree pressed her stomach to settle the bat-sized butterflies that had taken up residence there.

"Nope. Now I'll ask you again—you're wearing that on a date?"

"No?"

Rocki walked past Bree into her bedroom. "Let's see what our options are." She opened the closet door and started rummaging through it. "Girl, we really need to take you shopping." She pulled out an emerald green silk dress. It was sleeveless, with a very demure V-neck, and a tie at the waist—blousy and comfortable. "It's a little shapeless, and it certainly won't highlight your assets."

Bree pulled the dress from Rocki's clutches. "I don't want to highlight my assets. This isn't that kind of date."

"Not for lack of trying on his part. Besides, from what I hear, he's well acquainted with your assets. He'll spend most of the night staring at you and trying to catch glimpses of them. That dress might work out well after all. Do you have a bra to wear with it?"

"Yes." Bree rolled her eyes and tried to remember if she'd bothered to shave her legs. She had, thank God. She changed while Rocki went through her shoe collection, picking out two pairs. Bree tossed the stilettos back into her closet and slipped on the ballet flats—the ones that said comfortable as opposed to take-me-now.

"Now, what about your hair?"

"What about it?"

Rocki put her hand on her bony hip and tilted her head. "The ponytail isn't working for me."

"Then I guess it's a good thing it's not your ponytail. It's working for me just fine."

"No, it's not. Come on." She grabbed Bree's wrist, dragged her into the bathroom, and plugged in the curling iron. "Sit."

Bree knew better than to say anything when Rocki wore her give-me-a-hard-time-and-I'll-bust-your-chops look. "Fine."

Five minutes later, Rocki dropped the curling iron in the sink. "Now stand up, put your head down, and then flip it back up."

Bree followed her directions.

"Perfect." Rocki plucked at Bree's curls for a minute until satisfied. "Now hold your breath."

Before Bree could ask why, Rocki sprayed every strand with hair spray. After the air cleared, Bree blinked a few times and checked the mirror to see the results. Bree's hairstyle said exactly what her shoes didn't.

The knock on the door told her it was too late to rectify the situation. Besides, if she put it back in a ponytail, Rocki would kill her. "You did this on purpose."

Rocki shot her a cocky smile. "You bet your sweet ass I did. I just hope you're not wearing granny panties. You're not, are you?"

"No." Unfortunately. And it was way too late to change into a pair, especially since she didn't own any. Bree might not dress like the rock star Rocki did, but she had a real appreciation for nice lingerie. Not that Storm would have the opportunity to find out what color thong she wore. No, that ship had definitely sailed.

"Good." Rocki grabbed Bree's arm and dragged her to the door. Before Bree could say anything, Rocki had opened the door, scooted past Storm, and slipped into Pete's apartment, leaving Bree staring at Storm and wondering why he had to look so damn good.

# CHAPTER 12

Storm tried not to stare at Breezy. He was sure she did her best *not* to look too hot but had failed. Her dress might not be tight and the neckline left a whole lot more to the imagination than he liked, but he was well acquainted with what was underneath all that drapey silk. He knew it so well, he could pull up a detailed image from memory any second of the day—and he had, continuously. The woman could wear a Santa suit with a beard and padding and give him a hard-on. "You look incredible."

"Thanks, I think."

That was awkward. Storm covered the smile that threatened with a mask of seriousness. Poor little Breezy wasn't used to failing—even when it came to hiding her looks. The consternation that covered her face and wrinkled her nose was almost comical.

"You clean up pretty good yourself," she said as she looked at her shoes.

He was almost relieved to see she wore flats—almost. He would have preferred seeing her in heels even if he'd have to ask her to change them. "The car is downstairs. Are you ready to go?"

"We're not taking mine?" She grabbed her handbag and followed him out, locking the door behind her.

"No." The front of Bree's dress may have left a lot to the imagination, but the back didn't. It was formfitting, showing off her straight back, toned arms, tiny waist, the curve of her ass, and highlighted her long, long, long legs. He took her elbow and headed for the stairs.

"Where are we going?"

He followed her down and held the door open. "To dinner."

Her eyes widened when she saw the Lincoln Town Car and driver. He wasn't sure if she was impressed or horrified.

"I gathered that. Where are we going to dinner?"

Storm nodded at the driver and helped Bree into the car. She scooted across the leather seat, holding the short skirt of her dress down and giving him a nice outline of her very fine stern. "It's a surprise."

"I don't like surprises."

He slid in beside her and hoped to hell she liked this one. As they headed toward the Battery Tunnel, he snuck a glance trying to determine Bree's mood and wiped sweaty palms on his pants. He hadn't been this nervous since he launched his first boat.

"We're going into the city?"

"It sure looks that way."

With traffic, it was still only a twenty-minute drive — twenty long minutes. He'd never been this tongue-tied on a date. But then this was more than just a date; this was the only way to show Breezy who he was now. Part of him said it didn't matter what she thought, but then there was the part of him that knew instinctively it might change the course of both their lives. He wasn't quite sure how, but he learned a long time ago never to ignore his gut instinct. Every time he did, he either got arrested or hurt—sometimes both.

Storm tried to relax into the leather seat and snuck glances at Bree—little miss prim and proper with her hands in her lap and her legs crossed at the ankles. "You look as if you're headed to the firing squad. I'd offer you a final cigarette if I smoked."

"You're imagining things."

No, he wasn't, but he could. He was damn good at imagining things with Breezy. She seemed more intent on counting the tiles in the tunnel than in conversing with him. Since he wasn't sure there was a safe topic to discuss with a nervous-looking Breezy, he didn't bother trying to make small talk. The last thing he wanted was to stuff his size-thirteen foot in his mouth again.

When the car stopped at the end of North End Avenue, Bree frowned in confusion. "The only restaurants around the Winter Garden Atrium are lunch places, and they're all closed by now. It's Sunday, Storm, and this is the financial center."

"I've got it covered." He got out of the car and took a deep breath. He felt a thousand times better just being out of Red Hook. His gaze swept the area and focused on the masts in the distance. Here by the North Cove Marina he was on home turf. Home turf was any space, anywhere in the world, close to the water with an up-scale marina and racing or cruising yachts. They may have been only twenty minutes from Red Hook, but the North Cove Marina was a whole world away, and he couldn't wait to see how Breezy looked in it.

The driver tipped his cap. "You have my number to call for pickup, sir."

Storm shook his hand. "I do. Thank you."

Bree stood beside him, clutching her purse so tightly, her knuckles turned white. She watched the car pull away, then swallowed hard, looking resigned, as if waiting for the final shot to ring out.

"You sure you don't want that cigarette? I could buy you a pack."

Bree squared her shoulders. "No, thank you. So, where are you taking me?"

"For a walk. Come on." Storm took her elbow and led her toward the marina.

"I thought we were going to dinner."

"Dinner is coming to us, but not for an hour or so." They wandered across the plaza in the shadow of the ten-story Winter Garden Atrium. It was quiet. They'd lucked out. There were usually functions going on at the plaza. Tonight there were only a few people strolling along the riverfront and enjoying the summer evening. It was far from the usual mob scene.

Storm led Bree toward the marina, spotted *No Censor Ship*, and headed toward her. Someone had obviously prepared her for a sail. The mainsail cover had been removed and stowed, which meant less for him to do, and more time to enjoy Breezy.

"You're not going to steal another boat, are you?"

Storm chuckled before he realized she was as serious as Pete's heart attack. Breezy had that holier-than-thou tilt to her head—the one she always used before she lit into him. He swallowed back a smart-ass retort. "No, I'm not stealing her. I haven't stolen a boat since I was twelve. I'm borrowing her with permission." He helped Bree onto the dock, stopped at the stern, and clicked the remote on the key fob. He watched Bree's face as the transom folded open like the tailgate of a pickup truck, turning the back of the yacht into a deck, for diving or walking across to go aboard. It was ingenious if he did say so himself, and it sure beat climbing over the side. Storm stepped onto the transom, offering her a hand.

She looked from his face to the eighty-foot performance cruising yacht. "You seriously expect me to believe you're borrowing this gorgeous boat?"

"Yes."

"How did you manage it?"

"The usual way—"

"Blackmail?"

"I asked for a favor. No blackmail necessary."

"And the owner just said, 'Sure, here are the keys to my million-dollar yacht. Have at it'?"

"Pretty much." Storm rocked back on his heels. Bree knew nothing about yachts. *No Censor Ship* was a *ten-million-dollar* yacht, but then sharing that wouldn't help his case, especially since she still didn't believe a word he said. He couldn't help but wonder if this was all a huge waste of time. "Do you want me to call my friend Thomas, the owner, so you can question him?"

Bree seemed to weigh her options, scanning the area as if expecting a SWAT team to jump out from behind the bushes.

Storm worked on relaxing his jaw. He'd taken to grinding his teeth whenever Bree was around, and the way things were going, after a few more days with Bree, he'd be lucky if he had any molars left. "Thomas Danby is a real blue blood and bigwig with the *Wall Street Journal*. He was still at work last time I spoke to him. Of course, I can always call his assistant, Carly, to corroborate my story. She was good enough to help me arrange everything on short notice."

Bree's eyebrow shot up.

Maybe mentioning Carly wasn't such a good idea. Storm dug out his phone and offered it to her. "It's your call."

Bree looked around again and then took his arm instead of the phone before stepping aboard.

Storm let out a relieved breath and helped her across the transom and up the step to the deck. He unlocked the door to the companionway and looked inside. Perfect. An ice bucket with a bottle of champagne chilling sat on a tray; just waiting to be opened and poured.

"Come on down. You can stow your bag below and get a drink."

Bree swallowed hard—the only boat she'd ever been on was the ferry, and this was so not the ferry.

She stood in between two steering wheels—why the heck there were two was a mystery. How many captains did it take to drive this boat anyway?

She wasn't even sure what to call it exactly. A boat, a ship, a yacht? Whatever it was, she'd never seen anything like it before—well, except in pictures in fancy magazines or perfume ads with Greek gods wearing Speedos. She wondered what Storm would look like in one. She caught her breath when the picture became clear. But she needed to get her mind out of the Mediterranean gutter and back on the boat. "You want me to go down there?" Bree pointed a shaking hand to the entrance of the bowels of the boat.

"Yeah, I thought I'd give you the grand tour."

She had a vague idea what the inside would look like

from pictures, but she had always figured they'd been Photoshopped to keep it from looking like a tomb. She was a bit claustrophobic, and the thought of Storm sucking up all the oxygen in a confined space wasn't helping matters either. "Thanks for the offer, but I don't need a tour of your friend's boat." The boat was tied to the jetty, or dock, or whatever it was called, but the thing still moved—much more than she had expected it to. She grabbed the edge of the table.

Storm closed in on her and pried her fingers off. "Breezy, relax. What are you afraid of?"

"I'm not afraid."

He gave her a don't-bullshit-a-bullshitter look that he had down pat. She had every one of his looks catalogued. This one was straight out of her least-favorite file.

"I don't like tight spaces."

"You're claustrophobic?"

"No ... well, maybe a little." Only with him—with him every room seemed to shrink, making everything feel tighter than usual—even her clothes.

"You have nothing to worry about. It's really open and airy. It's designed to look as if you're not be-lowdecks." He tugged on her hand and moved her in front of the doorway. "Just look inside; you'll see."

Bree ducked her head and caught her breath. "Look at all those windows." They wrapped around the entire space above the walls.

"It's called a windscreen."

"Whatever." She waved a hand at him, stepped onto the top step, and she could see forever. She'd expected the interior to be utilitarian, not opulent. She continued down, and did a slow turn, taking in the whole place. "Wow, it's breathtaking."

"Beautiful."

Her stomach clenched when she realized Storm was staring at her, not the boat.

"This is the main salon."

Built-in curved couches that probably sat ten people comfortably, and tables made of beautiful burr elm were scattered throughout. The interior was all soft, sensual curves, with a warm gold, royal blue, and cream color scheme. It was rich but homey, and there wasn't one straight line in the joint. "It's . . . comfortable—like a really nice apartment."

"That's what the owner was going for. The lower level has another salon, the galley, a nav station."

"Nav station?"

"Navigational station—a desk, charts, GPS, the usual."

"The usual, huh? In what world?"

"In my world."

Soft lighting on the floor and ceilings looked like something out of a stage show. "Your friend has incredible taste." Bree looked around in amazement. "It's not what I expected."

Storm took the bottle of champagne out of the bucket and went about opening it. He didn't make a big deal of it; he just popped the top as he would a bottle of beer and poured two glasses, handing her one. "Here's to communication—in all its forms—and to exceeding expectations."

Bree felt her eyebrow spike and brought her glass to his, and then sipped the best champagne she'd ever tasted.

Storm turned her around. "Come on, I'll show you the rest."

"There's more?"

"Four staterooms."

"This place has more bedrooms than Pete's apartment?"

"Yeah, and three more heads . . ."

She must have looked confused, because he choked back a laugh and continued. "Heads are bathrooms." He walked toward the back of the boat; past the steps they'd come down, and opened a door. "Here's the main stateroom."

Bree stepped in and ran her hand over the coverlet on the queen-sized bed. It was silky and soft and made her want to strip just to see what it would feel like to roll around on it naked—with Storm. She'd been thinking about them wrinkling the sheets since he walked out on her the night before. She held back a laugh—the damn thing probably cost more than she made in a month. She slid back against a built-in leather couch flanking one side, and stared at the other wall made up of built-in drawers and doors. She wanted to look at anything but Storm; she was afraid he'd be able to read her dirty little mind.

"The head is through here." He opened another door and turned on the lights. It was all mirrors and marble, a shower, curved counters, a sink, and a toilet. She'd never thought of a bathroom as sexy, but then she'd never pictured Storm and her in the same bathroom naked before either. Damn, she was in way over her head.

He pulled her along to the next stateroom, which was G-rated and had twin beds. She didn't want to know if there was another sexy bathroom and was glad he just pointed to the door.

"The crew cabins are in the bow."

"I guess you need a whole crew to sail this thing."

"Nope, just one person can sail it; two is better, though. It's like a remote-control car — the engines, the sails, everything can be controlled from the helm."

"Then why are there two steering wheels?"

"Two wheels make it easier to enter the boat and for traffic flow on deck. There's nothing worse than having to maneuver around the wheel."

"I can imagine that would be a real drag." She didn't bother hiding her sarcasm.

"It also gives the helmsman a choice for the best visuals either to leeward or up to weather. Both wheels have the same controls, so it doesn't matter which you're using."

There was a knock at the door, or whatever it was called. Storm took her hand and led her to the deck, where three uniformed waiters held trays. "Right on time. Welcome aboard."

"Where would you like us to serve, Mr. Decker?"

Storm turned to Bree. "Would you like to eat up here or down below?"

"It's a beautiful evening; let's eat out here." She was afraid she'd spill something, and she was pretty sure everything on the deck could be washed down. Besides, right now, she could use the fresh air. She just wished she knew why he'd brought her here. When Storm asked her to dinner, she was thinking a restaurant, not catered yacht service.

She and Storm sat down to a five-course French meal. She was sure it was the best food she'd ever been served or ingested, but she barely noticed. Wine, soup, salad, escargot, followed by the main course of sea bass and vegetables in parchment; it was lovely, but the whole time they ate, she still couldn't figure him out.

Bree stuck her spoon into a poached pear topped with vanilla ice cream and covered with chocolate ganache, and she moaned. Okay, so maybe she did notice.

Storm cleared his throat. "You like it?"

Bree licked the chocolate-covered spoon. "Are you asking about the dessert or the date?"

"Both." He pushed his plate away and took a sip of port.

"There's nothing not to like, but this wasn't what I signed up for."

Disappointment flashed across his face and then disappeared into his typical cocky smirk. He'd been quiet, watching, and waiting. And she got the distinct impression that she wasn't giving him what he was watching and waiting for.

The waiters packed up their wares and set them on the jetty. She leaned forward. "Is this one of those games that's a series of tests or challenges, or something?"

"What are you talking about?" Ooh, she'd touched a nerve. His face looked like granite, except for the muscle that ticked in his jaw.

"I don't know, but I feel as if I'm playing a game without knowing the rules, the prize, or the players."

"Paranoid much?"

"No, not usually. I just don't know what you're after, Storm. I thought we were going to figure out how to deal with each other until you leave. Then Rocki showed up and said you were dressed as if you were headed to a cocktail party in the Hamptons."

"If we were going to the Hamptons, I'd take the boat anyway. Traffic on the Long Island Expressway is a real bitch."

"Very funny." She sat back and crossed her arms.

"Bree." He leaned forward. "This isn't a game. I want to spend time with you, get to know the woman you've become, and let you get to know me."

"Right, but how is our dining on your friend's boat helping me get to know you, Storm? The only thing it tells me is you have very wealthy friends with questionable judgment. I mean, who in their right mind would lend out a boat like this? I don't know what you're selling, but I'm not buying, so you might as well tell me why you brought me here in the first place."

"Dammit, Breezy." He stood and turned away. He took a deep breath and watched the staff leave the jetty before turning back to her. "I brought you here because this"—he spread his arms to encompass the entire boat, the meal, and the uniformed waiters—"this is part of me." Storm pressed the key fob; the back of the boat rose, and he stepped behind the wheel. Was he leaving? He pressed a button, and she heard the purr of a motor.

The floor beneath her feet vibrated, and she jumped.

Storm strode past her, climbed up on the side, and called out to a guy on the dock. "Toss me those lines, will you please?" He caught the ropes, and she watched the way his muscles moved as he made fast work of coiling them before jumping back toward her.

Bree stood and blocked him. "How is someone else's boat part of you?"

He didn't stop; he just walked right past her, stood behind the wheel, and glared. "It's part of me because she's one of mine." He pushed a lever, and the vibration increased with his anger—and man, was he angry. He practically vibrated with it, the jerk.

"Hold on. You just told me you borrowed it."

"*No Censor Ship* is my design, Breezy. She's as much a part of me as the Crow's Nest is a part of you." He pressed a lever, and the next thing she knew, the dock was moving.

Shit, it wasn't the dock that was moving; it was the boat—and it wasn't just shifting either. It was moving forward. "What's going on? Why are we moving?"

"Because we're going on a romantic sunset sail, even if it kills us both, and it's hard to sail staying still."

"You said dinner; you never said we were going sailing."

He spun the wheel and the boat turned smoothly, heading out of the marina and into the harbor. "It's part of the surprise. It's too late for you to make your escape, so unless you're up for a swim, sit the hell down."

Bree sat and grasped the table in front of her before finally remembering to close her mouth.

Storm steered with a steady hand through the entrance to the harbor. Once they were a hundred yards out, something hummed, and an enormous sail rose up the big mast. It fluttered for a moment and then caught the wind.

"I thought we'd cruise by Governors Island, and take a turn around the Statue of Liberty."

They were moving faster now, and the boat tilted. The vibration from the engines died, and then all she heard was the rushing of water. The wind made a mockery of the work Rocki had done on Bree's hair; it was flying all over and whipping against her face. She grabbed a handful of hair and stared, trying to take everything in. She didn't know which was more interesting, watching Storm or the New York skyline with the sunset turning it pink, orange, and purple—both were equally stunning. Storm looked every bit the competent captain—controlled, steady, and well, hot.

She was such an idiot. She *knew* he designed boats; the proof hung on Pete's Wall of Fame. Storm was always doodling and sketching—even in the bar on cocktail napkins, but seeing a sketch on paper didn't make it real. Sailing in New York Harbor on an eighty-foot luxury yacht was about as real as you could get. She was downright awestruck. "Am I allowed to get up now, or do I have to sit here for the duration?"

Storm looked as if he had forgotten she was even there—he was completely emotionless. She liked it better when he was angry—she knew how to deal with his anger, but this made her feel as if he were on the other side of the world.

"Feel free to roam around. You might want to take off your shoes, though. They're not exactly skid-proof."

She slipped out of the ballet flats, tossed them on the cushion beside her, and stood, holding on to the table for dear life. "The ferry never tilts like this, and it doesn't seem to move as fast either."

He nodded, his face a mask. Had she done that to him? Probably. After all, she had accused him of stealing the boat, which was pretty low considering he was what? Trying to impress her?

She went through all the things she'd said to him in the last few hours and cringed. What was it about him that brought out the worst in her? She was a nice person, except with Storm. She'd never been intentionally cruel. She tended to kill people with kindness. For the second time in her life she found herself in uncharted waters. She was confused; she didn't understand herself, no less what the hell he was doing with her. Rocki was going to have a field day when she heard about this.

Bree watched him and knew she had to apologize—again. She hated apologizing almost as much as she hated acting like a bitch without knowing why she was even doing it.

If she was going to apologize, she wanted to do it right, which meant talking face-to-face, not from across a boat. He wasn't that far away, just a few yards, but the way he looked at her, it might as well have been miles. Unfortunately, a face-to-face would also require her to leave the table she clung to.

He'd probably have a good laugh if he knew how afraid she was to let go. Bree swallowed hard, stepped away from the table, and felt as if she were walking the plank with one hand holding her hair and the other trying to keep her too-short skirt from blowing up and giving him a show.

Storm watched her but didn't say anything—he didn't need to. He looked wary, and who could blame him? She stopped next to him and did her best to smile. It was a wobbly smile, but right now, it was all she could do not to cry. If she'd wanted to push him away, she'd done a damn good job. "This is incredible."

"That's one word for it. An incredible failure. I got it, Bree. You only have to hit me upside the head a half dozen times before it sinks in. You're more like your mother than even *I* thought."

"My mother?" He couldn't have shocked her more if he'd slapped her. "I'm nothing like my mother. My mother is afraid to leave the damn house."

"And you're afraid of living. You might not confine

yourself to a house, but you're just as closed off, to me at least. You'd rather lick eleven-year-old wounds than try again. I get it."

"Oh really? You get it? Well, I sure as hell don't." She was screaming, and she really didn't care. Years of anger and hurt came to a boiling point. Every muscle in her body tightened, and she shook with it. "How am I supposed to forgive and forget something I don't understand? I still don't understand why you left without so much as a good-bye! Didn't I deserve that much from you? Now you show up after all these years, and I'm supposed to pretend it never happened and trust you?"

"Bree, I was eighteen years old. I may have been a dumb kid, but I was smart enough to know I had to leave. I had nothing to offer you, and God help me, I didn't want to get stuck in Red Hook and turn into my old man."

He'd never mentioned his real parents. The pain she saw in his eyes took her breath away; she wrapped her arms around herself to keep from touching him.

"The only thing my dad could do was work the docks. He hated it, he drank, and he took the fact that he was trapped in his shit-hole of a life out on my mom and me. I was lucky social services took me away after one too many visits to the ER. You, Pete, Slater, and Logan were the only good things in my life. Pete made me see what I could be. And Bree, I wanted more for you. I wanted more for us. I wanted an education, I wanted to design boats, and the only way I could make that happen was to get as far away from Red Hook as humanly possible."

"I would never have asked you to stay. I would have waited for you, Storm. I loved you."

"Don't you get it, Breezy? If we had made love, I

wouldn't have been strong enough to leave you. As it was, I felt like one of those dogs who had to chew off his own leg to escape a trap."

"Don't you dare put that on me, Storm Decker. I never wanted to trap you."

"It didn't matter what you wanted. That's not what I'm talking about. I was nothing but a punk kid with a record. I knew I didn't deserve you. I would have dragged you down with me, and I loved you too much to take a chance on hurting you. I loved you so much, I had to protect you from me, Breezy. I did the only thing I could to save us both—I ran. It was immature, and maybe I could have handled it better. I'm sorry I hurt you, but dammit, Breezy, I still believe I did the right thing."

"Why didn't you tell me that when you came home? It would have saved us a lot of time and trouble."

"I tried last night, but you weren't ready to hear it."

"I was angry."

Storm nodded. "I got that, and you had every right to be."

"Storm, when I said this is incredible, I was talking about the boat and the date." She released her skirt and touched his arm; his muscles tensed under her fingers. "No one has ever taken me on a date like this. No one has ever gone to this much trouble. Accusing you of stealing the boat was cruel and way out of line. And I'm sorry I sounded obtuse. I just didn't understand what you do—not really. I had no idea this boat was one of yours. It's just so beautiful...."

"And a guy like me is incapable of designing something beautiful?"

Even with the wind buffeting her face, the heat of a fierce blush hit her like a third-degree burn. "That's not what I meant. I know I don't deserve the benefit of the doubt, but I'm obviously capable of insulting you right to your face, so please, don't go putting words in my mouth."

She turned to face him—searching for the boy she used to love in the man beside her. "You've changed so much. I just didn't let myself see it. I think I was afraid to. I'm sorry I've been so hostile."

"It's okay, Bree. I'll take you home. I'm sure that's what you want."

"You're wrong." She watched the colors of the sunset lighting the horizon, trying to gather her fragmented thoughts before she stepped closer. "I hope you can forgive me. I'm sorry for the way I've been since you got here. It's just that you scare me, Storm, and I say horrible things and act like a complete bitch when I'm scared."

When she got the guts to look him in the face to see if he'd even heard her, she was shocked to see him grinning. It was not a happy smile, but a tortured, almost cynical, self-mocking grin.

"Wow, you must be really terrified."

# CHAPTER 13

Storm spared Bree a glance. She looked about to cry, and his gut tightened. He gripped the wheel with both hands to keep from reaching for her and cursed himself for even caring. After years of trying to forget about her and after everything she'd said and done in the last few days, he still cared. He was either a fucking lunatic or a masochist—probably both.

She stood within reach, looking about ready to crumble as quickly as his resistance. He adjusted the course and set the autopilot. He wasn't about to leave the wheel while sailing along the tip of lower Manhattan, but he had better things to do with his hands than steer. Way better.

She took a step back and started to dissolve before his eyes. "It's too little too late, isn't it?" Her voice sounded hollow. "I understand." One of those tears she'd been fighting escaped, and she turned away.

"No, you don't." He wrapped his arm around her waist, pulled her against him, and felt something shift inside. Holding her felt right. "I had to set the autopilot and increase our speed; the ferry is coming." He nodded in that direction. "We have the right-of-way, but I'm giving her wide berth. I don't want to sail through her wake."

"What are you saying?" Her hair whipped her face and hid it from him.

Storm tipped her face up to his and brushed back her hair, holding it before sliding his mouth over hers. It wasn't a long kiss; there was way too much traffic to be making out at the helm, for God's sake. He wasn't about to get carried away here—at least not until they had *No Censor Ship* neatly docked in her slip. But damn, it was a good kiss, and he relaxed, letting his tension fly away with the wind. "Now, do you want me to come about, or do you want to sail?"

"That's it?"

"What were you expecting?"

"I don't know. I figured you'd rake me over the coals at least a little bit. I wouldn't blame you." She looked at him as if she'd never seen him before, and maybe she really hadn't.

"Breezy, if we're starting over, we're starting over. That was our first kiss; we have a clean slate. Don't you think we've been raking each other over the coals long enough?"

She wrapped her arms around his neck, and he held back a groan when her body strained against his. She was dangerous. If being with him was like riding a roller coaster, being with her was like sailing through a typhoon—much scarier than any roller coaster could ever hope to be. Storm tucked her more securely against him and scanned the water. It was a perfect night for a sail, so he adjusted the course and leaned against the transom.

Five minutes ago he thought he'd lost Bree, not that he'd been delusional enough to believe he'd had her, but he'd thought she'd put a bullet between the eyes of their last chance, and the pain he'd felt almost brought him to his knees. Now she was in his arms, sailing across the harbor, and he'd be damned if it didn't feel as if she belonged there, as if they both did.

He held her a little tighter, afraid if he loosened his grip, the feeling would escape as quickly as it hit him. He didn't want to lose this, lose Bree. Shit, he felt as if he'd searched his whole life for what he had right this second. He didn't know if it would last; all he knew was that he never wanted it to disappear. For the first time in his life he felt at home, complete, happy. Nowhere else he'd ever been had felt this right.

"Storm?" She took his face in her hands, and those bright green eyes of hers bored into his. "I'm not going anywhere, but I'd like to be able to breathe."

"What?"

"You're crushing me."

"Shit." He relaxed his hold. "I'm sorry. Did I hurt you?"

"No, but I'd kill to know what was going through your mind when you did your impersonation of a boa constrictor."

She stared at him until it was clear he wasn't going to spill his guts—he'd already given her enough ammunition; any more could be deemed assisted suicide.

She looked as if a lightbulb had gone on, and she considered him with brows drawn together. "You really put yourself out there for me, didn't you?" There was wonder in her voice, something he hadn't heard since they were kids.

He did his best to laugh it off and scanned the water. What was he, an open book?

"You're as scared as I am, only you're braver. You don't let the fear stop you."

He shot her a get-real look and returned his gaze to a bright yellow water taxi.

"Oh, now you're doing that man-of-steel thing. It's as though you put on a mask."

They were sailing between Governors Island and Ellis Island. The Statue of Liberty stood as rigid as he felt. He forced out a breath. "I'm not doing anything but trying to figure out if we're on the same page here, Bree. This feels too right—you and me together, here, now—except for your play-by-play, that is."

"I just call 'em like I see 'em. It does feel right, but then we're sailing around on a yacht—not really a dose of reality, is it? I mean, how bad could it feel?"

"Pretty bad. I've been on a hell of a lot of yachts and never felt anything like this. The only thing different in the equation is you."

A smile lit her face. "Really?"

"Really." He scanned the water and then focused on her profile, her long hair blowing in the evening breeze. "With the sun setting all pink and purple, you look more beautiful than anything I've ever seen." He cleared his throat, swallowing back his emotions. "So where do we go from here?"

She stared at him for as long as it took to circle the Statue of Liberty and reset the autopilot. He snuck glances of her as she faced Lady Liberty with New York lit up in the background. Tension radiated off her in waves. Not good.

"I don't know. Everything has changed, but nothing is different. You still live on the other side of the world"— she pointed at Red Hook—"and my life is over there.

People depend on me—Pete, Nicki, my mother. So you tell me, where do we go from here?"

"I work all over the world, Bree. Just because I have to leave doesn't mean I won't come back."

"Really? But when? In another eleven years?" She shook her head and turned away.

His heart pounded out the drum of a dirge. He was going to lose her, and it hurt more than it did the last time. He felt as if he'd been kicked in the gut. He spun her around and wrapped his arms around her. He never thought he'd be one to beg. He'd been wrong. "Breezy, please."

"Why are you doing this, Storm?"

"Because I've been away from you for years, and in all that time, I've never stopped caring about you, no matter how hard I tried. I care about you because you make me want more, I care about you because you make me feel more, and I care about you because when I'm with you, I am more. All I'm asking for is a chance."

"A chance for what?"

"Everything. I want a chance to have everything with you."

"You don't ask for much, do you?"

"Breezy, with you, I can't imagine ever not wanting more."

Bree inhaled his scent—sea, soap, Right Guard, and Storm. She sank into the kiss while his words whipped around her like the wind through her hair. He anchored her against him, and she rode the wave of her rioting emotions. It was a good thing Storm was holding her, because if left on her own, she'd probably be kissing the deck.

A horn sounded and he groaned. "The middle of the

harbor is not the place to be doing this. Someone's gotta sail the damn boat."

"I guess that's my cue to leave." And it was a darn good excuse to get some space and pull herself together. She tried to step away, but his arms tightened around her. He tugged her behind the wheel and pressed his front to her back, sending heat rushing through her that all the wind in the world couldn't cool.

"Oh no you don't." His voice rumbled through his chest and into hers, and his warm breath fanned her ear. "I'm not going to let you go any time soon. Don't worry. We'll be back to the marina in no time." He kicked up the engines, and her pulse increased along with their speed.

"There's no rush." Lord knew, she was having a hard enough time coming to grips with what Storm meant when he said everything. She could dissect their conversation for the next year and still have trouble figuring it out. It didn't help that he held her so close, they were practically shrink-wrapped. There was no hiding her tension or ignoring his erection against her lower back.

"No rush? The hell there's not. I want to get to the marina where I can focus one hundred percent of my attention on you all night long."

Storm might as well have zapped her with a stun gun. Everything in Bree's body perked up. This was so not good.

The trip back to the marina didn't take nearly long enough. Before she knew it, Storm had the mainsail down, backed the boat into the slip, and tossed ropes to the men on the dock. Storm cut the engine and removed the key.

All Bree heard was water gently lapping against the

side of the boat, a distant clang of metal on metal, and the beat of her heart.

Storm walked past her. "Wait right here. I'm going to grab another bottle of wine."

"Why?"

"Why not? It's not as if we're driving, and I thought we could talk now that we're done fighting."

Bree was intoxicated enough just being around Storm; she didn't need to drink any more, but she couldn't very well say so.

Luckily he hadn't waited for a response, disappearing belowdecks and popping back up in no time. He wasn't gone long enough for her to get her bearings, but the way things were going that could take days, maybe weeks.

Storm handed her a glass of wine and sat beside her on the cushioned bench seat, drawing her close. He clinked his glass to hers. "Your turn. Make a toast."

She'd prefer wishing on a star—at least then she could keep it to herself. "Here's to Pete's health."

Storm looked disappointed but drank to it. "So, tell me why you got involved in the Revitalization Committee."

Thank God for safe topics. "My dad." She looked away from Storm and stared at the lights of the city. "My dad worked so hard to clean up the streets of Red Hook. He always said he did it for me and my mom, but even when I was a little kid, I knew how much he loved the community. He and Pete grew up in Red Hook, and he hated what had happened to his home. He wanted to make it better, and being a good cop was the only way he knew how to do that."

"So you're doing this in your dad's memory?"

She looked at him and thought about it. "Yes, it was

the only way I knew to stay close to him. Does that make sense? It was the reason I got involved, but that's not the only reason I've stayed involved. I got to know the people of Red Hook. I saw how much the committee could help, and I love being a part of something bigger than myself. The committee is making a huge difference in the lives of so many—it's very gratifying."

"Your dad would be really proud of all the work you've done." He kissed her temple. "I know Pop is. You really are amazing. You always were."

"Pete's easy."

"Yeah, maybe. After all, he's proud of me and Slater and Logan too. But you're his favorite. Plus, after last night, you and I both know I'm not easy, and you've impressed the hell out of me."

She leaned into Storm and kissed his cheek. "Thanks, that means a lot to me. You mean a lot to me." He really did, a fact that scared her but excited her at the same time. She reined in her emotions; it was safer to stay on topic. "I'll be happy if we can get the Harbor Pier Project off the ground. It would make a huge difference, bring in new businesses, jobs, a park. It will make that section of the waterfront a real destination. It's going to be great, provided I can get the zoning board to go along with the change."

"I'm sure you will."

She sank deeper into the cushion, letting the rocking of the boat and the wine lull her. "I hope so. I've worked for three months on the proposal. It's about as good as it's gonna get."

"I have all the confidence in the world in you."

"What about you? What are you passionate about?"

"Other than you?"

She rolled her eyes and took a sip of wine. "Other than me."

"My business, and a few years ago I started designing Class 40 racing yachts. It's a real challenge, and I'm having a good time with it. I have a few contracts, and I'm hoping to expand. Other than that, all I can think about is you."

Bree wasn't sure if it was Storm's kiss, or the way he looked at her as if she were the most precious thing on earth. Maybe it was the way he held her, his heartbeat racing under her palm, or the romantic setting, but it was getting easier and easier to ignore that little voice in her head telling her it was definitely time to cut and run. She put her empty wineglass down on the table and stood.

"I'll just go down and get my bag. Did you call the driver?" Maybe things would be clearer once she got back on dry land.

Storm followed her below. "I did. He'll be here first thing in the morning."

"What?" She spun around, clutching her purse, and ran right into Storm's chest. "I can't stay here with you."

"Sure you can." He drew her into his arms, ran his hands down her back, and nuzzled her neck. "I've got it covered. Rocki's babysitting; she'll call if there's a problem." His kiss was soft, almost pleading, and so mind-meltingly hypnotic, she couldn't think. All she could do was feel his fingers sliding over her backside, pressing her against him, his breath flowing into her lungs and filling her with wonder, his tongue teasing, tempting, tormenting. She reached up, encircling his neck, and her feet left the floor. She instinctively wrapped her legs around his waist.

"God, Breezy, you feel so good." Storm shifted his

hands, lifting her until his erection nestled between her thighs, and then it was her turn to groan.

Bree opened her eyes and stared into his. She saw so much—lust, hope, fear, and something more. Something she couldn't label, but whatever it was, it attracted her like nothing she'd ever seen. Storm might as well have been at the helm again—he was strong, certain, driven. His mouth was sure on hers, demanding, overpowering her senses as he carried her out of her safe, stifling existence and threw her right into the center of something so wonderful, terrifying, and all-consuming, she could do nothing but hold on. Her heart battered against her ribs, and nerve endings she didn't even realize she had came to life.

Storm slid her down his long, hard body until her toes curled into the plush carpet. She opened her eyes, surprised to be in the main stateroom. "What are we doing here?"

"Breezy, if I have to tell you"—he undid the tie at her waist—"I'm definitely losing my touch."

"I think your touch is working just fine."

Storm slipped the top button on her bodice through its hole, his knuckles sliding between her breasts and stealing her breath.

"I thought you didn't want me."

He closed his eyes as if in pain before resting his forehead against hers. "I didn't want to be your temporary boy toy, but I want you more than I want my next breath. God help me, I always have." He opened his eyes, looking straight into hers as he slowly slid the short skirt up her legs, his fingers brushing her thighs. "Let me love you, Breezy."

God, that was what she'd wanted for most of her life. His fingers slid across her panties, and her hips jerked. "You don't play fair." How could she resist him when he looked at her like that? One look at his heat-infused blue-green eyes and she was toast.

"All's fair in love and war, and with us, it's both. It probably always will be. I think it's a redhead thing."

She started to say something, but his fingers slipped under the elastic of her panties.

Storm watched Bree's face high with color, her eyes glazed and hooded, her lips red and swollen from kissing, and her chest rose and fell with short quick bursts. Visions of that night years ago floated through his mind; tonight seemed the same and different. He didn't know if they were starting anew or finishing what they'd begun. All he knew was that he had to find out if this connection with Bree was real or imagined. He needed to find out if it was as special as he remembered or if it was something he had built up in his mind all these years. He needed to find out if it would free him or keep him tied up in knots forever. He couldn't think that far ahead; right now, all he could think about was how much she'd changed and how much she'd stayed the same.

His lips traveled over her neck, zeroing in on the throbbing pulse point and nipping. He skimmed her skirt up to her waist and speared his leg between hers.

Her head fell back in invitation. He slid the dress up and over her head, tossing it on the couch behind him. She stood before him in an emerald green bra and panties.

"What's wrong with this picture?"

"Not a damn thing." Storm couldn't take his eyes off

her. She wasn't the same girl he dreamed about; she'd matured, and somehow she'd become even more perfect.

"Wrong." She slid her hands up his chest. "You have way too many clothes on." She unbuttoned his shirt but got sidelined when she kissed his neck, nipping his earlobe, sliding her tongue over his collarbone, and reaching down to run a hand over his bulge. If she didn't hurry, there'd be no reason to take his clothes off.

"The hell with it." He tugged his shirt from his pants, pulled it over his head, and sucked in a breath when she yanked on his belt. Finally.

Bree had no problem getting his pants down in record time, and the moment she slipped her hand in his BVDs, he almost lost it.

Nerves sparred with excitement, and memories collided with reality. A decade of wanting, waiting, wondering, and now they were either going to be amazed or disappointed. He didn't know which he wanted. Disappointment would be a real letdown, but that would end it. If they were as amazing as he thought they were going to be, it would seriously complicate his life.

His hands shook as they skimmed her sides, relieving her of her thong. Bree stared into his eyes, and it was like déjà vu. He slid her bra straps off her shoulders and, with a flick of his fingers, unhooked it, letting it fall along with his uncertainty, sailing straight into a category-six typhoon named Bree.

Breezy seemed as tentative as she was before, but then what did he expect? He had been down this road twice, only for it to end in disaster.

She looked her fill and then licked her lips. He groaned, and those lips spread into a seriously sexy, seductive smile. "You want me?" She pressed her palm over the sensitive head of his dick; he sucked in a lungful of air and then let it hiss between clenched teeth.

"God, yes." He grabbed her around the waist and laid her on the bed. "What do you want, Bree?"

"You." It sounded as if she forced the word out. She swallowed hard. "Naked. On the bed. Now."

Shit yeah, he had no problem with that. He ripped off the rest of his clothes, tossed a handful of condoms on the bedside table, and slid over her, feeling as if he were coming back to a home he'd never known but had always dreamed of. He eased onto her, letting her take his weight, seeing how they'd fit, his hands molding her breasts as his mouth ate hers, taking her breath, her taste, her scent, familiar and yet new—just like Breezy. The girl she once was and the woman she was now melded into one in his arms, in his mind, in his heart.

Fear slammed into him. She raised her hips to his and opened her eyes; he saw his fear reflected in hers.

He closed his eyes, kissing her and laving at that spot on her neck where her blood thrummed beneath his lips. His heart hammering against hers, he settled between her legs, his erection pressed against her heat. It took every ounce of self-control to keep from moving. One thrust and he'd be home, deep within her. Home, the one place he'd searched for his entire life. Home with Breezy.

Storm ripped the condom package with his teeth and rolled the rubber on. He kissed her as he'd been dreaming of for years, a full-body kiss, his heart pounding beneath her hands, his tongue stabbing its way into her mouth, hot, hard, demanding, and she gave it back tenfold. Sinking her claws into his shoulders, she wrapped her legs around his waist, and he slid into her heat. God, he didn't think he'd ever been squeezed so tight.

He stopped and kissed her lips. "Breezy, look at me."

When she opened her eyes and stared at him, he wasn't sure if he was seeing pleasure or pain. The only thing he knew was she wasn't as experienced as he'd thought. She might not be a virgin, but she sure as hell felt like one. He had to make this right. He couldn't screw this up. "Relax, baby. Let me in."

"It's been a while." She sucked in a stuttered breath. Not good.

Staying stock-still, he kissed her and soothed her until she relaxed around him. "That's it, Breezy. I'm gonna make it so good for you, for us." He slid in a little farther and pulled out, and when he heard her sigh and felt her moving beneath him, he finally breathed. He let her set the pace, all the while holding his control by a tenuous thread.

With every thrust of his hips, she took him in deeper, her muscles gripped him like a vise, and her gasps and moans sent him into overdrive. When her heels dug into his lower back and she rolled her hips, every muscle in his body tensed.

He'd never had a problem holding back before—he was good for as long as it took, but then he'd never been with Breezy. It was time for emergency measures. He slipped his hand between them, teased her bundle of nerves beneath his thumb, and took one of her nipples into his mouth, sucking hard in time with every thrust of his hips. Her moans turned into screams increasing in volume, her back arched off the bed, and her eyes opened wide. Increasing the pressure with his thumb, he worked the nipple between his teeth, his hips pistoning.

Bree exploded around him, her inner muscles gripping him and pulling him deeper, and when she screamed his name, he released her breast and rode out her orgasm before joining her. Every move she made amplified his climax until he was wrung out and collapsed on her. He knew he should roll over to take his weight off her, but he was unable to do anything but huff like a four-pack-a-day smoker.

Damn, he'd had a lot of sex with a lot of different women, but he'd never had sex like this.

No other woman moved him the way Breezy did.

No other woman tested his patience and his endurance the way Breezy did.

No other woman ever scared the hell out of him the way Breezy did.

When he was with her, she made him feel whole and alive, and when he wasn't, something seemed to be missing. It had been missing for so long, he'd forgotten he'd ever felt it—whatever *it* was. Storm had a very bad feeling that Pop was right. That elusive *it* had another name—love. Storm had fallen in love with Breezy.

Bree had no words to describe how exceptional sex was with Storm. No wonder people became sex addicts: If sex with Storm was always this good, addiction to him was a real and present danger.

She hadn't expected the avalanche of emotions. She wasn't prepared and wasn't sure she knew how to handle them.

Storm was supposed to be that wild-boy-toy-hot-spring-break kind of entertainment, not the oh-my-God-rock-my-emotional-world-and-tilt-everything-I-thought-I-knew-about-sex-so-far-off-its-axis-I'll-never-be-the-same-again love of a lifetime kind of man.

The way he touched her, the way he tasted her, the

way he focused all of his attention on her, making her feel cherished, fragile, adored, scared the crap out of her. But it also made her realize that she wanted to do the same for him. The biggest shocker was that she didn't just want him for the moment. She wanted him for-ever—and Storm wasn't a forever man.

She held on to him, afraid if she let go, he'd disappear, just as he always had in her dreams. She really didn't want to wake up clutching a pillow to her chest. Still, this was different. In her dreams, their stomachs never imi-tated suction cups stuck together with sweat; she'd never before felt as if her limbs weren't receiving signals from her brain; and in her dreams Storm never wormed his way into her soul as well as her body.

The connection she felt with Storm scared her more than anything in her life. Maybe it was better that they never had sex before; she was sure she wouldn't have been able to handle it then. Hell, she wasn't sure she could handle it now.

Storm groaned and flipped over onto his back, pulling her on top of him. She slid farther down on his erection— and it was still an erection, which shocked her. She thought that after a guy came, it deflated.

The movement sparked a cluster of little aftershocks. She caught her breath and tried not to moan. Maybe he hadn't come. Maybe he wasn't done. Maybe he was tak-ing a breather. She thought he'd come, his neck and face muscles delineated, his whole body tensed. He said something like "Fuck yeah, Breezy." But then what the hell did she know? The three times she'd had sex lasted maybe five minutes if she added them together.

Emotions ricocheted through her like the balls in a pin-ball game. She hadn't been prepared for his size—he wasn't quite porn-star material, but he was close. She hadn't been prepared for how long sex lasted, and she sure as hell hadn't been prepared to come like a freight train barreling out of control down the side of a mountain. She'd made herself come before, plenty of times—it had been ... pleasant. Comparing those orgasms to one with Storm was like comparing putting Mentos in a bottle of Coke to an eruption of Mount St. Helens. Pleasant certainly didn't fit the bill and, when added to her mental state, mind-blowing didn't cut it either.

"You keep moving around like that and I won't be responsible for my actions." Storm appeared to be in pain.

She hadn't realized she'd been rocking her hips. Storm's big hands gripped her, holding her still as he thrust one more time, setting off a new set of zingers a hell of a lot stronger than the last. She rocked forward, and her pelvis pressed against his, hitting that perfect spot. Rocking back and forth, she rolled her hips and grabbed his shoulders to keep from flying apart. She was so wanting to please him.

"Go for it, baby; make yourself come."

All that came from her mouth was a keening moan, as strong hands gripped her hips, pounding into her while she rocked. "Oh God!" She looked into his eyes, and the connection hit her again, leaving her emotionally drained and limp like a rag doll strewn across his chest.

When Bree's mind began functioning, she realized three things. First, Storm was peppering her shoulders and neck with kisses. Second, his hand was lazily tracing her spine, up and back, soothing, hypnotic, and, the way he slid his fingers to dip into the crack of her ass, just a little naughty. Third, he was still inside her and still not deflated. If anything, he was bigger than during round two.

What the hell had she done wrong? She was a failure at sex—even primates were better than she was. God, could a person die of embarrassment?

"Breezy? What's wrong? Your body is tighter than a drum all of a sudden."

"Nothing." She just had a soul-stirring, emotional life-altering experience, and he hadn't even been physically satisfied. She kept her head against his chest to avoid looking at him and tried to disengage herself, but his hands held her hips, making movement impossible.

Storm flipped them over, grabbing her hands and pulling them up beside her head. He held his weight on his elbows and stared straight into her eyes. "Don't do this. Don't pull away from me now. Don't shut me out, dammit." He didn't let up; he didn't blink; he just stared, demanding, hard, irascible.

Her face heated, and she blinked back tears burning her eyes. "I'm just no good at this. I'm sorry. I thought maybe it was everyone else, but no, it's me." She tried to move away from him.

"I've got you good and trapped. That's not going to change until you tell me what exactly *it* is you think you're not good at. Be specific, Breezy. I'm a guy, not a mind reader, and I need to know what the hell you're talking about. We've got all night."

God, he was so damn annoying. Couldn't he just let her die of embarrassment in peace? No, he had to twist the knife. "Sex. I'm a sexual pariah."

"Who the hell told you that? I'll kill him." And he looked mad enough to.

"No one. I have a brain, Storm. You didn't come. If

you had, you'd have ... Well, it would have deflated and it didn't; it hasn't, and it's still pretty hard."

Storm laughed, a deep belly laugh.

This was just getting better and better. He must have noticed her expression, because he stopped and pasted on a serious face. It took a while.

"Breezy, if you didn't notice me coming, it was only because you were having such a good time yourself. It was all I could do not to come the second I got inside you. You seriously tested my control. I came so hard, I thought my head was going to blow off from the pressure."

"You did?" She stared into his eyes, searching for the truth. "You're not just saying that to make me feel better?"

"Breezy, you're amazing. Hell, we're amazing together."

"Well, how come ... I mean, is it normal for you to stay that way?"

"What way is that?" He couldn't stifle his cocky grin.

She had a feeling she would be perpetually red faced around Storm. She didn't talk about sex to anyone. Hell, she hadn't had sex in over eight years, and the few times she had, there was nothing worth discussing. "Hard, engorged, turgid, tumescent."

Storm chuckled and nuzzled her neck, nipping her ear, which seemed to be hot-wired to her nipples. "God, Breezy, I love it when you talk dirty."

She smacked him on the shoulder. "Answer the question."

Storm pushed himself up on his elbows, which pressed his pelvis against hers. She sucked in a breath as more heat speared her nether regions. Shit, she didn't even know what to call it.

He shot her a satisfied look, knowing full well what he was doing to her. Thank God someone did, because she was clueless. It would have been like the blind leading the blind—which might have been why her past sexual encounters were so disastrous.

Storm was fighting to keep a straight face, but his eyes were laughing. "No. It's not normal, but I have a feeling that with you, normal doesn't exist. I've been a walking hard-on since you cracked me over the head with your frying pan."

"I didn't know it was you."

"If you had, you'd have made sure you did more damage."

She shrugged. "Maybe."

"There's something about you, Breezy. I wasn't this bad when I was a horny teenager—and believe me, I was bad then. With you, everything is different."

"Right, I know I'm not very—"

He kissed her, stopping her from pulling the lack-of-experience card.

"Listen to me. It's never been like this before."

She didn't want a line and started to say so, but he covered her lips with a finger.

"Not like this. With you everything is better, more intense, more beautiful, more fulfilling. I've had a lot of sex, Breezy, but I've never made love to anyone but you."

Bree didn't know what to say to that. He made love to her? He'd felt it too?

Storm's face fell; he must have expected a reaction. A blank stare obviously wasn't cutting it. He grabbed the edge of the condom and slid out and off her, gave her a quick kiss, and walked naked to the bathroom.

She took a deep breath and wondered what to do

now. A whole list of possibilities presented themselves, beginning with getting dressed real quick and running, and ending with following him into the bathroom. She settled on curling up and closing her eyes. Could he be thinking of staying? She was too afraid to even go there. It would be better to be happily surprised if he wanted to stay. Still she did her best not to picture Storm leaving and taking her heart with him.

A few minutes later the bed dipped and Storm slid in beside her, pulled her against him, and spooned her. "If we talk about whatever's bothering you, you might actually be able to sleep instead of pretending."

Tension rolled through her. "I'm not pretending. I'm resting my eyes."

"Sure you are."

She rolled over, exasperated. He wore a big smile, and another part of his anatomy was happy again ... or should she say still. She raised an eyebrow.

"I can't help it."

"What are you smiling about?"

"I was picturing your expression, which explains both the hard-on and the smile—at least part of it."

"What's the other part?"

He pulled her closer, rested her leg over his hip, and placed his hand on the base of her spine. "I was also thinking of cuddling up with you." He had free rein of her body, touching, stroking, discovering and hell, igniting—not that it took much. Within two minutes she was melting against him.

"Is this cuddling or foreplay?"

He slid his beard against her nipple, and she sucked in a lungful of air. Damn, the man knew just what to do to discombobulate her. "It's whatever you want it to be."

He seemed up for either or both.

Storm caught her nipple with his teeth and slipped his hand between her legs. Her hips rose to meet it. "Foreplay it is."

Bree thought she was quite imaginative when it came to fantasizing about sex with Storm, but she'd never dreamed of an orgasmic marathon. She tried to catch him, but he slipped out of her grasp, and when his mouth joined his fingers, she was too busy riding the big "O" roller coaster to do anything but scream and hang on.

God, she floated down, realizing she had landed back in his arms, his ever-present erection pressing against the thigh she'd tossed over his.

Once she recovered the use of her hands, she ran them over his chest, which, she had to admit, was one of the nicest she'd ever seen. The man could work as a cover model — washboard abs and all. She let her fingers do the walking and stepped down each ridge of his stomach, moving her thigh out of the way, giving her a clear path to her target. She slid her mouth over one of Storm's flat nipples and reached for Mr. Happy, when Storm stopped her progress.

Bree released his nipple with a pop. "What? Are you the only one allowed to cuddle?"

"No."

She smiled at the way Storm choked the word out. For the first time in her life she felt sexually powerful and in charge. It was a heady experience.

She curled her fingers around him and again was so fascinated by how hard and smooth it was. She slid farther down the bed and wondered if she was doing it right; Storm appeared to be in pain. She peered at him as she nuzzled his erection. "If I do anything you don't like, just tell me to stop."

He groaned, but it didn't sound like an I'm-not-enjoying-this groan—just the opposite.

"Bree, you don't have to."

She wasn't quite sure what she was going to do, but he seemed so on edge that it might not matter. She slid closer and looked over the top, right into Storm's eyes, and smiled. "Oh, but I want to. Don't worry. I'm not a complete novice." He grimaced, and she almost laughed. "With YouTube, there's nothing you can't learn. I just wish I'd paid better attention. Of course, at the time I thought I had as much chance of being in this position as I had of being hit by an asteroid while walking nude in Times Square." She took a swipe over the head with her tongue.

"YouTube?" he croaked.

"Uh-huh. I watched *Blow Jobs for Dummies*."

# CHAPTER 14

Storm held Breezy while she slept and wished his brain had an ON/OFF switch. His mind reeled with the implications of what had happened between them—implications he'd never before associated with sex. Words like *love* had never spun through his mind.

Breezy wasn't having the same problem. She slept like the dead.

He'd thought when he finally said the "L" word—even in the making love context—he'd get a reaction. Something. The porpoise-in-the-fishing-net look she'd sent him was not on his list of possibilities, but then Breezy was nothing if not surprising—case in point, *Blow Jobs for Dummies*. She'd proven to be an excellent student. Damn—she'd definitely blown his mind.

The sex was exceptional and Bree certainly seemed to be happy with that part of their relationship, but he wasn't dumb enough to think that just because he was making love meant she was too. He hadn't the first clue what she felt about him.

He blew out a frustrated breath. How in the hell was

he supposed to know if she was making love to him, or just using him?

"Are you always this cheerful in the morning?" Bree's bright green eyes stared at him while he'd been gazing into space.

He pulled her in tight, and her eyes widened before he kissed her, long, and slow, and deep. "Oh yeah, you can count on me always being this cheerful whenever I wake up with you." He didn't mention that he wanted to do that every morning from now on. No, that would scare her away.

"You sure didn't sound happy. Angry or frustrated was more like it."

"I was thinking about work." She knew he was lying— he could see it in her face—but she didn't call him on it.

"What time is it?" She rested her head on his shoulder and tossed her arm over his chest.

Damn, it felt so natural. She fit against him perfectly like no one ever had or probably ever would.

"Almost nine."

"What?" She grabbed the sheet and would have jumped out of bed if he hadn't held her.

"Calm down. I called Rocki earlier and everything is fine." Oh man, she looked like she wanted to kill him. He figured it was safer if he let her go.

"Fine?" Bree slid out of bed, pulling the sheet with her. "I have responsibilities, appointments—" She snatched her dress off the couch where he'd thrown it and found her bra on the floor. "I have to put in a liquor order, and I can't find my underwear."

Storm got out of bed, slid his arms around her, and smiled. So okay, he'd taken her thong and stashed it in his jacket pocket. "If you're trying to make me regret last night and this morning, it's not working. I'm not going to complain about your going commando. Damn, Breezy, just knowing you're walking around without panties is enough to make my whole month. I'm sorry about the appointments, though; I didn't know."

"It's my own fault. I should have set an alarm. I can't believe I slept so late."

Storm tried not to smile too much. "You may have slept late, but you didn't get much sleep."

Bree turned bright red and pressed her hot face into his neck. "God, I'm so not good at this morning-after thing."

He kissed her shoulder. "You go ahead and get dressed. I'll call the driver and make coffee."

She gave him a kiss and smiled. "Coffee sounds great. Thanks. I'll be out in just a minute."

She turned and ran to the head while he pulled on his clothes.

He heard the shower and was tempted to go and join her, but thought she'd appreciate breakfast more than another round of sex. He was fixing an omelet when she came out carrying an armful of sheets. "What are you doing?"

"Cleaning up and trying to find my underwear."

He tossed the filling on one side of the omelet and slid it under the broiler, shaking his head. "Bree, Thomas has a cleaning service. You don't need to do that."

"He does?"

"Babe, if a guy can afford a ten-million-dollar boat, he can afford to pay people to clean up after us."

She sat down on the closest couch. "Ten million dollars?"

"Yeah."

"U.S. dollars?"

He handed her a cup of coffee, gave her a quick kiss, and went to finish cooking.

"How did you and the owner get to be such good friends that he'd loan you his boat?"

"I don't know. He saw some of my designs and liked what I did, but he had some definite ideas about what he was looking for, especially in the interior. He wanted a home away from home. We went back and forth with e-mails, plans, phone conversations, and we got to know each other pretty well. Thomas flew out to Auckland for the sea trials and spent some time in the area. We've been close ever since."

"What if we crashed or something?"

"It's insured. And Breezy, I don't crash boats."

"No, you capsize them."

"That wasn't my fault. Hell, I was sleeping when that happened."

"Still, it happened."

"I wouldn't have taken you out in a gale. We were perfectly safe and so was the boat. What's the problem?"

"Nothing, I guess. It's just so different from what I'm used to."

"It's definitely a change from Red Hook." He set their omelet on the table and sat beside her. "But sometimes change is good."

She cut a bite of food and looked over at him. "Do you own a boat?"

"No, I don't."

"Wow, you're a much better cook than you used to be. So, how come?"

"How come I'm a better cook, or how come I don't own a boat?"

"Both."

"I'm a better cook because I like to eat. As for not having a boat, I don't know. I'm always sailing, doing sea trials, and racing, so I've never really felt the need; plus owning a boat is a big commitment."

"And you shy away from commitment."

"That's not true. I just take my commitments seriously. Maybe I haven't committed because I've never wanted anything or anyone badly enough before. Like I said, sometimes change is good."

Bree got out of the car, doing her best not to pull a Britney Spears, and cringed when she spotted Daniel Knickerbocker pacing the sidewalk. He was the last man she wanted to see while she was sans undies.

Daniel whirled on her and she took a step back. His hard eyes took too long looking her up and down, and then he licked his lips. Most people would think that was sexual, but Daniel reminded her of a Komodo dragon, flitting his tongue before he struck. "We had a ten o'clock appointment."

Arms crossed, nostrils flared, legs spread, Storm stood beside her, tension radiating off him. He didn't say a word. He didn't need to.

Bree's eyes went from Storm to Daniel. "You're right. I'm sorry I'm late. It's completely my fault." She dug through her purse for her keys and unlocked the outer door. "Daniel, why don't you wait for me in the bar. I'll just be a minute."

"I'm finished cooling my heels. I'm sure whatever you have to do can wait."

Storm stepped in front of her, blocking Daniel. "No, it can't. Bree will be down in a minute. You can wait in the bar, on the sidewalk, or you can leave." Storm took her keys, unlocked the door to the bar, and returned them to her. "Go on up, Bree. I'll wait here with your friend."

"Thank you." She had an awkward to-kiss-or-not-to-kiss moment. She chose the latter. Storm didn't look happy about her decision. She just wished she knew if it would pour gas on the fire the men had going, or extinguish it. Still, she wasn't willing to take the chance, so she ran up the steps holding her skirt down, feeling two sets of eyes on her ass.

Bree managed the world's fastest clothing change and was back in the bar wearing her usual business attire in less than three minutes.

The empty bar.

Well, empty except for Storm. "Where's Daniel?"

Storm didn't bother turning around. He met her eyes in the mirror. "Daniel left."

"Why? What did you say to him?"

Storm finished wiping down a bottle of rum, pulled down the next bottle, and turned toward her. "Care to rephrase the question?"

Bree pressed her nails into her palms. "Would you just tell me what happened?"

"Your friend Daniel is interested in more than a business relationship with you. He told me to leave you alone, and I told him to go to hell—nicely. I don't share."

Bree closed her eyes. and when she opened them, Storm was still staring and still angry, and damn sexy in a slightly Cro-Magnon way. "This is just great. I prefer to keep my private life private. I work with Daniel, and my personal life isn't his business."

"I don't like him."

"That's neither here nor there. The fact is, I have to

deal with him, I was late, and your getting into a pissing match with him doesn't help matters."

"What would you have me do? He told me to back off. He said you two were dating."

"I can handle Daniel."

Storm laughed. "From what I saw the other night, Daniel was the one handling you. I don't want him alone with you. I don't want him close enough to touch you. I don't trust him."

"You don't have to trust him, but you should trust me. If you don't, last night was a mistake." She turned toward her office when Storm jumped the bar and cut her off. Only Storm could piss her off and impress her at the same time—he even nailed the landing, but he didn't look happy about it.

"You don't throw a bomb like that and just walk away. Bree, let's talk." His jaw clenched, and the muscles in his neck bulged.

Bree's gaze strayed down to see if anything else was bulging, but it was hard to tell. If she didn't know better, she'd think he put it in the downward dog position just to avoid a zipper tattoo. She raked her hands through her hair, trying to get her mind back on the PG track and set some limits. "It's not a bomb, Storm. It's a fact. I have a business relationship with Daniel. I work with him. I've been handling him for over a year. I don't need a body-guard, a chaperone, or a jealous lover."

Storm took a step closer—close enough for her to catch a Storm-scented breath. "It's more than business if he's bringing you flowers, warns me off, and asks you out every chance he gets."

"How do you know that?" She was too shocked to

even deny it, not that she would, but damn, a girl was supposed to have some secrets.

"Nicki told me. She also told me that every time he comes in here, he tells her to get lost."

"She never said anything to me. . . ."

"Yeah, well, kids like Nicki would rather not know what your reaction would be. She's been told to get lost all her life, Bree. It would kill her if you did too."

"I would never . . . I didn't know." How could she not know? How did she miss that? She wrapped her arms around herself to ward off a sudden chill.

"I know that and you know that, but Nicki doesn't. I told her if Daniel ever said it again, to come and get me — I'd tell him to get lost. I don't want him around her, Bree. I don't want him around either of you."

"I would never let anything happen to Nicki."

Storm stepped closer, wrapped his arms around her, and rested his chin on the top of her head. She burrowed in. "I know that, babe, but you can't be everywhere. He's told Nicki more than once to take off. She's afraid of him, and the kid has great instincts. You're going to do what you have to do. I'd just appreciate it if you did it in a public place. I don't trust this guy, and I'm not blind. I knew you were about a minute away from taking him out the other night. You were channeling your inner Buffy. If Francis hadn't stepped in, you would have decked the asshole."

Bree blew out a breath. It really sucked that Storm was right. "Okay, I'll agree to be careful, and I'll arrange to have any meetings with Daniel in public, but don't think this changes anything. I'm a big girl, I can take care of myself, and I'm more than capable of decking Daniel should the need arise. You of all people should know that."

"Just be careful, Breezy. Your purse isn't big enough to hold a cast-iron skillet."

She couldn't resist, so she reached up, wrapped her arms around his neck, and kissed the smile right off his face.

Storm was just about to drag Bree into the back room, when their kiss was shattered by applause. Shit.

"Well, hot damn. It's about time." Francis pulled Bree out of Storm's arms, hugged her, and then smacked him on the back so hard, if Storm hadn't been prepared, he would have flown into the bar.

Bree's face turned as red as her hair.

"Great timing, Francis. You couldn't wait until I finished kissing her to applaud?"

"Hell no. You were ready to pick her up and carry her to the back room. Don't deny it. Been there, done that— only with Patrice, and I got two of the prettiest little girls to show for it."

If Francis's grin got any bigger, his face would split in half.

"I'm here to do inventory, so you two—carry on."

Like that was going to happen. Not with the embarrassment coloring Breezy's face.

Francis went around the bar and started counting bottles, ignoring them.

Bree rolled her eyes. "I'd better go place the liquor order, and you need to relieve Rocki. Pete's probably driving her nuts."

"Right. So I'll see you later?"

"I'm meeting with distributors today. I should be done in time to make dinner."

"I'll handle dinner—just be home by six." He gave her a quick kiss good-bye and watched her rush to the office. When he heard the door slam, he turned to glare at Francis behind the bar. "Great timing, Frankie."

"Shit, man, next time put a sock on the door or something."

"You couldn't quietly leave, or go back outside and give me a little warning?"

"I'll remember next time."

"You embarrassed the crap out of Bree."

"I wasn't the one with my tongue down her throat and my hands on her ass. So, your date went well?"

He turned around. "How do you know about our date?"

Francis shrugged. "Patrice and Rocki are friends, and the CIA could take lessons from my wife when it comes to interrogation techniques."

"I assume she already knows about the kiss."

"Yeah, I had to text her if I didn't want to spend the rest of the week sleeping on the couch."

"Shit, Francis. Why not put it on YouTube?"

"Come on, man, you know how it is. My couch is too short to sleep on, and I've got a bad back."

"Oh yeah, I know exactly how it is. Patrice has you so wrapped, you're on the verge of turning in your man card."

Francis smiled. "Takes one to know one, my friend, and you, like me, are loving every minute of it."

Storm left with a smile on his face; he couldn't help it. By the time he reached the apartment, the smile had disappeared. He opened the door and overheard Pop calling Rocki Nurse Ratched. D.O.G. let out a bark, tackled Storm, and licked half his face before he could get him to stop, and Nicki had the TV turned up to ear-splitting levels.

"Stop." D.O.G. hit the deck. Storm grabbed the remote and muted the TV. "Pop, behave and take your damn medicine." He heard Pop grumble something just before Rocki came out of Pop's room, walking like a model down the runway—except Rocki smiled and gave him a thumbs-up.

"Where's Bree?"

"In the office doing the liquor order."

Rocki rubbed her hands together. "Oh good. I'm assuming the date went well."

Storm rocked back on his heels. "Oh yeah—"

"Wait." Rocki held up her hand. "I want to be surprised."

"About what?"

Rocki waved. "Oh, don't you worry your gorgeous head about it. Have fun with your patient. D.O.G. ate about fifteen minutes ago, so you and Nicki had better take that boy for a walk. Pete's due for a nap, so he should be fine. I'm outta here."

"Rocki, do me a favor—go easy on Bree. She's not exactly comfortable yet with the idea of us together." And the last thing Bree needed was an inquisition.

"You think I don't know that? Geez, Storm, give me some credit, will you? I'm on your side. I think you're just what the doctor ordered."

Storm wasn't even going to ask what she meant. "Yeah, well, thanks for staying. I owe you."

"Don't worry. I'll collect. Just you wait."

Great, he could only imagine what Rocki would want to collect.

"Storm, get your butt in here."

Pop. Storm cringed and went to face the music. "You bellowed?"

Pop had a smile on his face when Storm stepped into the room. "I take it your date with Bree was a success."

Damn, he still didn't want to talk to Pop about Breezy. "We worked things out if that's what you're asking."

"I hope so since you spent the night with her. The only question in my mind is, what are your intentions?"

"Pop, Bree's an adult."

"She's like a daughter to me."

"And I'm your son."

"If you break her heart again, Storm, I'm going to have to hurt you."

Storm looked at Pop sitting propped up in bed. He wished the old man were strong enough to hurt him. "You don't have anything to worry about, Pop. If anyone's heart is going to end up broken, it will be mine." He turned on his heel. And wasn't that just the berries. Pop laughed, and Storm stopped and rested his hand on the doorknob before looking over his shoulder. "I'm going to take D.O.G. and Nicki for a walk, and then I'm going to try to get some work done. Behave yourself, old man."

Storm opened the door, only to find Nicki slinking away. "And just what do you think you were doing listening in?"

"Duh." Nicki rolled her eyes. "Listening in."

Storm gave himself a mental head smack. "It's bad manners to eavesdrop."

Nicki shrugged. "It's your own fault. You're the one who muted the TV. What else was I supposed to listen to?"

Damn, how was he supposed to compete with that logic? When he was Nicki's age, if he had been put in the same position, he would have done the same damn thing or worse. He tugged on her ponytail. "Get D.O.G.'s leash. We'd better take him for a walk before he has an accident. How about I give you your first drawing lesson, and then you can draw while I work."

"You're really going to teach me to draw?" Nicki tilted her head as if trying to figure out whether he was serious or not.

"I told you I would, and I always keep my word." She didn't look as if she believed him, but then if he had been Nicki, he wouldn't have believed him either. It seemed like Nicki was a smaller version of himself—only female, but not trusting people to keep their word wasn't necessarily a gender issue.

He called the dog and snapped the leash on his collar. "Let's go buy you a new sketchbook and some decent pencils. It's a beautiful day, so then we'll walk to the park and get started."

If he was going to make any headway with the two women in his life, he was going to have to prove himself—starting today.

# CHAPTER 15

Rocki banged through Bree's office door, which, unfortunately, was not surprising. The woman never met a door she didn't want to break down.

Bree didn't even need to look; she just stuck a finger in the air while she finished her daily phone call with Logan. She looked at her watch; Slater was due to call any minute. She had half a mind to just tell Logan to call Slater with the daily update on Pete, but she didn't. The two of them were worried sick about Pete, and for some reason calling her made them feel better.

Rocki had already made herself at home and had her legging-clad leg draped over the arm of the chair. Her orange toenails peeked out of what looked like the shoes Cinderella would wear if she took to hooking.

*That neon orange top should clash with the pink in Rocki's hair, shouldn't it?* Bree thought about it and decided it didn't, which was slightly disappointing, along with the fact that Rocki was the only woman alive who could wear those fake jean leggings and not come out looking like an overstuffed, lumpy scarecrow. Life just wasn't fair. Whenever they were in the same room, Bree felt like she faded into the wallpaper whereas Rocki stuck out like the Megatron in Times Square. Bree hung up the phone, took a deep breath, and met Rocki's eyes. "Okay."

"Wow, that was amazing. I deserve a gold star."

"Why?" Bree flipped through her wine list and looked over the week's specials—surf and turf and prime rib. She made a note to order an extra few cases of Mulderbosch Cabernet Sauvignon Rosé, which would pair perfectly with both.

"Because I waited."

"Nicki can wait longer than you. It's not necessarily something to be proud of."

Rocki looked at her compact and messed up her hair more than it already had been. "Sure, compare me to a ten-year-old after all I did for you."

Bree rested her elbows on her desk. "You set me up."

"And your problem is?"

"I didn't want to be set up."

Rocki fixed her lipstick, checked her teeth, and snapped the compact shut. "Oh sure you did; you just thought you didn't. I knew what the inner Bree needed and I gave it to you—and just between you, me, and your battery-operated boyfriend, you needed to get laid in the worst way. Speaking of which, it's fortune cookie time."

"Not again." Bree considered beating her head against the desk; unfortunately, it was so covered with paperwork, it was almost padded.

"Spill, girlfriend. I tell you all about my conquests."

"Only to torture me."

"Yeah, but that's just a perk."

Bree checked her watch. "I wish I could share"— which wasn't really a lie, not that she ever would, she just wished she could—"but it's a crazy Monday. I have a lunch meeting I can't be late to, and then I have liquor salesmen coming in all afternoon."

Rocki rose and put her hands on her hips. "A lunch meeting with who?"

"Daniel Knickerbocker. I was supposed to meet him this morning, and I was late. He wasn't happy. I went upstairs to change. When I came down, Storm was here and Daniel wasn't. God only knows what was said. So now, I not only have to go over everything I had planned to cover in the meeting, but I also have to smooth things over with Daniel."

Rocki made a face.

"Hey, I don't have to like Daniel; I just have to work with him, and Storm needs to deal with it. Just because we . . . You know—"

"Had amazing, crazy, wild, hot monkey sex?"

"Just because Storm and I are seeing each other doesn't mean anything has to change."

"So does that mean you didn't have amazing, crazy, wild, hot monkey sex?" Rocki stared at her, and a smile broke over her serious face. "You so did. Tell me everything."

"No." Bree was sure her face was the color of a Jersey tomato. "Something happened between Storm and Daniel while I was upstairs."

"I knew you were making a big mistake when you threw Daniel in Storm's face the other night. It serves you right. You broke dating rule number one: Never date a man with a high creep factor. FYI—Daniel's is off the charts."

"It wasn't a date."

"Oh yeah"—Rocki tapped her finger on her chin—

"where have I heard that before? Oh, I remember, last night before you went out with Storm Decker and got your groove on. Girlfriend, we really need to talk about the definition of the word *date*. It seems the only one who thought you weren't on a date with Daniel was you."

Bree groaned. "I went on one date with Daniel six months ago. It didn't work. I told him it didn't work, and I told Daniel the first time he asked me to the fund-raiser that we would go as colleagues. It's not my fault he's incapable of taking a hint."

"And now you're meeting him for lunch? It's no wonder he's confused. You're giving him mixed signals."

"I am not. This is the only time I have between now and the zoning board meeting on Wednesday night."

"Can't someone else on the committee take this meeting?"

Bree wished. "No, Daniel and I have been working on this proposal for months."

"Okay," Rocki said, opening the door. "Don't forget that Daniel's been working just as long trying to separate you from your panties. Think about how he must feel knowing that Storm waltzed into town and ripped them off you in only a few days."

Bree stood and stuffed a file in her briefcase to follow Rocki out and wondered again what became of her underwear. "Daniel doesn't know that."

"Maybe, but now I know I was right." Rocki turned around and looked her up and down. "Earth to Bree. Daniel was on the sidewalk when you pulled up in a limo with Storm this morning, wearing the clothes that spent more than a few hours on the floor, and you think he didn't notice?"

"You think he did?"

"Everyone noticed, Bree. Not to be crude or anything, but you have that just-got-fucked-within-an-inch-of-your-life look about you."

Bree brought her hands to her heated cheeks. "I do?"

"Yeah, and you really need to talk to Storm about shaving more often or you're going to have perpetual beard burn. Now get before you're late meeting Daniel."

Bree checked her watch again. "Shit. I'm going to have to make a run for it." She ran the two blocks to the Hope and Anchor, slowing to a walk as she turned the corner.

She wiped her brow, opened the door, and thanked the good Lord for air-conditioning. She was sweating like a whore in church. Sheesh. Of course Daniel was already seated, drinking his water with lemon, and looking as if he'd just stepped out of a boardroom. He stood when she approached the table and made a point to check the time.

"I'm sorry about this morning, Daniel." She sat and pulled the file with the proposal for a change of zoning out of her briefcase.

"Where were you?"

She didn't want to say it wasn't his business, which it wasn't. She was thankful to be saved from answering when the waiter stopped and set an iced tea on the table for her.

"I ordered our drinks when I arrived."

Bree took the lemon out of her tea and smiled at the server. "Thank you. I'll have the blue cheese sandwich with watercress and fig jam on Italian bread and a cup of gazpacho."

Daniel looked at her as if he smelled something bad. "I'll just have the Red Hook Burger, well-done."

The server took their menus and disappeared.

Determined to keep this meeting all business, Bree handed Daniel a copy of the proposal she'd spent the last three months preparing. She had every question answered, all the t's crossed, and all the i's dotted. "I thought you would present the proposal to the committee and then we could both take questions."

"No." He patted her hand and smiled.

Bree couldn't believe what she was hearing. Whenever there was a way for Daniel to get in the news, he was always front and center, not that Bree cared. She was more than happy to stay out of the spotlight. After all, she was doing this to improve Red Hook, she was doing this for her dad who died protecting the people in his hometown, she was doing this to fulfill her destiny. This wasn't about her. Daniel, on the other hand, thought the world should revolve around him.

"Breanna, I think it's best if you give the presentation. I'll be there for moral support, of course, as will the rest of the committee."

"Excuse me?" She took a sip of her tea and cleared her throat; a niggling feeling prickled the back of her neck. Daniel wasn't the type to let someone else hold the mic if there was one in reach. He wasn't the type to fade into the woodwork either. No, he could smell the digital pixels of a camera and made sure he was front and center. And Daniel Knickerbocker sure as hell wasn't the kind of man to sit back and let someone else take all the glory if he could snatch it away—unless he had a reason. "Daniel, we've been working the last year on this project, and now you're throwing me to the sharks?"

"I'm doing no such thing. You know this neighborhood, the committee members, and you know what we need to do to get our point across. You're well liked and highly respected, although your behavior for the last few days has me perplexed. Still, I think it's important for you to get the recognition you deserve."

"I'm not interested in recognition, only results. There's so much riding on this."

"Our lawyers think we should have no problem with the zoning board. Everyone wants another park. It will give all the tourists from the cruise lines and everyone who swarms like ants to Ikea another destination spot."

She wasn't buying it. "It still doesn't explain why we're not making a united front. We're heading up the fund-raising committee, the community relations task force, and the business association. Now you want to sit in the back of the room and give me moral support?" She rested her folded arms on the table and leaned in. "What's really going on, Daniel?"

The server dropped off her gazpacho, and suddenly it didn't look very appetizing.

"Breanna," he said, his condescending, Thurston Howell III tone making her bite her tongue to keep from saying something she would definitely regret. "I know how hard it was for you to take the Crow's Nest and change it from a dive into the halfway decent restaurant and bar it is now—"

Bree's forehead tightened. "Halfway decent?" The Crow's Nest was the best bar in Red Hook, maybe the best in all of Brooklyn, and he dared to call it halfway decent?

"Well, it's hardly Sardi's, now is it?"

She took a deep breath and blew it out in a nice, easy stream and glanced around the crowded restaurant. "Daniel, we're not trying to be Sardi's. We're an upscale neighborhood bar and restaurant with excellent service, wonderful food, and great music. The Crow's Nest is a place where real people gather, not a place on Broadway where people go to gawk at stars."

"The point is, Breanna," Daniel said, sitting forward and straightening his silverware, "your boss and his sons, not to mention a few of your friends, have questionable backgrounds, and I find myself—well, let's just say, I think it's best if I don't associate with you too closely until you come to your senses."

"Come to my senses? Now wait just a minute." She leaned in and placed her napkin on the table. "My boss was a decorated cop. He's taken in and raised three wonderful foster sons who are intelligent, enterprising, and successful members of society."

"Hardly. Every single one of them has a record."

"How do you know that? They haven't broken the law since they hit puberty. Their records have been sealed since the day they each turned eighteen."

He licked his lips. "I have my sources."

"The kind you have to bribe? Or the kind who owe you money?"

Daniel's face twisted into a sneer, and he spent one too many nanoseconds assessing her boobs. "You owe me." His voice slithered over her like an oil spill. "If not for me, no one would have ever taken a no-account waitress like you seriously."

Bree sat back, lost in the incredulousness of the moment. Was he serious?

"I made you respectable, and I won't have you running around acting like a well-heeled trollop while our names are connected."

Bree's face flamed. It didn't matter that what he said

wasn't true. But the lunch crowd sitting within earshot all shifted in their seats like a wave after a Rangers hat trick at Madison Square Garden. "You have one hell of a nerve." She flagged down the waiter. "Can you please pack this to go? I just remembered a previous engagement."

"Certainly." The waiter picked up her gazpacho and went to the kitchen pretty damn quick.

"Breanna." Daniel reached across the table and grabbed her elbow with crushing strength.

Bree yanked her throbbing arm out of his grasp so fast, she almost knocked over her chair. She gathered her things, threw her bag over her shoulder, tipping over her iced tea in the process, and left him sitting alone at the table in a puddle.

She headed to the far end of the bar and stood beside the familiar-looking man who stared at Daniel with a look of disgust on his face.

The man shot her a smile and an I-got-your-back nod, and made more room for her while she waited for her food. "You work at the Crow's Nest, right? I'm Jack Sanders—" The guy had sandy brown hair, a nice smile, and was built like a linebacker.

"Yes, I'm Bree Collins, the manager."

"Francis is a friend of mine."

"That's right." Bree smiled and slid onto the stool next to Jack. "I thought you looked familiar."

The waiter returned, and Bree handed him thirty bucks. "Thanks, keep the change."

Jack finished his coffee, tossed some money on the bar, and stood. "Francis mentioned he was working at the Crow's Nest today."

"He is."

"I was going to stop by. Would you mind if I walked over with you?"

"Not at all. As a matter of fact, I'd love the company, thanks."

"My pleasure." Jack took her elbow, which was still sore from the tug-of-war with Dickerbocker, and escorted her past Daniel, who looked like one of those cartoon characters ready to blow his stack. Bree waited for the whistle to pop out of the top of his head.

Jack held the door for her. "That guy a friend of yours?"

Bree stepped out onto the sidewalk and turned toward home. "We're most definitely not friends. Unfortunately, we're on the Red Hook Revitalization Committee together."

"Hmm." Jack took her elbow and guided her around a woman pushing a stroller.

Bree looked up at him and smiled. "Yeah, that about covers it." She gingerly straightened her elbow and rotated it.

Jack cursed under his breath.

"It'll be fine."

"It's going to bruise. You'd better put some ice on that when you get back."

"I will. Just do me a favor—don't mention this to Francis; he's a little overprotective." And the last thing she needed was Storm finding out.

Jack didn't look happy about it but held the door to the Crow's Nest open. "If you insist, but watch your back with that guy."

"Thanks, I will. And let me know the next time you come in. Dinner and drinks are on me."

"That's not necessary, but I'd be happy to take you out if you're free some night."

Bree smiled but shook her head. "Sorry. I'm seeing someone right now, but thanks."

Jack grinned. "Always a day late and a dollar short. If that 'right now' bit changes, you let me know."

"Definitely. I'll tell Francis you're here."

She turned toward the office and ran right into Storm—again. She wondered how much of her conversation he'd heard. "Wow, we've got to stop meeting like this."

"I came to see if I could interest you in lunch, but I see you've already gone out."

The words "with someone else" seemed to hang in a cartoon bubble above Storm's head—but that could have been just her guilty conscience, not that she had anything to feel guilty about. Jack asked her out, and she said no. Okay, so she felt a little guilty about saying she was seeing someone *right now*, as opposed to just *seeing* someone—as if her relationship with Storm had an unwritten expiration date. She thought back to the way he spoke last night; she wasn't sure if that had changed or not. "Um, yes. Lucky for you I have enough to share if you want. Let me just tell Francis that his friend Jack is here; then we can go back to the office and eat."

"You go ahead. I'll get some plates and holler for Francis."

"Okay, grab some spoons too."

Bree went into the office and threw her briefcase on the couch. That went well, not. She hadn't had a date for six months, and now men were popping up like freakin' Whac-A-Moles. Weird.

She put all her papers in a neat pile and made room to eat at her desk before opening the to-go containers.

Storm came in, set down the plates, and grabbed the

arms of her desk chair before leaning over and kissing her. Damn, she could get used to being kissed like that—the kind of kiss that went from hello to nuclear in under thirty seconds, leaving her breathing heavy and wanting more.

Storm pulled away, rubbed his nose against hers, and groaned. "I've missed you."

He had? "It's been less than three hours."

"Your point?"

She didn't have one, other than shock and awe. She supposed she should say she missed him too, but she hadn't had time to think about Storm. "I've been too busy to do anything but work." Man, maybe that wasn't the thing to say either.

He took a seat, looking resigned. "I took Nicki to the park for a drawing lesson."

Bree unwrapped the sandwich and flipped off the lid to the gazpacho.

Storm leaned forward. "The kid's got her own style. I didn't know a ten-year-old could have a style, but she tells a story on the page without writing a word. She's impressive."

Bree smiled and couldn't help but think Storm looked like a proud papa talking about Nicki the way he did. He clearly cared for Nicki, and for the first time, when she thought of them together, she didn't feel the need to protect herself or Nicki. Odd.

She took a sip of gazpacho and wiped her mouth. She was happy to see Storm. She liked watching him, and listening to him, and hearing all about his day—or at least the few hours they'd been apart. "Okay, I guess I did miss you. I went to the Hope and Anchor to meet

Daniel, which was a disaster. I left him in a puddle of iced tea and got my food to go."

Storm didn't say anything. He just raised an eyebrow.

"Jack was there eating lunch and offered to walk over here with me."

The tips of Storm's ears turned red, and his jaw looked like it was throbbing. "Did Knickerbocker touch you?"

"There's a big meeting with the zoning board on Wednesday night, and we were supposed to do the presentation together. Now Daniel tells me he wants me to do the presentation, which makes no sense. Anyway, things were said. I handled it. Now I'm giving the presentation, so I think I'm through with him except for our group meetings."

"Did he touch you?"

Bree ignored the deep dark gravelly texture of his voice and stuffed her half of the sandwich in her mouth to avoid answering.

"I take that as a yes. Did he hurt you?"

She shook her head, thanked God her shirt covered her elbows, and swallowed. "Are you going to eat or question me?" She pushed the rest of the sandwich toward him and let out a relieved breath when he finally took a bite.

"I don't know what the heck this is, but it's good."

"Blue cheese, watercress, and fig jam on Italian bread. It's my favorite."

"It's probably a good thing you didn't tell me before I tasted it."

"Not the adventurous type?"

The smile he sent her made her want to fan her face.

"I was talking about food."

"Uh-huh, sure. I'm plenty adventurous when it comes to just about everything. I'll prove it tonight—"

Bree's hormones rose up and did the hula.

"At dinner." Storm stuffed the last bite of his sandwich in his mouth and looked as if he were holding back a laugh, then licked his fingers.

She planted herself right on his lap so they were nose to nose, and did a bit of her own teasing. A knock on the door had her scrambling to her feet. By the time she turned, the beer distributor stood in the open doorway.

"Sorry to interrupt."

Bree tried to pretend she hadn't been caught making out in her office and grabbed her clipboard, holding it against her chest.

"No, it's fine. We were just about finished. With lunch ..."

Storm stood, wrapped his arm around her, and gave her another kiss. Damn him. "See you at home at six. Don't be late for dinner."

"Right." She turned to face her distributor. "Gary, this is Storm Decker, Pete's son. He was just leaving. Come on in. I've got the order all ready."

The two guys shook hands, and Storm shot her a grin before leaving her to deal with work.

Bree opened the door to her apartment, dropped her bag, and found Rocki and Patrice sitting on her couch. "How did you two get in here?"

Rocki twirled Bree's spare key around on her pointer finger.

"I left that at Pete's in case I got locked out. It's not there for your convenience."

Neither Rocki nor Patrice looked the least bit ashamed of ganging up on her.

Resigned, Bree went into the kitchen and grabbed a wineglass, the bottle of wine from the fridge, and pulled the cork out with her teeth. She filled the glass, wishing she had grabbed a red wineglass—they were larger. She'd learned that with certain parts of the male anatomy and wineglasses, size definitely mattered.

When Bree turned to face the music, she found Patrice leaning against the wall.

"Are you going to offer us any?" Patrice sashayed to the counter and held the bottle up to the light. "Damn girl, is there any left?"

Bree pointed to the wine rack. "Plenty—take your pick." She went to her favorite chair, pulled her legs up under her, and stared at the door as Patrice and Rocki argued about which bottle to open. For the first time all day, Bree let her mind spin like the carousel at Coney Island. She was able to block everything out at work, and figured the only reason she'd been able to sleep last night was because Storm had literally put her in a postorgasmic coma. She secretly hoped he would do the same tonight, or she'd be toast.

Bree had never slept so well, which was surprising because it was the first time she'd ever slept in the same bed with anyone, ever. She'd never even had girlfriends sleep over. Her mother had always teetered like a four-year-old gymnast on the balance beam of mental health, so having friends spend the night was not something Bree had ever encouraged. Keeping friends as far away from her mom as possible had been the goal, and at that, Bree excelled. If not for Rocki, Patrice, and Francis, she'd have no friends at all. Listening to the two of them argue, Bree wondered if she wanted the friends she had. Okay, so she loved them, but damn, they had terrible timing.

While Rocki and Patrice fought over red or white wine, Bree did her best to get a grip. She'd believed her life had been on track, but after last night, after Storm had taken her blinders off, she saw it for what it was— stalled. It had been stalled for a long time. Way too long.

Shit, she was twenty-eight years old, she'd been out of her mother's house for nine long years. After nine years she still had only a few friends, no love life—nothing but a job. If it hadn't been for Pete giving her a home, a job, and a career she loved, where would she be?

A picture of her in her mother's house fighting the same demons her mother had surrendered to a long time ago became crystal clear. It wasn't a pretty picture, and if she was being honest, neither was Bree's reality.

Storm had been right when he accused her of being afraid to live, of being more like her mother than she'd ever imagined.

There was nothing like having a mirror held up to her face and not liking what she found there. How had she gotten to this point without noticing?

Bree looked around her cozy apartment. It was comfortable, secure, boring—just like her life. There was absolutely nothing wrong with it, but there was nothing right with it either.

It was time for a change, and it had to do with her, not Storm. No matter what happened between them, Bree was going to change her life, starting today.

She was going to go for what she wanted and not let anyone stand in her way. In the end, if Storm left again, something she fully expected him to do, she'd be fine— once she figured out how to move on. And move on she would, because after last night, she couldn't imagine ever being happy living her life the way she had before.

Storm challenged her, showed her what she could have, and made her want more — with or without him.

Rocki sat on the couch and leaned toward Bree, invading her personal space without a hint of trepidation. "I gave you a brief reprieve so you could work, but that's over. Now spill. Patrice and I have been dying to find out what Storm is like in bed."

Patrice set her wine down. "I'm more interested in what happened outside of bed."

Rocki rolled her eyes. "She's just saying that because she doesn't want Francis to know that he's not the only man on the planet she dreams about getting hot and sweaty with."

Patrice slapped Rocki without ever taking her eyes off Bree. "Where were you all night?"

Bree shook her head, determined to just get through this. "North Cove Marina. Storm borrowed a boat he'd designed." She took a gulp of wine. "I asked if he was stealing it."

Rocki rolled her eyes. "Have I taught you nothing?"

"Rocki, you would have thought the same thing. This was a ten-million-dollar yacht. It's like something you see in the movies."

Patrice's eyes were wide. "No, shit! So that's what he's been doing all these years?"

Bree shrugged. "I guess. I knew he finished college and went to the Westlawn Institute of Marine Technology, but really what does that mean? I didn't have a clue. He could have been designing tugboats for all I knew."

Rocki was obviously handling the interrogation. "You accused him of stealing a yacht? Great way to start a date, Bree. I'm surprised he didn't push you overboard."

Bree took a sip of wine and shrugged. "I apologized

after I figured it out. I didn't know why he brought me there. He said he borrowed the boat from a friend to show me who he was now. How was I supposed to know he designed it? The yacht was beyond incredible."

Patrice let out a bark of laughter. "Isn't that just like a man? He might as well have killed a big woolly mammoth and dragged it over to your cave. Times may change, but male behavior stays the same. It's sweet if you think about it. Storm's proving to you he can be a good provider."

Bree choked on her wine, and she wondered if Patrice spent too much time in the psych ward at the hospital. "Do you know Storm Decker at all?"

Patrice sat forward and hammered her. "Do you? God, Bree, this is Psych 101."

Bree laughed. "I thought it had more to do with the length of the boat as it relates to the length of his . . ."

Rocki perked up. "And?"

"Both were equally impressive, not that I have much to compare either to, but the boat was an eighty footer."

"Damn." Rocki smiled and hit Patrice again. "Didn't I tell you I had a good feeling about this?"

Bree shook her head. "Storm was wonderful, and fun, and he definitely knew what he was doing, which was nice, but that doesn't mean he's going to stay, so nothing has really changed."

Rocki sat back and studied her. "You've changed. I didn't see it earlier, and maybe you didn't either, but you've changed. You've had a taste of a top-shelf man. Face it—you want more."

"Fine, you're right, but I'm not dumb enough to think it's going to be Storm. I'm not going to pretend just because we cleared up our past and we're sexually compatible that he's going to move halfway around the world to be with me."

Patrice took a sip of her wine. "Bree, this is Storm's home. His family is here. You're here. What is waiting for him in Auckland?"

Other than probably a dozen girlfriends? "His company, his life, his future. The Godzone is his world, and Red Hook is mine. He hates Red Hook. You know, that's okay. I'll take what I can get, and then when he leaves, I'll pick up the pieces and move on. He's not the only one who wants more. I want everything too. I'm just not delusional enough to believe I can have it with Storm."

# CHAPTER 16

Storm looked over the plans of his Class 40 design before e-mailing it to the boat builder. Deadlines sucked, and this one was written in stone. If he didn't get the design in on time, he'd lose the slot at the boat builder as well as his reputation, the final payment from his client, and his company's future. Nothing like a little pressure to stress a guy out. He'd worked his whole life for this opportunity, and he was on a precipice—one false move, one fuckup, one missed deadline, and he'd crash and burn. He checked the design weight for the thousandth time—everything added up perfectly.

"What are you doing?" Nicki asked from the other side of the desk where she sketched what looked like the rocks by the pier where they'd had their first art lesson. D.O.G. slept beneath her feet. His paws twitched, and he let out muffled barks in mid–puppy dream.

Storm took a deep breath. "I'm checking my work." He turned the computer toward her. "I'm designing a racing yacht and there are very specific rules, so I need to figure out how much the finished boat will weigh. If the bulb weight is off, it would affect the whole design."

"Huh?"

"Well, think about it. If the boat weighs too much, then it will sit lower in the water, changing the mast height, which is measured from the waterline. There are rules about maximum mast height, and no one wants to buy an eight-million-dollar racing boat that won't be allowed to race. The change in weight also changes the stability and causes a domino effect. Plus, maximizing the bulb weight is the art behind building a faster yacht."

"Sounds complicated."

Storm looked over the design, splitting the screen. "Most things in life are complicated if you look at the bigger picture."

"What do you mean?"

"If you look at things from the surface, all you see is what's on top of the water, but if you look beneath the surface, you see a whole lot more, and everything below changes everything above it."

"In boats maybe."

"No, not just in boats; it's that way with people too. I understand you a lot better knowing where you come from than if I ran into you on a street corner. If I ran into you somewhere, I wouldn't see how similar we are."

"You think we're similar? How?"

Storm sat back and looked at her. "We both had parents who gave us up; we were both lucky enough to end up in a better place. Sometimes I look at you and see myself when I was a kid. We have a lot in common that you wouldn't realize until you take a closer look."

Nicki slid off her chair and moved closer, studying his face in that way she had. "You think we're lucky?"

"Heck yeah. Think of all those kids who never had a guy like Pop to steer them in the right direction, to love them, to care for them. Hell, I could have had to stay with my real parents. I'm damn lucky, and I think you are too. Would we have been better off if we were born into the perfect family?"

"Like Francis and Patrice's kids?"

"Maybe we would have been better off, but then I don't know. I've seen plenty of people who grew up with great families who can't hack the real world. We have something kids who seem to have everything sometimes never get. We're tough; we never let anything stop us."

Nicki slid closer and leaned against his side.

Storm's arm wrapped around her, and he sat her on his thigh. "Nicki, you're smart enough to rely on yourself when you have to. You listen to your gut, your instincts, but you're also smart enough to accept all the help and the love that Bree and Pop and I give you. You don't take anything for granted, and you use all the knowledge you have. You're a survivor. When you're all grown up, you're going to go places, kid. No one will ever be able to stop you because when you hit a brick wall, you figure out how to go over it, around it, or through it. That's what people like us do."

Nicki leaned into him, resting her head against his chest. "Is that what you did? Is that why you left?"

"I guess that's what I thought I was doing at the time. I might have been wrong, though. I should have talked to Pop about it. I didn't look below the surface. If I had ... I don't know." He tossed the pencil he'd been twirling between his fingers onto the desk. Maybe if he had looked beneath the surface, he wouldn't have hurt Bree.

"But you came back." Pop's gruff voice startled Nicki, and she jumped off Storm's lap and woke D.O.G.

Storm shot her a smile. "Pop always had great hearing." He didn't say anything about Pop's frequent eavesdropping even though if the shoe were on the other foot, Storm would have heard about it.

Nicki rubbed D.O.G.'s floppy ear between her fingers. "Bree didn't like you much before, but she seems to like you well enough now. Did you have fun on your date?"

"I did. I hope she did too. I took her out on a boat I designed."

"Did she look beneath the surface?"

"Maybe, but seeing and believing are two different things, kiddo."

"I know. It's like what you taught me today at the pier. Per—"

"Perspective?"

"That's it. I was thinking about what you said about seeing things from different perspectives; I guess that goes for people too. Maybe Bree is changing her perspective."

"Maybe we all are." Storm bit the bullet on his design, saved it, and hit Send. He'd gone over it enough times and could tweak the design here and there, but when it came down to it, it wouldn't get any better. It was time to let it go and start making dinner.

"What's the plan for tonight?" Pop dragged Nicki's chair farther away from the table and sat.

"I'm cooking. Bree will be here by six, and since I ate half her lunch, she'll be hungry."

Pop checked his watch and stood. "She should be back at her place by now. I think I'll go over and see her."

Storm rose too. "I don't know why you just don't wait for her to come to dinner."

"Because I can't. I'll make sure we're back by six."

Storm watched Pop walk through the apartment. He looked tired as he let himself out and rested against the wall between the two apartments before closing the door behind him.

Nicki followed Pop's progress as closely as Storm had.

Storm couldn't imagine what Pop had to talk to Bree about that would chase him out two days after he came home. He just hoped it had nothing to do with him. "Okay, Nicki, I've got to get dinner started. Let's clean up our mess, and then maybe you can help."

Nicki wrinkled her nose. "I'm not much of a cook."

"Well, neither am I." At least not heart-healthy stuff. He grabbed the recipe he'd picked up at the Fairway Market and read it. "But hell, if I can design boats, I should have no problem following a recipe, right?"

"I guess. How old were you when you decided you wanted to design boats?"

"I don't know. I've loved boats ever since I can remember. I used to go down to the water and watch them whenever I could sneak away from my house. I always thought if I could just get on a boat, I'd be free."

He didn't tell her he was trying to steal one and run away the first time Pop had caught him. "When Pop took me in, he bought an old sailboat that was falling apart and we stripped it, fixed it all up, and made her seaworthy again. Pop taught me how to sail. That was when I knew what I wanted to do for the rest of my life. I wanted to design sailboats and race them." He'd never thought about it before, but he owed Pop for so much more than just taking him in. He owed him for showing him how to use his passion for boats constructively. Storm owed his father everything.

"Maybe I can be a boat designer too."

"You want to be a marine architect?"

"Yeah, that." Nicki wrinkled her nose. "'Cause I know I don't want to be a cook."

"That makes two of us. Yet if we want to eat, we've got to cook. So what do you say we give it a try?"

At the sound of the knock, Bree's heart banged against her ribs. It had been hours since she'd seen Storm. Just picturing the way he'd look when she opened the door had her running. Maybe he needed to borrow a cup of sugar, or maybe he just wanted to kiss her senseless again. Either way, she couldn't get to the door fast enough.

She wrenched it open, only to find Pete leaning uncomfortably against the wall; he looked like hell. "Are you okay?" She wrapped her arm around him and led him to her chair.

"I'm fine. Would you stop hovering?"

"Hey, I'm not the one who looks like a zombie from *Dawn of the Dead*."

Patrice and Rocki both stood. The deserters that they were took off with a cheerleader's wave.

Pete watched as the girls left, as if waiting for them to be alone before he said anything. The click of the door was like a ringing of the bell in a prizefight. "I was worried about you. You've made yourself scarce since Nicki brought home her furry friend."

Bree sat beside him and clasped her hands between her knees to keep from touching him. His color wasn't good, but then it could be from walking through the apartments; he'd only been home two days.

"Storm told me you're afraid of dogs."

"Wasn't that nice of him?" Bree didn't bother to hide her sarcasm. "I suppose he told Nicki too. It's one thing to look like a wuss in front of the two of you, but I really don't want Nicki to think I'm—"

"Human? God, Bree, you don't have to be anything more than you are for Nicki, me, and Storm to love you. But don't worry. I'm sure Storm hasn't said anything to Nicki. He means well, you know. The only reason he told me was because you disappeared and I was worried about you."

"I'm fine. What's this about?"

Pete pulled his robe around him and shivered.

"Are you cold? Do you want me to turn up the thermostat?"

His hand on her knee stopped her from jumping. "No, I'm fine." He shot her a tortured look, rubbed his forehead, and then slicked back his hair with a shaking hand.

"Calm down. I'm sure we can work out whatever it is." She didn't have a clue what was wrong, but it must have something to do with Storm.

"I see the way you and Storm dance around each other. I don't pretend to know what happened between you two before Storm took off, but whatever it was hurt you both."

Bree let out a relieved breath. "It was a long time ago. And we're working through it, getting to know each other again. We've buried the hatchet and are seeing where to go from here."

"It must have been one hell of a big hatchet. I'm not blind, Bree. It didn't escape my notice that Storm went out of his way to avoid seeing you all these years."

"He said he came home, but you never mentioned he visited."

"Whenever he came home, you were away at school. Probably by design. He didn't come home nearly often enough, and for whatever reason, he made me promise not to mention it to you."

Bree didn't say anything and didn't bother pretending it didn't hurt. If what Storm said last night was true, she wasn't the only one afraid. She must have really scared the hell out of him.

"Storm said your date went well."

"We did get a lot of things worked out."

"You spent the night with him, Bree. I was hoping things went beyond burying the hatchet."

"It did, but it's confusing. You know how he feels about Red Hook. And Red Hook is my home."

"It's Nicki's home too."

"Of course it is."

"So you spent the night together and didn't talk about the future? For two people who have no problem communicating with everyone else, you sure do a crappy job with each other."

Bree winced. Most of the fault for their lack of communication rested squarely on her shoulders—something else that she would have to change. "Tell me about it."

Pete took her hand and squeezed. "Bree, it's important that Storm stays here now. I hoped you'd tell me you think he's back for good."

"He said he'd stay until you were back on your feet and able to take care of Nicki by yourself. We haven't talked about anything beyond that."

"That's the thing. Nicki should have more than just me taking care of her."

Pete was beating around the bush again. She'd never seen him like this in all the years she'd known him. She faced him and covered his shaking, cold hand in hers. "What are you not telling me?"

"I hope to God I'm doing the right thing telling you this. When I took Nicki in, I thought I had plenty of time—"

"Time for what?"

"Time to get things settled. But then I had the heart attack. I need to know Nicki will be taken care of should anything happen to me."

"You don't have to worry about Nicki. I'll always be there for her."

"I know you will." Pete put his arm around her and kissed her temple. "And I love you for it, but Nicki needs at least one of her parents."

"Don't tell me you're going to try and contact her mother." Rage she hadn't known existed boiled to the surface. She had to move. She brushed off Pete's arm and paced the room, trying to calm her temper before turning back to him. "Pete, the woman abandoned her. She left Nicki with a total stranger. She hasn't even tried to contact her in the three months she's been with us."

"I'm not going after Marisa. Bree, I'm talking about Nicki's father."

Bree felt as if her legs wouldn't hold her any longer, and her stomach ended up in her throat. She sank into the couch beside Pete. "You know who her father is?"

"I have an idea. A possibility. A few possibilities, actually. Marisa used to work as a waitress at the bar when the boys were all still home."

Bree's scalp tightened, and fear of whatever it was Pete was having such a hard time spitting out raced through her with every beat of her heart. It was something bad enough to shake the once-unshakable man she'd known her whole life. She took a deep breath. "Okay."

"I thought if Storm was planning to move back here, it would be easier to talk to him about this. Bree, when Marisa left Nicki with me, Nicki was hysterical. Marisa was halfway out the door when she said I was Nicki's grandfather and that Nicki would be better off with me."

"If you're Nicki's grandfather, who did she say Nicki's father was?"

"She didn't. She took off. It could be a lie for all I know, but then I suppose it could be any one of my boys."

"And you think it's Storm?" Bree hadn't realized she'd said it aloud until Pete shook his head and ran his hand through what was left of his hair.

"I'm not sure. If I remember correctly, Logan had a girlfriend back then, and Slater had his head stuck so far into his computers, I don't think he discovered women until after he went into the navy."

Bree wrapped her arms around herself. "You think Storm is Nicki's father?"

"I don't know how to ask him." Pete scrubbed his face with his hand. "Bree, when Storm left, he wasn't supposed to have joined the merchant marines for another few months. He ran away. He left the hemisphere on the first ship he could get out on. I never would have thought he'd run out on his own child, but I think the idea of being a father could have scared the hell out of him."

Bree looked into Pete's pain-filled eyes. "Storm told me he left because of me."

"Do you believe him?"

"I did. I had no reason not to."

"Until I told you what Marisa said. Shit. This was a

mistake. I thought with you and Storm getting closer, you'd have a better handle on how he might react to this. I thought . . . Aw hell, I thought if Nicki was his, that you and Storm would finally get your shit together and—"

"Do what, Pete? Storm might be here now, and we're seeing each other, but that doesn't change the fact that everything—his life, his business—is in New Zealand."

"His family, you, and Nicki are here."

She was on the outside looking in again. Bree went back to pacing. "You can't tell Nicki until you know for sure. You need to talk to Storm."

Bree's mind raced. Storm could be Nicki's father. That couldn't be bad, could it? Nicki loved him, and from everything she'd seen, Storm was falling hard for Nicki too. She looked into Pete's rheumy eyes. "What are you afraid of?"

Pete shook his head. "You probably don't remember what Storm was like when he first came to me. Bree. You don't know the kind of abuse Storm suffered."

"Abuse? I thought his parents were dead and that you fostered him after you caught him stealing a boat."

"I caught him, all right. I caught him and returned him to his parents." Pete was quiet for a long time, seemingly lost in the painful memories. Regret and guilt rolled off him in waves. "After I'd left them, his father went after him with a tire iron. It was my fault. Storm begged me not to tell his parents. I knew he was scared; I thought it was because he'd been caught. His father almost killed him."

"Oh, Pete. You had no way of knowing—" Bree wanted to comfort him. The pain in his eyes amplified the rawness of the regret in his voice.

"Sure I did. I should have taken him back to the precinct. I should have gone by the book. If I had, I would have seen the history of domestic disturbances and emergency room visits. Broken ribs, a broken arm, black eyes, a bruised spleen . . . His medical file was the size of the New York phone book. When I saw it, I thought I was going to be sick. But I liked the kid. By taking him home, I thought I was doing him a favor. Kids make mistakes; I wanted to cut him a break. I heard the domestic disturbance call less than a half hour later. When I arrived, it was all I could do not to shoot the bastard who fathered him."

"Pete—"

He waved away any platitudes she may have given him. Storm hadn't been much older than Nicki when Pete took him in. Her heart broke for the little boy he'd been and the man she loved.

"I did the only thing I could do to make it right, to make up for failing him. After he got out of the hospital, I made sure he never had to go back to his parents again. I worked the system. I took him in. I was responsible for him."

"You loved him."

"How could I not? He didn't have an easy time of it, Bree. He ran every chance he got. Every time he did something wrong, if I so much as raised my voice, he'd run. By the time he hit sixteen, I thought he'd stopped running all together. Until that night. He ran again, and I'm not sure why.

"If Marisa had told him she was pregnant, he may very well have run. Not for himself, but to protect the child from the monster he thought he might become. Even if he's not Nicki's father, the idea of fatherhood is going to bring up all kinds of painful memories for him."

"Oh God. But since he ran, he's grown up. He's responsible, an adult; he's made something of himself. He's not that scared boy anymore."

Bree blinked back tears. Bree loved Nicki and wanted to protect her from the hurt that gets buried so deep, there can be no digging it out. She wanted to protect Storm. She wanted a family with Storm and Nicki—she wanted it all.

She'd thought she'd had no illusions. She'd thought any illusions she once had were shattered years ago. She'd thought wrong—the ringing in her ears was the sound of her last illusion shattering. Bree cleared her throat, hoping she wouldn't sound on the verge of falling apart. There would be time enough for that later. "Maybe Nicki's not his. Have you talked to Logan? If anyone would know what happened back then, it would be him."

"No, I haven't said anything to any of the boys. None are in a position to take on Nicki right now. Well, maybe Storm—if he doesn't rabbit again, but Logan and Slater aren't, and I can't hit them with this over the phone. Hell, they can't leave work. Both their careers depend on their finishing their commitments."

Pete stared at his hands. "Nicki comes off like a tough kid, but she's fragile. I need to be the one to tell them, Bree. Nicki is my grandchild in my heart if nothing else. She's my responsibility, my family."

"Okay." And once again, she was on the outside looking in.

"Then it's decided. I'll talk to Logan when he comes home. Maybe he'll know if Storm and Marisa were together."

"I don't like it, but as you said, it's your decision." She didn't like it at all, but this wasn't her family. It was Pete's.

*    *    *

Storm helped Nicki set the table and looked up when Pop trudged through the door. "Where's Bree? Dinner is almost ready."

Pete looked like he'd aged a decade since leaving not twenty minutes ago. Storm pulled out his chair and helped lower Pop into it. "Are you okay?" he asked under his breath.

"Would you stop asking me that? Damn, you'd think I have one foot in the grave. I'm fine."

Storm put his arm around Nicki, who seemed to shrink into herself. "It's okay, Nicki. Why don't you wash up? Bree will be here in a minute." Storm waited until he heard the bathroom door close. "Give it a break, Pop. You look like shit."

"Yeah, well, what the hell do you expect? I just got out of the hospital. You look like shit too, and all you have to complain about is missing a good night's sleep."

Storm held on to the end of the table and bent to eye level. "I don't know what crawled up your ass today, but you'd better cut it out. You're scaring Nicki, and so help me, if you do anything to screw up what Bree and I have going, I'll kill you myself."

Pop raised an eyebrow and looked pleased.

"Are you pulling that reverse-psychology crap again? It didn't work when I was a kid. It's not going to work now."

"Really? It seems to be working just fine. But if you want to keep Bree, you had better tell her things have changed."

"I don't want to scare her away. Hell, I've been home less than a week. Rome wasn't built in a day."

"No, but it burned in one. She still thinks you're going to leave as soon as you can."

Storm shrugged and went into the kitchen to check on the salmon; he had to step over D.O.G., who was sprawled out on the linoleum floor, in the way of everything. Storm was stirring the rice when Bree came into the kitchen looking a little pale, and skirted the dog. He gave Bree a quick kiss. "Are you feeling okay?"

"I'm fine."

The flat tone of her voice had Storm doing a double take.

"What can I do to help?"

He shrugged, hoping he was imagining things, and handed her the pot of rice. "Just put this in a bowl. I have everything else covered." He took the asparagus out of the microwave and tossed it on the platter next to the salmon. It wasn't pretty, but it was definitely edible.

Bree stared at him, holding the spoon. She looked as if she were a million miles away.

"Do you need some help with that?"

"What?" She looked at her hand as if she'd never seen a spoon before. "Oh no. It's fine."

Something was definitely up. He took everything out to the table and served Pop and Nicki—who wore identical faces of discontent.

Nicki took her fork and pushed a piece of fish away. "What is it?"

Storm laughed. "If you'd helped with dinner, you'd know. It's salmon."

"It's fish?"

Bree brought the rice to the table, and Storm held her chair for her. "Yes, Nicki. Salmon is fish."

"I don't like fish. Neither does Pop."

Bree scooped some rice onto her plate and then

served Nicki before handing it to Pop. "Lox is fish, and you like that."

It was obviously news to Nicki.

"Take an adventure bite. You know the rules."

Storm shot Bree a sideways glance. "An adventure bite?"

"Yes, everyone has to taste everything on their plate. They don't have to eat it, but they do have to try it." She shot Pop a pointed look. "Isn't that right, Pete?"

Pop made a good show of it for Nicki's benefit and took a bite of salmon. He chewed and seemed pleasantly surprised. "It's not half bad, Storm. What did you say you put on it?"

"Maple syrup, ginger, garlic, and soy sauce."

Bree dug in and made all the appropriate noises. "It's great. Thanks for cooking." She looked from him to Nicki. "Nicki?"

"Bree, I've tried fish. I don't like it."

"You haven't tried Storm's fish, so you might as well get it over with."

Storm held back a laugh. "Thanks for the vote of confidence." He knocked Bree's knee with his, and she just about jumped out of the chair. Good thing Nicki was working so hard avoiding the fish; she didn't notice, but Pop did.

Bree's gaze darted from him to Nicki and back again. Storm couldn't figure out what the hell was going on.

Nicki finally tasted her food and said it wasn't terrible. Which was good enough apparently for her to take seconds. Bree didn't eat much; she was more interested in moving her food around.

When dinner was finished, he cleared the table and

took Bree by the hand. "Come on, we're going for a walk."

"You go ahead." Bree dug in her heels. "Nicki needs a bath, and I need to do the dishes."

"Nicki." He stared at Bree. "Bree and I are going to take D.O.G. for a walk. You hit the shower."

"But I want to watch TV."

Storm didn't break the connection. "After you take a shower, you can watch TV. We'll be back in a little while, and I'll take care of the dishes." He picked up D.O.G.'s leash, and the dog sprang to life, causing Bree to jump. "He's not gonna hurt you. He just likes our walks. You will too; you'll see."

Bree didn't look like she was buying it.

Storm got the puppy down the stairs without breaking his own neck and waited for Bree to join them. He pressed her against the wall, kissed her within an inch of her life, and then rested his forehead on hers. "Now, do you want to tell me what's going on with you and Pop?"

"Nothing I can talk about, so please, let's just drop it." She moved to kiss him again, but he pulled away and led her and D.O.G. out the door, keeping her hand in his as he scanned the block.

"If something is bothering you, Breezy, I'm the one person you should always be able to talk to. About anything. That's part of the deal."

Bree stopped to look in the window of a new art gallery and watched his reflection in the glass while D.O.G. sniffed the telephone pole. "What deal?"

Storm pulled her against him and looked into those bright green eyes of hers, the ones he'd dreamed about for the last decade. "Bree, we're together. When you're involved with someone, you share things, or at least you're supposed to."

"Do you share things with your other girlfriends?"

"I don't have other girlfriends."

Bree laughed. "You mean to tell me you don't have a flock of women you're dating in New Zealand? Come on, you've been here less than a week, and after one night at the bar, they were following your every move."

"Jealous?"

"No, just observant."

Storm gnashed his teeth and did his best not to lose his temper. "Okay, if this wasn't made clear last night, we'd better correct the situation. We're together—"

"For now."

"For however long we're together, there will be no other girlfriends or boyfriends, no other lovers, period. You're mine and I'm yours and that's the end of it. Agreed?"

"That's hardly a problem for me."

She might as well have said, "But it's a problem for you." It wasn't, but he didn't think Bree would believe him. He didn't mention he'd heard that guy Jack asking her out earlier, or the way he felt about her "I'm seeing someone right now" answer. In Bree's mind he was temporary, and that didn't set well with him.

Maybe she needed time. Time to see how good they were together. Time to learn to trust him. Time to get used to being a couple—not that he knew the first thing about being a couple. He'd never been part of anything, but if there was one person he'd like to figure it out with, it was Breezy. After seeing the way Pop looked when he returned to the apartment, the one thing Storm could count on was that he would be in Red Hook for a while. He just hoped it was long enough.

They walked in awkward silence for a few blocks until D.O.G. wrapped them in his leash. Storm had never been so grateful for the mutt's lack of training. He took Bree's hand to help her out of the quagmire, and he thought it was a good sign when she didn't drop his hand after they were free of the leash.

Breezy took him on a tour of the neighborhood, showing him the new restaurants and stores that had opened up in the time she'd been on the Revitalization Committee; talking about the owners, the menus, and the artists, who seemed to be turning Van Brunt into Gallery Row; and introducing him to everyone she knew—almost everyone they met. They strolled toward the Fairway, the evening wind whipping her hair around as they passed the market and walked out onto one of the piers where more artisans set up shop.

The sun was going down and there were still people milling about. That was something that didn't happen when he last lived there. People used to think twice about walking in broad daylight—dusk or night was out of the question.

Seeing this part of Red Hook with Breezy, Storm hardly recognized the place he'd spent much of his youth in. He hardly recognized the girl he'd known in the vibrant, beautiful, self-assured woman she'd become. He hardly recognized the man he was when he was with her. With her, he wanted to be that man. The man she wanted. Her man.

They stopped and shared a piece of cannoli cake at the Fairway's outdoor café and talked about the Revitalization Committee's plan for Red Hook. They bought a water for D.O.G., who had yet to master drinking from an open cup, and got more water on Storm than he drank, and relaxed.

When the place started emptying out, Bree picked up their trash and stepped over a lazy D.O.G. She was starting to get more comfortable with the mutt. "What now?"

"We go home." Storm wrapped his arm around Bree's waist before giving D.O.G.'s leash a tug. "This is nice." He leaned in and stole a kiss.

Bree's hand was on his chest, and she smiled up at him. "It is. We haven't had one argument."

But she still hadn't told him what was the matter, and whatever it was, he could still sense her tension. Storm didn't think it was the dog.

"Did you get a lot of work done today?"

"Not as much as I would have liked. I did get the plans sent to the boat builder for a new Class 40. When I get back, I need to call the office and have Sandy e-mail me a few contracts. I have to plan my work schedule since I'll be doing it from here instead of my office."

"Is that manageable?"

"I miss my drafting table and my desktop computer, but I can work from just about anywhere. It's a good thing. This is a busy time for me."

"I thought the winter months would be slow."

"Oh no, this is when everyone is planning and building the boats they want to race during the summer. At least in Australia and New Zealand, which are about sixty percent of my business."

"And the rest?"

"Thirty percent European and ten American."

"You build boats in the United States?"

"No, we build them in Auckland, do the sea trials there, and then ship them over on a freighter. With the New Zealand dollar, it's still cheaper than building them here. It's handy; sometimes I have to go to the boat builder if there's trouble." They went inside and up the steps. Bree turned to go to her place. "You're not coming in?"

"I wasn't planning on it, why?"

Was she serious? Damn, he'd spent the entire day reliving every moment they'd spent together—every kiss, every touch, every look. "You weren't planning on staying with me tonight?"

"You were?" She even looked shocked.

"Hell yes, I've been waiting all day to get you alone again." He dropped the dog's leash and pulled her into his arms.

She was tense and stiff for a second and then relaxed.

He brushed the hair from her face. She was holding something back, but he didn't have a clue as to what it was. He'd hoped to weasel it out of her in bed after she was satisfied and sleepy. "So, what's it gonna be, your place or mine?"

"What about Pete and Nicki? Someone needs to be there in case something happens, and we can't sleep together with them right there."

"We're adults, Breezy, and Pop knows we're together."

"Nicki doesn't."

Storm figured Nicki knew a hell of a lot more than Bree suspected, but he wasn't about to tell her that. "We'll make sure we get up before Nicki does, and you'll have to be a little quieter. Not that I don't enjoy hearing you scream, but I wouldn't want to be the one to explain that to Nicki." Bree blushed so fiercely, he laughed. "Don't worry. We'll sneak off to your place every now and then, and I promise to make you scream as much as you'd like." God, he loved that a twenty-eight-year-old woman could still blush like a schoolgirl. Making Breezy blush was his second-favorite thing to do. He tipped her chin so she couldn't avoid his gaze and put all kidding aside. "I just want to make love to you and hold you all night long. Stay with me from now on."

Her eyes widened, and she thought about it long enough to make him sweat. "Yes." Then she kissed him, and he was lost.

# CHAPTER 17

Bree escaped Storm, telling him to text her after Nicki went to bed. She stood in the shower and let the hot water run over her head while she tried to wrap her mind around everything that had happened: Daniel calling her a whore and telling her the only reason she got on the Revitalization Committee was because of him; Pete telling her Storm's history and that he could be Nicki's father; Storm acting like this thing between them was more than a fling and her heart agreeing with him. Next came the thought of Storm leaving her, leaving Nicki—Bree's heart ached from one virtual body blow after another. Okay, so Storm hadn't dealt her a blow—but as wonderful as he seemed, she couldn't help but wait for it. Telling herself to live, enjoy Storm while he was here, and not worry about their future was a hell of a lot easier in theory than in practice.

Was it really possible? Could Storm be Nicki's father? Had Storm slept with Marisa instead of her eleven years ago? She'd spent the entire dinner looking for a family resemblance between Storm and Nicki and found none. Still, Bree was the spitting image of her mother and had looked nothing like her dad. There was no resemblance except in personality, but she and her dad had a special connection. Nicki had taken to Storm right away.

She rested her head against the cool tile wall, letting the hot water soothe the aching muscles in her neck and shoulders while visions of Storm, Nicki, and her as a family floated through her mind. She loved them both and didn't want to lose either of them; yet she felt them slipping away. If Nicki was Storm's, they would be a family, and, as usual, Bree would be outside looking in, not really a part of anything, not fitting in, not enough.

The shower curtain was yanked open, and Bree gasped, spinning around to see Storm grinning at her. She covered herself, or tried to. The fluorescent lighting wasn't doing her any favors. Her wet hair lay in stringy clumps around her shoulders, and if any makeup was still on her face, it was running like a racehorse down her cheeks.

"Hey, is there room in there for one more?" Storm's gaze traveled from head to toe and back again; then the corner of his mouth quirked up. "I could spend a lifetime looking at you. You're so beautiful."

The man was clearly insane. Bree knew what she looked like. She wouldn't scare small children, but she was hardly beauty-queen material. But that knowledge didn't seem to matter. The heat in Storm's eyes had all systems firing; with one look he took her to that dangerous place she'd been trying to avoid. One look and he had her body and her heart welcoming him.

He was already pulling his T-shirt over his head and kicking out of his Top-Siders.

The air-conditioning chilled her overheated skin, goose bumps covered every square inch of her body, and she shook as she watched him lose his pants.

He was tan, ripped, and hard—everywhere. "Are you going to answer the question?"

She had no idea what he was talking about. What question? But no words came out of her mouth.

"Can I come in?"

She still stared.

"In the shower, can I join you?"

"Oh," she said, running her hand over her wet face in the hope of wiping away any residual mascara, wiping away the tears, and wiping away the signs of her tumultuous emotions. She stepped back under the shower spray. "Of course."

When Storm stepped into the shower, the oversized tub she'd loved so much shrank. She'd never showered with anyone before. He drew her to him and kissed her before pulling back and looking into her eyes. He nudged her back under the water and ran his hands through her hair before pulling her out of the spray and depositing a dollop of shampoo on her head. He stilled her hands, turned her around, and lathered her hair, massaging her scalp. "Have you gotten everything figured out? You were in here for fifteen minutes before I came in. Are you okay, Breezy? I can't help if you don't tell me what's wrong."

She pressed her palm against the cold tile. "It's just . . . nothing and everything." She puffed her cheeks out and released a slow I'm-at-the-end-of-my-soap-on-a-rope breath.

He looked her up and down. "Shit, what's this?" He wrapped his hand around her forearm and pulled it toward him, staring at the bruise.

She'd forgotten all about it. "It's nothing."

"That's a handprint-shaped bruise, Breezy. It's definitely not nothing. Did Dickerbocker do this?"

"Yes, and I handled it. I told you."

"You didn't say he hurt you. I asked, remember?"

"I said I handled it. Please, let's just change the subject."

"Are there any other subjects we're not supposed to talk about? If there are, I'd better make a list."

"No, dammit. Storm, in the last week I've had the rug pulled out from under me more than a few times—with you, Pete, the Revitalization Committee and Daniel, not to mention D.O.G. I'm trying to get a grip and not doing a very good job of it."

"How can I help?"

"You can't." The words came out as a defeated sigh. "But thanks for asking. It's something I have to deal with on my own. There's so much that's up in the air, I'm sure after the zoning meeting, things will settle down on that front at least."

"Pop is doing better."

"He is, and before you know it, Logan will be home."

Storm turned her around. "Is that what this is about?"

Bree rinsed her hair, and after she wiped the water from her eyes, she couldn't miss Storm's anger. "Why are you glaring at me? I just stated a fact. Logan will come home, and you'll be free to leave."

Storm took a menacing step toward her. "I thought you were done with wishing me away to Auckland."

Bree felt the hold on her emotions slip down the drain with the cooling water. She took a shuddered breath and lost the battle with her tears. Her shoulders shook. "I love you, Storm." She looked away from him and stared at the white tile wall. "I probably always have, but I'm not depending on you or anyone else for my happiness anymore." She wrapped her arms around herself to keep from shaking. "You were right last night when you said I was afraid to live." She snuck a glance in his direction and then lost her nerve and stared at the tile wall again, with tears running down her cheeks like rain. "I've been surviving, not living. Then you step back in my life and change everything. You changed me. I realized so many things. I'm determined not to go back to living a half life, with or without you. I have no control over whether you stay or go. I can only control my actions." She filled her lungs to steady herself and stared him straight in the eye. "And that's what I'm determined to do."

He pulled her into his arms and did his boa constrictor imitation again. "You love me?"

She pressed her forehead against his shoulder and wished she'd kept her mouth shut. "You sound a whole lot happier about it than I am."

"I was afraid I was the only one falling in love in this relationship. At least we're in the same boat."

"Let's just hope it's not the *Titanic*."

Storm wasn't too happy with the *Titanic* allusion. But since their first time around was a big disaster, he wasn't too surprised Breezy wasn't jumping for joy over the realization. "She'll be right, you'll see."

Bree raised her gaze to his, her eyes shiny. He wasn't sure if it was from her tears or the shower water. "There you go, sounding all Kiwi again. It's not helping."

He wasn't sure anything would help, except maybe a good night's sleep, so he got her out of the shower as quickly as he could, dried her off, and watched her put on another pair of ridiculous pajamas before they went back to Pop's place.

The apartment was quiet and he turned out the lights as they made their way to their room.

Bree stood just inside the door. "What if Nicki gets up in the night?"

Storm hadn't bothered putting his shirt back on. Hell, it and his boxer briefs were probably still on Bree's bathroom floor. "Does she usually?"

"No."

"We'll lock the door." And he did exactly that. "Besides, Nicki always knocks before she comes in here. I laid down some ground rules the first time she walked in on me shaving."

"She walked in on you?"

"I was wearing a towel, so it could have been worse, but we made a deal to respect each other's privacy." He took Bree's hand and pulled her away from the door before she ran. "Come to bed. You didn't get much sleep last night." Which might explain why she was so upset. Lack of sleep on top of a stressful day couldn't be helping matters. He turned the bed down and pulled up her T-shirt.

"What are you doing?" she whispered.

He pulled it the rest of the way off. "Getting you naked."

"These are pajamas." Bree reached for her top.

He tossed it over her head onto the chair before he slid down her shorts and panties. "And they're really cute, but unnecessary. The only thing I want you to wear to bed is me."

She slid into bed, pulling the top sheet around her chest as if they hadn't spent the last half hour together naked, as if he hadn't explored her entire body with his mouth, as if they hadn't had the most amazing sex of his life several times in the last twenty-four hours.

He tugged off his pants and got in beside her, knowing that she needed to sleep, not make love. Still, he pulled her into his arms, spooned her, and wondered if he'd ever be able to sleep with her, just sleep. His hand rested on her belly, far enough away from the breasts he wanted to hold and the thatch of curls he wanted to explore, and did his best to keep his raging hard-on from touching her. It was going to be a long and painful night. He kissed her bare shoulder. "I love you, Breezy. Get some sleep. Things will look better tomorrow."

She flipped over, pushed him onto his back, and went nose to nose with him. "Get some sleep?" she hissed, her eyes flashing like fire in the light coming off the street. "You drag me to bed, strip me naked, tell me you love me for the first time, and now you expect me to sleep?"

He tried to sit up, only to be pushed down again. "I was trying to be understanding. You're exhausted. You've had a tough day."

"I'm not tired; I'm frustrated, Storm. The last thing I need is to lie here and think."

Okay, she was pissed, and he was confused. Maybe she wanted to talk about everything—again. Women were always into communicating. Not usually Breezy, but then he'd never expected her to vent like she had in the shower either. Maybe she wasn't finished? "You want to talk?"

She threw her leg over him and none too gently sat on his stomach, forcing the breath he'd been holding out of his lungs with a whoosh.

Storm found himself looking up at an enraged goddess.

"Try again."

Damn, he hoped to hell she wanted to make love, because seeing her like this had him panting like a kid with his first *Penthouse*.

Before he could respond, she crushed her mouth against his and kissed him like a woman possessed. Teeth clashed, and she sucked his tongue into her mouth and raked her teeth over it, ripping a groan from his chest.

He was surrounded by her scent, her taste, her emotions. He was on the verge of becoming totally engulfed.

Bree slid over his erection, and she stole the air from his lungs once more.

If this was what she meant about being in control of her own happiness, he was all for it. She was hot and wet and wild, and she was his. Gone was the tentative lover from last night. Tonight she was a demanding hellcat, with fangs and claws and a rabid determination. He loved the dichotomy—hell, he loved everything about her. "Breezy?" He grasped her hips—one more inch and he'd be inside her.

She let out a frustrated groan. "What?" Exasperation was evident in the way she spit out the "t."

"Protection, babe, unless you've got that covered too."

"Oh God." Her breath ragged, she collapsed on him, her heart raging in time with his. "I wasn't . . . I didn't . . . I'm not . . ."

"It's okay." He rolled them over, brushed the hair off her face, and kissed her swollen lips before he took care of it. When he reached for her, he found her lying right where he had left her, minus the urgency, the anger, the tinge of desperation. He lay beside her, pulled her onto her side facing him, and ran his hand from shoulder to thigh. "I believe you were in the middle of having your way with me."

"I attacked you." She looked mortified. A blush

spread from chest to cheeks, and she rested her forehead in the crook of his neck, hiding from him again.

"Breezy, if you attack me like that every time you're mad, you can count on me pissing you off every chance I get."

"I wasn't mad."

He kissed her, sucking on her lower lip, and nipped at it as he pulled her on top of him, tugging her closer, right where she sat before he called a time-out. She was so close, her heat teased his erection, her scent tantalized, his dick twitched.

Bree sucked in a breath and rose above him. "I was frustrated."

"You're not the only one." His voice came out sounding strangled even to his own ears. He clenched his jaw to keep control. He held still, every muscle tensed and twitching like a bucking bull in a shoot when his rider takes his seat. Storm waited for his chance to explode out of the gate and shook with anticipation.

Bree leaned over and traced his lips with the tip of her tongue. "I just wanted you." The pebbled tips of her breasts brushed his chest. "I got a little crazy." She nipped his ear, her hot breath spiking his temperature even higher. "I wanted to feel the way only you make me feel. I need you, Storm."

She didn't know how Storm managed it, but in one move he had control of her entire body—she was a marionette, and Storm was pulling all her strings. His hand on the back of her neck brought her mouth to his in a kiss that was hard, demanding, explosive, and everything she'd dreamed of. With one thrust of his hips he filled her to overflowing.

He held her, sent her flying, and tugged her back to

earth, only to shoot her off again. His kiss captured her screams, and the heart, heat, and love in his eyes held her captive as he gave her everything she'd ever imagined, everything she'd wanted, everything she needed. When he looked at her like that, Nicki, Pete, her mother—all the responsibilities, all their differences, their problems, all the things she couldn't control, ceased to exist. All she could do was experience Storm and the love she was powerless to fight, the love she'd known most of her life, the love she wore like a tattoo on her heart.

"Breezy, I can't hold out. Come with me, babe." His entire body tensed and shuddered, and he groaned, and though she didn't think it possible, he set her off again.

The last things she remembered were his kiss, his hands soothing the tremors still racking her body, his heart pounding under her ear, and the way he said, "Love you, Breezy," just before she gave in to her exhaustion and fell into a dreamless sleep.

# CHAPTER 18

Storm found himself sitting at a bar a block away from the North Cove Marina and thinking about Breezy. He took a sip of his beer and saw Thomas Danby strolling toward him. Storm stood. "Thomas, good to see you."

Thomas shook his hand with a surprisingly strong grip, and his smile showed off his gap-tooth grin. The man looked like a forty-year-old with prematurely gray hair. The seventysomething-year-old still ran ten miles a day, and his daily constitution put Storm to shame.

Storm fingered the key fob for *No Censor Ship* and reluctantly handed it over. "Thanks for letting me borrow her. She's as much fun as she was in the sea trials."

Thomas raised a bushy eyebrow. "And the girl?"

"Once I convinced her I wasn't committing grand theft, things went extremely well."

"Glad to hear it." Thomas sat back and waved to the bartender, who brought over his favorite scotch. "So, how long are you in town?"

"At least another month. But then if all goes well, I'll be spending a lot more time here."

Thomas let out a low whistle. "Well, that is certainly a

change. Last I heard you wanted to be anywhere but Red Hook. I guess you weren't kidding about the date going well."

"It's too early to tell for sure. We have a lot of history to get through, but things are definitely looking up."

"So, what does this woman do?"

Storm took a sip of his beer. "Bree manages my dad's bar and restaurant, and she's on the Red Hook Revitalization Committee. As a matter of fact, she's presenting a request for a change of zoning tomorrow. Speaking of which, do you know anything about a guy named Daniel Knickerbocker?"

"Daniel Knickerbocker? The name rings a bell." He took out his smartphone and typed something.

"I don't like him—something is off; I'm just not sure what. He's been bothering Bree, and he's on the committee with her. He supposedly owns a bunch of real estate in Red Hook, but when I did a search of county records, his name didn't come up. I was hoping you could do a little snooping for me."

"Are you sure it's not just that he's after the woman you care enough to jump through hoops for?"

"Hell, I don't know. That's probably part of it, but when I did my search, I kept coming back to one thing: Why is he so interested in Red Hook? He strikes me as more of a predator than a philanthropist, and he doesn't seem to have any ties to the community except for his attraction to my girlfriend."

"What makes you think he owns real estate?"

"Just the neighborhood scuttlebutt. But then Red Hook is a close-knit community, and my source has always been pretty solid."

Thomas stood and took the last swallow of scotch.

"I'll have the reporter who handles Red Hook snoop around and see what she finds."

"Is she going to the zoning board meeting tomorrow night?"

"She could."

"Daniel Knickerbocker will be there, and for some reason, he's having Bree present the proposal for the zoning change for the Harbor Pier Project. He told Bree it was so that she could get the recognition she deserves. I think it's because he's trying to keep a low profile."

"Okay, you have my antenna twitching too. I'll get back to you." Thomas shook his hand and clapped him on the shoulder. "I'm glad you're here. Keep in touch, and let me know if you want to bring your lady friend out for another sail. I'd like to meet the woman who snared the Storm."

Storm shook his head. "Really, Thomas? Snared the Storm? You couldn't do any better than that? You're supposed to be a wordsmith; yet that's so cliché. I'm disappointed."

"Me too. I've been sitting on the sidelines too long. See you around."

Storm followed him out and headed toward the bar and Bree. It had been hours since he'd seen her. She'd been all strung out over practicing her presentation. She was going to be great, but he figured he was good for more than just a captive audience. He hoped to hell she'd use him for stress relief.

"Does my butt look big in this?" Bree looked over her shoulder at Storm, who sat on her bed with D.O.G., his shadow, and all the color left his face. "Yeah, that's what

I thought too. I'll change." She dug through her closet, looking for something more suitable.

Storm's arms came around her from behind. "Your butt looks amazing. I just don't like the thought of anyone but me admiring it."

Her gaze returned to the mirror when she asked, "Too slutty?"

"No, you look tempting." He kissed her neck, and his hands inched higher. "So tempting, I want to unbutton this prim and proper business suit and find out what you're wearing beneath it. I'm just glad no one but me knows your taste in lingerie."

Bree rolled her eyes. "Storm, I'm hardly a vestal virgin."

His grip went from seductive to possessive. "Did you sleep with him?"

She had absolutely no idea who Storm was referring to—not that it really mattered. "Do I ask you who you slept with?" And God, how she wished she could. She had a vague memory of Nicki's mother from years ago, dark hair, hot body, way too much makeup—her direct opposite. And if Storm was Nicki's father, that meant he'd chosen Marisa over her.

"Knickerbocker. Did you sleep with him?"

"Eww, no, so would you please stop this testosterone-charged chest pounding and let me breathe?" She should be completely disgusted by his behavior. She was a smart, independent woman. She didn't need a man. She'd survived all this time without one. Well, except for the other night, but even Gloria Steinem had great sex once in a while, didn't she? What shocked her was that a little part of her liked it—the little girl who had dreamed of wearing a tiara and of being rescued by a white knight. That little girl inside had Bree fighting back a sigh and questioning her sanity.

Storm loosened his hold and looked as shocked as she was by his reaction. "Sorry."

Bree shook her head and waved his apology away. "I'm nervous enough about the meeting; I don't need anything else to deal with."

"You've practiced; you'll be fine." He looked so sure of himself.

"I've practiced using a spatula as a microphone, and a blank wall for my PowerPoint in front of you, Nicki, and D.O.G. Hardly an unbiased audience."

"The PowerPoint is more for you than for anyone else. It will keep you on track. As for the rest, just pretend that everyone on the board is your employee. You have no problem talking to them, making your needs known, and asking for results."

Bree shook her head and checked her computer again. "Why couldn't Daniel just do this?"

"You're better off without him. You'll be fine."

Stampeding footsteps prevented any response as Nicki rounded the corner into Bree's room and stopped short, wrapping her arm around D.O.G.'s neck. Bree still couldn't believe they'd talked her into allowing the monster of a dog into her apartment. Still, he was growing on her ... slowly. She was getting used to being licked awake by man and dog. She still preferred the man, probably always would, but the mutt was pretty cute.

"Pop said I could come over and give you this." Nicki held out her hand. "It's my lucky rock."

"Lucky rock?" If Bree had expected a pebble, she was mistaken. She accepted the loan of a rock big enough to fit neatly in the palm of her hand, her fingers wrapped around the cool stone.

"If you get scared, just hold on to it. It always helps me."

"Thanks, Nicki." Bree wondered if it was a ten-year-old's equivalent of brass knuckles. She reached for Nicki and gave her a hug. "Are you sure you're going to be all right tonight with Pop?"

"Bree, I'm not a baby." She rolled her eyes and shot Storm a conspiratorial look. "Rocki and Francis are downstairs, and they promised one of them would come up to take D.O.G. and me for a walk later. And it's not as if you're going to stay out all night again. Are you?"

Bree saw a little kernel of insecurity bleed through Nicki's bravado and wished she and Storm hadn't spent the other night on the boat. They should have come home. She knew it then, but Storm had been too persuasive. "No, we'll be home right after the meeting."

Storm cleared his throat. "I thought we might stop for a late dinner to celebrate, but I guess we could do that downstairs at the bar. But either way, we'll be home tonight, kiddo. I promise."

Nicki's smile popped out with Storm's words, and she gave Bree another hug. "You'll do great. Just pretend you're in the kitchen practicing."

"I will."

"And Storm will be there if you get scared. Plus, you have my lucky rock."

"I'll be fine. Thanks, Nicki."

Storm picked up her briefcase. "Let's go. We don't want to be late."

Bree took one last look at herself in the mirror and then at the picture of her and her father—he was the reason she started this whole crusade. Her father's vision of Red Hook became hers, and with her hard work, it was becoming a reality. She hoped her dad was looking down and smiling on her just as he was in the picture. She needed all the help she could get and figured it was too late to do anything but pray.

Storm held the door to the meeting room open for Bree and was surprised to see it was standing room only a good fifteen minutes before the meeting was to start.

Bree looked from the dais to him, her nervousness palpable. "Could you do me a favor?"

"Anything."

"Hold this"—she handed him Nicki's rock—"and this." Her purse hit him in the chest.

He looked around for a place to stash it, but every seat was taken. "I'll just stand in the back against the wall."

"Thanks." She turned and walked away before he could kiss her for luck, which was probably a good thing since Daniel Knickerbocker was paying an awful lot of attention to them.

Storm watched her back as she made her way through the crowded meeting room and then he fumbled with her purse. He'd never been asked to hold a woman's purse before, or if he had, he had blocked it from his memory. He was holding a hot pink bag with JUICY COUTURE written in big white letters across the front and large enough to garage a Mini Cooper. If it wasn't before, his man card was history now.

Storm looked to see if anyone noticed, only to find Thomas a few yards away fighting a laugh. Storm gave him a what-the-hell-am-I-supposed-to-do-with-it look, and Thomas pantomimed slinging it over his shoulder,

Storm took the rock and, throwing it in her bag, cringed when he heard it clunk hard against something else. He eased the strap over his shoulder and leaned back against the wall, wishing he'd blend into the woodwork.

He had one eye on Knickerbocker, who sat in the third row, looking as cool and smug as Storm remembered, and one eye on Breezy, who wore her nervousness and emotions on her sleeve. He watched and waited, praying they'd move the reading of the meeting minutes along and get down to new business before Breezy lost her nerve.

A few minutes later, Bree took the mic, and Storm felt something he'd never felt for a woman—pride. Bone-deep pride, which was stupid since he had nothing to do with Bree's success, but damn, he had never been so proud of anyone before. Bree nailed the presentation and then sailed through the questions. It was the longest half hour of Storm's life; never before had he felt as invested in anyone or anything outside himself and his business.

The motion to change the zoning passed unanimously—not surprising after Bree's presentation. He didn't see how anyone could vote against it. His Breezy was a superstar.

When the meeting broke up, cameras flashed, and reporters peppered her with questions. Daniel made his way to the front. Just as Storm suspected, Daniel couldn't resist the allure of the limelight for long. When Daniel wrapped his beefy arm around Bree's waist, Storm's adrenaline kicked in, his heartbeat sped up, and every muscle tensed. He took a deep breath and checked the urge to go up to the guy, rip his arm out of the socket, and shove it down his throat.

Thomas worked his way over to Storm through the throng of people. "That man sidling up to Ms. Collins is Knickerbocker, I take it?"

"That would be him." Storm clenched his fist and released it, spreading out his fingers, only to fist them again.

Bree took a step away, but Daniel moved in tandem as if they were connected at the hip, and he pulled her closer.

Thomas gave Storm's shoulder a warning squeeze. "She can handle herself. You have to let her. The last thing she needs right now is you stirring up trouble."

Storm let out a frustrated breath. "I know. You're right, but the man makes me want to punch him like a bag at the Y."

Bree shook hands with everyone on the board and, as discreetly as she could, separated herself from Daniel before catching Storm's eye and smiling. She headed for him with a look of triumph on her face.

The moment Daniel noticed Bree had escaped his clutches, he followed her, made eye contact with Storm, a smug smirk twisting his lips, and reached for Bree's shoulder.

Daniel wrapped his arm around her waist from behind, tugging her against him, and whispered something in her ear.

Surprise, shock, and revulsion crossed her face.

That was it. All bets were off. Storm crossed the room in three strides. "Bree." He eyed Knickerbocker as he spoke—it was all he could do not to haul off and knock that smarmy smirk off the guy's pretty face. For Bree's sake, Storm gave Daniel a heartbeat to rethink his actions.

Knickerbocker released her, and Bree stepped into Storm's arms. "You were amazing, babe." He gave her a kiss on the temple, slid her purse off his shoulder and passed it to her, and then took her briefcase. "Come on, there's someone here I'd like you to meet."

"I just want to leave." She took a deep breath and wrapped her arm around Storm's waist.

"I know, but you can't let him chase you off. Come meet my friend Thomas Danby."

"What's he doing here?"

"You're news, babe. He wouldn't miss it."

She gave him a get-real look but pasted a genuine smile on her face.

"Thomas, I'd like you to meet Breanna Collins. Bree, this is Thomas Danby of the *Wall Street Journal,* and the owner of *No Censor Ship.*"

Bree shook Thomas's hand. "Thanks for lending us your boat. *No Censor Ship* is incredible."

"You're welcome, but Storm deserves most of the praise. I didn't have much to do with it."

Storm laughed. "Right, thanks for the props, but Bree is too smart to believe that. She thought I stole it."

Bree elbowed Storm and smiled at Thomas. "It's wonderful to meet you, Mr. Danby. I'm surprised you're here."

"Call me Thomas, please. You make me sound old enough to be your father—something I'd like to ignore even if it is the truth. Congratulations on the decision. Your presentation was thorough and very convincing. I should know; I'm a professional fact checker. Storm tells me you've been on the Revitalization Committee for the last five years. I've been impressed with the changes the Committee has effected."

"Thank you. They are a wonderful group of people, and it's been a real team effort."

"I'd like to hear more about it. How about over dinner?"

"Sure." Bree took a breath and looked over at Storm. "We can go to the Crow's Nest."

"Sounds good. Storm's told me all about the bar. He said you've turned it into a real neighborhood gathering place." He stepped aside to allow Bree to pass. "I hope you two will come out on the boat with me sometime soon. Unfortunately, summer doesn't last forever."

Storm gave her an it's-up-to-you tilt of his head and drew a relieved breath when she aimed one of her thousand-watt-smiles at Thomas. Taking that as a yes, Storm gave her a quick squeeze. "The Crow's Nest is closed on Sundays and Mondays. Just let us know when, and we'll be there."

She turned up the wattage at Storm. "Maybe on our next trip, I'll be able to pay more attention to the view."

Bree walked into the Crow's Nest to a round of applause, but this time at least it wasn't because she was caught necking. Still, she wasn't sure why everyone was applauding.

One look at Storm told her that he had a hand in this, and, before she could stop herself, she pinched him just below the ribs. "You set me up."

He let out a pleasing grunt. "No, I just answered a few dozen texts. I didn't want to get on the bad side of both Rocki and Patrice, so I agreed to a party. They'd probably send Francis in the ambulance with full lights and sirens for the impromptu celebration." He pulled her around in front so she was in full view of the crowd and brought his mouth to her ear, making her wish they were alone. "Don't worry. We'll celebrate privately, later."

"We'd better, or you'll be sleeping on the couch." Even to her own ears she sounded breathless. She was disgusted with the way her hormones raged whenever he was in the vicinity. It was bad enough she found herself thinking about him constantly. She'd been waiting for Storm's effect on her to dissipate, waiting for a time that just seeing him didn't make her heart race like a drum-roll, when his touch didn't make her catch her breath, or the sound of his voice didn't make her drool. It hadn't happened yet, and she was still waiting for the Storm Surge—as she thought of it—to recede.

Everyone important in Bree's life was there—Storm and Nicki, Francis and Patrice, Rocki, even Pete. Every-one was there—everyone but her own mother who had sentenced herself to life in a prison of her own making, something, Bree reminded herself, she was determined not to do.

She soaked in the moment, watching all the people she loved and the bar she'd worked so hard to turn around, in the neighborhood she helped improve, and felt as if everything in her life was finally moving in the right direction.

Her gaze zeroed in on Storm with his arm around Nicki while he talked to Pete and Thomas and a bunch of the regulars. She took a deep breath, walked right up to Storm, and slid under his other arm, hoping to be-come part of the circle.

Storm kissed her temple, tightened his hold on her, and it felt right, and natural, and real, and so wonderful, she had to blink away tears.

For the first time since her dad died, she felt truly part

of a family. Her family—Storm and Nicki and Pete—right here in Red Hook.

For the first time since her dad died, she felt complete.

For the first time since her dad died, Bree was happy.

Bree let Nicki stay up past her bedtime, but when she saw Pete drooping, she herded them upstairs, putting up with whining on both their parts.

When she returned, Storm caught her hand. "Dance with me." He led her to the dance floor and held her too close, not that she minded. "Happy?"

"Yes, very happy. Thanks for doing all this."

"I didn't do anything. Everyone here planned this; all I did was drag you back. Did Pete and Nicki give you a hard time?"

"No more than usual. Pete made it all the way up the stairs without looking as if he were going to pass out. It was a big improvement." She rested her head against his shoulder and breathed him in while Rocki sang a ballad—another perfect moment. She wanted to dance with Storm forever.

"What do you think of Thomas?"

"He seems really nice. I've always wondered what one of those guys looked like."

Storm ran his hand down her back, stopping just short of the point of indecency. "One of which guys?"

"The guys who can drop ten million on a toy."

He leaned back, dipped his chin, and stopped dancing. "*No Censor Ship* is a hell of a lot more than a toy."

"I'm sorry. It wasn't my intention to demean it. But still, I can't imagine buying a house for a tenth of that price, and I'd be able to live in it."

He pulled her hip to hip and started moving again. "You could live on *No Censor Ship* if you wanted to."

"But Thomas doesn't."

"No, he's more of a penthouse-on–Park Avenue kind of guy."

She pulled away to look at his face. "What kind of guy are you?"

"You don't know?" He seemed surprised.

"I thought I did, but then I see you with Thomas and you seem to fit right in. It's obvious that you're good friends. How many of your friends are like Thomas?"

"Rich? I'm not rich if that's what you're asking. Not compared to most of the people I know through business. They're clients, Bree. I design boats, see that they're built correctly, and spend a lot of time with my clients during the design process. Some become friends; some don't."

"But you have no trouble mixing with them. You're as easy with Thomas as you are with Francis and Patrice."

"Some of them, sure. People are people—no matter how much money they have in the bank. If there's one thing I've learned, it's that money is not the measure of a man. That should be clear to you when you look at Dickerbocker."

Bree raised her eyebrow. "I don't think Daniel is rich."

"He dresses as if he is. A guy doesn't walk around in thousand-dollar suits and handmade Italian shoes unless he makes a good living."

She gave him a Brooklyn shrug. "I guess, but I never looked at him as anything but a coworker."

"You went out with him once."

"Who told you? Patrice or Rocki?

"Both."

"Of course they did. Sometimes I wonder about my friends."

Storm kissed her forehead. "They love you; we all do."

"Yeah, I know, but I'm more concerned about us than our friends."

"And my having rich friends is a concern?"

"I don't know. I worry that I wouldn't fit in with Thomas's crowd."

"No one who gets to know you would ever think you're not incredible. You impressed the hell out of Thomas, and believe me, not many people do."

"You do."

Storm spun her around and dipped her. "I'm just an impressive guy." He pulled her up and then kissed her, proving his point.

# CHAPTER 19

Storm had been home for more than a month without having had a morning to sleep in. The first morning he thought he'd be able to started with a crash. The sound of Nicki charging through the living room like a herd of elephants was followed by D.O.G.'s excited bark. She had a few days off school for Rosh Hashanah, so he'd worked until three in the morning, knowing today would be spent with Nicki underfoot. He wiped the sleep out of his eyes, dragged on a pair of jeans and a T-shirt, stepped out of the bedroom, and found his laptop swimming with . . . "Orange juice?"

Nicki froze, tears welling in her eyes. "I'm sorry. I cleaned it all up. I even washed it."

He spotted the trail of water from the sink to the table. "In the sink?"

Her head bobbed up and down like the bobble-head doll Bree had on her dashboard. "Whenever I spill anything, Bree rinses it off in the sink."

Storm sat down, held his aching head, and silently fired off a long list of curses. He'd gotten better about not cursing out loud, but no one said he couldn't think them.

He'd been there a month. He juggled his work with taking care of Pete and Nicki. He followed the Daniel Knickerbocker investigation Thomas had waged, making sure Bree wasn't caught up in whatever illegal activities Daniel seemed to be up to his eyeballs in, and kept a close eye on her so that she wouldn't be caught in the middle when the story hit the presses. Added to all that were working at the bar and spending time with Bree.

He'd been pushing his limits for so long, he'd forgotten what it felt like to rest. Most nights he got out of bed after Bree fell asleep and tried to catch up on his work. He was tired, dog tired, and he couldn't remember the last time he'd backed up his computer. Fuck.

It had been days, which meant he had probably lost a week's worth of work. It was, he reminded himself, his own damn fault, not Nicki's.

"I'm s-s-sorry." She hiccoughed and dissolved into gulping tears.

"It's okay." He closed his eyes and scrubbed his hands over his face. He wanted to kick himself for being so stupid, for leaving his computer on the table, for not backing it up, and for not getting enough sleep.

When he opened his eyes, Nicki wasn't only crying; she was shaking. "Hey." He went to put his arm around her and she flinched, not just a blink but a full-body flinch, arms protecting her face, torso bent, ready to flee. Damn, she was terrified. Nicki thought he was going to hit her. It stopped him cold. Memories of his father's hand, the one thing he never wanted to get in the way of, flashed before his eyes. His insides churned but not in fear, not like he was headed for a bruising, not like sitting in the back of a cruiser with his hands cuffed, and definitely not like the night he ran out on Bree. This fear was the realization that he was on the other end. No, he was not his father. He'd never turn into the monster his father was. He took a deep breath. A strange sense of calm enveloped him, and the huge weight he'd carried his whole life lifted off his shoulders. He'd never turn into his old man. Never. "Nicki, I'm not going to hurt you."

He tapped his knee, and D.O.G. came over to him. He gave the dog a pat, and Nicki stepped closer—within reach, but she still didn't trust him. He tried not to take it personally. He knew how it felt to be on the wrong side of an irate man. He wasn't irate at anyone but himself, but that could be hard for a little kid to figure out.

He took a deep breath, picked up the computer, and took it back to the kitchen, letting it drip over the sink. "I guess we need to go shopping."

"We do?" She took a gulp of air and wiped her face with sticky hands.

"It looks like I need to buy a new computer." And see if anything could be salvaged from the hard drive. He grabbed a handful of paper towels, did his best to soak up whatever liquid was left, and then stood the computer on its side to dry on the drain board while he got ready to go. "Do you want to come with me, or would you rather go down to the bar and stay with Bree and Pop?"

"You're not mad?"

"At you? No, it was an accident. I'm mad at myself. I've told you to clean up after yourself how many times? I should have followed my own rules."

Nicki ran to her room, and he wondered if he should get Bree. He didn't want to go after Nicki if he was going to scare the crap out of her again. Damn, the look on the kid's face brought back so many memories, memories he thought were dead and buried. Spilling juice at the breakfast table had earned him a smack on the side of his head that ruptured his eardrum. He wondered what his dad would have done to him if he had single-handedly destroyed a computer and a week's worth of work.

He shook his head and turned to find Nicki standing there with her hands behind her back. "Hey." He forced a smile and hoped it didn't look menacing. He crouched down in front of her. "I wondered where you went. I was just going to call Bree to help me find you."

Nicki held her hands out. "I went to get my money. It's not much, but I want to help buy you a new computer since I wrecked yours by accident. I didn't mean to."

This smile came naturally. God, he loved this kid. "How much you got there?"

"Twenty-four dollars and sixty-seven cents." Most of which was change.

"Wow, that's a lot of money."

Nicki nodded. "I save whatever I find." Her eyes went from young and innocent to way-too-old. "You never know when you'll need it."

"Thanks for the offer, Nicki, but I don't want to take your money. You keep that for something special, okay?"

She looked at him with her big brown eyes still spiked with tears. "But you are special."

Storm tried to swallow a tanker-sized lump in his throat, reached out, and grabbed the kid to pull her into a hug. Damn, his eyes were tearing like a freakin' pansy. "So are you, Nicki. If I ever have a kid, I hope she's just like you." He kissed the top of her head.

Nicki clung to him like a little monkey, and he was in no rush to get away. He'd walk all over Brooklyn with her attached if that was what she wanted. He'd proved to himself that he wasn't his old man, never would be, and it was as if a whole new world opened up to him. If all kids were like Nicki, he wouldn't mind a few of his own—as long as he kept his computer away from them. He wondered what his and Bree's kids would look like. He hoped to hell they'd take after Bree; Lord knew he caused enough trouble as a kid to make him wary of their taking after him. But with a normal family, maybe they wouldn't be so set on getting into trouble.

"If I ever get a dad of my very own, I hope he's just like you too."

"I love you, Nicki." He held her away a little bit so they were eye to eye. "You never have to be afraid of me. I don't hit little girls, or even big girls. Ever. Understand?"

She looked at her sneakers, which were covered in orange juice, and dug her foot into the carpet.

He put a finger under her chin and made sure she was listening. "No one should ever hit you. If anyone tries, you come get me, and I'll take care of him, okay?"

She nodded.

"Good." He smiled at her tear-stained face and held her sticky hands in his. "You're a hot mess, kiddo. You go wash up, change your clothes, and then we can go computer shopping."

Bree stood in the kitchen, eavesdropping on the two people she loved most in the world and wondering if she hadn't made the biggest mistake of her life.

Nicki and Storm loved each other. They might very well be father and daughter, and Bree had kept them apart. Not in a physical sense, of course; the way Nicki clung to Storm showed that much, but not telling Storm what she knew was wrong and so much worse than she'd ever imagined.

Why could she see it now and not a month ago when she and Pete had talked? What she'd done was selfish. Bree had never thought of herself that way; now, she wasn't so sure.

The last month with Storm had been perfect, and no matter how many times Pete told her that Storm might run if he found out Nicki could be his child, she'd known in her heart he would never leave a child of his own. He would never leave Nicki.

What became glaringly obvious as she watched Storm and Nicki together was that she wasn't so confident he wouldn't leave her. Maybe that was why she'd promised Pete she wouldn't say anything to Storm. She was afraid he'd leave her.

Guilt stole the air from her lungs and burned her eyes. She had to tell him. He might never forgive her and she might never forgive herself, but he had a right to know. She'd already waited too long. She needed to talk to Pete first. She couldn't break his confidence. Together, they'd have to figure out how to tell Storm.

"It's just a computer, Bree. It's not that bad."

"What?"

Storm had spotted her and pointed to the computer sitting in the dish rack. "I think the hard drive is fried. Nicki spilled her juice on it and then tried to wash it off in the sink."

"Oh God. You have a backup, right?"

Storm rubbed his neck. "If the hard drive is fried, I figure I've lost about a week's work."

"You've been working every night and not backing up?"

He looked guilty. "You knew I was sneaking out of bed to work?"

Bree shrugged. "I don't sleep well without you anymore. I rolled over one night to throw my arm around you and found the dog there instead."

Storm slid his arms around her and laughed. "I'm sure D.O.G. enjoyed the attention."

"To say the least. But why would you think you had to hide your work from me?"

"I wasn't hiding. I was just working during business hours in Auckland. There's a seventeen-hour time difference, babe. Things like conversations on Skype have to be had on their time, not mine. My assistant needs questions answered, and assignments to complete."

"What happened when you found your computer?"

"I did a lot of silent cursing, and when I looked up, Nicki was shaking. She thought I was going to hit her, Bree. The kid flinched when I reached for her."

"I know."

"You were here?"

"No." Great, now she wasn't only selfish, but she was also a liar. "I just know Nicki gets scared when she does something wrong. If someone waves a hand near her, she flinches. I took her to a game once, and she was terrified. She doesn't talk about what happened to her, but it doesn't take a rocket scientist to see the signs."

Storm fisted his hands. "She's a great kid, Bree. She should never have to be afraid."

"And so were you. Look at what you went through."

"I was a guy."

"A little boy. I remember when you came here. You had a broken arm, and a cast as big as my whole leg. It went almost to your shoulder."

Storm shrugged it off.

"You were two years older than Nicki and as skinny as any of those kids from Ethiopia I used to see in *National Geographic*."

"I could take care of myself."

"Not when your dad went after you with a tire iron."

He flushed.

"I overheard Pete talking." She shrugged and took his fisted hand in hers, and felt the tension leave him. "Life isn't fair. At least Nicki will never have to be afraid again. I'll make sure of that."

"We'll make sure of it." He slipped his arms around her and held her too tight again. Tension and anger flowed through him into her before he relaxed. "We need to talk. Later. But right now, I need to get a new computer. It's going to take forever just to load the programs I need. Shit." He let out a frustrated breath. "This couldn't have happened at a worse time. I'm expecting a call from my boat builder at three about a problem."

"Okay, do you want me to keep Nicki with me at the bar? She's supposed to have a playdate at Patrice's this afternoon."

Storm shook his head. "No, I need to take her with me. I want to make sure she doesn't think I'm mad at her. I'll drop her off at Patrice and Francis's place on the way home."

"Okay." Bree looked into his eyes and saw a sadness that stole her breath.

"Nicki's been hoarding all the money she finds. It's her emergency stash. I used to do the same thing. Hell, I still do. I guess old habits die hard. It's her food money, her escape money, and she offered to give it to me."

Storm looked as if his heart were breaking, for Nicki and for the little beaten boy he used to be, and he was sharing it with her.

He trusted her, and she didn't deserve it.

# CHAPTER 20

Pete jumped when Bree barged into his office, hair flying, red faced, and near tears. The Bree he knew didn't cry.

"We gotta talk."

He slid the cigar he'd been sniffing into his drawer and hoped to hell she didn't see him. She'd open a can of whoopass on him in a heartbeat, and he really didn't need that right now, especially since she was already upset. He was man enough to know there was no winning against a pissed-off Irishwoman. "What the hell happened?"

She slammed her hands on his desk, whether to stop herself from falling over it or make a point, he wasn't sure. "We have to tell Storm. Keeping it from him was a mistake."

"Take a breath and sit down. What's the matter?"

Bree looked at him, but it was as if she were somewhere else. "Nicki spilled juice on Storm's computer and then washed it off in the sink."

"You gotta be kidding."

"No, I'm not." She straightened and turned away. "We have to tell him. I should have told him the second I found out. God, Pete, what kind of monster am I?"

"Monster?" He heaved himself out of his chair, went around his desk, and patted her back. "Bree, you're a lot of things, but a monster isn't one of them. You did what you thought was best at the time. We both did."

"No, I was so afraid Storm would leave, I didn't want to tell him."

"It's not surprising; he's left before."

"But not because of Nicki. Storm would never leave his own child. I'm just not so sure he wouldn't leave me. Especially now. Who would blame him? He trusted me and I didn't trust him, and to think I might have been keeping him from his own daughter."

"You haven't been doing anything of the kind. You know as well as I do that those two are always together; it's as if they're connected at the hip. I've never seen Storm connect with anyone like that except for you and his brothers."

"He thinks of Nicki as a little sister. It's wrong."

"It might not be, Bree. We don't know that. We don't know anything."

"They love each other. Storm told her if he ever had kids, he'd want them to be just like her."

Pete felt a smile crack his craggy old face. "Really? Wow. He's always said he never wanted kids. I wonder what changed his mind. A man who says things like that is thinking about the future."

"What kind of future will he want when he finds out the woman who supposedly loves him has been keeping such a secret from him?" She threw herself in the chair and pulled her hair off her face. "This whole situation is like a bad movie of the week, the ones you watch and think the heroine is too stupid to live."

"You're not stupid; you're just human. It's my fault. I

asked you not to tell him. Give yourself a break. Storm will understand."

"That's what I'm afraid of. Pete, he really knows me. He's going to know I didn't trust him enough to tell him when I should have."

"Storm loves you. He's loved you most of his life."

"Is love enough, Pete? Am I?"

He hoped to hell it was enough; if it wasn't, they were all screwed.

For Storm, shopping for computers with Nicki was almost as bad as shopping for school supplies. It had been almost a month since they braved Staples, and the flashbacks had only just subsided. He ended up having to put Nicki up on his shoulders, afraid he'd lose her in the crush. He learned a lot that day—mothers on a mission were scary creatures, and spoiled kids were even scarier.

Nicki pulled the bag away from her chest and looked inside as if to check that her prize was still there. "Tell me again why you bought me an iPad?"

He didn't think guilt for scaring the crap out of her was a good answer even if it was partially true. "So that when I have to go away, we'll always be able to talk and see each other. Plus, you can play games, listen to music, whatever you want . . . within reason." He had also bought one for Bree. If the call he was expecting from the boat builder was bad, he might be leaving sooner than expected.

Nicki stopped right in the middle of the sidewalk; people walked around her. "You're leaving, aren't you?"

Storm took her by the hand and led her closer to the building, squatted in front of her, and with his hands on her waist, he looked her right in the eye. "I might be. But,

Nicki, I have to travel for work sometimes. If I don't do my job, I don't get paid. But no matter where I go, I'll always come back, and with your iPad you can use Face-Time and see me whenever you want."

Nicki squinted her eyes and looked almost angry. "You promise that you'll come back? No matter what?"

"I promise, and I always keep my word."

"Can't me and Bree go with you?"

Storm smiled at the thought of showing them Auck-land, of Nicki wearing a little hard hat at the boat builder's. . . . "If you and Bree came with me, who would take care of Pop and the bar? Besides, you can't miss school. Maybe if I have to travel during summer vaca-tion, you can come with me."

Nicki threw her arms around his neck, her bag flopped against his back, and she held on tight. "But I don't want you to go."

Storm picked her up and grabbed his bag. "I don't want to go either, but I might not have a choice. That's the bad part of being a grown-up. You have to do stuff you don't necessarily want to do. I made a promise to the man who paid me to design his boat, and if something is wrong with it, I might have to go down there and figure out where the problem is."

"You promise to come right home after you fix what-ever's wrong at the stupid boat builder's?"

"I promise; I'll always come home to you and Bree." And he would. Nothing in the world would keep him away from Bree and Nicki.

"Okay." She smiled and gave him a big smacking kiss on the cheek. "Let's go to Miss Patrice's house and show her and the girls my iPad. I'm supposed to have a play-date with them anyway."

"Sounds good. I told Bree I'd drop you off when we finished shopping. You'll have a lot more fun over there. I'll be stuck in my room for the rest of the day on a call and doing computer stuff."

"You won't leave before I get home, will you?"

"I'm not even sure I have to go." But he had a bad feeling about it all the same. "I'll tell you what, if I have to go, I promise to stop by Patrice and Francis's to say good-bye. How's that sound?"

"Okay."

Storm put her down and took her little hand in his as they made their way to Pop's car. If he was going to be spending more time in Red Hook, he'd have to buy a car, because he sure as shit wasn't going to be tooling around in Bree's little windup toy. He and Bree would also need a bigger place to live. Yup, they definitely needed to talk. Right after he found out what the hell was going on with his Class 40.

Bree left her office when she heard Pete's bark of laughter and found Pete and his cronies bellied up to the bar. She slid under the pass-through and grabbed Pete's whiskey, then tossed the contents into the sink.

"Aw, Bree."

"Don't 'aw, Bree' me. You heard the doctors. No booze yet." She set a seltzer in front of him and raised an eyebrow. "Don't make me kick you out of my bar."

"As if you could." Pete sounded more like a ten-year-old than a middle-aged man with a heart condition.

"It would be a piece of cake if Storm and I helped her."

The deep bass baritone voice had all the hair on the back of Bree's neck standing straight up. "Logan!" She was part ecstatic and part horrified. She wasn't ready for Logan to come home. Not yet. It was too soon.

Logan tossed a piece of very expensive luggage on the floor and grabbed Pete in a bear hug. "How you doin', Pop?"

"Happy to be alive and getting better every day."

Bree ran around the bar and hugged Logan as soon as he let go of Pete. "Why didn't you call and let us know you were on your way?" She held him at arm's length and looked him over. His ink black hair was styled within an inch of its life. "Are you using hair gel?"

Entering the bar through the kitchen, Storm stopped short at the sight of Bree in the arms of a tall, dark-haired man. He'd never been the possessive type, but then he'd never been in love before either. He saw red until he realized the man in question was Logan. He wasn't sure what surprised him more—that Logan had suddenly appeared or that he used hair gel. His damn brother still hadn't let go of Bree, and Storm bit down on the urge to pummel him.

He caught Logan's eye roll, but even his tanned olive skin didn't hide the pink around his chiseled cheekbones. Leave it to Breezy to put Logan in his place with the hair gel crack. The small diamond in his ear gave him a pi-ratelike quality, which contrasted with the expensive look of his clothes. Logan might be wearing jeans, but they were a far cry from 501s.

Storm never saw any of his brothers as a threat be-fore, but he figured any woman—even Bree—would think Logan was really good-looking if she was into the exceptionally tall and lanky. Storm let out a breath of relief when Logan released her.

"The crush is over at the vineyard, so I caught the first flight out. I thought you were in a hurry to get rid of someone."

The man looked like Logan, but he certainly didn't sound like him. Gone was the Brooklyn boy, and in his place was a cultured man with a strange accent. Storm planned to flatten his big brother for that last crack as soon as they were alone together.

Bree shook her head. "God, I've missed you."

"Lucky for me. I heard you hit Storm with a frying pan. Way to go, Bree." Logan high-fived her, which just increased the urge to pummel him. "Storm saw stars, and not just because it was his first glimpse of you in a long time."

Storm was just about to make his presence known when Bree's face flamed.

"I thought he was a burglar."

It didn't escape Storm that she had yet to mention their relationship to Logan.

The corner of Logan's mouth quirked up in a wry grin. "Lucky for him. If you knew who it was, you'd have killed him. Speaking of Storm, where is he?"

"Computer shopping. There was a little accident this morning involving orange juice and his laptop. The laptop didn't make it." Bree took his brother's hand and gave it a tug. "Logan, why don't you come upstairs and bring your things." Bree caught Pete's eye and widened hers.

"I don't even get a beer?"

"Not now, Logan. We need to talk."

Bree was nervous about something. Storm looked around the quiet bar—nothing was amiss, and Simon had everything under control. He couldn't imagine what she was worked up over.

Logan cocked his head. "Problem?"

"Maybe. I don't know." Bree shrugged. "Pete and I have to talk to you and Storm in private. He should be home soon."

"Sounds serious."

No shit. Logan must have sensed her tension—there was no sign of his normal teasing tone. A feeling of dread crawled its way up Storm's spine and clawed the back of his neck. He stepped forward and cleared his throat. "Did I hear my name mentioned? Hey, Logan, welcome home." He pulled his brother into his arms and slapped him hard on the back.

Bree's face lost all color when she turned to face him. She pasted on a fake smile, as if she'd just been caught doing something bad. Really bad. Other than hugging his brother, which, as much as he'd like it to be, was not against the rules, he couldn't imagine what caused the look of guilt that ping-ponged across her face.

Storm waited for her to come to him and give him a hug—anything. She didn't move. Had she found out he was leaving?

"It's good you're home. Let's go upstairs where we can talk." She might have said it was good, but the look of dread on her face belied her words. She wasn't happy about something, and that was putting it mildly. He hadn't seen her this nervous since he pulled her off the counter after she met D.O.G. the first time.

As soon as they entered the apartment, Logan dropped his bag and put his hands on his hips. "What's going on, Bree?" He looked at Pop, who was winded and coughing but otherwise looked almost normal. "Pop, are you all right?"

Pete sank into his recliner. "I'm fine. This is about Nicki."

"The kid you took in?"

Storm stood beside Logan and mirrored his pose. "What about Nicki? Is she okay?"

Bree cut in. "Yes, she's fine."

Logan shot him a confused look. "Nicki's the kid, right?"

Storm wanted to pummel him again. Nicki wasn't just a kid. "Nicki's a little girl. A ten-and-a-half-year-old little girl."

Bree didn't come near him. She didn't look at him. She just sank onto the couch, hugged her legs to her chest, and rested her chin on her knees.

"So?" Logan stood, feet shoulder-width apart, rolling on the balls of his feet as if he expected an attack. Storm didn't blame him.

Pete leaned forward and looked from Logan to him and back again. "Nicki's mother is Marisa Sotto. She was a waitress at the bar before you boys left. Do you two remember her?"

Logan nodded and paled.

Storm couldn't believe it. "Fuck, Marisa is Nicki's mother? Why am I just finding out about this now?"

Logan looked from Bree to Pete. "And what does this have to do with us? What's the deal?"

Pete ignored their questions and continued without skipping a beat. "Marisa didn't work here long; she was a much better flirt than a waitress. A few years later, she came back asking for work, hauling around a toddler, and God forgive me, I didn't give her the time of day."

"Why should you have?" Logan asked.

Logan had never liked being kept in the dark; neither did Storm. What Storm didn't like even more was that he and Logan were the only ones shocked by this news, which meant Bree already knew all about it.

"Because I could do the math, son, and there aren't

enough Hail Marys in the world to make me worthy of forgiveness for that one stupid, selfish mistake."

"I'm not following you, Pop."

Storm crossed his arms. "Neither am I. What the hell are you trying to say?"

"When Marisa left Nicki with me, she said Nicki was my granddaughter and that she was better off with me."

Logan turned white and Storm felt as if he'd just taken one in the solar plexus. Nicki was Pete's grandchild? What the hell?

"I've racked my brain trying to remember what went on back then. Logan, if I remember correctly, you had a girlfriend that summer, and Slater kept himself closeted with his computers." Pop looked Storm in the eye and then down at his hands. "Storm—you were always the impulsive one back then, and you took off."

Logan's shocked face twisted into an angry grimace. Storm had rarely seen Logan mad; he'd always been the calmest of the three of them. "Is that what this is all about? You want to know if Storm or I fucked Marisa? Why didn't you just ask us?"

Storm shook his head, his embarrassment choking him. He couldn't deny what Pop had said about him being impulsive back then; it was the truth. He took a step back, as if putting more distance between them would stop whatever it was that was happening. "I was just wondering the same thing." He felt sick, the same sick he'd felt when he was a kid and knew he was in for a beating from his old man. He planted his feet, ignoring the inner voice that screamed at him to run. This was Bree and Pop. They loved him. They'd never hurt him. He took a deep breath and told himself he was imagining things.

"Storm." Bree finally looked him in the eyes. And what he saw there was horror, guilt, and fear.

His heart sank. How long had Bree suspected Nicki was his? How long had she kept it from him? Why? Did she tell him she loved him, thinking he was Nicki's father and she'd be getting a twofer? Was she in love with him, or the idea of having a ready-made family? "How long have you known?"

She made a move to get up, but his warning look kept her rooted to her chair.

"Answer the question." His voice shook with anger; his gaze shot between Bree and Pop. The two of them looked guilty as hell. "Never mind. It doesn't matter. Right now the only thing that matters is Nicki, and unfortunately, she's not mine." As he stared at Bree, blood rushed through his ears, drowning out the sound of the air conditioner; sweat dripped between his shoulder blades; disbelief coated his throat and tasted like bile. "There was only one girl I was interested in back then, and it wasn't Marisa. As much as I wish she were, Nicki isn't my daughter." He took a shaky breath and stared at the woman he loved and his own father. "You thought I was capable of running out on the mother of my child, my own kid?"

Neither said a word.

"I take that as a yes." He turned, then gave Logan a crushing hug and a clap on the back. "I'm glad you're here. If Nicki is yours, you're one lucky son of a bitch." He cleared his throat—forcing the words past the lump of what was probably the remains of his heart. "She's a daughter any man would be blessed to have. I've got somewhere I have to be. I'm on the six forty-five to Auckland."

\*       \*       \*

Storm didn't spare Bree or Pete a glance as he went to the room he'd shared with Bree and slammed the door. He made it to the bed before his legs gave out. He'd been beaten up, broken, and thrown away before, but he'd never hurt this bad. His hand shook as he scrubbed it over his face.

The door opened and Pete stepped in.

Storm stood on wobbly legs and stared down the man he respected more than any other—the man who was the only father he'd ever really had; the man who had just betrayed him. "Why?"

Pete cleared his throat. "You never told me why you ran, son. I knew how you felt about having children. You were afraid you'd hurt them. You told me you'd rather die than turn into a monster like your old man. If Marisa told you she was pregnant ..." Pete's face crumbled, and he raked his bony hand through his hair. "I asked you why you left, and you wouldn't tell me. I didn't want to believe it, but shit, Storm."

"And you asked Bree."

Pop nodded and put a hand on the dresser to steady himself. "She said you left because of her."

"But she didn't believe she was the only reason, did she? She had so little faith in me, she thought I not only ran away from her, but from the girl I supposedly knocked up, and my baby?" Storm turned away from his father. He needed to get out of there. He dug out his duffel bag and ripped his clothes off the hangers, stuffing them inside.

"Bree loves you."

"How could she love a man she could even think would do that? How could you?"

"You're my son."

"Maybe." Storm dropped the bag and looked at his father, shoving his hands in his pockets to keep from shaking him. "But I never thought the father I trusted and loved would keep the fact that I might have a child from me. What am I supposed to think, Pop? Since Nicki isn't my kid, do you think you're off the hook? Am I supposed to say, no problem? No harm done? Am I supposed to just forget about it?"

"I'm sorry, son. Everyone makes mistakes. I hope in time you'll forgive me. I'm not perfect, but I love you. I always will."

"Yeah, I'm just not sure I want that kind of love."

Storm watched his dad leave looking like he'd aged ten years; then he turned and set the duffel bag on the bed beside D.O.G., who let out a sympathetic whine. "I know just how you feel."

"Do you?"

The sound of Bree's voice had every muscle in his body tightening as if someone had taken a ratchet to them. He rubbed his stiff neck. "I was talking to the dog."

She walked into the room they'd shared, sat on the bed beside D.O.G., and toyed with his floppy ear as if gathering her thoughts while his whole world shifted off its axis.

She straightened her shoulders, raised her chin, and looked him in the eye before angrily wiping away a tear. "We were wrong not to tell you. Pete wanted to wait until Logan returned. It was his decision to wait, but I'm just as guilty. I agreed to it. I promised not to say anything. This morning when I saw you and Nicki together, I knew how very wrong we were to keep it from you. I should never have agreed not to tell you. I'm sorry."

"How could you think I'd run out on Nicki? I love that kid."

"I knew you'd never run out on her. I just wasn't sure you wouldn't run out on me."

"You were wrong, Bree. I'm not running out on you. I got a call from the boat builder. There's a problem, and it's costing eight thousand dollars plus penalties for every day work stops. I'd have to leave regardless. Now that I know the truth, I guess the timing is actually fortuitous."

"Fortuitous?" Silent tears rolled down her cheeks unhindered. "I was wrong. I'm a coward. I know that and I'm sorry. Forgive me, Storm. I love you."

"You say you love me, but I'm not even sure you know your own mind. Is it me you love, or the family we could have had together if I were Nicki's father?"

Her mouth opened as if she intended to deny it, and then closed.

The pain he'd been fighting slammed into him again. "You don't even know, do you?"

She jumped off the bed. "I never thought that. You have to believe me." She came toward him, reaching for him, her arms open.

"Don't do this, Bree." He held up his hands. He couldn't take it if she touched him. If she touched him, he might just fall apart. He took a giant step back and almost ran into the closet door. "I have a plane to catch. I can't do this now. I just can't." He turned away and wished he could leave all his clothes. If he thought they'd let him on a plane without luggage, he'd be gone.

"Storm, no matter what you think, I love you. I have since I first met you, and God help me, I always will. If I could go back in time, I'd tell you as soon as I found out. I'm so sorry—"

Her words shot through him like bullets, leaving his heart bleeding. He sank down onto the bed and stared at his feet. "Me too."

He didn't breathe again until he heard the snick of the door. He dragged in a breath, and then another, and then another just as he used to when he was beaten until his body hurt so bad he thought he'd pass out.

If he kept breathing, he'd keep living. He didn't have much of a choice. He had promises to keep and a little girl who needed him. Even if Nicki wasn't his daughter, she was still his kid.

His phone rang and he thought about not answering it, until he saw it was Thomas.

"Yeah." Storm hardly recognized his own voice.

"Storm, I got everything I need. The story is going to print."

"You got Knickerbocker?"

"He's as crooked as you thought. He owns all the property the city is buying for the Harbor Pier Project, and with the zoning change, that property, and all that surrounds it, is worth millions more today than it was a month and a half ago. Can you say conflict of interest?"

"You're keeping Bree out of it though, right, Thomas? I don't want her hurt by this."

"It won't touch her. She'll come out smelling like the rose she is. You have my word."

"I'll hold you to it. I'm leaving on the six forty-five to Auckland. I have a problem to take care of down there."

"What's going on?"

"The bulb weight on a Class 40 is more than two hundred pounds off, and I have to figure out what the hell is going on. I have to get down there."

"Understandable. When will you be back?"

"I don't know. I'll be in touch."

"I'll e-mail you the article. Look for it, and thanks for the tip—I owe you, my friend. We're going to blow this whole thing wide open."

"Just make sure it doesn't touch Bree and we'll call it even."

"Storm, are you okay?"

"I'll live." He just wasn't sure he wanted to. "I have to go. Talk to you soon."

Storm disconnected and called for a cab. Five minutes later, he was packed and stacked at the front door ready to go.

"Whatever you said to Bree had her running out of here in tears." Logan sat at the table, peeling the label off his beer. "Are you sure you want to leave like this?"

Storm checked his watch. "I'm not sure of anything anymore. All I know is that I have to get back to Auckland to see if I can save my contract, my professional reputation, and my company. After today, they're about all I have left."

Logan pulled him into a guy hug, clapping him on the back. "Say good-bye to Pop at least. He didn't look too good after you talked. He's in his room."

Storm dropped his briefcase and nodded. When he knocked on Pete's door, he heard a grumble and let himself in. "I'm taking off."

"Are you planning on coming back home?"

Damn, he wanted to think of Red Hook as home. He'd felt more at home here with Bree than he'd ever felt anywhere before in his life. Even the pain he felt now couldn't tarnish the sense of peace coming home had given him. He hoped it wasn't lost. "I promised Nicki I'd be back to see her."

"Good. I just hope it doesn't take you another five years."

"It won't. Try to behave, Pop. I'll see you."

Pop got out of bed and grabbed him in a hug. "I love you, son. So does Bree. It's my fault. I made her promise not to tell you."

Storm's eyes burned. "I've got a cab waiting. Bye, Pop."

Pop released him. He grabbed his luggage and took the steps two at a time. The cab screeched to a halt when he hit the sidewalk. He climbed into the backseat, gave the driver Patrice and Francis's address, and steeled himself to say good-bye to Nicki.

Patrice and Rocki banged on Bree's door until she opened it. Her eyes were swollen. She'd finally stopped crying, but the second she saw Patrice and Rocki, she broke down again.

Patrice pulled her into a hug. "Storm stopped by the house to say good-bye to Nicki."

"How did she take it?"

"Much better than I expected. Within a few minutes she was smiling and playing with the girls again. It was weird. I don't know what he said to her, but she only shed a few tears."

Rocki looked Bree up and down, "You, however, did not take it as well. You look like a snot factory. What happened?"

It took Bree a few minutes until she could talk; then she went to the couch and collapsed. "Pete thought Nicki might be Storm's child, and I didn't tell him."

Rocki crossed her arms and tapped the toe of her leopard-print kitten heels. "Why?"

Patrice passed Bree a handful of tissues.

"Because I was afraid that when he found out, he'd leave me. Because I'm selfish and stupid and a coward. Because I was too blind to see how much he'd changed, and I didn't trust him."

Patrice stood with her mouth open. Rocki just shook her head and, for the first time, kept silent.

Bree looked from one to the other. "Well?"

Rocki cocked her hip and rested her hand on it. "For once in your life, you're right. So what are you going to do about it?"

"What can I do? I apologized. When I told him I loved him, he said he wasn't sure I even knew my own mind, and then he left. He's gone. He's flying back to the Godzone. What can I do?"

Rocki rolled her eyes. "Is he the only one who can jump on a plane and fly to Auckland?"

"I don't even have a passport."

"So, get one. It will take some time to find people to cover for you. Oh, and remember, I'm not good behind the bar."

"As if I could forget."

Patrice perked up. "Francis has some vacation time coming. I'm sure he'd be happy to help. It might take a few weeks, though."

Rocki smiled and sat back in the chair. "It will take her at least that long to get her big-girl panties on to do what needs to be done."

"Storm doesn't want anything to do with me. I can't go all the way to Auckland. What if he tells me to get lost?"

"Then you find a nice beach, drink too many umbrella drinks, and have your way with a hot cabana boy. Next question?"

Patrice waved away Rocki's suggestion. "Bree, what if he doesn't? Do you want to spend the rest of your life wondering if you could have gotten him back?"

"Patrice, I've never gone any farther away from home than the Jersey Shore. I've never been on a plane. My mother will have a heart attack."

Rocki smirked. "Only if you tell her. But then, maybe you should. After she gets out of ICU, she could recuperate in the psych ward. It would do her good."

Rocki evaded Patrice's punch. "What the hell do you think I am, a Bozo the Clown Bop Bag, for heck's sake?"

Patrice laughed. "If only."

"Hey, I just say what everyone else thinks."

"You need a filter."

"Bree has a filter. She's filtered her entire life, and look where it's gotten her. Face it—sometimes you just have to put everything you got out there and screw the consequences. Sometimes you have to jump and trust someone else to catch you. Sometimes you have to put your dignity aside and beg. And earth to Bree—this is one of those times."

# CHAPTER 21

Bree got out of bed with the knowledge that Storm was still in the air. She thought about him every second. Every minute put more distance between them; every hour the pain of her loss increased. She'd held a slim hope he'd land in LA, turn around, and come home. If he had, he'd have been home by now. He wasn't.

She hadn't slept. Oh, she'd tried—she'd drowned her sorrows with more than a half bottle of wine until she figured out it only served to make pacing and mental self-flagellation more dangerous. She'd never realized how many things there were in her apartment to run into.

Now, not only did she feel as if she'd gone nine rounds with a heavyweight prizefighter; she also had a few new bruises to add to her collection.

There was nowhere in her world she could go that didn't bring back memories of Storm. Her shower, her bed, every room of Pete's apartment, the bar, heck, even the grocery store. Together they'd walked D.O.G. down every block in Red Hook. She'd started running with Storm, so even Carroll Gardens wasn't safe. There was nowhere to escape the memory of him, and after fourteen hours, she was tired of fighting it, especially since it did no good. She stood in the shower and let the memories flow. She leaned against the tile wall and cried until the water went cold; then she went downstairs, grabbed the morning paper, and headed to work.

Tossing the paper on her desk, she poured her first cup of coffee, popped a few Excedrin in her mouth, and looked at the paper as she took her first sip. She choked on both the pills and the headline.

### RED HOOK ROCKED BY SCANDAL. KNICKERBOCKER DUPES CITY IN HARBOR PIER PROJECT SCAM.

"Scam?" The air whooshed from her lungs as she started coughing, sputtering, and choking on her coffee. She slammed her mug on the cluttered desk and knocked it over in the process. Grabbing the paper, she waved it like a flag. Coffee flew everywhere, reminding her of D.O.G. after a bath. She grabbed a handful of tissues to dab up the remaining moisture before the paper disintegrated.

What the hell was going on? She recognized the name of the reporter who worked for Thomas. She'd met her at the zoning board meeting. "Shit. Does everything in my life have to fall apart at the same time?"

She scanned the article. Daniel owned a series of shell companies that owned the pier and all the surrounding land. With the zoning board change that she personally effected, the zoning of the pier and surrounding area went from industrial to mixed commercial, thereby increasing its value tenfold. The city had a written agreement for the sale of the pier, but Daniel would make a killing off all the other land. She wasn't sure it was illegal, but it stank worse than a garbage strike in an August heat wave. "That slimy bastard."

She sank back into her chair and slumped her ass to the edge of the seat. How stupid was she? She had played right into Daniel's hands and had allowed him to use her. She paved the way for the humiliation of the entire board. The worst part was that he couldn't have done it without her help, making her just as guilty— maybe not of any real wrongdoing, but the guilt of stupidity was a hard pill to swallow. Harder than the Excedrin.

If she could have the wool pulled over her eyes so thoroughly, she had no right being on the board of anything. She'd have to resign her position. She'd let herself down, let her community down, and worst of all, she'd let her father down. She had lost everything.

Her cell phone rang and she reached for it, hoping it was Storm, which was ridiculous because he was halfway over the Pacific by now. When she saw Thomas's name on the screen, she considered not answering. But then what was the point in ignoring it? She was sure between her fellow board members and the press, her phone would be ringing off the hook. Rocki's voice rang out, loud and clear in her head, ordering her to put on her big-girl panties and get on with it. "Bree Collins." Just because she had to speak to him didn't mean she had to be happy about it.

"Congratulations, Bree."

"Congratulations? On what? On being exposed as the biggest patsy in all of New York? Thomas, I'm not making any statements to the press. I'm sure we'll be convening an emergency committee meeting shortly. I'll let you know when we have a statement."

"Did you read the article?"

"No, I choked and spit my coffee all over it. I did get the first paragraph read, though."

"Bree, I just got off the phone with the mayor's office. He'd like you to be at the press briefing today."

"Excuse me?"

"My driver can pick you up at noon. The mayor would like to speak with you before the briefing. He mentioned something about an opening on the New York City Council on Community Development."

"But Thomas, I played right into Daniel Knickerbocker's hands. I was publicly made a fool of. I'm practically a political pariah. He tried to scam the city with my help."

"You played an integral part in the development of the Harbor Pier Project. Honey, it took one of my best reporters weeks of research to connect Knickerbocker to the half dozen shell companies that own the land—the man knows how to cover his tracks. It was your questioning his dissociation at the zoning board meeting that convinced me there was a story there." Thomas waited a beat before he continued. "If you'd read the entire article, you'd find that Daniel has become a true philanthropist and has gifted the pier to the city for the park you've worked so hard to bring about."

"He's getting away with it?"

"Oh, I wouldn't exactly say that. Knickerbocker never got far enough to actually break any laws, although I'm sure he would have, had you and Storm not alerted the press to your suspicions. But don't worry, my dear. He's on the DA's shit list now. He'll have the entire office watching his every move, and I'm sure the state auditors are sharpening their pencils."

Bree pinched the bridge of her nose and released a long where's-my-fairy-godmother-when-I-need-her sigh. "I don't know what Storm told you, but I was completely clueless when it came to Daniel. I plan to tender my resignation from the Revitalization Committee today. I'm the last person the mayor should want on the city council."

"I think you're wrong about that. Storm didn't tell me anything you didn't tell him. And he was adamant you not be touched by this. Luckily, that was an easy condition to meet. You've been impeccable in all your dealings, and everyone we've interviewed has had nothing but the highest praise for your work and commitment to Red Hook."

"They're wrong."

"Bree, take some advice from an old man who's been around the block more than a few times. Come to the mayor's office this afternoon. You don't have to make any commitments. All I ask is that you listen. There's plenty of time to resign if that's your decision, but no decision like that should be made in haste. I've told you before, and I'll tell you again, you're going places, young lady. All you have to do is get out of your own way."

"When will you be home, Storm?"

He did his best to smile at Nicki's pretty little face on his phone. "I don't know, kiddo. I'm on my way from the airport to the boat builder, so it's too early to even tell what I'm dealing with."

"I miss you and so does Bree."

"Did you have fun at Patrice and Francis's?"

"I guess." She shrugged her little shoulders. "We had a sleepover, and Ms. Patrice was at a party with Bree, so Mr. Francis ordered pizza and let us stay up late."

Storm's shoulders tightened when he heard Bree's name. "What kind of party?"

"A pity party. He said it involves a weenie roast, too much wine, and tissues. He made us be real quiet this morning. He even took us to the park."

"That's good. So, have you seen Bree since you got home?"

"Nope. Logan said she's hanging with the mayor. She was on TV and everything. Cool, huh?"

"Are you sure?"

"Did you know Logan puts girl stuff in his hair?"

"What's Bree doing with the mayor?"

"You don't put girl stuff in your hair, do you?"

"What? No, but I'm sure Logan uses guy stuff, not girl stuff."

"It smells girly." Nicki wrinkled her nose, and the picture bopped up and down as if she were prancing. The jiggling on his FaceTime screen wasn't helping his headache.

"You okay, Nicki?"

"Yeah, I just gotta go to the bathroom. I love you, Storm. Come home soon." The picture changed from Nicki's face to what looked like the light fixture in her bedroom. She must have thrown the iPad on her bed and run for the head.

The sound of her footsteps meeting him from thousands of miles away made his heart ache more than his head, and that was saying something. He looked at the familiar landscape and missed the sights and sounds of home. He had felt more comfortable in Red Hook than he felt on the waterfront of Auckland. He didn't know how it happened, but there was no arguing with the truth. He rubbed his gritty eyes and then his chest, and disconnected FaceTime. He had work to do. At least work might keep him from thinking about Bree.

Rocki stepped into Bree's office and quickly exited. She stopped, looked around, and then returned.

Bree was used to her theatrics. She didn't like them, but she was used to them. "What do you need, Rocki?"

Rocki panned the entire room. "Where are all your files?"

"Put away." Bree stepped over D.O.G., who had taken to following Bree around since Storm left, and sat at her desk.

Rocki held her sleeve and wiped the top of Bree's desk. "You even dusted. Are you feeling okay?"

"I'm fine."

"I thought I was in the wrong office, seriously." She flopped into her chair and tossed her leg over the arm. "I've heard of spring cleaning but never fall gutting. Who knew the top of your desk was mahogany? Alert the media—oh, never mind, you've already done that, haven't you? So, how was your meeting with Mikey?"

"The mayor was very nice. The meeting was fine."

"Fine? You rub elbows with the mayor and that's all I get? Time to dish, girlfriend. How big are his feet?"

"Let's just say he has a big presence and leave it at that."

"Really? So are you trying to get the Good House-keeping Seal of Approval, or are you nesting? Is there something you need to tell me?"

Bree looked up from the pile of mail she was sorting and raised an eyebrow. "Other than get out?"

"If I didn't know any better, I'd think you were cleaning up in case you get a wild hair and feel the need to fly the friendly skies."

"Rocki, I let a lot of things slide since Pete got sick. With Nicki back in school, Pete coming down to help out on occasion, and Logan working full-time, I'm able to do some catching up. You don't have to make a federal case of it."

"I'm not, but now that you brought it up, you didn't happen to stop by the post office to get your passport, did you?"

Bree tossed the junk mail she'd sorted into the trash before standing. "Yes, okay? I got my freakin' passport — or applied for it at least. Are you happy now?"

Rocki gave her one of the few rare glimpses of her heart. "Yes, I'm happy. I hate seeing you like this. Storm's been gone a week and you're miserable, you've lost weight, and it doesn't look as if you've gotten a good night's sleep since before that. I'm just worried about you."

Bree sank back into her chair, deflated. "I'm sorry. Look, getting a passport is a far cry from flying to New Zealand."

"But at least having one gives you the option. Has Storm called?"

"Not me. Pete said he talks to Nicki every day. She said he's growing a beard."

"Really?"

Bree started to say something and Rocki put a hand up to stop her. "I'm trying to come up with a mental picture here. Not bad, not bad at all. Anything else?"

"Only that Nicki insists that Storm is coming home. If he does, it won't be to see me." She laid her head on the desk. "God, how long is it going to hurt like this?"

Rocki jumped up and ran around Bree's desk to hug her. "I don't know, Bree, but since you never got over him the first time, I think you should just bite the bullet and go after the man. Honestly, when you weren't at each other's throats, you were great together. Even when you were ready to kill each other, you ended up with beard burn." She stepped away, "Face it, Bree. You're pretty much toast anyway. What do you have left to lose?"

As much as Bree didn't want to hear it, Rocki was right. She'd either have to go after Storm or enter a nunnery.

"You made one mistake, but over time, even someone as stubborn as Storm should be able to see you didn't mean to hurt him. You were only protecting yourself, and you promised Pete. And let us not forget, you weren't the only one invested in this relationship. That man had it bad for you. He's probably hurting as badly as you are."

"Doubtful. I'm sure there are plenty of rich women after him, who are more than happy to help him take his mind off me."

Rocki shook her head. "Oh no. Storm only has eyes for you. You're not the only one who never got over her first love. You don't give yourself enough credit." Rocki clapped her hands. "You know what you need?"

"A bottle of sleeping pills?"

Rocki shot her a disgusted look. "No, retail therapy. What do you say we make a run to the city and hit Macy's and Nordstrom Rack? We can shop for the perfect dream vacation. If things work out with Storm, you won't need clothes, but if not, you'll have to wear something fabulous to pick up that cabana boy we talked about."

"I have plenty of clothes."

"None that I'd be caught wearing. Really, Bree, you're supposed to dress to attract men, not scare them away."

Rocki pulled Bree's purse out of her bottom desk drawer. "Logan's manning the bar, so that's covered, and Nicki's not going to be back from school for hours."

"Okay." Bree threw her hands in the air. "I give up. I'm not strong enough to fight you." She accepted her purse from Rocki, shooed the dog up the back stairs, and called up to Pete; then she took one more look around her office to be sure there was nothing left to catch up on. "Maybe retail therapy will help. It's worth a try anyway."

"Lucky for you my fee is only a mani-pedi and a new pair of shoes."

Storm awoke with his assistant standing over him. The look on her face made him move to protect his genitals. In the six years Sandy had worked for him, he'd never seen her pissed, but he'd heard her husband describe the phenomenon. Brad didn't do her justice—she looked like the Tasmanian Devil on a bender.

"You look like you're going bush. I could smell you as soon as I entered the office even though your door was closed."

"You couldn't knock?"

"I thought something that smelled as bad as you carked it."

"As you can see, I'm alive and well."

"I'll give you alive; well is another story all together. What the hell are you doing sleeping in your office?"

"What does it matter?" Storm had gone to his condo, and the place seemed as empty as his life. He didn't bother unpacking; he just picked up his bag and brought it to the office. He'd been at the boatyard pulling eighteen-hour days for almost two weeks, trying to figure out where the extra bulb weight was. He'd gone back and forth over his plans, and they'd all checked out. He'd spent the rest of the time crawling around the yacht. In the last few days he'd contorted himself into positions that would make the author of the Kama Sutra blush. He hurt everywhere.

Sandy held her hand over her nose and mouth. "Listen, mate, this has got to stop. I can't take it anymore. You've been narking at me ever since you returned, and when you're not narking, you look like you're off with the fairies."

"Off with the fairies? What the—"

"Daydreaming, woolgathering, whatever else you Yanks call it. You smell like you belong in a zoo."

"I didn't get a chance to shower last night. I was so knackered, I just passed out."

"Did you find the problem?"

"The extra weight? Of course I did."

"Was it the builder's fault?"

"Was there ever any doubt?"

Sandy laughed. "The only doubts were yours. Half the reason you smell as bad as you do is because you were so worried about it, you forgot to bathe. So what did they do this time?"

"I came up with a clever structural matrix that allowed minimal frames and bulkheads and maximized strength with a very light structure. The builder had never seen anything like it, so he added a few extra frames on his own. It's a good thing the bulb weight was off. If I hadn't caught them, the extra frames would have taken the majority of the load and would have failed."

"Problem solved, then?"

"If only all my problems were so easy to solve."

With a face to match her mood, she swept his legs off the couch. "Now do you want to tell me why you came back looking like a dingo with the mange and madder than a croc after a root canal?"

He let out a low groan. "God, my head didn't hurt this bad when Bree walloped me with the frying pan."

"What?"

"It's a long story."

"We've got time — after you shower. I'll make coffee."

Storm stood and stretched, rubbing his chest. Oh man, he definitely needed a shower.

"Don't forget to shave — again."

Fifteen minutes and half a bar of soap later, Storm sat across from Taz, wolfing down Marmite and toast.

"Okay, mate, get on with your story."

"There's not much to tell. Whatever I thought I had with Bree was an illusion."

Sandy sat back, crossed her arms, and thrummed her fingers on her surprisingly toned biceps. "Not that part; I already heard the whole thing from your friends Rocki and Patrice."

"You talked to the two stooges?"

"Three, Pete was on the line too."

"Oh God."

"It was like a long-distance intervention. You have a fascinating group of friends, and your family sounds lovely."

"That's one way to put it."

"What I want to know is the story about the frying pan. They left that out, little else, but they never mentioned an attack using an unconventional weapon."

"I got home in the middle of the night and let myself into the apartment. I didn't even think. I just headed to my old room, and Bree walloped me over the head with a cast-iron frying pan. She wasn't expecting me and thought I was a burglar."

"Are you sure it wasn't in retaliation for running out on her?"

"I think if she'd known who it was, she would have finished me off."

"She might still. After all, you ran away from her again."

"I did not run. I had to leave. They'd stopped work on the boat. They were charging us eight thousand dollars a day."

Sandy laughed in his face. "Oh right, so you were forced to take the six forty-five flight. You couldn't have talked your problems out and caught the nine fifty? I'm sure the three hours and five minutes made all the difference in the world. Face it, mate; you ran. You got your feelings hurt and you ran."

Storm dropped his head. Shame flooded his face, radiating to his hands that blocked Sandy's view. He'd run all right, but not because he was scared. He'd run because he was hurt—hurt because Bree hadn't trusted him enough to tell him about Nicki, hurt by Pete for thinking he could run out on his own child, and hurt by life because he'd never realized before how much he wanted to be Nicki's dad. "Fuck. Bree's gonna kill me."

"Possibly. Still, if you stay here, I'm definitely going to quit, and that's only if I don't kill you first. I think you'll have better luck going back to Bree; at least she claims to love you. So, what are you doing here talking to me instead of getting your arse on the first plane to the States?"

*             *             *

*It's here.* Bree ripped open the envelope, pulled out her new passport, and ran her fingers across the embossed gold lettering before flipping it open. Yep, that was a picture of her. The thought of using it sent her heart pounding like a steel drum.

Could she really do it? Could she get on a plane and cross the Pacific, land in a foreign country, and take a chance on Storm? She closed the cover and stuffed the passport in her top desk drawer. The answer at that moment at least, was no. Besides, it was a Monday. She had shopping to do, and her liquor salesmen were slated for that afternoon. She rose, grabbed her purse, and slid the top desk drawer shut. "The more things change, the more they stay the same."

Bree drove to the Fairway Market with her collection of lists—hers, Pete and Logan's, and her mother's. She didn't know why she bothered wasting paper on a list for her mother, because every week she bought the same damn thing. The only variation was when her mother ran out of laundry and dishwashing detergent.

Bree roamed the aisles, and everywhere she looked brought back memories of Storm. She walked by the bakery and remembered the piece of cannoli cake they'd shared. She passed the flowers and pictured him grabbing a bunch and tossing them in the cart just because. She thought about the day he'd run to the market because he thought they actually needed chocolate syrup with their ice cream and then snuck it into the bedroom later that night.

God, she missed him.

By rote, Bree pulled up to her mother's house and grabbed her mother's green reusable bags. An early-fall wind had her pulling her sweatshirt around her more tightly before slinging two bags over her shoulder, grabbing two more, and shouldering her mother's side door open. "Mom, it's me."

"Breanna, did you remember to check the list?"

As if she needed to. "Yes, and they had a special on tomatoes, so I picked up a few extras."

Her mother stepped into the kitchen wearing the same clothes, the same sour look, and making the same annoying tsk, tsk, tsk she'd heard all her life. "I wish you'd follow the list I gave you. The tomatoes will probably go to waste."

"Fine, if you don't want them, I'll take them home with me." She left the damn tomatoes in the bag and put away the rice.

"Coretta told me that Storm Decker left again."

Bree really needed to ask Patrice not to feed information to her mother—it always got back to Bree's mom in the end.

"Poor Pete must be beside himself. I told you Storm would leave. Men like him always do. I suppose you're upset."

"I—"

"I don't know why. I told you before and I'll tell you again, dangerous men always leave. You're better off without him."

"I don't want to talk about this, Mom."

"I understand. You're hurt."

"Yes, I'm hurt, and you're not helping matters. I love Storm and he's gone. Leave it alone, all right?" She turned her back to her mother and did her best to stop the tears welling in her burning eyes. God, leave it to her mother to put a healthy dose of salt on the wounds.

"I don't know why you don't date that nice man Daniel Knickerbocker. He's rich, he has a good, safe job, and he'll take care of us."

"Us?" Was she mad? "I guess you didn't hear the news, Mom. Daniel tried to scam the city and is under investigation."

"Oh? Well, that is a shame." She wore the same pinched look she'd worn since Bree's father died. "You just need to find another safe, stable man who will be there for you."

"Mom, I love Storm. The last thing I want is another man."

"What's love got to do with anything? Forget about those romantic notions. Love should never be on your short list. It will do nothing but leave you hurt and broken."

She was hurt and broken, all right, but how much of that was her own fault? How much of it was because she was paralyzed by fear? How much of it was because she was as trapped as her own mother, only in a larger cage? God, she had to get out. The walls closed in on her and she could hear every door and window slamming shut, trapping her and making it hard to breathe.

"I'm going to leave the bags for you to empty. I'll pick them up later."

"But you always unload my groceries."

"Not today, Mom. Today I'm shaking things up. Bye." She ran out of the house so fast, she wasn't sure the door had even closed behind her, and she didn't care. Her mother could close the damn door by herself. Bree was finished being suffocated by her mother. She was finished with a lot of things.

\*     \*     \*

Bree rushed into the bar like a diver kicking to the surface, gulping air as she broke through the door. She walked in on what looked like a private powwow over beer. She didn't bother asking what everyone was doing there on a Monday. She had too much to do to care.

Pete, Logan, Rocki, Patrice, and Francis wore matching stunned expressions. What the hell was going on? She didn't bother to ask for fear she'd lose her nerve.

Bree pushed her hands into her pants pockets to keep them from shaking, took a deep breath, and jumped off her virtual cliff. "I have an announcement to make. I've decided to take a vacation, starting immediately. Logan, you have the bar. The liquor orders are all ready to go; just give them to the salesmen. Next week Pete can help you with the orders if you have questions. Francis, did you get that time off? Can you cover me?"

"No problem, Bree."

Patrice elbowed him, and Francis gave her the please-don't-make-me-sleep-on-the-couch-again look, which made no sense. Patrice and Rocki had both pushed her to get her passport, they'd pushed her to take time off, and they'd pushed her to chase after Storm. Bree shook the questions from her thoughts. She couldn't afford to slow down; if she lost momentum, she'd be sunk. "Good, then it's all taken care of. I'm going upstairs to pack."

Bree power-walked to her office with the click, click, click of Rocki's high heels trailing behind her. Bree pulled out her brand-spanking-new passport and shoved it into her back pocket. She was really going to do this even if it killed her. She was going to escape her cage and find Storm. She wasn't going to die without ever going more than a hundred miles from home. She wasn't her mother.

Rocki blocked the door. "What the hell is going on with you?"

"If you want to talk, you'd better do it while I pack. I don't have time to screw around. I've got to get the next plane out."

"What's the rush?" Patrice took up whatever space Rocki left in the doorway.

"Move or I'll knock the both of you on your asses."

They moved, but they followed her into her apartment.

Bree needed to pack but realized she didn't even own a freakin' suitcase. How sick was that? "Pete," she hollered, "I'm borrowing your luggage." Not waiting for a reply, she stepped into the storage closet and took the largest piece of luggage she could find. It looked like something she'd seen tied to the back of the Beverly Hillbillies' truck. Fabulous. At least it would be easy to spot.

"You're using that?" Rocki and Patrice asked in stereo.

"I don't have luggage of my own—I've never been anywhere."

Rocki spread her legs and arms, blocking the hallway, and looking like a sexier punk version of Elastigirl. "You can't take those relics. They belong in a museum. Use mine. I just have to run home and get them."

"No time."

"When is the plane?" Patrice asked.

"I don't know. I have to call and book a flight."

Patrice stepped in front of Rocki. "Where's the fire, Bree? It took you two weeks to make the decision, and now you're racing to leave? What are you running from?"

"Nothing. It's what I'm running to. I can't stay, and

I'm afraid if I slow down, I'll lose my nerve and I'll be trapped here forever."

Patrice looked hurt. "You think we're trapping you?"

"No, not you, me. Storm was right. I'm turning into my mother. I have to find him and make things up to him. You two will look after my mom and Pete when I'm away, won't you?"

Patrice and Rocki both gave her a stunned nod.

"Good. That's good." Bree pushed her hair out of her eyes. "I have to go, don't you see? I have to, or I'll spend the rest of my life regretting it. Even if it doesn't work out between us, he's worth the risk. If Storm doesn't want me, at least I'll have done something, I'll have put my heart out there on the line, I'll be living—really living and not trapped in some kind of sick half life. I love you guys, but I have to go."

A look passed between Rocki and Patrice as if they made a silent agreement. Patrice grabbed Bree's shaking, slightly clammy hand and squeezed it. "Okay. Come on Rocki. Let's run to your place and pick up your luggage. Bree, we'll be back in twenty minutes, thirty tops."

"What am I going to do for thirty minutes?"

Rocki rolled her eyes. "Primp, of course, and then get everything together to pack."

"I need a ticket." Bree left them staring after her and ran down to her office, got on the computer, Googled plane tickets, and clicked on the first recognizable name.

She was really going to do this. The words blurred on the screen, and she had to remind herself that people flew every day. She wasn't afraid of flying. She just had never done it before. The whole taking off and landing thing made her nervous, so she chose the fewest number

of stops—one. New York to LA and then direct to Auckland.

"Twenty-three hundred dollars? Damn, who knew
last-minute flights were so expensive?" Bree reminded
herself that she'd saved money all her life, saving every
last cent without even knowing what she was saving for.
God, she was worse than she'd ever imagined.

Bree typed her credit card information, took a deep
breath, and with a shaking finger clicked the Purchase
button. Fear mixed with exhilaration and filled her as the
printer spit out the boarding pass and itinerary. Now all
she had to do was pack and find several pairs of big-girl
panties. She just hoped they didn't look like Depends.

# CHAPTER 22

The last time Storm had made the trip from JFK to Red Hook it had been the middle of the night, and, in the heat of summer, it had felt like a drive straight into hell. It was amazing how his entire life changed in just two months. The bright blue skies and chilly temperatures welcoming him home would have made the trip enjoyable if he hadn't been sweating his reception.

He'd screwed up royally—again. He scrubbed his hands over his face and imagined what Breezy would hit him with when he came through the door this time. He was just glad New York had strict gun laws.

Storm had spent the last twenty-four hours trying to come up with a way to win Bree back. When his cab pulled up to the Crow's Nest, he still hadn't come up with a sure thing. And that was what he needed—a sure thing. He couldn't afford to lose Breezy again. He couldn't imagine his life without her in it. He didn't want to. Being away from her for a few weeks had been worse then the eleven years they'd been apart. He couldn't go on like this.

Storm got out of the cab and found Francis backed up against the wall with fear in his eyes and Rocki and Patrice bearing down on him like a couple of rabid dogs—cute dogs, but dogs all the same.

Patrice poked Francis in the chest, sharpened claws enunciating every word. "If you let her leave, Francis Salvatore DeBruscio, you'll spend the rest of your natural life on the couch. Got it?"

Storm heaved his duffel over his shoulder, grabbed his computer case with the other hand, and stepped into Francis's line of vision.

A look of pure relief crossed his face. He stood straighter and pointed right at Storm. "He's here. He's here."

Rocki and Patrice turned, spotted him, and shot him matching grins. He wasn't sure if they were happy to see him or looking forward to planning his funeral.

Francis wiped beads of sweat off his forehead. "Bree's upstairs. I hope for your sake, and mine, it's a warm welcome. I'll say a prayer."

"Thanks, man. You'd better light a candle for me too. I'm going to need all the help I can get."

Patrice put her hands on her hips, stepped in front of him, and got in his face. "Well, Storm, what the hell are you waiting for, an engraved invitation?"

"Calm down, Patty." Storm adjusted his duffel, sliding it against his back so he could fit through the door when Patrice hauled off and slugged him right in the diaphragm. The air whooshed out of his lungs, and he put his free hand up to block her.

"You leave Bree again and you'll answer to me. Do you know how painful broken kneecaps can be?"

"I have a picture in my mind."

"Good, keep it there." She turned to Francis and said, "Come on, we're going to pick up Nicki from school."

"We are?"

Patrice rolled her eyes. "Just get in the car, honey. I'll explain it all to you on the way." She patted his shoulder and grabbed Rocki. "Come on, Rocki. We'll give you a ride home." Patrice was already pushing them in front of her toward the car.

Storm looked around the neighborhood he grew up in with new eyes. He was home—in Red Hook, a place he'd known all his life but had to search the whole world to find.

He drank in the scent of home, climbed to the top of the stairs, and found Bree's door wide open. She'd just walked into her bedroom. He slipped down the hall and peeked in.

Breezy had her head buried in her closet, taking clothes out, examining them, and either putting them back or tossing them on a pile on the bed. "How long does it take to pick up a freakin' suitcase? Where the hell are they?"

Storm needed to say something. He'd intended to surprise her, but the longer he watched, the more he felt like a creepy stalker. "I saw Rocki, Patrice, and Francis leave just a minute ago."

Bree stumbled out of her closet and sat hard on the bed, crushing a slanted pile of clothes beneath her. Her mouth hung open, her eyes confused and unblinking, her face devoid of color. He'd seen that look before—it was the same look she wore when he'd told her that he'd made love only to her. It was as if she thought she was hearing things, or in this case seeing things.

"Breezy, can I come in?"

She blinked once, so he took it as a yes.

He held his breath and stepped inside. Damn, he

should have stopped to get her some flowers, a ring, something. He just stood there, looking stupid with his duffel bag and computer case. Maybe he did deserve a crack on the head. He dropped his bags on the floor, pulled her off the bed and into his arms. "Now that's much better." He nuzzled her neck, drinking in her scent of citrus, spice, and Breezy. "God, I've missed you."

"What are you doing here?" She seemed more shocked than angry, but she didn't push him away.

"I fixed the problem with the boat and came home. I never should have left like I did. I should have taken time to talk to you and hear you out. I'm sorry."

"You ran."

"I kept telling myself I had to leave — and I did. I have a lot riding on this boat, but it was an excuse for running. You're right. But it was different this time: I didn't run because I was scared; I ran because I was hurt. I was hurt that you didn't feel you could trust me. I was hurt because the man I love and respect most in the world thought I was capable of deserting my own child."

She wrapped her arms around him and kissed his cheek. "I'm so sorry."

"Breezy, I loved you when we were kids, but what I feel for you now — it's not even in the same galaxy. I fell in love with you all over again. I fell in love with a woman who would take down a grown man with a frying pan to protect a child she loves. I fell in love with the woman who single-handedly dealt with Pop and turned a run-down longshoreman's dive into a classy, thriving restaurant and bar. I fell in love with a woman who worked tirelessly in her father's memory to make her home the incredible place Red Hook is becoming. I fell in love with you, Nicki, and my hometown. I want to come back to you, Breezy, if you'll have me. I want to be here with you and our family. I don't think I can go on without you. I don't want to try."

She blinked back tears, and she hadn't kicked his ass to the curb yet. He took it as a good sign. She still wore that shell-shocked look, but that was okay. She'd process it in her own time.

He looked pointedly at the bed covered with clothes. "So, what are you doing with all this stuff?"

"I was packing, but I remembered I don't even have luggage."

"Where are you going?"

"Patrice and Rocki goaded me into applying for my passport after you left. I was mad at you and I was hurt, but most of all I was scared. You've been right since day one. I was becoming my mother."

"Hold on. I didn't mean—"

Bree rested her finger on his lips. "I was. I didn't see it at first. My mother doesn't leave her house except to go out into her backyard. She's afraid of life, and I've been enabling her for years." She shook her head as if to rid herself of something. "Storm, did you know that I've never gone more than a hundred miles from Red Hook?"

He shrugged. "So. It's not a federal offense. A lot of people don't travel."

"It wasn't because I didn't have the opportunity. I could have gone to Europe for a semester abroad; I had a job offer in California. I just didn't have the guts. And I was afraid to love you, afraid to let you love me."

"Bree, you love Red Hook. It's your home."

"Yes, but Red Hook is a place. I wanted to fulfill my father's dream and make Red Hook everything it can be. But that was his dream. I finally figured it out. Red Hook is home, but the only place I've ever felt complete was with you. So today I bought a plane ticket."

"What?"

Bree pulled a bunch of papers out of her pocket and held them over her chest. "I just spent twenty-three hundred dollars on a ticket to Auckland because that's where I thought you were. I was going to see if you'd forgive me and come back to me. I love Nicki and Pete, and I love my job, but I don't want to live without you ever again. Storm, I loved the boy you were and the man you've become. I'll love you forever."

"Thank God." Storm kissed her and couldn't believe his luck. He pulled the ticket from between them and let out a laugh.

"I don't see what's so damn funny. It's a nonrefundable ticket, and the plane leaves in three hours."

He tossed the ticket and her passport onto the floor. "Looks like you're gonna be missing your flight, babe." With one swipe of his hand, the pile of clothes flew off the bed, and then he kissed her, backing her up to the bed. He had her pants unbuttoned and was pulling her shirt up, which meant he had to release her mouth.

Her eyes sparkled with excitement and anger—his favorite combination. "Are you telling me I just blew twenty-three hundred dollars?"

"No, we just need to change the ticket." He hoped. He loved seeing the fire in her, but he wasn't about to push it.

Her shirt hit the ground, and he tackled her onto the bed. His body covered hers and he was almost home; he just needed to lose his pants and hers. He looked down at her, her hair wild, her eyes flashing, and her lips swollen from his kisses.

"What the hell are we going to do with the ticket?"

"I guess there's always the honeymoon." He was getting used to her shocked look. It didn't scare him half as much as it used to. Still, he felt the need to clarify. He'd never proposed to anyone before and hoped to hell he never had to again. "You know that thing you do after you get married?"

"Uh-huh."

"Was that a yes?"

There was that fire in her eyes again. Only now the heat danced with anticipation and promise. "Uh-huh. Welcome home, Storm."

# CHAPTER 23

Bree parked her car outside the Crow's Nest and looked over at her mother. "Are you doing okay?" It had been almost three weeks since her mother, with much arm-twisting, had agreed to get help for her problem. The medication and biweekly visits to a caring therapist were working wonders.

Her mother gave her a shaky smile. "The therapist said it was going to be difficult, but it's something I'm strong enough to do. I'll be fine."

Bree reached over and hugged her. "I'm so proud of you, Mom."

Noreen teared up. "I'm so sorry, honey. I should have done this so long ago. . . . I wasted so much time. If I had known—"

"Stop. You're doing something about it now. That's all that matters, right?"

Noreen took a deep breath, wiped her eyes, and pasted on a smile. "Right."

"Good. Coretta will be there with Patrice and Francis and their kids, Pete and Nicki, of course, Storm and Logan, and probably Rocki."

Bree got out of the car and placed her hand on top of the door, her new engagement ring clinking against the frame. She still wasn't used to wearing it and couldn't help but admire the way the pear-shaped diamond caught the light. She'd never been happier and did her best not to sigh.

When she looked up, her mother smiled at her—a real honest-to-goodness smile. Noreen Collins lit up like the Christmas tree at Rockefeller Center. Bree had even talked her into Internet shopping, and she wore a new outfit. "Mom, you look amazing. I'm so glad you're here." She walked around the car and took her mother by the hand like she used to. Instead of stifling, it felt as natural as she suspected it should. Hand in hand they walked toward the Crow's Nest.

The outer door opened and Storm stepped out, engulfing Bree in a hug before turning to her mom. "Hi, Mrs. Collins."

"Hello, Storm. Please call me Noreen."

"Okay." He looked from Bree to her mother. "Look, there's something I have to tell you." He wiped his face with his hand. "I didn't have anything to do with it, but it seems they've planned a surprise party. I'm sorry, babe." Storm took her mother's hand. "Noreen, if you're not up for it—"

"It's fine." Her mother looked Storm in the eye and smiled—two genuine smiles in less than a few minutes. "Pete called and asked if a party was okay with me. I haven't been to a party in years, and I wouldn't miss this one for the world."

Bree wondered if she was hearing things. "You knew?" Wow, the medication was really working. A huge weight she hadn't even been aware she'd carried slipped from her shoulders.

Storm opened the door and ushered them in. "Noreen, we're here for you if the gang gets to be too much, but from the way you look, I think you're going to have fun."

Bree watched Storm take her mother's arm and fell a little bit more in love with him. She didn't think it was possible, but she did. This ranked right up there as the happiest day of her life. Stepping inside, she took it all in and blinked back tears. Everyone was there. Everyone — Nicki and Logan, Rocki's band, Storm, Bree's favorite customers, the liquor distributors, Pete's entire crew, Patrice and her whole family, even Thomas Danby.

Storm gave her his good-time grin and a what-are-you-gonna-do shrug before pointing out the banner hanging over the bar that said CONGRATULATIONS, BREE AND STORM!

She sucked in a lungful of air and tried to calm her racing heart.

Pete stepped out of the crowd wearing a smile so dazzling, Bree was tempted to reach for her sunglasses. He wrapped his arms around her mother and hugged her close. "Noreen, it's so wonderful to have you back where you belong. I've missed you." He gave her a smacking kiss on both cheeks. "Quinn is looking down on you and smiling."

Noreen placed a hand on Pete's cheek. "I'm so sorry—"

"Now, none of that. We're celebrating a wonderful new beginning, for you, and for Bree and Storm. It's a fine day for it, don't you think?"

Noreen nodded, and Pete kept his arm around her as they made their way to the bar. "Now sit yourself down and I'll get you a drink. What will it be?"

"Just a sparkling water, Pete."

Bree caught Nicki, who'd run right into her arms, hugging her tight. "Hi, sweetie." Nicki wore a frilly dress. "Look at you!" Nicki held out the skirt of her dress. "Miss Rocki bought it and made me wear it. It's pink." Nicki obviously wasn't a fan of the color or the dress.

Storm put his arm around Nicki. "I think you both look beautiful."

Nicki beamed, and Bree was pretty sure she was doing her fair share of beaming too. But then she had been ever since Storm came back to her.

One of Patrice's kids called Nicki; she said a quick good-bye and ran off to play.

Storm tugged her away as Patrice's mother took the stool beside Noreen. "Your mom's doing great, huh?"

"Yes, she's doing amazingly well." She saw the tension in her mother's stiff back, but Bree supposed that was to be expected. Life was good. Pete too was getting better and stronger every day. It was great to see him behind the bar again.

Bree rested against Storm's chest as he kissed the side of her neck. "Let's take a few minutes to say hello to everyone else. Coretta's keeping an eye on your mom. We won't go far."

Bree turned in his arms. "How do you know the exact right thing to say?"

"I know you, Breezy, and I love you."

Bree and Storm spent the next hour talking with friends and dancing to the "For Lovers Only" playlist Rocki performed with her band.

Storm held her close, swaying to "Someone Like You." "Uh-oh."

Bree leaned back to look into his eyes. "What's wrong?"

"Thomas and your mother have their heads together, and Pop looks . . . Damn, he looks jealous."

"What?" Storm spun them around so Bree could see. Thomas definitely seemed to be cozying up to her mom, and Pete looked put out. "Maybe Thomas is just being friendly and Pete's being protective."

"Thomas is definitely being friendly—real friendly. Your mom's a beautiful woman, Bree, and Thomas is single. His wife died years ago, and he's a great guy, but Pop doesn't like it at all. Your mom, on the other hand, looks as if she's having a great time."

"She's never dated anyone other than my dad. As far as I know, she's never even looked at another man."

"Hate to break it to you, babe, but she's lookin' now."

Once Rocki finished the song, she told everyone to head over to the bar for an announcement, and Bree and Storm followed the crowd.

Pete, as usual, took charge. "Okay, everyone. We're here to celebrate Bree and Storm's engagement."

Everyone cheered.

Pete signaled for quiet. "But that's not all. Bree, come up here, sweetheart. We have a little something especially for you."

Bree felt her face flush as Storm led her to the end of the bar. She couldn't imagine what he and Pete had up their sleeves. Her mother joined them, looping her arm around Bree's waist.

Pete brought a large, thin, beautifully wrapped box from behind the bar. "This is for you from all of us. We're so proud of you, Bree."

"Me? Why?" Bree pulled the wrapping paper off the box, set it on the bar, and lifted the top. She took out a plaque with the *Wall Street Journal* article about the

Harbor Pier Project and her work on the Red Hook Revitalization Committee. "Oh my, it's beautiful." It took her breath away. Next to it was an artist's rendering of the Harbor Pier Project. She'd never seen the drawing before. She looked at the artists' signatures—it was signed *Storm Decker and Nicki.*

"Storm, you and Nicki drew this?"

Storm shrugged. "I looked over the plans and thought it would be a fun project for us to take on."

Nicki stood in front of Bree's mother. Noreen's hands rested on Nicki's shoulders as Nicki bounced with excitement. "Do you like it, Bree?"

"Like it? I love it. I love you, Nicki." She pulled her into a hug and then kissed Storm as he wrapped his arms around the two of them, pulling her mom into the group hug. "It's the best gift I've ever received. Thank you."

Storm brushed away a tear from her cheek. "Okay, Pop. Hand it over."

She wasn't sure what Storm was talking about until Pete handed him a hammer and nail. Storm walked right up to the Wall of Fame and hung her plaque as the crowd applauded.

Bree stopped him. "Storm, that's for your family."

Storm kissed her again. "You're right, which is why we're putting it here in the center, just where it belongs. You're the heart of our family, Bree. You always have been."

"The head cook just quit." Logan looked from Rocki to Francis.

Francis did a double take. "Rex would never just up and quit."

Logan rubbed his forehead where the mother of all headaches was forming. "He's an only child and his mother just had a stroke. She's paralyzed on the left side—and she lives in Florida. It's not as if he really had a choice."

Rocki tapped her foot. "Bummer."

Logan couldn't believe this. "Come on, guys, you're supposed to help me out. Can either of you cook?"

The two of them looked like a pair of bobblehead dolls in a crosswind.

"Neither can I. This is just great. What am I supposed to do now?"

Rocki shrugged one shoulder. "I suggest you start looking for a cook."

"It's Sunday. How the hell am I going to find a cook by opening on Tuesday?"

A grin split Francis's face. "You can put a help-wanted sign in the window."

Rocki went around the bar and poured herself a soda, missing the glass and making a mess of the bar Logan had just scrubbed. "Have you asked Pete?"

"No, I didn't want him to have another coronary."

Both Rocki and Francis shot him matching glares.

"Bad joke. He's had a rough morning. I caught him smoking his cigar on the roof and we had words." Logan was definitely not ready for the role reversal. "All I need to do is tell Pop his cook just quit. He's supposed to be recovering, and I'm supposed to be managing the place, remember?"

Rocki took a long sip of her soda and watched him over the rim of the glass. "It's not as if you're going to be able to hide it from him for long. He'll notice on Tuesday. Maybe he has a backup chef."

Francis shook his head. "I doubt it. He's never needed one before."

Logan's phone vibrated. He didn't have to check to know it was his fiancé, Payton; she'd been calling constantly crying desertion since he'd traveled from California to Brooklyn to help out his father. He let the call go to voice mail. "Fine. I'll tell Pop, but first I'm going to put up a help-wanted sign. Maybe an incredible cook will walk by and want the job."

Francis laughed. "Yeah, and maybe I'll win the New York lottery."

Logan got busy with the sign, figuring he had nothing to lose, and other than putting an ad on Craigslist later, he didn't have a plan B.

Logan taped the sign up in the front window and wondered if temp services had cooks—it was worth a try.

He was still running his finger over the tape when a beautiful dark-haired woman dragging a suitcase shouldered the door open. She was a little thing with shoulder-length black hair, pale, almost translucent skin, and the darkest blue eyes he'd ever seen.

"You're hiring a cook?"

Logan shot a glance at Rocki and Francis, who stood beside the bar with their mouths hanging open.

"That's what the sign says. Can you cook?"

"Honey, there's nothing I can't do in a kitchen." She had a deep, smoky voice that made him think of tangled sheets.

Between her voice and her comment, Logan's mind spun directly into the gutter. What was wrong with him? Not only was she not his type, but he was engaged—to a woman who could double as a centerfold. He cleared his throat, temporarily speechless.

"Lucky for you, I'm looking for a job. May I see the kitchen?"

"Why?"

"I won't work in a dirty or unsafe kitchen."

"Where have you worked?"

"Here and there. You know how it is in the restaurant business." She pulled a menu out of the rack on the side of the hostess stand and paged through it. "There's nothing on here I can't handle. How many people do you seat a night?"

Logan looked at Rocki and Francis, but the two of them simply shrugged.

"I don't know. I just took over the place last night. The manager got married yesterday, went on her honeymoon. I'm just filling in for the month. It was a really bad time for the cook to quit."

She smiled and it transformed her from beautiful in a girl-next-door kind of way to simply stunning. "It's a good thing I walked by, then." She looked around. "I assume the kitchen is through there?" She pointed at the swinging double doors.

"Yes, it is."

"Okay, then, let's take a look." She set her backpack and suitcase on the bench of a booth, and he found himself following her to the kitchen.

"Did you close today because you lost your cook?"

"No, we're only open Tuesday through Saturday."

She shot him another heart-stopping grin. Nope, he hadn't imagined it. She was absolutely staggering. Her lips were full, rose colored, and bare. She wasn't wearing all that lip crap Payton was always applying—most of which tasted bad enough to put him off kissing for life. If this woman wore makeup, he couldn't detect it—not that she needed it. Her eyelashes were coal black, full enough to create shadows on her pale cheeks.

"So I'll only have to work five days a week? It'll seem like a vacation."

The way she spoke, he'd have thought he'd already given her the job. He hadn't. Still, he followed her and couldn't help but notice that her back was as attractive as her front—not that he was looking or anything. His cell phone vibrated. He snuck a peek—Payton—and shoved his phone into his pocket as the woman inspected the kitchen like a general inspecting her troops. She even ran her finger under the hood. "Your cook kept a clean kitchen. I like that." She took a turn through the walk-through refrigerator, stepped out, and closed the door behind her. "Okay, I'll take the job."

"You will?" He shook his head. "Hold on. I haven't even offered it yet. Hell, I don't even know your name."

She stepped toward him and held out her hand. "Skye. Skye Sinclair."

He took it—her hand was small, warm, and as callused as his. Her shake was surprisingly firm, considering she barely came up to his shoulder, and her touch sent a shock wave through him that had him holding on to see if it would continue. It did.

Once this guy tasted her cooking, there was no question that he'd hire her on the spot and she really needed the job. The kitchen was first-class, and the dining room was large enough to keep the menu interesting, but still small enough to cook everything to order.

Since the man seemed completely clueless when it came to running a restaurant, she'd have total control of the kitchen for at least the month he was scheduled to be in charge. It was the one thing she'd always longed for— her very own kitchen.

This was a real lucky break—she fingered the four-leaf clover she wore around her neck.

When she'd walked through the doors and spotted him, he'd looked familiar. Tall, really tall, he was at least a foot taller than her five feet two. Sometimes it really sucked being short. He had dark brown, almost black hair, a narrow nose, a square jaw, and high cheekbones sharp enough to fillet meat. His eyes were the color of rich caramel—her favorite decadence other than chocolate. He was tan and lean, and hotter than a desert afternoon during a heat wave. He looked like one of the models she'd seen while paging through the stack of magazines she'd picked up to read on the plane—the man was gorgeous. But the more she watched him, the more he reminded her of someone specific. She just couldn't put her finger on who.

When he took her hand in his to shake, she wasn't sure if the shock she felt running through her arm straight to her breasts was because he touched her, or if it was God's way of zapping her for lying about her name.

Then it hit her; he reminded her of that vintner who was engaged to Payton Billingsly. She'd never met him in person, but she'd seen him once at her parents' country club from a distance. She took a closer look and laughed at her ridiculousness. As if Payton would ever lower herself to marry someone who hadn't come out of a penthouse on Park Avenue. Besides, according to the society pages, Payton's fiancé was on the other side of the country running Billingsly Vineyards and helping the ice princess to plan their New Year's Eve wedding. He was not freaking out over finding a chef for his dad's bar and restaurant in Brooklyn.

"It's nice to meet you, Skye. I'm Logan Blaise."

Oh, God, no! It was him. She did her best to smile through the shock, but the way his smiled flattened told her she failed.

"About the job—"

She did a mental eye roll. Her patience slipped another notch, so she decided to just go with it. "Yes, about the job. How much are you paying me?"

His mouth dropped open.

"And is there a reason you're still holding my hand?"

"What?" Logan looked down, seemingly stunned to see their joined hands, and broke the connection.

Thank God.

"I'm sorry. Um . . . I don't know how much the job

pays. I'm going to have to figure it out. But I haven't even offered it to you yet."

"Well, Logan, from where I'm standing, I don't see that you have much of a choice. What are you going to do, call Rent a Chef?"

His brows drew together—she'd shocked him. Good. "Do they have Rent a Chefs?"

"If they did, I'd be the last person to tell you."

"I have to discuss this with my dad. He owns the place."

"Then why isn't he interviewing me?" She'd much rather deal with the man in charge than Payton's plaything.

"He had a heart attack and bypass surgery a few months ago, so my brothers and I are taking turns coming home to help out. The manager just ran off and married one of my brothers, which is why I'm here. She'll be back in a month, and then I'll return to my life."

"Good to know." She let out a relieved breath. She could work with anyone for a month. After all, she'd put up with her overbearing brothers for years. "I can wait if you want to discuss this with your father. Are you hungry? Do want me to throw together lunch while you ferret out the paperwork and talk to him?"

"Um . . ."

"Think of it as a working interview. You wouldn't hire a band without hearing them play, would you?"

"No."

"I'll even clean up after myself. What are you and your friends in the mood for? Or would you rather me go off the menu?"

"You want to cook?"

She shrugged. "It's what I do. Besides, I haven't cooked in two days, and not cooking makes me antsy."

"Okay. It'll get me out of having to cook lunch. If you could make something heart-healthy that doesn't taste it, it would be great. Pop's on a pretty strict diet, and he's not happy about it. Oh, and try to make it something a kid wouldn't mind eating."

"You have a child?"

"Um . . ." Was it her imagination or did he just blanch? "Nicki is my dad's foster child. She's ten." He headed out the swinging doors toward the bar, so she followed. "Hey, Rocki, Francis, this is Skye Sinclair. She's going to cook for us as part of her job interview. Are you staying for lunch?"

Skye looked toward the ceiling and cursed silently. God was having a good ol' time at her expense. This had to be some kind of cosmic joke.

She'd never met Logan Blaise, but she'd grown up hearing all about Payton. Skye's parents always suggested their daughter try to emulate her. A woman so plastic, if she took up smoking, she'd melt. People like Payton made her skin crawl, and this guy was engaged to her.

She smiled through Logan's introductions to Rocki, the lead singer of the house band, and Francis, who looked more like a bouncer than a bartender. She watched him speak. He even sounded like her brothers — not a hint of the Brooklyn accent his friends had. He was gorgeous, polished, shallow, and fake.

At least Logan hadn't recognized her. Not that they traveled in the same circles — she'd always avoided his circles. Still, it was a darn good thing she'd thought to use her mother's maiden name. "So it's five for lunch, right?"

Logan raised his brows. "Six including you. You do eat your own food, don't you?"

"Not usually with the people for whom I'm cooking."

"Make an exception today. I'm sure Pop would like to talk to you."

"Fine. Any food allergies I should know about?"

They all shook their heads. "Okay, I'll go see what there is to make. Give me about forty-five minutes. I have to start everything from scratch."

"No problem. Take your time and holler if you need any help."

"You know your way around the kitchen?"

Rocki and Francis laughed, and then Francis stepped forward and threw his arm over her shoulder. "My man Logan knows a lot about a lot of things. He knows his way around a lab, a distillery, a brewery, and a vineyard definitely. But the kitchen is one place he has little or no experience. I'm Italian, so I'm no stranger to the kitchen. If you need anything, just call my name."

Skye took a relieved breath. She liked Francis immediately, even if he could bench-press her using only his pinkies. Rocki seemed nice too. She just wasn't sure what they were doing with a guy like Logan Blaise.